"What are y...

"You said you di... ...ew
they weren't really... ...ut
he reveled in the r... ...she couldn't
hide in spite of her scowl.

"You're being outrageous."

"Good."

"Stop. Now," she said firmly.

Okay, he'd pushed her far enough for today, but he could see that while their love for each other might have burned out, their passion still had plenty of fire left.

He buttoned his shirt again and tucked in the tails. "Spoilsport."

She brushed papers into a stack. "The pilot's waiting."

"Damn waste of an empty desk," he said with a smile.

* * *

One Good Cowboy
is part of the Diamonds in the Rough trilogy:

The McNair cousins must pass their grandmother's tests to inherit their fortune—and find true love!

ONE GOOD COWBOY

BY
CATHERINE MANN

Published in Great Britain 2014
by Mills & Boon, an imprint of Harlequin (UK) Limited,
Eton House, 18-24 Paradise Road, Richmond, Surrey, TW9 1SR

© 2014 Catherine Mann

ISBN: 978 0 263 91462 7

51-0414

Harlequin (UK) Limited's policy is to use papers that are natural, renewable and recyclable products and made from wood grown in sustainable forests. The logging and manufacturing processes conform to the legal environmental regulations of the country of origin.

Printed and bound in Spain
by Blackprint CPI, Barcelona

USA TODAY bestselling author **Catherine Mann** lives on a sunny Florida beach with her flyboy husband and their four children. With more than forty books in print in over twenty countries, she has also celebrated wins for both a RITA® Award and a Booksellers' Best Award. Catherine enjoys chatting with readers online—thanks to the wonders of the internet, which allows her to network with her laptop by the water! Contact Catherine through her website, www.catherinemann.com, find her on Facebook and Twitter (@CatherineMann1) or reach her by snail mail at PO Box 6065, Navarre, FL 32566, USA.

To my husband, Rob, always my hero.

One

"Gentlemen, never forget the importance of protecting your family jewels."

Unfazed by his grandmother's outrageous comment, Stone McNair ducked low as his horse sailed under a branch and over a creek. Gran prided herself on being the unconventional matriarch of a major jewelry design empire, and her mocking jab carried on the wind as Stone raced with his cousin.

Alex pulled up alongside him, neck and neck with Stone's quarter horse. Hooves chewed at the earth, deftly dodging the roots of a cypress tree, spewing turf into the creek.

Even as he raced, Stone soaked in the scents and sounds of home—the squeak of the saddle, the whistle of the wind through the pines. Churned earth and blue-bonnets waving in the wind released a fragrance every bit as intoxicating as the first whiff of a freshly opened bottle of Glenfiddich whiskey.

This corner of land outside of Fort Worth, Texas, had belonged to the McNairs for generations, their homestead as they built a business empire. His blood hummed when he rode the ranch. Ownership had branded itself into his DNA as tangibly as the symbol of the Hidden

Gem Ranch that had been branded onto his quarter horse's flank.

Outings on the ranch with his grandmother and his twin cousins were few and far between these days, given their hectic work schedules. He wasn't sure why Gran had called this little reunion and impromptu race, but it had to be something important for her to resort to pulling them all away from the McNair Empire.

His other cousin, Amie, galloped alongside Stone, her laughter full and uninhibited. "How're the family jewels holding up?"

Without waiting for an answer, Amie urged her Arabian ahead, her McNair-black hair trailing behind her just like when she'd been ten instead of thirty. Rides with their grandmother had been a regular occurrence when they were children, then less and less frequent as they grew older and went their separate ways. None of them had hesitated when the family matriarch insisted on an impromptu gathering. Stone owed his grandmother. She'd been his safe haven every time his druggy mother went on a binge or checked into rehab.

Again.

Damn straight, he owed his grandmother a debt he couldn't repay. She'd been there from day one, an aggressive advocate in getting the best care possible to detox her crack baby grandson. Gran had paid for her daughter to enter detox programs again and again with little success. Year after year, Gran had been as constant as the land they called home—for his cousins, too.

And she'd given each one of them a role to play. Alex managed the family lands—Hidden Gem Ranch, which operated as a bed-and-breakfast hobby ranch for the rich and famous. Stone managed the family jewelry design house and stores. Diamonds in the Rough featured high-end rustic designs, from rodeo belt buckles and stylized bolos to Aztec jewelry, all highly sought after around the country. If everything went according to plan, he intended to expand Diamonds in the Rough with international offices in London and Milan, making the big announcement at a wild mustang fund-raiser this fall. And Amie—a gemologist—was already working on designs for new pieces to meet the expected increase in demand.

Yes, the world was finally coming back together for him. After his broken engagement knocked him for a loop seven months ago…

But he didn't want to think about Johanna. Not today. Not ever, if he could avoid it. Although that was tough to accomplish, since Johanna worked for Hidden Gem Stables as a vet tech. He'd missed her this morning when they'd saddled up. Would he bump into her after his ride?

The possibility filled him with frustration—and an unwanted boot in the libido.

Gran slowed her favorite palomino, Goldie, to a trot near the pond where they'd played as kids. Apparently race time was over. Maybe now she would explain the reason for this surprise get-together.

Stone stroked along Copper's neck as the horse dipped his head to drink. "So, Gran, care to enlighten us on the reason for this family meeting?"

His cousins drew up along either side of her.

She shifted in the saddle, her head regal with a long gray braid trailing down her stiff spine. "The time has come for me to decide who will take over the reins of the McNair holdings."

Stone's grip tightened on the pommel. "You're not actually considering retiring."

"No, dear..." Gran paused, drawing in a shaky breath at odds with her usual steel. "The doctor has told me it's time to get my affairs in order."

Her words knocked the wind out of him as fully as the first time he'd been thrown from a horse. He couldn't envision a world without the indomitable Mariah McNair.

Amie reached across to touch her grandmother's arm lightly, as much contact as could be made without everyone dismounting, and Gran didn't show any signs of leaving the saddle. Which was probably the reason their grandmother had chosen this way to make her announcement.

"Gran, what exactly did the doctor say?"

Alex patted Gran's other shoulder, he and his sister protecting her like bookends. They always had.

Amie's and Alex's childhoods had been more stable than Stone's, with parents and a home of their own. As a kid, Stone had dreamed of stepping into their house and becoming a sibling rather than a cousin. Once he'd even overheard his grandmother suggest that very arrangement. But Amethyst and Alexandrite's mother made it clear that she could handle only her twins. Another child would be too much to juggle between obligations to her daughter's pageants and her son's rodeos.

In one fell swoop, Stone had realized that while his family loved him, no one wanted him—not his mother, his aunt or his grandmother. They were all looking for some way to shuffle him off. Except Gran hadn't bailed. She'd taken him on regardless. He respected and loved her all the more for that.

Mariah patted each twin on the cheek and smiled sadly at Stone since he held himself apart. "It's inoperable brain cancer."

His throat closed up tight. Amie gasped, blinking fast but a tear still escaped.

Their grandmother shook her head. "None of that emotional stuff. I've never had much patience for tears. I want optimism. Doctors are hopeful treatment can reduce the size of the tumor. That could give me years instead of months."

Months?

Damn it.

The wind got knocked out of him all over again. More than once, Stone had been called a charmer with a stone-cold heart. But that heart ached right now at the thought of anything happening to his grandmother.

Shrugging, Mariah leaned back in the saddle. "Still, even if the treatments help, I can't risk the tumor clouding my judgment. I won't put everything I've worked for at risk by waiting too long to make important decisions about Diamonds in the Rough and the Hidden Gem Ranch."

The family holdings meant everything to her. To all of them. It had never dawned on him until now that his grandmother—the major stockholder—might want to change the roles they all played to keep the empire rock-solid. He must be mistaken. Better to wait and hear her out rather than assume.

Amie wasn't so restrained, but then she never had been. "What have you decided?"

"I haven't," Mariah conceded. "Not yet, but I have a plan, which is why I asked you three to come riding with me today."

Alex, the quiet one of the bunch, frowned. "I'm not sure I understand."

"You'll each need to do something for me—" Mariah angled forward, forearm on the saddle horn "—something to help put my mind at ease about who to place in charge."

"You're testing us," Amie accused softly.

"Call it what you like." Gran was unapologetic, her jaw set. "But as it stands now, I'm not sold on any of you taking over."

That revelation stabbed pain clear through his already raw nerves.

Enough holding back. He was a man of action, and the urge to be in control of something, anything, roared through him. "What do you need me to do for you?"

"Stone, you need to find homes for all four of my dogs."

A fish plopped in the pond, the only sound breaking his stunned silence.

Finally, he asked, "You're joking, right? To lighten the mood."

"I'm serious. My pets are very important to me. You know that. They're family."

"It just seems a…strange test." Was the tumor already affecting her judgment?

His grandmother shook her head slowly. "The fact that you don't know how serious this is merely affirms my concerns. You need to prove to me you have the heart to run this company and possibly oversee the entire family portfolio."

She held him with her clear blue gaze, not even a whisper of confusion showing. Then she looked away, clicked her horse into motion and started back toward the main house, racing past the cabins vacationers rented.

Shaking off his daze, he followed her, riding along the split rail fence, his cousins behind him as they made their way home.

Home.

Some would call it a mansion—a rustic log ranch house with two wings. Their personal living quarters occupied one side, and the other side housed the lodge run by Alex. His cousin had expanded the place from a small bed-and-breakfast to a true hobby ranch, with everything from horseback riding to a spa, fishing and trail adventures...even poker games, saloon-style. They catered to a variety of people's needs, from vacations to weddings.

The gift store featured some of the McNair signature jewelry pieces, just a sampling from their flagship store in Fort Worth.

Alex was one helluva businessman in his own right. Gran could be serious about turning over majority control to him.

Or maybe she had someone else in mind. A total stranger. He couldn't even wrap his brain around that unthinkable possibility. His whole being was consumed with shock—and hell, yes, grief—not over the fact that he might lose the company but because he would lose Gran. A month or a year from now, he couldn't envision a world without her.

And he also couldn't deny her anything she needed to make her last days easier.

Stone urged his horse faster to catch her before she reached the stables.

"Okay, fine, Gran," he said as he pulled alongside

her, their horses' gaits in sync. "I can do that for you. I'll line up people to take, uh…" What the hell were their names? "Your dogs."

"There are four of them, in case you've forgotten that, as well as forgetting their names."

"The scruffy one's named Dorothy, right?"

Gran snorted almost as loudly as the horse. "Close. The dog looks like Toto, but her name is Pearl. The yellow lab is Gem, given to us by a friend. My precious Rottie that I adopted from a shelter is named Ruby. And my baby chi-weenie's name is Sterling."

Chi-what? Oh, right, a Chihuahua and dachshund. "What about your two cats?"

Surely he would get points for remembering there were two.

"Amie is keeping them."

She always was a suck-up.

"Then I'll keep the dogs. They can live with me." How much trouble could four dogs be? He had lots of help. He would find one of those doggy day cares.

"I said I wanted them to go to *good* homes."

He winced. "Of course you do."

"Homes approved of by an expert," she continued as she stopped her horse by the stables.

"An expert?" Hairs on the back of his neck rose with an impending sense of Karma about to bite him on the butt.

He didn't even have to look down the lengthy walkway between horse stalls to know Johanna Fletcher was striding toward them on long, lean legs that could have sold a million pairs of jeans. She usually wore a French braid to keep her wavy blond hair secure when she worked. His fingers twitched at the memory of slid-

ing through that braid to unleash all those tawny strands
around her bare shoulders.

What he wouldn't give to lose himself in her again,
to forget about the thought of his grandmother's illness.
Even if the best scenario played out, a couple of years
wasn't enough.

For now, he would do whatever it took to keep Gran
happy.

"Your expert?" he prodded.

"All adoptions must be approved by our ranch vet
tech, Johanna Fletcher."

Of course.

His eyes slid to Johanna closing the gap between
them as she went from stall to stall, horse to horse. Her
face shuttered the instant she looked at him, whereas
once she would have met him with a full-lipped smile,
a slight gap between her front teeth. That endearing im-
perfection only enhanced her attractiveness. She was
down-to-earth and sexy. He knew every inch of her
intimately.

After all, she was his ex-fiancée.

The woman who had dumped him in no uncertain
terms in front of all their friends at a major fund-raiser.
A woman who now hated his guts and would like nothing more than to see his dreams go up in flames.

Stone McNair, the CEO in a business suit ruling the
boardroom, commanded respect and awe. But Stone
McNair, cowboy Casanova on a horse, was a charismatic charmer Johanna Fletcher had always been hard-
pressed to resist.

Johanna tamped down the urge to fan herself as she
stood just outside a horse stall and studied her former

lover out of the corner of her eyes. Damn it, he still made her hot all over.

She busied herself with listening to a horse's heart-beat—or pretending to listen at least. The palomino was fine, but she didn't want anyone thinking she was still pining for Stone. Everyone from Fort Worth to Del Rio knew her history with him. She didn't need to feed them any fodder for gossip by drooling every time he strutted into the stables.

Lord help her, that man knew how to strut.

Jeans hugged his thighs as he swung a leg over his horse, boots hitting the ground with a thud that vibrated clear through her even from twenty yards away. The sun flashed off his belt buckle—a signature Diamonds in the Rough design—bringing out the nuances of the pattern. Magnificent. Just like the man. All the McNairs had charisma, but Stone was sinfully handsome, with coal-black hair and ice-blue eyes right off some movie poster. Sweat dotted his brow, giving his hair a hint of a curl along the edges of his tan Stetson. She'd idol-ized him as a child. Fantasized about him as a teenager.

And as a woman? She'd fallen right in line with the rest and let herself be swayed by his charms.

Never again.

Johanna turned her focus back to the next stall with a quarter horse named Topaz, one of the more popular rides for vacationers. She had a job to do and she was darn lucky to work here after the scene she'd caused during her breakup with Stone. But Mrs. McNair liked her and kept her on. Johanna hadn't been able to resist the opportunity to work with so many unique horses in the best stable.

Her career was everything to her now, and she refused to put it in jeopardy. Her parents had sacrificed their life's savings to send her to the best schools so she had the educational foundation she needed to pursue her dreams. Although her parents were gone now after a fire in the trailer park, she owed them. Perhaps even more so to honor their memory. Her father's work here had brought her into the McNair world—brought her to Stone, even if their romance ultimately hadn't been able to withstand the wide social chasm between them.

She had no family, not even the promise of one she'd once harbored while engaged to Stone. She had her work, her horses. This was her life and her future.

Hooves clopped as Mariah and Stone passed off their rides to two stable hands. Johanna frowned. Even though the McNairs were wealthy, they usually unsaddled and rubbed down their horses themselves. Instead, the grandmother and grandson were walking directly toward her. Tingles pranced up and down her spine. Ignoring him would be impossible.

She hooked her stethoscope around her neck. Her own racing heartbeat filled her ears now, each breath faster and faster, filling her lungs with the scent of hay and leather.

Trailing her hand along the plush velvet of the horse's coat, she angled her way out of the wooden stall and into the walkway. "Hello, Mrs. McNair—" she swallowed hard "—and Stone."

Mariah McNair smiled. Stone didn't. In fact, he was scowling. But there was also something more lurking in his eyes, something…sad? She hated the way her heart pinched instinctively, and hated even more that she could still read him so well.

Mariah held out a hand. "Dear, let's step back into the office where we can chat in private."

With Stone, too? But Mariah's words weren't a question. "Of course."

Questions welled inside her with each step toward the office, passing Hidden Gem staff barely hiding their own curiosity as they prepped rides for vacationers. Alex and Amie eyed them but kept their distance as they hauled the saddles off their horses. The twins wore the same somber and stunned expressions on their faces that she saw on Stone's.

Concern nipped like a feisty foal, and Johanna walked faster. She'd all but grown up here, following her stable hand dad around. Her family hadn't been wealthy like the McNairs, but she'd always been loved, secure—until the day her family had died when their malfunctioning furnace caught on fire in the night.

She'd lost everything. Except rather than making her afraid to love, she craved that sense of family. These walls echoed with memories of how special those bonds had been.

Custom saddles lined the corridors, all works of art like everything the McNairs made. Carvings marked the leather with a variety of designs from roses to vines to full-out pastoral scenes. Some saddles sported silver or brass studs on horn caps and skirting edges that rivaled the tooling of any of the best old vaqueros.

Her job here had spoiled her for any other place. She couldn't imagine living anywhere else. This was her home as well as her workplace.

Stone held open the office door, which left her no choice but to walk past him, closely. His radiant heat brought back memories of his bare skin slick with perspiration against hers as they made love in the woods on a hot summer day.

His gaze held hers for an electrified moment, attraction crackling, alive and well, between them, before she forced herself to walk forward and break the connection.

Red leather chairs, a sofa and a heavy oak desk filled the paneled room. The walls were covered in framed prints of the McNair holdings at various stages of expansion. A portrait of Mariah and her husband, Jasper, on their twenty-fifth wedding anniversary dominated the space over a stone fireplace, a painting done shortly before Jasper had passed away from a heart attack.

Mariah's fingers traced lightly along the carved frame before she settled into a fat wingback chair with an exhausted sigh. "Please, have a seat, Johanna. Stone? Pour us something to drink, dear."

Johanna perched on the edge of a wooden rocker. "Mrs. McNair? Is there a problem?"

"I'm afraid there is, and I need your help."

"Whatever I can do, just let me know."

Mariah took a glass of sparkling spring water from her grandson, swallowed deeply, then set the crystal tumbler aside. "I'm having some health problems and during my treatment I need to be sure I have my life settled."

"Health problems?" Concern gripped Johanna's heart in a chilly fist. How much could she ask without being too pushy? Considering this woman had almost been her family, she decided she could press as far as she needed. "Is it serious?"

"Very," Mariah said simply, fingering her diamond horseshoe necklace. "I'm hopeful my doctors can buy me more time, but treatments will be consuming and I don't want the business or my pets to be neglected."

Mariah's love for her animals was one of the bonds the two women shared. The head of a billion-dollar empire had always made time for a stable hand's daughter who wanted to learn more about the animals at Hidden Gem.

Johanna took the glass from Stone, her hand shaking so much the ice rattled. "I'm sorry, more than I can say. What can I do to help?"

Angling forward, Mariah held her with clear blue eyes identical to Stone's. "You can help me find homes for my dogs."

Without hesitation, Johanna said, "I can watch them while you're undergoing treatments."

"My dear," Mariah said gently, but with a steely strength, "it's brain cancer. I believe it's best for my dogs to find permanent homes."

The pronouncement slammed Johanna back in her chair. She bit her bottom lip to hold in a gasp and blinked back tears. There were no words.

A firm hand landed on her shoulder. Stone's hand. She didn't have to look. She would know his touch anywhere.

God, he must be devastated. She angled around to clasp his hand, but the cool look in his eyes stopped her. Apparently, he was fine with giving out sympathy, but his pride wouldn't allow him to accept any from her.

Johanna reached to take Mariah's hands instead, holding them in hers. "I'll do whatever you need."

"Thank you." Mariah smiled and squeezed Johanna's hands. "Stone will be finding homes for my dogs, but I need for you to go with him and make sure the matches are truly right for each one. It should take about a week."

"A week?" she squeaked.

Go off alone with Stone for a week? No, no and hell, no. The torture of running across him here was bad enough, but at least they had the buffer of work. Stone had stolen her heart then trounced all her dreams of having a family of her own. He'd refused to consider having children or adopting. They'd argued—more than once—until finally she'd broken things off. He'd thought she was bluffing.

He was wrong.

Did Mariah think she was bluffing, as well?

Johanna chose her words carefully. "I don't mean any disrespect, ma'am, and I understand your need for peace, especially now..." She pushed back a well of emotion. This wasn't about her. It was about Mariah, and yes, Stone, too. "You have to realize this attempt at matchmaking isn't going to work. Stone and I were finished a long time ago."

Johanna shot a pointed look at him in case he might be harboring any thoughts of using this situation to wrangle his way back into her bed. Even when she'd broken things off, he'd been persistent for a solid month before accepting that she wouldn't change her mind.

He simply arched an arrogant eyebrow before shifting his glacial gaze toward his grandmother. Only then did his eyes warm.

Mariah shook her head. "I'm not trying anything of the sort. I have trusted you with my animals for years. I've watched you grow up, known you since you were in elementary school. You also understand Stone. He won't pull off anything questionable with you watching him. Can you think of anyone else he can't charm?"

Johanna conceded, "You have a point there."

Stone frowned, speaking for the first time, "Hey, I think I'm being insulted."

Mariah reached up to pat his cheek. "If you only *think* it, Stone, then I must not be making myself clear enough. I hope you will be successful in proving yourself, but I have serious reservations."

He scratched along his jaw, which was perpetually peppered with beard stubble no matter how often he shaved. "You trust Johanna over your own flesh and blood?"

"I do," Mariah said without hesitation. "Case in point, you wanted to keep the expansion a secret, even from me."

"Just until I had the details hammered out, to surprise you. To impress you."

"Our company isn't a grade-school art project to tape to the refrigerator. You need to show me you understand the importance of teamwork and compassion. That's the reason I came up with this test." Mariah's calm but unwavering tone made it clear there would be no changing her mind. "Johanna, you'll go with him to all the interviews with prospective families that I've lined up."

"You've already found the families? You're making his test too easy," Johanna said suspiciously. "There must be a catch."

"No catch. But as for easy?" Mariah laughed softly. "That depends on you two and your ability to act like grownups around each other."

"Civility during a few interviews," Johanna echoed. "We can handle that." Maybe.

"More than during interviews. There's travel time, as well."

"Travel?" So there was a catch. She glanced at Stone who was looking too damn hot—and smug—leaning against the fireplace mantel. He simply shrugged, staying tall, dark and silent.

"These families I've lined up don't live around the corner, but the corporate jet should make the journey easier." Mariah patted her diamond horseshoe necklace. "You should be able to complete the meet and greets in a week."

Stone stepped forward. "Gran, I can handle our travel arrangements."

"You can. But you're not going to. I'm calling the shots on this. My plan. My test," his grandmother said succinctly.

Stone's jaw clamped shut, and Johanna could see the lord of the boardroom holding himself back because of his grandmother's condition.

"A week…" Johanna repeated. A week away from work, a week of more than just crossing paths for a few meet and greets. "Alone together, jetting around the country on the McNair corporate airplane?"

"I don't expect the two of you to reunite. This truly is about Stone showing me he's capable of the compassion needed to run a company." Her hand slid up behind her neck and she unclasped the chain. "But I do hope the two of you can also find some way to reconcile your way back to friendship."

Understanding settled over Johanna. "You want to be at peace—knowing your dogs are loved *and* that Stone and I won't hurt each other again."

Mariah's fingers closed around her necklace and

whispered, "My grandson's well-being is important, more so than any company."

Mariah had found Johanna's Achilles' heel. Was it an act from Mariah, to get her way? Heaven knew the woman could be every bit as wily as Stone. But given Mariah's illness, the woman did deserve peace in every realm of her life.

"Okay," Johanna agreed simply.

Mariah pressed the necklace into Johanna's palm. "Good luck, dear."

Johanna started to protest such an extravagant gift, but one look in Mariah's eyes showed her how much it meant to her...a woman at the end of her life passing along pieces of herself. The horseshoe was so much more than diamonds. It was a gift of the heart, of family, a symbol of all Johanna wanted for her life.

All that Stone had thrown away without a thought.

She pitied him almost as much as she resented him for costing them the life they could have had together.

Her fist closed around the necklace, and she stood, facing Stone with a steely resolve she'd learned from Mariah. "Pack your bags, Casanova. We have a plane to catch."

TWO

Staring out the office window, Stone listened for the door to click closed as his grandmother and Johanna left, then he sank into the leather desk chair, his shoulders hunched. He couldn't believe Johanna had actually agreed to a week alone on the road with him.

Heaven or hell?

He'd started to argue with Mariah, but she'd cut out on the conversation, claiming exhaustion. How could he dispute that? If anything, he wanted to wrap her in cotton to protect her even as she made her way to her favorite chaise longue chair up in her sitting room.

The prideful air that had shone in Mariah's eyes kept him from following her. Not to mention the intuitive sense that she needed to be alone. He understood the feeling, especially right now. He and his grandmother were alike in that, needing privacy and space to lick wounds. A hard sigh racked his body as he tamped down the urge to tear apart the whole office space—books, computers, saddles and framed awards—to rage at a world that would take away his grandmother.

The last thing he wanted to do was leave Fort Worth now and waste even one of her remaining days flying around the country. Even with Johanna.

What exactly was Mariah's angle in pairing them up on this Mutt Mission of Mercy? Was she making him jump through hoops like one of her trained dogs to see how badly he wanted to run the company, to prove he had a heart? Or was she matchmaking, as Johanna had accused? If so, this wasn't about the company at all, which should reassure him.

More likely his multitasking, masterminding grand-mother was looking to kill two birds with one stone—matchmaking and putting him through the wringer to make him appreciate what he'd inherit when he took the reins of the company.

He just had to get through the next seven days with his former fiancée without rehashing the train wreck of their messy breakup where she'd pointed out all his emotional shortcomings. He couldn't give Johanna what she'd wanted from him—a white picket fence fam-ily life. He wasn't wired that way. He truly was aptly named. He might have overcome the rough start in life, born with an addiction, spending most of his first ten years catching up on developmental delays—but some betrayals left scars so thick and deep he might as well be made of stone.

He understood full well his grandmother's concerns about him were true, even if he disagreed about the company needing a soft-hearted marshmallow at the helm. Although God knew he would do anything to give his grandmother peace, whatever her motivation for this doggy assignment. The business was all he would have left of her and he didn't intend to throw that away because hanging out with Johanna opened him up to a second round of falling short. His hand fisted on the chair's armrests as he stared out at the rolling fields filled with vacationers riding into the woods.

No, he didn't expect a magical fix-it with the only woman he'd ever considered marrying. But he needed closure. Because he couldn't stop thinking about her. And he was growing weary of her avoiding him.

Truth be told, he would give his right arm for the chance to sleep with Johanna again. And again. And most certainly again, because she ruled his thoughts until he hadn't been able to touch another woman since their breakup seven months ago. That was a damn long time to go without.

The life of a monk didn't suit him. Frustration pumped through him, making him ache to punch a wall. He dragged in breaths of air and forced his fists to unfurl along the arms of the chair.

A hand rested lightly on his shoulder.

Stone jolted and pivoted around fast. "Johanna? You've been there the whole time?"

He'd assumed she'd left with his grandmother.

"I started to tell you, but you seemed…lost in thought. I was searching for the right moment to clear my throat or something, and that moment just never came."

She'd stood there the whole time, watching him struggle to hold in his grief over his grandmother's announcement? The roomy office suddenly felt smaller now that he was alone with Johanna. The airplane would be damn near claustrophobic as they jetted across the country with his grandmother's pack of dogs.

"What did you need?" His voice came out chilly even to his own ears, but he had a tight rein on his emotions right now.

Johanna pulled her hand off his shoulder awkwardly. "Are you okay?"

There was a time when they hadn't hesitated to put their hands all over each other. That time had passed. A wall stood between them now, and he had no one to blame but himself. "What do you mean?"

Her sun-kissed face flooded with compassion. "Your grandmother just told you she has terminal cancer. That has to be upsetting."

"Of course it is. To you, too, I imagine." The wall between him and Johanna kept him from reaching out to comfort her.

"I'm so sorry." She twisted her fingers in front of her, the chain from the diamond horseshoe necklace dangling. "You have to know that regardless of what happened between us, I do still care about your family...and you."

She *cared* about him?

What a wishy-washy word. *Cared*. What he felt for her was fiery, intense and, yes, even at times filled with frustrated anger that they couldn't be together, and he couldn't forget about her when they were apart. "You *care* about my family, and that's why you agreed to my grandmother's crazy plan." It wasn't that she wanted to be alone with him.

"It influenced my decision, yes." She shuffled from dusty boot to dusty boot, drawing his attention to her long legs. "I also care about her dogs and I respect that she wants to look after their welfare. She's an amazing woman."

"Yes, she is." An enormity of emotion about his grandmother's health problems welled inside him, pain and anger combatting for dominance, both due to the grinding agony that he couldn't fix this. Feeling powerless went against everything in his nature.

It made him rage inside all over again, and only exacerbated the frustration over months of rejection from Johanna.

Over months of missing her.

Something grouchy within him made him do the very thing guaranteed to push Johanna away. Although arguing with her felt better than being ignored.

He stepped closer, near enough to catch a whiff of hay and bluebonnets, and closed his hands over her fingers, which were gripping the necklace his grandmother had given her. Johanna's eyes went wide, but she didn't move away, so he pressed ahead.

Dipping his head, Stone whispered against the curve of her neck, "Do you feel sorry enough for me to do anything about it?"

She flattened a hand on his chest, finally stopping him short. But her breathing was far from steady and she still hadn't pushed him away.

"Not *anything*." Her eyes narrowed, and he knew he'd pushed her far enough for now.

He backed away and hitched a hip on the heavy oak desk he'd climbed over as a kid. His initials were still carved underneath. "You've come back to offer comfort. Mission complete. Thanks."

"You're not fooling me." Her emerald-green eyes went from angry to sad in a revealing instant. "I know you better than anyone."

He reached for her fist, which was still holding the necklace from his grandmother, and drew Johanna toward him until her hand rested against his heart. "Then tell me what I'm feeling right now."

"You're trying to get me to run by making a move on me, because I'm touching a nerve with questions about your grandmother," she said with unerring accuracy. He never had been able to get anything past her. "You're in pain and you don't want me to see that."

"I'm in pain, all right—" his eyes slid down the fine length of her curvy, toned body "—and I'm more than happy to let you see everything."

She tugged away from him, shaking her head. "For a practiced, world-class charmer, you're overplaying your hand."

"But you're not unaffected." He slipped the necklace from her fist deftly.

Standing, he put the chain around her neck as if that had been his reason for coming closer. He brushed aside the tail of her thick braid. Her chest rose and fell faster. As he worked the clasp, he savored the satiny skin of her neck, then skimmed his fingers forward along the silvery links, settling the diamond horseshoe between her breasts. Her heartbeat fluttered against his knuckles.

"Stone, our attraction to each other was never in question," she said bluntly, her hands clenched at her sides and her chin tipping defiantly. "Because of that attraction, we need to have ground rules for this trip."

"Ground rules?"

She met his gaze full-on. "No more of these seduction games. If you want *me* to play nice, then *you* be nice."

"Define *nice*." He couldn't resist teasing.

"Being truthful, polite—" Her eyes glinted like emeralds. "And above all, no games."

"I thought your only agenda here was making sure the dogs end up in good homes." He toyed with the diamond horseshoe, barely touching her. A little taste of Johanna went a long way.

"I can place the dogs without you," she said confidently. "I'm agreeing to your grandmother's plan to give her peace of mind on a broader spectrum. She wants us to make this trip together, and the only way I can manage that is if you stop with the practiced seduction moves. Be real. Be honest."

"Fine then." He slid the horseshoe back and forth along the chain, just over her skin, like a phantom touch. "In all honesty, I can assure you that I ache to peel off your clothes with my teeth. I burn to kiss every inch of your bared skin. And my body burns to make love to you again and again, because, hell, yes, I want to forget about what my grandmother just told me."

He dropped the charm and waited.

She exhaled long and hard, her eyes wide. "Okay, then. I hear you, and I believe you."

Shoving away from the desk and around her, he strutted right to the door and stopped short, waiting until she turned to look at him.

"Oh, Johanna, one last thing." He met her gaze dead-on, her eyes as appealing as her curves. "I wanted you every bit as much before my grandmother's announcement. This has nothing to do with me needing consolation. See you in the morning, sunshine."

Johanna had until morning to pack her bags and get her hormones under control.

Moonlight cast a dappled path through the pine trees as she walked the gravel lane from the barn to her cabin. Her heart ached as much as her muscles after this long day. Too long.

She opened her mailbox and tugged out a handful of flyers and a pizza coupon. Laughter from vacationers rode the wind as they enjoyed a party on the back deck of the main lodge, the splash of the hot tub mingling with the trickling echo of the creek that ran behind her little hideaway house.

Since graduation from vet tech school four years ago, she'd lived in a two-bedroom cabin on the Hidden Gem Ranch, the same cabin model used by vacationers. She liked to think of it as home, but truth be told she hadn't had a home since her parents' trailer had burned down when she was eighteen. She'd lived in an apartment during her two years of vet tech training, thanks to a scholarship from Mariah McNair. Then Johanna had accepted a job at Hidden Gem after graduation, her girlhood crush on Stone flourishing into full-out love.

Day by day, she'd earned a living, marking time, doing a job she adored but never putting down roots of her own, waiting on Prince Charming to pop the question. Once he did, she discovered her prince was a frog. A hot, sexy frog. But a frog nonetheless. She couldn't blame Stone for how things shook down between them. She was the one who'd worn blinders, refusing to accept the truth until it was too late.

But with the silver chain around her neck, the diamond horseshoe cool against her skin, she could only feel the weight of impending loss, the finality of closing the book on this chapter of her life. Once Mariah died, there would be nothing left holding Johanna here. Nothing other than her tenacious attraction to Stone, but that only kept her from moving on with another man, finding a future for herself with the family she craved.

She pushed open the gate on her split rail fence. The

night air carried the refrain of square-dancing music from the sound system that fed the pool area. Maybe she needed this trip away from the ranch for more reasons than she'd thought. Perhaps this wasn't just about finding peace for Mariah, but snipping the last bonds that held her to Stone so she could move on without regrets.

She climbed the three wooden steps up to her dark log cabin, katydids buzzing a full-out Texas symphony. A creak just ahead stopped her in her tracks. She searched the railed porch, wishing she'd remembered to leave on a front light, but she hadn't expected to come home so late. She blinked her eyes fast to better adjust to the dark and found a surprise waiting for her in one of the two rocking chairs.

Amie McNair sat with a gray tabby cat in her lap, a Siamese at her feet, both hers, soon to have feline siblings when Mariah's pride joined them.

"Well, hey, there," Amie drawled. "I didn't think you would ever get home."

What was Amie's reason for waiting around? Was she here to talk about Mariah's announcement? The impending loss had to be hard on the whole family. She and Amie weren't enemies but they weren't BFFs, either. They were more like childhood acquaintances who had almost been related. And because of that connection, she felt the need to hug this woman on what had to be one of the most difficult days of her life.

Johanna unlocked the front door and reached inside to turn on the porch light. "I worked late preparing to leave tomorrow, but I'm here now." She let the screen door close again. "Is there something I can do for you?"

"Ah, so you're actually going through with my grandmother's plan." Amie swept her hand over the tabby, sending a hint of kitty dander wafting into the night air as her bracelets jingled.

Even covered in cat hair and a light sheen of perspiration, Amie was a stunner, totally gorgeous no matter what she wore. She'd been the first runner-up in the Miss Texas pageant ten years ago, reportedly the first beauty competition she'd lost since her mother had teased up her hair and sent Amie tap-dancing out on the stage at four years old. She'd tap-danced her way through puberty into bikinis and spray tans. Johanna remembered well how Amie's mama had lived for her daughter's wins.

Johanna settled into the cedar rocker beside Amie and the cats, reluctant to go into her cabin. Inside, she had nothing to do but pace around, unable to sleep because of this crazy, upside down day. "I don't have a choice but to go with Stone and the dogs."

"Sure you do." Amie kicked off her sandals and stroked her toes over the kitty at her feet. "Tell my grandmother no, that it's not fair to play with your life this way. You know as well as I do that you can find homes for those dogs all on your own."

"True enough, and of course I've thought of that. Except any…unease…I feel doesn't matter, not in light of what's important to Mariah. She's dying, Amie." The reality of those words still stole her breath for a long, humid moment. "How can I deny her anything, even if the request is bizarre?"

Amie blinked back tears and looked away, her sleek black ponytail trailing over one shoulder. "I refuse to accept she's going to die. The doctors will buy her enough time so she can pass away at a ripe old age." Her throat moved with a long swallow before she looked at Johanna again, her eyes cleared of grief. "Mariah can be reasoned with…unless you don't really want to say no."

An ugly suspicion bloomed in Johanna's mind. "Or is it you who wants me to walk away so your cousin loses?"

Amie's perfectly plucked eyebrows arched upward. "That wouldn't be very loyal of me."

"Yet you're not denying anything. What's really going on?" She hated to think Amie could be so coldly calculating, but then she'd always had the sense the woman wanted more power in the family business.

The former beauty queen spread her hands. Long fingers that had once played the piano to accompany her singing now crafted high-end jewelry. "I've never made a secret of the fact that I want my family to take me seriously." Her hair swished over her shoulder, the porch light catching on the gems in the Aztec design of her hair clamp. "I'm just weighing in with my thoughts on this whole 'test' game. This is not the way to decide the future of our family legacy."

"What's *your* test?"

"Gran hasn't told me yet. Or Alex, either, for that matter." Amie scrunched her nose. In frustration? Or at the smoky scent of a bonfire launching an acrid tint to the night breeze? "But after what she set up for Stone, I'm not hopeful mine will make sense. I'm just trying to protect us all."

Johanna thumbed a knotty circle on the armrest. "How is talking to me going to accomplish that?"

"You're the only one who has ever come close to getting through the walls Stone puts around himself. I just hope you'll make sure he's okay."

Johanna sat up straighter. "Excuse me?"

"Be sure he doesn't crack up over this."

"Crack up? Stone? He's rock-solid—no pun intended."

Amie clamped Johanna's arm in a surprisingly strong grip. "I'm worried about him, okay? He doesn't have a support system like I do. My brother and I can tell each other everything. Stone is our family, but he's never let himself get close to us. And I'm worried about him right now."

There was no denying the sincerity in her voice.

"That's really sweet of you." Johanna felt bad for assuming the worst. "I do care about Stone, even though we can't be together. He's a strong man. He will grieve for Mariah—we all will—but he will haul himself through. He always does."

Even as she said it, she couldn't ignore a niggling voice in the back of her mind reminding her that Stone's childhood had been very different from her own or that of his twin cousins. His grandmother had been his only bedrock of support.

Amie's hand slid away. "Just keep what I said in mind. That's all I ask." Cradling her cat in her arms, she stood. "Good night and good luck with your trip."

"Thank you…" She had a feeling she would need luck and more to get through the coming week. She needed a plan and stronger boundaries to protect her heart.

"Anytime," Amie called over her shoulder as strolled down the steps as though she were taking a runway scene by storm, leaving her shoes behind, her other cat following her into the night.

Scooping up her junk mail, Johanna shoved to her feet. She needed to start packing now if she wanted any chance of getting to bed at a reasonable time. Not that she expected to sleep much with her brain whirling a million miles an hour.

She'd tried to make this place her own, with everything from sunflowers in the front yard to a quilted wreath on the door. Hokey? Maybe. But she'd dreamed of hokey and normal as a kid listening to the rain rattling along the tin roof of their trailer.

She pushed her way inside. The scent of freshly waxed floors and flowers greeted her, but not even a cat or dog of her own. So many times she'd wondered why she never chose a pet for herself, just took care of other people's....

Wait.

Her nose twitched.

Waxed floors and...flowers? She didn't have any inside, not even a floral air freshener.

Patting along the wall, she found the switch and flipped on the light. A wagon wheel chandelier splashed illumination around the room full of fat stuffed furniture in paisley patterns, a girly escape for a tomboy in a dusty, mucky profession. She spun to scan the room, her eyes landing on her shabby chic sofa.

Where a man was sprawled out asleep.

Her gaze skated from the boots on the armrest, up muscular legs in jeans, past a Diamonds in the Rough belt buckle, to broad shoulders in a blue flannel shirt. For a second, she thought Stone had followed her here. A straw cowboy hat covered the man's face as he snored softly.

Although once she looked closer, she realized it wasn't Stone at all. It was his near twin. His cousin

Alex was asleep on her sofa, with a fistful of wild daisies on his chest.

As she saw him waiting there for her, she couldn't help but think, Amie and Alex didn't tell each other everything.

Three

Johanna swept the cowboy hat from Alex's face. "What are you doing in my house?"

He peeked out of one eye lazily, scrubbed a hand over his face and yawned. Stretching, he sat up, keeping his hold on the daisies, apparently in no hurry to answer her question.

Alex rarely rushed. Yet he always seemed to get crazy amounts done. He was a fascinating individual, like all the McNairs. And while he'd been in her cabin often, she hadn't expected to see him here tonight.

"Well?" She hitched her hands on her hips. "Do you have anything to say for yourself? I locked the door, so you're breaking and entering."

"As your *landlord*," he drawled, his voice like Southern Comfort on the rocks, smooth with a bite. Stone spoke in more clipped, bass tones—like boulders rumbling. "I used my master key. I own the place."

She'd known Alex as long as she'd known Stone. She'd met all of the McNairs when her father took a stable hand job here during Johanna's third-grade year. Where Stone was the outgoing, bad-boy charmer, Alex had been the brooding, silent type, a tenacious rodeo champ even as a kid, breaking more bones by eighteen than any pro football star.

After she'd ended her engagement to Stone, she'd realized Alex's resolute nature had hidden a longtime attraction to her. Six months after the split, Alex had made his move by asking her out to dinner. She'd been stunned—and not ready to consider dating anyone. He'd taken the news well. Or so she'd thought. She was beginning to grasp how persistent, patient and downright stubborn this quiet giant could be.

With that in mind, she should have realized their grandmother's plan would not go over well with Alex. "Even though you own my rental cabin, I didn't realize landlords slept on the sofa," she joked, needing to keep things light. Her emotional well was running on empty. "Do you have a specific reason for being here?"

"I'm making sure you don't fall under my evil cousin's spell again." He swung his legs to the floor and thrust out the fistful of daisies.

Roots straggled from a couple of the stems. He definitely was a unique one with a charm all his own. At another time in her life she might have been tempted.

She took the daisies from him. "You're trying to persuade me by giving me flowers?"

"Consider it elaborate bribery," he said with a self-deprecating grin directed at the raggedy bouquet.

"You stole them out of the garden by the back deck," she shot over her shoulder as she stepped into the kitchen area to get a large mason jar.

"The garden belongs to me."

"To your family." She slid the flowers into the jar and tucked it under the faucet.

"Same thing." His smile faded. "Are you okay with this trip?"

"Your concern is sweet and I do mean that." She smiled, then jerked as water overflowed from the jar and splashed onto her hand.

"My motives are purer than Amie's were out there on the porch."

"You heard her?"

"I did, since you always leave your windows open rather than use the air conditioner." He stretched his legs out in front of him, crossing his boots at the ankles as he extended his arms along the back of the couch. "You would be wise to remember she's the most ruthless of all of us."

"That's not a very nice thing to say." She placed the flowers on the end table by the floral sofa, a perfect match for the rustic charm of her place.

"I only mean that you're my friend." He reached for her hand and tugged her down to sit beside him. "You and Amie don't have that kind of relationship. She's thinking of the family. I'm worried about you."

Johanna looked into his eyes, the same unique shade of light blue as Stone's. Though born three years apart, the men could have been twins. Alex was actually better suited for her. They had more in common. Alex ran a family ranch, whereas Stone was the king of the boardroom, such a workaholic he'd made it clear he had little room in his life for white-picket dreams.

Yet, as she sat here inches away from this incredibly sexy cowboy who'd just given her the sweetest flowers, she could only think of how much she'd wanted Stone to kiss her earlier. And Alex left her lukewarm, and it wasn't fair to keep stringing him along.

She touched his wrist. "Alex, we need to talk about—"

The front door opened with a knock in progress, no real warning at all. Johanna jolted, nearly falling off the sofa as she turned to face the intruder.

Stone stood in the open door, scowling, holding a handful of purple tulips.

What the hell?

Standing in Johanna's doorway, Stone cricked his neck from side to side, trying to process what his eyes told him. His cousin Alex sat on the sofa with Johanna. Close to Johanna. So near, their thighs pressed against each other and before she'd jolted away, she'd been leaning in, her hand on Alex's arm.

And there were fresh flowers on the end table.

Stone strode inside and tossed the tulips—ones that he'd pulled out of a vase in the lobby of the main lodge—onto the end table beside the daisies that looked remarkably like ones in the garden by the deck.

"Sorry to have interrupted..." Whatever had been about to happen. His pulse hammered behind his eyes; his head pounded in frustration over a hellish day that was spiraling down the drain faster and faster by the second.

Nibbling her bottom lip, Johanna rubbed her palms along her jeans. "At the risk of sounding cliché, this isn't what it looks like."

"What does it look like?" Stone smiled, somehow managing to keep his tone level in spite of the jealousy pumping through him.

"That Alex and I are a couple. We're not." She glanced at Alex apologetically.

That apologetic look spoke volumes. His cousin had

been trying to make a move on her. His cousin—as close as any brother—had fallen for Johanna. The thought stunned and rattled Stone into silence.

Alex stood, a gleam in his eyes just like when he'd reached the boiling point as a kid—just before he decked whoever had pissed him off. He leveled that gaze at Stone and slung an arm around Johanna's shoulders. "Who says we're not a couple?"

She shrugged off his arm. "Stop riling him up on purpose. You two are not teenagers anymore." She jabbed a finger at Stone. "That goes for you, too. No fights."

"I'm just looking for a straight answer." Stone spread his arms.

Johanna went prickly. "What this is or isn't doesn't concern you."

"Sure it does," he said, his tone half-joking, but his intent dead serious. "If you've been seeing each other and didn't bother to tell me, that's damn inconsiderate of my feelings."

Alex snorted. "Your *feelings?* You're joking, right?"

Stone resisted the urge to punch Alex in the face and forced reason through the fog. "You're yanking my chain on purpose. Why?"

"Just making a point. Johanna is important to this family and not just because she was your fiancée. If you hurt her," Alex said softly, lethally, "I'll kick your ass."

Fair enough.

They had the same goal: protecting her. Stone respected that. He nodded curtly. "Message heard and received."

Johanna whistled sharply between her teeth, like when she called a horse. "Hey, boys? Don't I get any say here?"

Stone shifted his focus from Alex to her. "Of course. What would you like to add?"

She rolled her eyes. "Nothing. Absolutely nothing. I'm completely capable of taking care of myself. Thank you both for your concern, but I need to pack for this trip tomorrow."

"Of course you can look after yourself," Stone said, gesturing for Alex to go out the door ahead of him. Then he took that moment's privacy to lean toward Johanna. "Just wanted to bring the tulips and say thank-you for caring about my grandmother's happiness."

She went still, most likely in shock, her hand drifting down to rest on top of the purple tulips. He used her moment of distraction to kiss her, just once, on the mouth, but good God, even a brief taste of Johanna was more potent than…anything. After seven months without the feel of her, his body shouted for more.

For everything.

Desire cracked like a whip inside him. He pulled back before he lost control and pushed his luck too far. "See you in the morning at the landing strip."

He closed the door behind him, the night sounds of bugs and owls, the wind in the trees, wrapping around him. He sucked in two deep breaths to steady himself before facing his cousin again.

Alex leaned against the porch post, tucking his hat on his head. "I meant what I said in there about kicking your ass."

"How serious is it? Whatever the two of you have going on?" What the hell would he do if his cousin was all-in? Or worse yet, if Johanna harbored feelings, too?

"If you care so much who she's seeing," Alex said ambiguously, "then do something about it." Without an-

other word, he shoved away from the post, jogged down
the steps and disappeared into the dark.

Stone stood on the porch, the smell of the tulips and
the feel of Johanna still fresh in his senses even though
he'd left her and the flowers inside. But then she'd been
in his thoughts every damn second since their split.

His cousin was right. Stone was still attracted to Johanna, and it was time to do something about it.

Stone's kiss still tinged her lips and her memory.

Johanna hauled her suitcase out from under the bed
and tossed it onto the mattress with a resounding thump.
What the hell had he been thinking, kissing her like
that? Although he hadn't lingered. Some might call it a
friendly kiss. Except they had this history together....

Need coursed through her, hot and molten, with just
a splash of sweetness, like the scent of the tulips she'd
brought with her into the bedroom. They rested under
the lamp, purple splashes of color on the white table.

She'd tried her best to tamp down her attraction to
Stone these past months, which was easier to do when
their paths rarely crossed. How would she survive a
week of time alone with him?

She dropped to sit on the edge of her bed, the white
iron headboard tapping the wall. She tugged one of the
purple tulips from the bunch and skimmed it against her
mouth lightly. She knew he'd certainly stolen them from
a vase in the lodge, and she couldn't help but note how
both cousins had snagged the closest flowers at hand.
They could drape women in jewels from their family
business, yet they still understood the value of a well-
timed bouquet.

Stone's tulips, and his kiss, were picking away at her

defenses. Too bad she couldn't wedge a coat of armor into her suitcase to withstand the barrage on her hormones.

Laughter with a hysterical edge bubbled out of her, and she flopped back on the bed into the cushiony softness of her pink-and-gray chevron quilt. She clasped the tulip against her chest, watching the ceiling fan click lazy circles above her. She and Stone had spent entire weekends in her bed making love. She hadn't wanted to go to his quarters in the main house, not even after they'd gotten engaged, not with his grandmother in a nearby suite. So he'd taken her on elaborate trips, vowing that he did so because then he could at least feel like she was staying with him.

Now Johanna wondered if she'd known they were destined to fail even from the start. Their time together had been a fantasy that couldn't withstand the light of harsh reality.

She hadn't traveled much before Stone. During her year dating Stone, he'd flown her to exotic locales and swanky fund-raisers held by influential billionaires, a world away from her ranch and Stetson day-to-day life.

What should she expect from this trip?

She rolled to her side and stared into the empty suitcase. What did a girl take to a week of doggie dates with mystery families and her ex-fiancé? More importantly, how would she react if he gave her another one of those impromptu kisses?

A tap on the window snapped her out of her daze.

She jolted upright, her heart pounding in alarm. Before she could even reach for the cell phone her eyes focused on the face in the glass pane.

Stone stood outside like a Lone Star Romeo.

Her pulse leaped. Damn her traitorous body.

She rolled from the bed and to her feet. She shoved the window up, the muggy night breeze rolling inside and fluttering the lace curtains. "What are you doing out there?"

"I forgot my flowers. You didn't seem to want them, so I figured I would give them to someone who would appreciate them." He hefted himself up and through the window before she could blink.

She stumbled back a step, watching him eye her room, walk to the flowers then peer out the door.

Realization dawned, along with a spark of anger. "You're checking to make sure your cousin didn't come back here."

"Maybe I am." He turned on his heels to face her again. His gaze fell to her bed, right where the lone tulip lay.

Feeling vulnerable, she rushed to scoop up the flower and said, "I'm trying to decide what to pack for the trip. Since I don't know where we're going, I'm not making much progress."

"Pack comfortably." The gleam in his eyes projected loud and clear that he wasn't fooled. "If we need something more, I'll buy it for you."

"We're not engaged anymore. You're not buying me clothes or other gifts." She'd returned all the jewelry after she'd broken up with him—everything, including a yellow diamond engagement ring with a double halo setting. The night he'd given it to her, she'd thought all of her dreams of a family and a real home had come true.

She'd grown up a lot in the past seven months, alone with her disillusionment.

"Johanna," he drawled, "we may not be engaged, but you are an employee of Hidden Gem Ranch and if you're

on Hidden Gem business and need clothes, the company
can pick up the bill."

"Clothes for what, exactly?"

"There's a gem trade show I want to catch while we're
out."

She knew how elaborate and hoity-toity those events
could get. Being with him at one of those shows would
feel too much like a fancy date. "I'll stay at the hotel
with the dogs."

"We'll see," he said in that stubborn, noncommittal
way of his just before he swung a leg out the window
again. "Good night."

"Stone?"

He stopped shy of stepping all the way through the
window. "Yes?"

"Thanks for the flowers." She strode closer—just
to be ready to close the window when he left, not to be
nearer to him. Right? "It really is sweet how much you
care about your grandmother's happiness. I always admired that about you, your family loyalty."

"Glad you have good memories, not just bad."

Guilt pinched her over how their breakup had hurt
him, too. She touched his shoulder lightly. "There's nothing between Alex and me."

"I'm glad to hear that."

Was it her imagination or had he swayed closer?

She pressed a hand to his chest. "That doesn't mean
there will never be someone. Am I not allowed to have
another relationship again?"

A smile played with his mouth. "I'm not answering that."

He looked over his shoulder at the yard.

She frowned. "Is something wrong?"

"Uh, actually—" he glanced back at her sheepishly "—I was taking the dogs for a run. Hope you don't mind they're digging up your yard right now."

She laughed, enjoying this Stone, more like the man she remembered falling for, playful and open. "We're just lucky they didn't jump my little split rail fence."

"Since they're going to be spending the next week with me flying around in a plane, it would be a good idea to remind them who I am."

She allowed herself to fall just a little more under his spell again, even if only for a minute. "That's very sweet of you."

"Sweet? First you make out with my cousin and then you call me sweet. Twice." He shook his head, tsking. "This is not my night."

Before she could help herself, she blurted out, "I wasn't kissing your cousin."

"Good." Stone cupped the back of her neck and drew her in for a kiss, the full-out kind that proved to be a lot more than mouth meeting mouth.

His body pressed to hers in a familiar wall of muscle. Her lips parted and heaven help her, she didn't regret it. She sank into the sensation of having his hands on her again, the warmth of his tongue boldly meeting hers. Kisses like this could lure her into forgetting a lot. In their time apart, somehow she'd lost sight of how intensely their physical attraction could sweep away reason.

Heat gathered between her legs until she gripped his arms, her fingers digging deep. A husky moan of pleasure and need welled up in her throat. She was so close to losing control altogether, what with a bed only a few short steps away. They may have had so many issues in their relationship, but when it came to sex, they were in perfect synchronicity.

How was she going to walk away from him after a kiss like this?

The ground tipped under her feet…or wait…Stone was stumbling into her. She braced a hand on her dresser for balance and realized Ruby the Rottweiler had both paws on the open window and she was nudging Stone in the back. Gem the yellow lab sprung up to join the Rottie, a symphony of barking echoing from beneath them. A quick glance down confirmed that Pearl the terrier and Sterling the Chihuahua-dachshund mix danced in the bushes below.

Breathlessly, she whispered, "I think it's time for you to go."

"Sleep well, beautiful." Stone winked once before sliding back out the window.

She should have slammed the window closed after him. Instead, she stood between the parted curtains and watched him gather the pack with ease. He guided the larger dogs to jump her fence while scooping up the two little ones.

No question, she was in serious trouble here with only one way to cope during the coming week. She had to make absolutely sure she and Stone did not touch each other, not even accidentally. First thing in the morning, she intended to make her hands-off edict clear. Her eyes clung to the breadth of his shoulders and lower to his perfect butt that rivaled any blue jeans ad ever.

Gritting her teeth, she slammed the window closed and spun away fast.

Damn, it was going to be a long, achy night.

* * *

The morning sun crept upward at the McNairs' private landing strip, which was located on the ranch. Johanna had given up waiting for Stone in the limousine an hour ago and had moved inside the small airport offices. The space held a waiting area, a control desk and a back room with a cot for a pilot to take naps if needed. There wasn't much else to do but sit. She could understand Stone being late to meet her, but his grandmother was here with her dogs, prolonging a farewell that already had to be horribly difficult.

Mariah held herself rigidly in control, Ruby and Gem each resting against one leg. Pearl and Sterling curled up together on a seat beside her. Johanna couldn't help but wonder how well the pack would adjust to being separated.

She checked the large digital clock above the door. The red numbers blinked nearly ten o'clock while the pilot kept busy with some paperwork outside beneath a Texas flag flapping lazily in the soft breeze. She bit back anger. She was exhausted from lack of sleep and frustrated from bracing herself to appear blasé in front of Stone.

Only to have him freakin' stand her up.

She was mad. Steaming mad. And completely confused. If he was playing mind games with her, that was one thing. But to involve his grandmother? That was plain wrong, and not like him.

Shuffling a seat to move closer to Mariah, Johanna put a reassuring hand on the woman's arm. "You don't have to do this, Mrs. McNair. The dogs can stay with you. They can stay here now and even if the time comes…" She swallowed back a lump of emotion. "Even if the time comes when you're not here. This is their home."

Mariah patted Johanna's hand. "It's okay, really. I love them enough to do what's best for them. I'll be in and out of the hospital quite often, and they deserve attention."

"Everyone here will take care of them." She held on tighter to this strong, brilliant woman who was already showing signs of fading away. She had new gaunt angles and a darkness around her eyes that showed her exhaustion in spite of keeping up appearances of normalcy with a red denim dress and boots. "You must realize that."

"I do, but I need to know they're settled permanently, for my own peace of mind." Mariah stroked the scruffy little terrier, adjusting the dog's bejeweled collar. "They deserve to be a part of a family and not just a task for the staff, or an obligation for a relative who doesn't really want them."

"They could be a comfort to you. Even if you kept one of them, like Pearl or Sterling, maybe…"

Mariah's touch skimmed from pup to pup until she'd petted all four. "I couldn't choose. It would be like playing favorites with my children or grandchildren."

There was an undeniable truth in her words and a selflessness that made Johanna ache all over again at the thought of losing her. "I wish there were more people like you in the world."

"You're dear to say that." She cradled Johanna's face in her hands. "And I wish you could be my granddaughter."

There it was. Out there. The unacknowledged big pink elephant that had sat in the middle of every one of their conversations for the past seven months. Mariah had never once interfered or questioned her decision to break it off with Stone.

If only there'd been some other way.

Johanna leaned in and hugged Mariah, whispering in her ear, "I'm so sorry I can't make that come true for you. I would have liked very much to have you as part of my family."

Mariah squeezed her once before easing away and thumbing a lone tear from the corner of her eye. "I just want you to be happy."

"My job makes me happy." True, but she'd once dreamed of much more. "If it weren't for your scholarship, I never could have afforded the training. I know I've thanked you before, but I can never thank you enough."

"Ah, dear." Mariah brushed back a loose strand from Johanna's braid. "This isn't goodbye. Even worst-case scenario, I'll be around for months, and you're only going to be gone a week. I intend to fight hard to be around as long as I can."

"I know." Johanna fidgeted with the horseshoe necklace. "I just want to be sure all the important things are said."

"Of course, but I don't want us to use our time on morbid thoughts or gloominess." Mariah smoothed her denim dress and sat straighter. "Stone in particular has had enough disappointment from the people he loves."

Johanna looked into the woman's deep blue eyes and read her in an instant. "You're sending him away this week so he won't be here as you start your treatments."

"Just until I get settled into a routine."

The closeness of the moment, the importance of this

time, emboldened her. "What if he wants to be around to support you?"

"My choices trump anyone else's right now," Mariah said with a steely strength that had made her a business-woman of national stature. "Keep Stone busy and take care of placing my dogs. Enjoy the time away from the ranch. You work too hard, and if I've learned anything lately, it's that we shouldn't waste a day."

Mariah eased the lecture with another squeeze of her hand, which Johanna quickly returned.

"Yes, ma'am."

"Good enough, and for goodness' sake, quit calling me Mrs. McNair or ma'am. If you can't call me Gran, then call me Mariah." She sighed, before shoving slowly to her feet. "Now how about we track down my tardy grandson so you can start your journey?"

"I'm sure he's on his way…Mariah." Johanna glanced at the wall clock again. This wasn't like him. Could something have happened?

Johanna's cell phone chimed from her purse, play-ing a vintage Willie Nelson love song. She glanced at Mariah, a blush stinging her cheeks faster than the fierce Texas sun. Damn it, why hadn't she changed her Stone ringtone? She should have swapped her ringtone to some broken heart, broken truck country song. There were sure plenty to pick from. She fished out her cell, fum-bling with the on button before putting it to her ear. "Where are you?"

"I'm at the office downtown." Stone's bass rumbled over her ears sending a fresh shiver of awareness down her spine. "A few unavoidable emergencies came up with work. I'll give you a call when I'm ready to leave."

Not a chance in hell was he getting off that easy, but

she didn't intend to chew him out with his grandmother listening. She would go straight to the Diamonds in the Rough headquarters and haul him out with both hands, if need be. Not that she intended to give him any warning. "Sure, thanks for calling."

She disconnected and turned to Mariah. "He's fine, just delayed downtown at the Fort Worth office. He wants me to swing by with the dogs, and we'll leave from there. Would you like to help me load the dogs in the car?"

"Of course." Mariah brightened at the task. "But please, take my limo. I'll have the airport security run me back to the house."

Johanna started to argue, but then the notion of rolling up to Diamonds in the Rough, Incorporated in the middle of downtown Fort Worth, dogs in tow, sounded like one hell of an entrance.

Her Texas temper fired up and ready, she was through letting Stone McNair walk all over her emotions.

Four

Stone hated like hell being late for anything, but crisis after crisis had cropped up at the office even though he'd come in at five in the morning to prep for his week-long departure.

Parked at his desk in front of the computer, he finished with the last details, clearing his calendar and rescheduling as much as he could for teleconferences from the road. He loved his grandmother, but she had to know the CEO of Diamonds in the Rough couldn't just check out for a week without major prep. That was the primary reason for her test, right? For him to prove he was best suited to run the company.

She couldn't have chosen a worse time.

Their CFO had gone into premature labor and had been placed on bed rest. His personal assistant was stuck in an airport in North Dakota. Their showroom was still under repairs from tornado damage and the construction crew's foreman had gone on strike.

And his grandmother was dying of cancer.

His hands clenched over the keyboard. For her, he'd put together detailed plans for taking Diamonds in the Rough to an international level, to expand the company as a tribute to his grandparents who'd been there for him

over the years. Yet now she might not even live long
enough to see that dream come to fruition. It cut him
to the core to think he'd somehow let her down, but he
must have since she felt she needed to concoct tests for
him to prove himself.

His eyes slid to the wood drafting table littered with
new designs, most of them done by Amie, but a few of
his own were scattered through the mix. He sketched
late at night, after hours, to ease the tension of the corporate rat race, more so since his breakup with Johanna. His pieces incorporated a larger emphasis on
metal work and carvings than Amie's. He still included
signature company jewels inlaid into the buckles, bolos
and even a few larger necklaces. Each piece also carried the expected Western aura.

Amie was the true artist in the family, but his pieces
usually landed well, too. Johanna had always encouraged him to design more....

He scratched his head and leaned back, desk chair
squeaking in protest. What had he been thinking,
climbing through her window last night like some out-
of-control teenager? Except...he had been out of control, jealous over seeing her with his cousin. He hadn't
thought. He'd simply acted. That kiss had left him with
a need for her that clawed like metal shards scraping
his insides raw. Even hearing her voice on the phone
forty-five minutes ago had increased the ache of wanting her in his bed again.

A quick buzz from the temp serving as a stand-in
personal assistant gave him only a second's warning
before his door flung open to reveal Johanna, fire spitting from her eyes. "You missed your flight."

God, she was sexy all riled up.

"I called you." He creaked his chair back even further, taking in the sight of her in white jeans and layered yellow tank tops. "And it's a private plane. *My* private plane, for that matter. There's no way to miss a flight that's waiting for me to give the go-ahead for takeoff."

Speaking of taking off... What he wouldn't give right now to peel away those tanks of hers, one at a time, with his teeth. He'd left her place last night to give himself space to regain control. Instead, their time apart had only taken his need to another level.

"Would have been nice to know you had other plans for your day before I reached the landing strip. I could have worked, too, or slept in. Or..." She held up her hand, four leashes in her fist. "I could have let the dogs play and run around in the yard longer."

She dropped the leashes and the four-pup pack stampeded into his office. Stone barely had time to bark, "Heel, damn it!" before Gem launched into his lap, the full force of the yellow lab almost tipping his chair over. Stone regained his balance then knelt to greet the dogs. Ruby, Sterling and Pearl licked over his face with slobbery wet tongues. He liked animals—clearly, since he'd grown up on a ranch—but these guys in full force were a little much, even for him.

Barks and yips continued until Johanna dipped into sight again, regaining control of the pooches one at time until all four mutts sat in a perfect line. Which only proved she could have controlled them right away. She'd let them overrun him on purpose.

Wincing, he stood, swiping an arm across his face. He shrugged off his suit jacket. Thank goodness he hadn't bothered with a tie today.

He draped his jacket over the back of his leather

chair. "My apologies for inconveniencing you. Even if my grandmother questions my ability to run the company, I do still have obligations here that needed to be taken care of before I could leave."

"Is that what this is about?" She crossed her arms, which threatened to draw his eyes to her chest just when he needed to keep his wits about him and focus on her words. "Showing your grandmother you're indispensable?"

"That's not a nice accusation."

"Is it true?" she pressed.

Damn it, she always saw right through him. But that was only part of the picture. "My primary goal is to bring my grandmother peace. A crisis here at the office will only add to her stress level at a time when she can't afford any additional drain."

Silently, Johanna assessed him through narrowed eyes while the dogs panted, lazy tongues lolling.

"What?" he said. "You don't believe me?"

"I'm skeptical," she said slowly. "Are you still sulking because Alex brought me flowers?"

Did she have to read his every thought? "I don't sulk. I'm charming. Everyone says so."

She cocked an eyebrow. "Yep, you're sure charming the socks off me right now."

Really? He recognized a challenge when he heard one. He flattened a palm to the heavy oak desk that mirrored the one in the ranch office. "If memory serves, I charmed off more than your socks right on this desk about ten months ago."

Her jaw dropped, then clamped shut before she finally said, "Never mind. If you're finished, let's leave so we can get this trip over with sooner rather than later."

All the more reason, in his mind, to prolong this little chat.

She leaned down to gather the leashes.

Kneeling, he clasped her wrist. "Wait, you started this. Let's talk."

"Let's not." She tugged her arm free.

"Fine. Not talking is okay with me, too." Standing, he swept off his desk.

Her eyes went wide. "What are you doing?"

"You said you didn't want to talk." He fingered a button on his shirt. Sure he knew they weren't really going to have sex on his desk, but he reveled in the regret in her eyes that she couldn't hide in spite of her scowl.

She shook her head, blond hair loose and silky sliding along her shoulders. "You're being outrageous."

"Good." He untucked his shirt.

"Stop. Now," she said firmly.

Okay, he'd pushed her far enough for today, but he could see that while their love for each other might have burned out, their passion still had plenty of fire left.

He buttoned his shirt again and tucked in the tails. "Spoilsport."

"Let's clean up the floors first before we go." She brushed papers into a stack. "The pilot's waiting."

"Damn waste of an empty desk." He stacked a haphazard pile of Diamonds in the Rough promo flyers and placed them on the drafting table.

She glanced up at him through long lashes. "Are you trying to chase me off? Because if you don't stop with these stunts, I am out of here. I will place the animals because it's the right thing to do, but you, however, are on your own."

For some reason, her words caught him off guard.

He leaned back against the desk, a weary exhale bursting from him. "Honest to God, Johanna, I don't know what I'm doing. Ever since my grandmother dropped her bombshell, I've just been reacting."

Standing, she clutched a stack of files to her chest, the dog leashes still trailing from her grip. "That's understandable."

"So you're not going to threaten to leave again?" he couldn't stop himself from asking.

She chewed her lip for an instant before responding, "If you keep being honest with me, I will stay."

"Deal." He extended a hand.

She slid hers into his. "Deal."

They stood there with their hands clasped for a few seconds longer than a handshake, seconds that crackled like static in the air just before a thunderstorm.

He enjoyed the hell out of a good drenching downpour, every bit as arousing as a blazing fire.

Her tongue slid along her lips as if to soothe where she'd chewed moments before. His body throbbed in response.

She tugged her hand from his self-consciously and rubbed her fingers along her white jeans. "Where's the first stop on our journey?"

"You don't know?" He would have expected his grandmother to tell her. Yet, even without knowing the specifics, Johanna had signed on for Mariah. That giving spirit was one of the things that had always drawn him to Johanna, even as it simultaneously scared the hell out of him. Because he'd always known she was too good for him. And too wise. Eventually, she would see through him and leave.

He'd been right.

"My grandmother has put me completely at your mercy." He spread his arms wide.

She thrust the leashes at him. "Feels more like I'm at your mercy, but whatever. You can start by helping me with the dogs."

Pivoting away, she strode out of his office, those white jeans showcasing the perfect curve of her hips, her butt. His fist clenched around the leather leads.

Hell, yes, the fire between them was alive and well.

Johanna gripped the leather armrests of her chair during takeoff. The private jet climbed into the sky and she still didn't know where they were going. Yet she'd gotten back into the limousine and onto the plane with Stone and the dogs without demanding more information. She'd been grateful to use the animals as an excuse to end their sexually charged exchange in his office.

Although the confined space of the plane didn't do much to ease the tight knot of desire inside her. The plane leveled out, and she wished her own emotions were as easy to smooth. She sank deeper into the fat chair, its brown leather and brass gleaming.

Each of the pups was now secured in a designer crate bolted to the floor in the back, complete with a luxurious dog bed and a pewter bowl. Engraved nameplates marked each crate and dish. Mariah hadn't been at the landing strip when they returned. Apparently, one set of goodbyes had been as much as she could take. These past two days had been some of the most emotional Johanna had experienced. The only other days that could compare were when her parents had died and when she'd broken her engagement.

And what about Stone? She glanced across the aisle

at him, sympathy whispering through her, mingling with the frustrated passion she'd experienced in his office. Okay, to be frank, that frustrated desire flared every time she saw him, regardless of whether he said outrageous things.

He continued to work, even on the plane, just as he'd been doing when she'd burst into his office earlier. He'd opened his tablet and fired it to life, sitting on the plane's sofa. In days past, she would have curled beside him, close, touching. Now they sat on opposite sides of the jet.

As if he felt her gaze, he spoke without looking up. "We're flying to Vermont to interview a family for Gem first."

"Nice to know you're finally giving specifics for this trip. Please do carry on about Gem, Vermont and this prospective adoptive family."

He flashed a quick dimple without looking up from his tablet. "They have a newborn, so they prefer an adult dog that's already trained."

"They're wise to know that adding a puppy is like having another baby." Sounded promising. "Who's this family?"

"Troy Donavan and his wife, Hillary."

"Donavan?" she repeated in shock. She knew the McNairs had connections, but they acted so down-to-earth sometimes their power still caught her unaware. "The Robin Hood Hacker Donavan? Your grandmother chose a former criminal for her dog?"

"Where's your sense of forgiveness?" He glanced up. "His criminal past was a long time ago. He went to reform school as a teenager."

She snorted on a laugh of disbelief. "For breaking into the Department of Defense computer system. That's more than some teenage prank."

"True," Stone conceded, setting his tablet beside his Stetson. "But he's led a productive and successful life as an adult. Well, once he got past the playboy stage."

"People in glass barns shouldn't throw stones."

"I've missed your humor."

"Thank you."

She'd missed a lot of things about him, which had made her question her decision more than once. Except Stone wasn't known for his forgiving nature. While he'd made it clear he still desired her, she didn't expect he would get over being dumped or change his stance on having children. So all this flirting was counterproductive.

"We're getting off the subject," she said. "Back to the Donavans, please."

"Regardless of Troy's past, all signs indicate the Donavans are a happy couple. But the whole reason for this visit is to be sure Gem is going to a good home. They understand there's no promise the dog will be theirs."

"Good." She nodded tightly. "I have no problem leaving with her if we don't trust them to take the best care of her."

His full-out smile pushed dimples into both cheeks, his skin weathered from the sun. "I've also missed the way you get fearless when it comes to your love of animals. You never were impressed with my money. That's a rare thing."

His genuine compliment moved her as much as his touch and that was dangerous to her peace of mind. "Back to the dogs," she insisted. She pulled a manila folder from her carry-on backpack. "I have questionnaires for the families to fill out to help ensure they are a good fit."

He cocked a dark eyebrow. "A meet and greet is one thing, but you have an adoption application for them to fill out, as well?"

"I prefer the word *questionnaire*," she said primly. "But yes, it could also be called an application."

He leaned back, arms along the sofa. "You do realize they could just buy a dog."

"They could. That doesn't mean we have to give them Gem simply because they have money. If anything, adopting Gem will show their child that love can't be bought." Tapping the folder, she sighed sadly. "It's becoming clear now that your grandmother was right to send me with you."

"What if they're awesome but Gem isn't a good fit or doesn't like them? How will you explain it to them?" he asked, appearing to be genuinely interested. "What will you tell my grandmother?"

"Your grandmother will understand. That was her reason for sending us rather than just shipping the dogs directly to the families."

"And the Donavans?" he pushed for more.

That would be awkward but not enough to make her go against her principles. "I will suggest they go to their local animal shelter to find a forever furry friend." She couldn't resist adding, "Hopefully, they'll make a huge donation while they're there."

"You've thought a lot through since just yesterday."

She rolled her shoulders in a shrug. "I'm also trusting you to roll out that charisma to smooth over any rough patches if need be."

"Somehow I don't think you're complimenting me."

Were his feelings really hurt? He seemed so confident most—all—of the time. She unbuckled and walked across the aisle to sit beside him and oops, she hadn't given much thought to the fact that his arms were extended along the couch, which in effect put his arm around her.

She held herself upright to keep from leaning into his hold. "Why don't you just keep Gem? Didn't some client give him to you?"

"He's not really mine. He may have been given to me, but he always preferred my grandmother." He picked up a lock of her hair. "Truth is, Gem was a gift from a guy who had the hots for my grandmother and was trying to wrangle an in with the family, since she loves dogs."

"Run that by me again?" How had she not known that?

"After my grandfather died of a heart attack, a lot of guys made moves on Gran," he said darkly. "She was a rich widow. Pretty. Guys were lining up. Some were genuine," he conceded. "Some were fortune hunters."

"Yet she never remarried."

"She says no one matches up to my grandfather."

Johanna's parents had felt the same way about each other. She wanted a love like that for herself and she wasn't willing to settle. "That's sweet and sad at the same time, loving that much and losing it."

He shifted in his seat. "Back to the story of how we got Gem as a puppy…"

"Not so at ease with the emotional stuff, are you?" How many other times had he dodged speaking about deeper feelings when she'd just assumed he was jaded or insensitive?

"Puppy. Gem." His firm voice made it clear he wasn't

taking her bait. He would stay in control of the conversation, going only as far as he decided to go.

"This guy thought he was being original giving me a dog to get to my grandmother. Little did he know, he wasn't the first dude to try that. The first guy brought a puppy—Gem number one—when I was around nine. The guy who'd given him to me to get to my grandmother... Boy, did that ever backfire on him. The puppy hated kids, had zero interest in playing ball or sleeping at the foot of my bed. He just wanted to go on lazy walks, which sounded boring to me at that age."

An image unfolded in her head of Stone as a little boy. And what little boy wouldn't be thrilled over a puppy? How sad he must have been to have the first Gem ignore him, reject him. He wouldn't have understood.

She leaned toward his hand ever so slightly as he toyed with her hair. "That's why all the family members should meet a pet first before deciding on the best fit for their family. Otherwise, it's not fair to the dog or the people."

"So the guy learned as my grandmother showed him the door." He wrapped the lock of hair around his finger as the jet engines hummed in the background. "The guy offered to drop the puppy off at the local shelter, which was totally the wrong thing to say to my grandmother. She dumped the guy flat and kept the puppy for herself." He smiled fondly at the memory, his gaze shifting to the yellow Labrador asleep in her crate. "So the next time a guy brought a puppy trying to win Gran over, we named him Gem II. Both Gems were her favorite walking companions."

Affection for his grandmother wrapped around his

every word. Saying goodbye to Gem would start that
letting go, the beginning of a grieving process Johanna
wished she could take from him or make easier. Even
thinking about all the pain he would face watching his
grandmother's health fail squeezed at Johanna's heart.

Before she could stop the impulse, she wrapped her
arms around Stone.

Five

Kissing Johanna had rocked his world, always had. But since they'd begun this trip, he'd been the one to make the first move each time they'd touched. Having Johanna reach for him sent Stone rocketing into another orbit altogether.

He didn't need any further encouragement.

Sliding his arms around her, he breathed in her flowery scent and savored the silky tease of her braided hair gripped in his fist. The plane engines hummed an echo of the desire buzzing through his veins.

And to think, he'd almost messed this up.

His first instinct when she'd offered consolation had been to shrug off her sympathy. Then his better sense had kicked in. He had Johanna in his arms. Touching him. Sighing.

He skimmed a hand down her pulled-back hair, releasing more of that floral scent. Her slim body molded to him, the softness of her breasts against his chest so familiar. So damn perfect. He nuzzled her ear, right beside the filigreed dream catcher dangling from her lobe. Her arms tightened around him, her hand cupping his neck. Just the feel of being skin to skin sent his heart slugging against his ribs.

Her fingers stroked through his hair, and he couldn't hold back any longer. He kissed her, fully and thoroughly, with his mouth, his hands, his body. From the first time he'd touched her and tasted her, desire had pulsed through him. Stronger than any attraction he'd ever experienced. He'd known then. Johanna was special.

For years he'd seen her as only that kid wandering around the stable yard. Everything had changed the day she'd come riding in after getting caught in a rainstorm. Her clothes had been plastered to her body. He'd gathered a couple of towels to give her. Two pats in and he'd known. He'd wanted her.

Still did.

That had been two years ago, a couple of years after she'd finished vet tech school and taken a job at the Hidden Gem Ranch. A year later they'd been engaged. Five months later, she'd returned his ring.

His mind shied away from that part and back to the passion, the connection, the need. He stroked along her spine until he reached the waistband of her jeans. Her layered tank tops had ridden up to expose a patch of skin. He palmed her waist, drawing her closer. She wriggled nearer, her fingers gripping his hair, her mouth moving along his, meeting him kiss for kiss, touch for touch.

She might have only meant to console him, but she was clearly every bit as moved as he was by the moment. She wanted him every bit as much as he wanted her. There wasn't a question in his mind.

He reclined her onto the sofa, stretching out over her. Her long legs twined with his. A husky moan vibrated in her throat. Her head fell back and she arched into the press of his mouth as he kissed down her neck.

Tucking a hand between them, he slid the button free on her jeans, then flicked her belly button ring. His thumb recognized the jewelry from touch, a tiny silver boot with spurs and a diamond stud at the top. Possessiveness stirred deep in his gut. He'd given it to her early in their relationship, when she'd still wanted to keep their connection a secret. She'd been nervous about people calling her an opportunist.

That she still wore the gift stoked his passion and made him bolder. He eased her zipper down link by link then dipped his hand inside. He knew the feel of her, had memorized every inch of her, but after months without her, there was also a newness to this moment. He slipped his fingers lower, lower still until he found...

Yes.

The slick proof of her arousal set his skin on fire. Her hips rolled as she surrendered to his touch. Her husky, needy whispers caressed his ears.

Her hands roved his back restlessly, her nails scoring a needy path down his spine, tugging the hem of his shirt from his suit pants. With a frenzied yank, she popped the buttons of his shirt. He pushed up her tank tops, and bare flesh met bare flesh, damn near sending him over the edge.

This was getting out of control fast. The pilot was a simple door away. Stone had hoped to steal a kiss but he hadn't dared hope things would go this far. He needed to ensure their privacy. The sleeping area in back was small but plenty sufficient to make thorough love to her. He'd done so more than once as he'd sought to romance her around the world.

Easing his hand from her jeans with more than a little regret over losing her sweetness for even a brief break, he rolled from her, keeping his mouth sealed to hers. He tucked both arms under Johanna and lifted her against his chest. More than once he'd carried her to bed or to his desk or to a field of bluebonnets. On this realm, at least, they were in perfect synch with one another.

"Stone—" she nipped his ear with a husky sigh "—you have to know this isn't a wise idea, but for some reason I can't bring myself to say no."

"I never claimed anything about our relationship was logical." He shouldered open the door to the jet's sleeping quarters.

She cupped his face in her hands. "What do you mean by that?"

He adjusted his hold on her as he neared the bed covered in a thick comforter. Dim pot lights overhead illuminated the small jet cabin. "I've always known that you are too good for me. It was only a matter of time until you figured it out."

Her forehead furrowed. "Is that really how you felt, or are you manipulating me because I'm having a weak moment?"

Manipulating her? Is that what she really thought of him?

Her words splashed cold reality over him. This wasn't the right time to take her back into his bed again. He'd made considerable progress just now and he didn't intend to lose ground by pushing for too much too soon. If he slept with her now, she might never trust him enough for a second time…and hell, yes, he knew once would not be enough.

He lowered her feet to the ground. The glide of her

body against his made him throb all the harder, almost changing his mind and to hell with wisdom. He wanted—needed—her now so damn much his teeth ached.

Almost.

"You'll have to decide that for yourself." He backed away, his hands up between them, trying to keep his eyes firmly focused on her face rather than on the gorgeous tangled mess of her hair and the open vee of her jeans. "And when you do, if you still want us to sleep together again, just say the word and I'll be there before you can say 'let's get naked.' But I need to know you're in one hundred percent, no regrets."

He pivoted away and out the door before he made a liar out of himself and tangled up in the sheets with her for what he knew would be the best sex of their lives.

Five hours later, in Vermont, Johanna's brain was still spinning with confusion after how close she'd come to sleeping with Stone again.

Sleeping? More like unraveling in his arms at just one touch.

At least she had the distraction of a picnic lunch with the Donavan family while she gathered her thoughts. She and Stone had brought Gem along to meet them, while the other three dogs unwound in a fenced area around the guesthouse where Stone and Johanna would be staying tonight.

The late lunch with the Donavan family was an intriguing surprise. Johanna sat at a rustic picnic table while Hillary Donavan pushed her snoozing infant son in a baby swing under a sprawling sugar maple tree. Hillary was so down-to-earth she could have been Johanna's redheaded cousin, complete with freckles and a high swinging ponytail. Johanna felt at ease, something she hadn't expected once she'd heard who they would be visiting first.

Hillary's husband was every bit as approachable in spite of his notorious history as the Robin Hood hacker. Wearing a fedora with his khaki shorts and T-shirt, Troy ran alongside Stone playing fetch with Gem in a field of red clover.

The Donavan homestead was as understated as the couple. A 1920s farmhouse perched on a low rolling hill. A porch wrapped around the first floor and black shutters bracketed the windows.

Bit by bit she saw the amenities added into the landscape so artfully she'd barely noticed. A pool nestled near a wooded area with rock ledges and a waterfall gave it the appearance of a stream feeding into a pond—a clear, chlorinated pond. A child's playhouse had been built from wood under a massive tree. A security fence enclosed the entire two-acre property—which enabled her to check a box on the adoption application. A lab like Gem would need a safe place to run out her energy with this wonderful family.

She sipped her iced tea, finally beginning to relax now that part one of their mission appeared to be a success. The lunch together had been just what Johanna needed to unwind after the tension of the past twenty-four hours. The meal had been beyond delicious without being overly elaborate. A juicy fruit salad accompanied loaves of hearty peasant bread and deli meats, cheeses and spreads of their choice. Fresh-squeezed lemonade. And the ice cream… Her mouth watered as she finished off another bite of fresh maple walnut ice cream. These parents were clearly trying to give their child as normal a life as possible, given little T.J.—Troy Junior—was the offspring of one of the wealthiest men in the world.

Hillary wrapped her arms around her knees as she hitched her feet up onto the bench by the redwood picnic table. "We appreciate you going to so much trouble to bring Gem to us. He's such a great dog, playful but well trained."

"Thank *you* for letting us invade your home. We could have met in a park or somewhere generic for you to see Gem."

"I loved time at the park as a child, but I'm still nervous about taking T.J. out in public for security reasons." Hillary's hand fell protectively to stroke the baby's head.

The Donavan compound clearly had top-of-the-line security that could rival Fort Knox, including computerized keypads discreetly hidden and staff that could have doubled as bouncers. Johanna had never thought about the safety issue with Stone's upbringing. How difficult it must have been for his family to balance all that wealth with values. He'd clearly been born into a vast dynasty, but he had a strong work ethic. She'd always admired that about him.

Apparently, the Donavans felt the same.

"Well, Hillary, I have to say this is definitely more comfy than a park. It's generous of you to host us overnight."

The thought of being alone with Stone tonight was starting to sink in. Her skin tingled at the notion.

Hillary's gaze scanned the low rolling hills around their home. "We bought this place to give T.J. the kind of upbringing neither of us had."

Johanna angled her head to the side. "Where did you grow up?"

"Here in Vermont actually, but much more scaled back and...well...not secure." She looked back at Johanna. "I love my mom, but she was troubled. Actually, she was an alcoholic. It took us a long time to reconcile, but I'm glad we found a way to make peace before she passed."

"Oh, um, I'm sorry you had to go through that," she said, feeling totally inadequate. *Sorry* was such a lame, overused word. "Is the rest of your family still nearby?"

"My sister, yes. Troy and I have extended family, as well, the kinds of friends that are as close as relatives. We visit each other as often as we can, but we all bought vacation homes in Monte Carlo so our kids can have a sense of growing up together like cousins."

Hillary's shoulders lost much of their tension at the mention of her husband's close friends, and she launched into a story about their most recent trip to Monaco for a Formula One racing event.

The baby boy squawked awake in his swing, stopping Hillary midstory. With already expert hands, she scooped up her newborn and declared, "He needs changing and I didn't bring enough diapers out here. If you'll excuse me for a few minutes, I'll be right back."

"Of course. Take your time. I'm enjoying the sunshine." And trying so very hard not to be envious of Hillary's glowing happiness.

As if to rub salt in the wound in her aching heart, Troy noticed his wife's departure and took off after her in a slow jog, Gem loping alongside him having already transferred his doggy allegiance to the Donavans.

Stone peeled away and strode back toward her, so

damn handsome he took her breath away. Yet she knew even if he turned gray and paunchy, the essence of the man would be the same.

Strong. Driven. Accomplished. Charismatic.

And still determined to deny himself—both of them—the family happiness she craved. As much as she wanted him, she couldn't bring herself to settle for less than everything.

Taking a seat beside Johanna at the picnic table, Stone saw the wistfulness in her eyes as she watched the family tableau. He knew, without question, he'd put that pain there. Guilt threatened to drive him to his knees.

This whole afternoon of domestic bliss had been tough for him, as well, reminding him of all the times he'd seen his cousins with their parents while he sat on the periphery. He'd moved past wanting that for himself and realized he was better off not inflicting the same disappointment on offspring of his own. He knew his limitations. He didn't have the emotional capacity to be a parent, and he refused to let down a kid. A parent had to be 100 percent in. Otherwise it wasn't fair to the child. Johanna would expect—and deserved—to have a spouse every bit as committed to home and hearth as she was, rather than some stonehearted guy with a crack baby past.

He didn't want to think overlong about the man who would offer her that fairy-tale future, especially not with the feel and taste of Johanna still so fresh in his memory. The sun kissed her shoulders, which were bared in her sundress. He allowed himself at least a small indulgence and grazed his knuckles along the tanned skin, sweeping aside her golden French braid.

He cupped the back of her neck and massaged lightly. "Are you okay with the Donavans adopting Gem?"

"What do you think?" Her head lolled back into his touch. "I'm thrilled. Gem is going to a wonderful family. There's nothing not to love about this."

"I have to confess, it's going even better than I'd hoped." His thumb worked at a knotted muscle at the base of her skull. The silkiness of her skin and the light sigh passing her lips stirred him.

Her eyelids fluttered closed, her face a study in bliss. "Your grandmother will be relieved to hear the news."

"I already texted her." He waggled his cell phone before tucking it away again.

"You what?" Her emerald-green eyes snapped open, surprise and a hint of something else sparking. "That was mighty confident of you. What if I'd disagreed? I am a part of this process, you know."

"I could tell you were okay with this about thirty minutes in." His thumb brushed along her cheek before returning to the back of her neck again. "I may not be the right man for you, but I know you well."

She swatted at his chest lightly. "Then why did you bother asking when you sat down with me a few minutes ago?"

"It was an excuse to talk to you, and God knows, I wasn't going to pass up an opportunity to touch you." His voice went gravelly. His self-control was shot around her these days.

Her chest rose and fell faster in a tangible mirror of his arousal. "Why are you torturing us both this way?"

Hell if he knew the answer. "How about we both just enjoy the outdoors and sunshine? We have red clover instead of bluebonnets, but the love of the land is still here. Nothing is going to happen between us out here in the open, especially not with the Donavans nearby. There's no harm. Accept the neck massage and relax."

Some of the anger melted from her kinked muscles and she sagged back into his touch. "You always did give the best neck rubs."

"It's been a stressful couple of days." He hadn't wanted to leave Texas and now he couldn't envision what life would be like after they returned. "I sent my grandmother photos of Gem with the Donavans."

"That was thoughtful of you."

"She texted back that she's happy and relieved." And he had to confess knowing he'd eased that worry for her made him as happy as if he'd landed a big new contract. "So yes, our task is twenty-five percent complete."

"I know those photos must have brought Mariah a lot of joy." Angling toward him, Johanna stroked along his eyebrows before cupping his face. Her fingertips were callused from work, but gentle, soothing, the hands of a healer. "We may not be meant to be married, but there was—is—so much about you that's special. Otherwise I never could have fallen for you."

"Yet, here we are."

Silence settled between them, highlighting nature's sounds of branches rustling in the wind and birds chirping.

Johanna's eyes went sad, unshed tears glistening. "I wish things could be different for us, I truly do."

He agreed 100 percent. But where did that leave them? "We haven't talked about what happened between us earlier on the airplane."

"What *almost* happened," she amended.

"Right." That sure put him in his place. Still, he

couldn't stop the urge to indulge in a week of no-strings sex, to make the most of one last chance to be with Johanna. "Do you still feel like I was trying to manipulate you?"

She eased back, her hand falling from his face, and she ducked her head to avoid his touch. "Nothing's changed. We both know an affair can't lead anywhere."

"Not even a temporary fling," he said in a joke, though he was more than half-serious.

She didn't laugh. But she didn't say no, either. She simply sat in silence as the wind sent a couple of stray maple leaves skittering across the picnic table.

Hope surged through him along with a pulse of heat in his veins. He knew they couldn't have a long-term relationship, but he could feel her giving in to this week together. He pressed ahead. He just had to figure out what was holding her back. "Is there someone else?"

She choked on a laugh. "Are you serious? I live on your land, and I work at your family's ranch. There aren't any secrets."

No secrets? She was wrong there. He'd been clueless about Alex's feelings for her. "My cousin has a thing for you, and I didn't know about that."

She crossed her arms over her chest, plumping the gentle curves of her breasts along the neckline of her yellow sundress. "I told you there's nothing between Alex and me."

"But he wants there to be more." Stone's jaw clenched at the thought of her with someone else. The possibility that someone could be his cousin, and that Stone would have to watch them together every day for the rest of his life, was still more than he could wrap his brain around without blowing a gasket. "That's clear to me now. Although why I didn't see it earlier is a mystery."

"I can't control what your cousin feels, but I can assure you those feelings are not returned." She touched his wrist lightly, tentatively. "This isn't Alex's fault. People don't always make wise choices about who to... be drawn to."

"Are you talking about us now?"

Chuckling wryly, she squeezed his hand. "You truly are clueless if you even have to ask. No wonder you didn't notice how Alex feels."

Even though she insisted she didn't want Alex, Stone still had to know more. "How far did things go with Alex before you realized you weren't interested in him that way?"

For a moment, he thought she would refuse to answer his question, but then her shoulders lowered, defensiveness melting from her. Her answer was important to him, too important. His heart pounded in his ears.

"Alex asked me out once. I said no, because I'm not into rebound relationships. I also didn't want to cause trouble between the two of you."

"You care about both of us," he realized. How much did she care about Alex? Was she holding back?

"Of course I care about you both." Her hand stayed on his. Did she know her thumb stroked along his wrist? "I practically grew up on the ranch with both of you. In fact, I played more with Alex and Amie since they're younger than you. Of course I spent a lot more time studying you because of my monster crush. Sometimes it amazes me how I can know so much about you in some ways and so little in others."

He flipped his hand over to grip hers. "We saw what we wanted to see."

"I know you and Alex are as close as brothers. The last thing I want to do is cause trouble between you."

"We don't always see eye to eye on everything, but we're close. We'll get through this, too." The thought of losing any more of his family was beyond considering. "We grew up like brothers."

Except they weren't, in spite of all the times he'd wished they could be.

"You guys definitely had troublemaker moments." She grinned, lightening the mood and taking them back to safer ground. "Remember when the two of you put Kool-Aid in Amie's showerhead right before the Miss Stampede Queen pageant? I didn't think she would ever forgive either of you for turning her hair pink."

"That was Alex's idea."

"Um, I don't think so. And if it was, that's probably because you whispered the idea in his ear when he was sleeping."

Or because he'd left a gag book open to a particular page right on Alex's desk. Stone grinned. "I may have instigated some—okay, *most* of the pranks." He recognized her attempt to get off the subject and he didn't intend to lose sight of what he needed to know.

"Both of you were fantasy material for all my school friends—rich, sexy cowboys. What's not to drool over?" Mischief sparkled in her eyes. "But as you know, my crush was firmly placed on you."

"What about now?"

The pool filter kicked on, the fountain spewing higher. He looked over his shoulder and found staff clearing away the dishes discreetly. Once they left, Johanna leaned toward him again.

"You and I are not engaged anymore, and our core reason for the breakup hasn't changed. You know that," she said gently but firmly.

"Yet, we were kissing a few hours ago." Kissing and more.

She pulled her hand back. "This kind of conversation is exactly what I wanted to avoid."

"If I weren't in the picture, would you and Alex be together?" He hated the way this discussion made him feel, the jealousy, the doubts. But damn it, he couldn't let it go.

Her lips went tight with frustration for an instant. "I've already told you I'm not seeing Alex."

"I heard you." He remembered everything she'd ever said to him. "I'm asking if you have romantic feelings for him. That's different."

She shoved to her feet, walking absently toward the trunk of the maple tree before glancing back over her shoulder. "You're not going to let this go, are you?"

"You broke up with me, not the other way around." And the days following that breakup had been some of the darkest in his life.

"Your cousin and I are very much alike." She sagged against the trunk. "Too much so to be a couple."

His shoulders dropped with relief. "I'm glad to hear that…." He stood and walked to her, grabbing a branch just over her head. "Even though I know I have no rights, the thought of you being with him drives me crazy."

"Is that why you made a move on me at my place, in your office—on the plane?"

"I kissed you because I wanted to." Like now.

"And that's the first time you've wanted to in seven months?"

"Hell, no." He thought about having her every day—and every night.

"Then something changed to make you act on the impulse. Is that 'something' jealousy?" Her eyes searched him with genuine confusion. "If you can't have me, no one can?"

Put that way, he sounded like a jerk. "I don't know how to explain it other than to say that since my grandmother dropped her bombshell news on us, it feels like the world is off-kilter."

"So if your grandmother was healthy, you would still be keeping your distance, like before."

Was she hinting that she'd wanted him to fight harder to get her back? One wrong move and he could wreck the moment. The only thing he knew to do was be honest.

"Hell, I don't even really know what I mean except that we are here, together. And the thought of never being with you again is tearing me apart."

She swallowed hard, chewing her bottom lip as she stared up at him.

Stone continued, "I also know I can't just stand around and pretend to be unaffected. So either leave now or prepare to be fully, thoroughly kissed."

"I, I just… I can't." She stuttered, shaking her head slowly, sidestepping away from the tree, then rushing past him.

She couldn't be any clearer than that.

Disappointment delivered a kick to the gut even though he hadn't expected anything different.

He gave her enough time to make it inside before he released the tree branch and started back toward the main house. He only had an afternoon and dinnertime to get his head together before they spent the night alone together in the guesthouse.

One afternoon didn't sound like nearly long enough when even seven months hadn't helped him get over Johanna.

Johanna had busied herself caring for the other three dogs, taking them on a hike, feeding them, hiking again, and still restless energy whirled inside her well into suppertime.

Their evening was coming to an end with coffee on the covered back porch, a lazy ceiling fan rustling the air. Soon, she wouldn't be able to hide behind the Donavan family any longer. She would be spending the night alone with Stone.

Of course she could go to a hotel. Nothing in Mariah's agreement said she had to sleep under the same roof as Stone. She just had to help him place the dogs. Except she didn't want to cause an embarrassing scene for him in front of the Donavans....

Oh, hell, who was she kidding? She wanted to finish their afternoon conversation and learn more about why he was pursuing her now. He'd said his grandmother's terminal illness had flipped his world. If he was reevaluating, could he change his mind on things that had kept them apart before?

If so, could she trust her heart to him a second time?

Walking away the first time had nearly destroyed her with grief and loss. They were barely a day into this trip and her willpower was fading fast. She finished the last of her iced decaf coffee.

Stone set aside his empty mug and leaned toward Johanna. "We should say our good-nights. Do you have the gift from my grandmother?"

"Oh, right." She jolted and reached into her woven satchel. "We have a present for your son, to thank you both for having us here and for giving Gem a good home."

She pulled out a Diamonds in the Rough gift sack and passed it to Hillary. The bag glistened with the pattern of diamonds and spurs, the company's bold, black logo scrolled at an angle.

"How thoughtful," Troy said. "You didn't have to do this, but thanks. Hillary, how about you do the honors."

"I do love surprises." She passed over the snoozing infant to Stone.

A momentary panic flashed in his eyes, quickly masked before he cradled the baby carefully in his arms. His broad hands cupped the tiny bottom and supported the head. His sun-bronzed skin contrasted with the newborn alabaster of the baby.

Johanna's heart melted. How could it not? Her fondest dream in her heart of hearts was playing out in front of her. Stone rocked the baby in his arms as if by instinct. A lump lodged in her throat as big as the welling emotion filling her heart.

She vaguely registered the sound of rustling paper as Hillary unwrapped the gift they'd brought. Stone's gaze flew to Johanna's and held. The rawness in his eyes tore at her. She saw…pain. She saw a hurt so deep she ached to reach out and wrap her arms around him.

Clearing his throat, Stone pivoted away and passed

the baby back to Troy. Johanna shook off the daze and looked at Hillary again.

The baby's mother pulled out a box, untied the fat orange ribbon and pulled out... "A tiny rodeo buckle! How adorable."

Hillary held up the tot-sized leather belt with a rodeo buckle, the leather crafted and studded with one of Amie's originals. It was a one-of-a-kind design with a cartoon horse and baby cowboy engraved on the pewter oval.

Stone picked up the bag and tucked the box inside. "He'll have to grow a bit for it to fit."

"Thank you," Hillary said, tracing the design with her finger. "This is fabulous. We'll be sure to take a photo of him wearing it and playing with Gem."

Troy held the baby in one arm like a seasoned dad, clapping Stone on the shoulder with his other hand. "Thank you again for thinking of us for Gem. He's a great dog. And you're welcome to visit him anytime."

Stone nodded tightly. "Thank you for giving her a good home and easing my grandmother's mind."

Johanna's heart ached all over again for Stone. No wonder he was having a tougher time hiding his feelings. If they'd still been a couple, she could have comforted him, even if all he would let her do was hold his hand.

She couldn't help but be reminded of when he was about twenty-one or twenty-two and his favorite horse had gone lame. Even with the best vets money could bring, nothing could be done to save Jet. She'd found Stone grieving in the stable with his horse afterward. She'd just been a gangly teenager and hugging him would have been out of the question regardless. So she'd just sat beside him quietly, being there. He hadn't asked her to leave, and she liked to think her presence had made things somewhat easier for him.

God knew, Stone would need someone now as he dealt with his grandmother's illness, and he'd always made a point of being stoic, as if the problems rolled right off him. Mariah had been the most important person in his life, the only parental figure he'd had after his grandfather had passed away while Stone was still young.

Hillary smiled gently, tucking the belt back into the bag. "It's our pleasure to have Gem as a part of our family. He will be T.J.'s best buddy and a treasured friend." She patted Stone on the arm, seeming to understand that was as much tenderness as the man would accept right now. "The guest cabin is fully stocked with food and drinks, but please let us know if you need anything at all. Otherwise we'll see you after breakfast to say goodbye before you leave."

In the morning?

Johanna's heart leaped to her throat. Of course it was time to call an end to the evening and go to the guesthouse. Resisting Stone had been difficult enough when occasionally crossing paths at the ranch. But tonight, with the memory of him cradling that tiny infant in his powerful arms?

She didn't know how she would hold strong once the doors closed behind them.

Six

Johanna's stomach tightened with each step closer to the guesthouse. A barn perched on a hill behind the Donavan's main home had been converted into a guesthouse with soaring ceilings. One side had been removed and replaced with glass windows.

Tonight, she and Stone would sleep under the same roof together for the first time in seven months. They walked side-by-side silently, not touching. But the wind twined around them as if binding them with whispering bands of air carrying his scent mingling with hers.

The desire that still simmered between them was out in the open now. Discussed. Acknowledged. She'd told him no, and he'd respected that. But to be honest with herself, she wasn't so certain she could hold out through tonight, much less through this whole week without succumbing to the temptation of one last fling. One more chance to lose herself in being with him. To immerse herself in total bliss. If only they didn't have to face the morning.

Once the guesthouse door closed behind them, there would be no more delaying. And she was feeling all the more vulnerable after watching him hold the Donavan baby. The evening seemed to have been tailor-made to play with her emotions.

Stone opened the gate to the picket fence around the guesthouse. Cuddly Sterling, impish Pearl and loyal Ruby raced up to greet them, barking and sniffing their hands. Little Pearl's head tipped to the side quizzically.

Crouching, Johanna scratched the cairn terrier's head. "It's as if she's asking about Gem. I wish there was a way to keep them all together. I have to admit I'm going to miss that goof of a dog."

"Life doesn't always work out the way we'd hoped and we're just left with doing the best we can." Stone ruffled the Rottweiler's ears, then the dachshund mix's. "Thank goodness Mariah made sure all her dogs and cats were placed in good homes."

Johanna glanced up through her eyelashes at Stone. His broad shoulders against the sentimental moonlight made for a mouth-watering silhouette. "You're right. I'm just…feeling emotional about Mariah. I know it must be so much worse for you."

He cricked his neck from side to side. "Let's get through the week as best we can."

"Of course, there's satisfaction to be found in doing something tangible for Mariah." She scooped up the dachshund. Seven-year-old Sterling cuddled closer as if sensing the ache inside her. "We should, uh, turn in. We have a lot of ground to cover this week for the other dogs."

Nerves pattered as quickly as racing dog feet as she made fast tracks along the pavers toward the guesthouse.

Stone followed—she could hear the steady even tread of his long-legged stride. He reached past her, thumbed in the security code and pushed the large door wide into the sweeping great room.

Pearl and Ruby raced past, sniffing and exploring, closing in on the large dog bowl of water even though they'd had plenty to drink outside, as well. She set Sterling down to join them. Three fat, fluffy dog beds were lined up behind the sofa. The Donavans were thoughtful hosts.

As she turned toward the expansive glass wall, she couldn't help but think the winter must be magnificent with the view of a snow-covered countryside. Even now, the sight was beyond magnificent, lush and green with cows grazing. She worked with large animals as a vet tech every day and had seen farms across Texas, but even she found this place breathtaking. What would it be like to have visited these people when she and Stone had been a couple? Most of their outings had been to more pretentious social gatherings, high-end fund-raisers or business functions.

Nothing like this day or this place.

The Donavans clearly had embraced the Vermont experience, complete with dairy cows. Although not all Vermont farms came with an ice cream parlor just for their kids.

Stone whistled softly from the state-of-the-art kitchen. "When they said they'd stocked the kitchen for us, they weren't joking. Do you want something to drink? Just pick, I'm sure it's here. Snacks, breakfast pastries, fruit and ice cream. Holy cow—so to speak."

Listening to him ramble off the flavors, she realized he was doing his best to ease the tension between them. Definitely a wise idea if she wanted to get through this week with her sanity intact. "I'll take a scoop of the maple nut."

"Coming right up," he said, opening cabinets and drawers.

She walked to the kitchen island and hitched a hip up onto a bar stool. "They're a surprisingly normal family, given all their wealth."

He passed her a bowl and spoon. "Are you saying that my family is pretentious because of our money?"

"Not at all. But some of your friends…" She stabbed her spoon into the generous mound of ice cream in the blue stoneware bowl. "They looked right through my father in the stables."

Scowling, he stood across from her, his bowl in front of him. "I'm sorry to hear that."

"You were more than just sorry about it," she answered, remembering well how he'd stood up to snobs. "You did something about it. I remember this one time when I was about eleven and one of your college friends was ordering my dad around. You made sure that guy was given the slowest, least cooperative horse in the stable. The horse even sat in the middle of a stream and got the guy soaking wet. I knew it wasn't accidental on your part. Was it?"

He winked, his scowl fading. "You seem to have me all figured out."

"You always treated everyone with respect." Her trip down memory lane reminded her of the reasons she'd fallen for this man in the first place. "You took care of your own horse. But that day when I was eleven, I officially developed my crush on you."

"You never told me that story before." He shoveled a spoonful of ice cream into his mouth, his eyes tracking her every movement with an intensity that tingled through her.

"I had insecurities of my own in those days," she admitted now. It was tough to share her self-doubts around someone as confident and, yes, arrogant as Stone. "I was a tomboy, freckled and gangly, living in a trailer park. I was brought up with strong values and I loved my parents, the life they made for me."

"They loved you. The pride on your dad's face when he talked about you was unmistakable."

"Thank you…" Her eyes misted just thinking about them. She understood all too well the pain Stone was facing, losing his mother figure. "I miss them so much, especially lately."

He ate silently, letting her find her way through. She wasn't sure where her thoughts were taking her, but she felt the need to make him understand something she couldn't quite define herself.

Johanna set her spoon aside. "I know your family is full of good people, open-minded and generous. A part of me didn't want to show just how vulnerable I felt. Even growing up on the ranch, I was on the periphery as an employee's child."

She shook her head, her voice trailing off, and she ate a bite of ice cream to cover her silence. The maple flavor melted over her taste buds.

"Johanna…" He clasped her wrist. "Go ahead. I'm listening."

Licking the spoon clean, ever aware of his eyes on her mouth, she gathered her words. "It's strange how you said you felt you weren't good enough for me…. Learning which fork to use for an occasional meal at the big house is a long way from walking in billionaire circles on a day-to-day basis. Keeping up appearances during our engagement and constantly worrying I would do something to embarrass you was exhausting."

"You never let it show." His frown turned to a scowl. "Don't you think that's something I would have cared to know? We were engaged to be married, for God's sake. If we couldn't tell each other even something basic like that, then what did we even have together?"

"You're angry?"

"I'm frustrated, yes. All this time I've been thinking that I let you down." He shoved aside his bowl and leaned on his elbows, closing the space between them. "Right now, I'm realizing we let each other down. Except you weren't interested in shouldering your part of the blame."

Anger sparked along her already raw nerves. "I open up to you, and now you're pissed off? That isn't very fair."

He sidestepped around the island to stand in front of her. "Nothing about what has happened between us has been fair or we wouldn't still be hurting this much."

She swallowed hard, certain to her toes he was about to kiss her and she wouldn't be able to tell him no. They would pour all those frustrated emotions into passion. It wouldn't solve anything, but at least they would have an outlet, a release.

Except he turned and left.

Her jaw dropped.

What the hell? Stone had just walked away from her?

She almost leaped from her seat to charge after him and demand he finish the conversation. How dare he just leave? They had unfinished business....

But hadn't she done the same thing to him? Not only had she run away from him after the picnic, scared she couldn't resist the temptation to do more than kiss him. But she'd also walked out on their relationship and very publicly, at that. His words settled in her gut along with the sting of guilt. He was right. She'd let him shoulder all the blame for their breakup when she hadn't given her all to him, either.

The realization echoed hollowly inside her. She gathered both bowls and rinsed them out carefully, wishing her confusion was as easily swirled down the drain. Or that she could just shake off her worries and go to sleep like the three dogs curled up on their beds, snoring. The thought of going to her room alone was more than she could bear tonight after watching all-day family bliss with the Donavans, not just as parents but as a couple.

She yanked a blanket from the back of the sofa and curled up on the couch to count stars instead of sheep.

Stone woke the next morning with a throbbing headache and an aching erection.

His shower took care of the visible sign of his arousal, but didn't do much to cool the fire inside him. Walking away from Johanna the night before had been one of the most difficult things he'd ever done. But he'd been too angry, too on edge. He didn't trust himself and damned if he would ever put her at risk.

So he'd left her alone. He'd worked for hours before falling into a fitful sleep just before sunup.

Tossing his shaving gear into his bag, he was still steamed over his conversation with Johanna last night. He'd spent most of the night reviewing their time together and he kept coming back to how she'd broken up with him at one of his grandmother's major fundraisers. That couldn't be coincidental. If he'd known how she'd felt, he could have done things differently. Hell, he could have—

What? Given up his job and all the responsibilities that came with that? Dismissed his background and offered to give her the family she wanted? Last night he'd learned of yet another reason they weren't meant to be together.

Who would he be if he didn't run Diamonds in the Rough?

He tossed his bag on the thick four-poster bed beside a stack of discarded sketches for a new kids' line with a horse logo. The images just wouldn't come together on paper the way he saw them in his mind. Visions of a misty-eyed Johanna kept interfering, thoughts of her struggling to hold back tears when he'd held the baby.

Damn it.

He flipped open his suitcase, pulled out a pair of well-worn jeans and tugged them on. One day into this mandated week together and he was already losing his damn mind. He scratched his hands through his wet hair, needing to get his head together.

Barring that, he could at least let the dogs out.

He opened his bedroom door, wondering if Johanna was up yet. He didn't hear her so he assumed not. The wide-open barn space sprawled in front of him. The dogs sat up, one, two, three—tails wagging, tongues lolling out. They launched off their beds behind the sofa in unison but thank God, not barking. He knelt, petting each to keep them quiet. Then he snapped his fingers to lead them to the door. Walking past the couch, he almost stopped short. Johanna slept on the sofa, wrapped in a quilt, still wearing her sundress from yesterday.

His gaze stayed on her even as he waved the dogs

outside, then he turned to face her fully and enjoy a view that far exceeded anything outside. Many nights he'd watched her sleep, her face relaxed, her stubborn chin softened a bit. Her long lashes brushed her sun-kissed cheeks. His body went hard all over again, his jeans more and more uncomfortable. He needed to get himself under control before she woke.

Padding barefoot across the room, he quietly put together the coffeepot. A crystal cake plate and cover displayed a selection of pastries big enough to feed them twice over. He grabbed a bear claw, wishing his other hunger was as easy to satisfy.

As the coffee gurgled the scent of java into the air, he felt the weight of eyes studying him. He already knew. Johanna. The connection that threatened to drive him mad was alive and well.

He pulled two stoneware mugs off the hooks under the cabinets. "Sorry I woke you."

A rustle from the sofa sounded, and her reflection came to life in the window pane over the sink.

"It's okay. I was just catnapping anyway." Johanna stretched her arms over her head. "It was tough to sleep after we argued."

"That wasn't an argument. I consider that a very revealing discussion we should have had a long time ago." He poured coffee into both mugs. Black. They both drank it the same way, strong and undiluted by sugar or cream. The only thing it seemed they still had in common. He picked up both and walked toward her.

"What would talking about my insecurities have changed?" Her bare toes curled against the rustic braid rug. "Do you think our breakup would have hurt any less? I can't imagine how."

"True enough." He passed her a mug, wishing he could find a way to be with her without tearing them both apart. "Truce?"

She took the mug, wrapping both hands around the mug, brushing his fingers. The ever-ready attraction crackled. He saw it echoed in her eyes, along with wariness.

"Truce," she repeated, sipping the coffee carefully. "Where to next?"

"Travel day, actually. I've got work to catch up on this morning." Not a total lie, since he always had work. "Then we'll fly out this afternoon to take Sterling to his new family in South Carolina."

"I'm almost afraid to ask who your grandmother lined up next. The president?"

"Just a former secretary of state."

She coughed a mouthful of coffee. "I was joking."

"I'm not." His grandmother moved in influential circles. He hadn't given a second thought to the families she had chosen. They were longtime friends. But he hadn't thought of how visiting these high-profile people would go over with Johanna. How many times had he tossed her into the middle of unfamiliar, perhaps even intimidating gatherings with no warning? Hell, he hadn't even given her any direction on how to pack, just offering to buy what she needed.

He'd hoped to use this time together to find peace for his grandmother—but also to find closure with Johanna. Okay, and also to have lots of sex with Johanna until they both were too exhausted to argue about the past. Then they could move on.

Clearly, his plan wasn't working out because he was falling into an old pattern of charging ahead and expecting her to follow. She didn't trust him and if she didn't trust him, there wasn't a chance in hell they could sleep together again.

He couldn't change the past, and he'd accepted they couldn't have a future together.

Although he could damn well do something about the present. For starters, he could share the details about their travel plans. But he would have to dig a lot deeper than that to fully regain her trust.

He sat beside her on the fat sectional sofa, trying to start right now, by including her in the plan for the week. "We'll be visiting the Landis-Renshaw family in Hilton Head. They've vacationed at the ranch before. As a matter of fact, they rented the whole place once for a family reunion."

"That would be quite a who's who of family reunions."

And he hadn't even told her their third stop would be to meet with a deposed European king.

Johanna welcomed the bustle of their travel day to Hilton Head, South Carolina. Stone had arranged for accommodations in a pet-friendly beach cottage with plenty of space for the dogs to run. They would meet with the Landis-Renshaw family in the morning.

Other cottages dotted the shoreline, but with an exclusivity that brought privacy. One other couple and a small family played in the surf, but otherwise she and Stone were on their own. She'd sensed a change in him earlier as he'd shared his plans for the South Carolina portion of their trip. He was genuinely attempting to include her, rather than simply taking charge.

So far, the truce they'd declared had held, due in

large part to how he'd included her. That helped her
relax, taking away a layer of tension she hadn't even realized existed. She'd been worrying about the unknown.

She sat cross-legged on the wooden deck, a dozen
steps away from him. The dogs curled up around her
and she checked over each of them, making sure they
hadn't picked up ticks in Vermont or sand spurs from
their run along the beach earlier. She finished with
Pearl, the search more extensive given the cairn terrier's longer fur.

Stone walked out of the surf like Poseidon emerg-
ing from the depths of the ocean. Big. Powerful. The
hazy glow of the ending day cast him in shadows, his
dark hair even blacker slicked with water. She'd always
known Stone the cowboy entranced her more than Stone
the CEO.

But Stone nearly naked absolutely melted her.

She forced her attention back to Pearl to keep from
drooling over Stone in swim trunks. Her skin prickled
with awareness as he opened the porch gate and walked
past her. She heard the rattle of ice as he poured a glass
of sweet tea before he dropped into one of the Adiron-
dack loungers.

"How was the water?" She released Pearl to play
with the other two dogs on the fenced deck.

"Good, good." He set his glass aside. "Everything
okay with the dogs?"

They sounded like any other couple catching up at
the end of the day, except there was this aching tension
between them. "They all checked out fine. Just a couple of sandspurs on Pearl. I trimmed their nails, and I'll
want to bathe them all after they run on the beach again.
Otherwise, they're all set to meet their new families."

He swung his feet around, elbows on his knees. "You're a nurturer. It's in your blood."

Her hands clenched into fists to resist the urge to sweep sand from the hair on his legs. "Are you trying to needle me with the nurturer comment?"

"I'm just stating a fact. You'll make a great mother someday."

The humid night air grew thicker, her chest constricting. "You're good with children. The natural way you held little T.J....I just don't understand you."

"I'm good with horses, too. That doesn't mean I'm supposed to be a jockey," he said wryly.

"I wasn't insinuating you should be a father. You've been honest about your feelings on that subject. It just took me a while to stop thinking I could change your mind." Hugging her knees, she studied him in the fading light.

"I've always tried to be careful that women didn't get the wrong idea about me and wedding bells...until you."

That should have meant something, but it only served to increase the ache. "You're a playboy married to your work." She exhaled hard. "I get that. Totally."

Stone went quiet again for so long she thought they might be returning to the silent truce again. Awkward and painful.

Then Stone stood, walking to the rail and staring out at the ocean. "My father."

Rising, she moved to stand beside him, wind pulling at the whispery cover-up over her bikini. "What do you mean?"

His father had been an off-limits topic for as long as she'd known him. Not even Mariah brought up the subject. Stone had always said that according to his mom, his paternity was a mystery. Was he opening up to her on a deeper level, including her in more than a few travel plans?

"I found out." His voice came out hoarse and a little harsh as he continued to look out at the foaming waves.

She rested a hand on his arm tentatively, not sure how he would react but unable to deny him some comfort during what had to be a difficult revelation. "I wish you would have told me."

"I've never told anyone."

"I was supposed to be more than just 'anyone' to you," she reminded him softly.

He glanced sideways at her. "Touché."

"Did you hire a private investigator?"

"Don't you think my grandmother already tried that hoping to find someone who actually wanted me around?"

His words snapped her upright in shock. "Your grandmother loves you."

"I know that. I do," he said with certainty. "But she'd already brought up her kids. She was supposed to be my grandmother. Not my parent."

"Did she tell you that?" She knew full well Mariah never would have said anything of the sort to Stone. Johanna just wanted to remind him of how very much his grandmother loved him.

"She didn't have to say it." He went silent for the length of two rolling waves crashing to the shore. "When I was eleven, I found the private detective's report of her search for my biological father."

"Of course she would want to know everything about you. Perhaps she was worried that he might try to take you away. Did you ever consider that?" When he didn't answer, she continued, "You said she didn't find him. So how did you locate him?"

"The report uncovered a wealth of data about my mother's activities then." His face went darker. "Suffice it to say, my mother led quite an active party life."

"That reflects on her." She squeezed his arm. "Not on you."

"I understand that." He braced his shoulders, his eyes cold with an anger Johanna knew wasn't directed at her. "I'm not a drug addict like my mother. And while I'm not a monk, I'm monogamous during a relationship. I am my own man. I control myself and my destiny."

She rubbed soothing circles along his arm. Even if this conversation wouldn't change things between them, she knew he needed to get these words out and for some reason she was the person he trusted most to tell.

She drew in a bracing breath of salty air before continuing, "How did you find out about your father?"

"My mother told me."

"That simple?"

"Apparently so. She was high at the time and to this day doesn't remember telling me." He pinched the bridge of his nose. "I was twenty-five when she let it slip about the man who fathered me—Dale Banks."

Johanna gasped in recognition. "*The* Dale Banks? The country music star?"

"My mom was a groupie back in the day." He shrugged. "She hooked up with him and here I am."

She studied his features with a new perspective. Wind whipped her hair over her face, and she scraped the locks aside. "You do look a little like him. I never noticed until now...."

"I needed more reassurance than a look-alike contest. So I confronted him."

"How did you get past his security guards?"

"I have influence of my own." He smiled darkly. "Remember the benefit concert we sponsored a few years back?"

She did the quick math and realized Stone would have been in his mid-twenties then. She couldn't imagine how difficult that meeting must have been. "You arranged that to speak with him?"

"I'm not above using philanthropy for my own good, as well."

"You don't need to be sarcastic to cover your emotions." She slid her hand to his back and tucked her body to his side as if it was the most natural thing in the world to share his burdens. And it was. She drew in the heat and salty scent of him, her senses starved after months without him. "That had to have been difficult for you, confronting him."

"I didn't. I got a DNA sample during dinner."

"What?" She looked up sharply, unable to believe she'd heard him correctly. "You tricked him?"

"Easier than forcing the matter with a conversation where he denied it and I had to prove him a liar."

He didn't fool her for a second with this blasé act.

"What did he say when you finally told him?"

"He doesn't know. Why should he? He slept with a woman he didn't know and didn't care enough to follow up."

"Stone!" She cupped his face and made him look at her. "Maybe he's changed. Perhaps he has regrets and would like to know you now."

"I don't need him in my life," he said in a cold tone that left no room for negotiation.

"Maybe *he* needs *you*," she suggested. "People are so much more important than money or fame."

"That's right. You grew up poor but loved," he said sarcastically.

Again, he didn't fool her. She patted his cheek just a touch harder than a love tap. "Don't be a jerk."

"Maybe I'm letting my real side show." He turned his face to kiss her palm, then nipped it gently.

She wouldn't let him divert her with sex. She slipped her hand back down to his shoulder. "How did we spend so much time together and never talk about these things?"

"You were right in saying I was holding back."

She couldn't believe he'd admitted it. "Why are you telling me now? And please be truthful."

"I'm not really sure." He snagged a strand of her hair and stroked the length with gentle pressure. "Maybe because there's nothing left to lose between us. You've already ditched me. Why bother working my ass off to impress you?"

"You were working to impress me?" She couldn't resist smiling.

"Clearly, I failed." He looped the lock around his finger until he cupped the back of her head.

"Not totally." She stepped closer, unable to resist the sizzle, especially not combined with the vulnerability he'd shown in sharing what he'd found out about his father. "I did agree to marry you."

She arched up on her toes and kissed him. How could she not? Her body ached to be with him. They were two consenting adults, alone together, attached to no one else and both so very aware of the price of being together.

His arms banded around her, thick, muscled arms that held her with such gentle power she leaned closer until her breasts pressed to the hard bare wall of his chest. His mouth tasted of the salty ocean and sweet tea, a heady combination for a woman already teetering on the edge of losing control.

She sketched along the hard planes of his back, still damp from his swim and perspiration. So many nights she'd lain awake yearning to be with him again and now those restless fantasies were coming to life. Being away from home gave her the freedom to act on those impulses.

Stone caressed down her back to her hips, molding her closer to him, his arousal pressing against her stomach.

"Johanna," he groaned against her mouth. "You're killing me here. If you want to stop, we need to put the brakes on this now. It's up to you what happens next. How are we going to handle this attraction that's tearing us both apart?"

She dipped her hands into his swim trunks. "We're going to sleep together again. Tonight."

Seven

Finally, he had Johanna back in his arms again, even if just for a night. Only a fool would pass up this chance, and he was not a fool.

Taking her face in his hands, he kissed her, fully, tongues meeting and inhibitions gone. A perfect fit, just like before. Familiar and new all at once—their time apart added an edge to the need.

He backed her into the cottage, their bare legs tangling as they walked, notching his desire higher and higher with each provocative brush of skin against skin. Her fingers linked behind his neck as she writhed against him in a lithe dance of desire denied for far too long.

Impatiently, he pushed open the door with such urgency it slammed against the wall. His hands slid low, cupping her bottom and lifting her over the threshold. Once inside the cottage, he set her down, the bamboo floor cool under his feet in contrast to the heat searing through him.

Their bathing suits offered thin barriers between them, but too much right now. He bunched her whispery cover up in his hands and swept it over her head. He'd seen her in her bikini earlier—had seen her in far less—but she still took his breath away. Her simple black two-piece called to his hands, triangles begging to be peeled away.

She smiled with a siren's gleam in her eyes. "This is usually the point where you drop your Stetson on my head."

"I left it on my suitcase. Not too many cowboy hats on the beach while a guy's riding a wave."

"That's a damn shame." She traced the rope tattoo around his biceps, which ended in a lasso loop.

He and his cousins had gotten tattoos together when the twins had turned eighteen. He'd been twenty-one. Johanna had wanted to go with them. He'd forgotten that until just now. She'd wanted to get paw print tattoos on her ankle, but he'd known her parents wouldn't approve.

Tracing the length of her collarbone, he lifted the diamond horseshoe necklace she wore all the time now. "I would drape you in gems, design entire lines of jewelry dedicated to your beauty."

"Who knew you were poetic?"

"You inspire me."

She stroked up his arms. "I'm just as happy with wildflowers and bluebonnets. That day we made love in the open and you covered me in petals is one of my all-time favorite memories."

"Another reason you're special. I never have to wonder with you. I know you're here—or not here—based on me. It has nothing to do with my family or our money." He plucked the strings behind her neck. The top fell away, revealing her breasts, pert and a perfect fit in his palms.

"You're a savvy man," she gasped, her nipples beading against his hands, either from his touch or the cool swoosh of the air conditioner. "I imagine you see through the sycophants right away."

"That discernment came from practice." He thumbed along her taut peaks, teasing them tighter until she swayed ever so slightly.

She covered his hands with hers. "You shouldn't have to wonder about people that way. Thinking of you wondering, learning from practice—that makes me so sad."

"I definitely don't want you sad right now—or ever." He hooked his thumbs in the strings along her hips and snapped them before the thought formed in his mind.

Her swimsuit bottom fell away.

She kicked aside the scrap of fabric. "If I were the sort of woman who wanted to be draped only in jewels, what would you design for me?"

"Ah, now you're talking." He let his imagination take flight. "I've always liked yellow diamonds for you. I can see long earrings that trail in a sleek, thin cascade to your shoulders." He skimmed each spot with a kiss. "Each piece would echo the golden lines of your beautiful body. And a long, gold rope chain with a pendant that trails right…here…between…"

His mouth landed along the inside of one curve, then the other. Her breath hitched, her fingers twisting in the band of his swim trunks. Tugging at the elastic, she peeled the damp suit down and off into a pile around his feet.

He stepped out and then swept her up against his chest. "And since the jewelry would be for our eyes only, I dream of you in more erotic designs, as well."

"Oh, really?" She looped her arms around his neck. "I can't decide whether to be nervous or intrigued."

One step at a time, he carried her closer to the white

iron bed with a view of the water. "A thicker rope chain would circle low on your waist, resting on your hips."

"Ah, like a lasso." She thumbed his tattoo. "That works both ways, you know. I could pull you to me, especially perfect if you wore chaps and nothing more."

He arched an eyebrow. "Not very businesslike."

"We're not in the boardroom."

"True." He tossed her onto the mattress.

She landed with an enticing bounce that made all the right parts jiggle just a hint. She stretched out along the puffy quilt, her creamy shoulders propped up by a pile of seashell-patterned pillows.

Part of him wanted to take in the sight of her for hours on end, and another more urgent part of him couldn't delay any longer. He kneeled on the edge of the bed and crawled up over her, tasting his way up her bared flesh, along her stomach, teasing the diamond belly button ring with his teeth. Higher still, he took her breast in his mouth, rolling the nipple with his tongue until her needy sighs begged him for more, faster, sooner.

He glanced up to see her head thrown back, pushing into the pillows. From the flush blooming over her skin he knew she was close to coming apart. He understood the urgent sensation well and slid the rest of the way up to take her lips, his erection nudging against the slick core of her. Ready. For him. Just as he was ready for her, only her, always her.

With a hoarse growl, he thrust deep inside her.

Gasping, she grabbed his shoulders. "Stone, wait." She gripped harder, her fingernails digging into his flesh. "What about protection?"

He arched back to look into her eyes. "Aren't you on the pill?"

"Not anymore," she said. "Once we broke up and it was clear we weren't going to reconcile, I stopped taking it."

She'd thought about reconciling with him? For how long? How many opportunities had he missed to get her back only to lose her because of stubborn pride?

Have her back?

Wasn't this just about sex now?

All thoughts too weighty for him to consider with his brain muddled from being buried to the hilt inside her again.

He hadn't packed condoms.... And if they discussed this much further it was going to lead to a serious mood buster of a conversation. He rolled off her with a groan of frustration.

Johanna sat up with a gasp. "Wait." She snapped her fingers. "I saw some in the honeymooners' welcome basket on the bedside table."

Crisis averted. Thank heavens the staff had assumed they would need the romance special basket. He stayed on his side while Johanna raced into the living area, and yes, he enjoyed the hell out of the view. He'd dreamed of her, but fantasies couldn't come close to the reality of being here with her.

The sound of rustling carried from the next room before she returned. Grinning, she held a condom in one hand and a plump pear in the other. She sank her teeth into the fruit and tossed him the square packet. He snatched it out of midair then grabbed her wrist to tug her back into bed with him.

Laughing, she settled on top of him and pressed the

pear against his mouth. He took a bite, then set the fruit
aside to have her. Johanna. His again.

He flipped her onto her back and thrust inside her.
Gasping, she closed her eyes and welcomed him with a
roll of her hips. Her legs wrapped around him, her heels
digging in and urging him deeper, faster, leaving no
room for misunderstanding. She wanted him, too, with
the same hungry edge. He kissed her hard and insistent,
the taste of pear mingling with the sweet warmth of her.

He knew her body as well as he knew his own. He'd
made a point of learning each sensitive spot and how
to tease her pleasure higher. And she'd done the same
for him.

Touch for touch, they moved in synch with each
other. Her hands roved a restless path until perspiration dotted his forehead in spite of the ocean breeze
gusting through the window.

Wind chimes sang louder and louder as if kicked
up by a spring storm. He whispered in her ear about
husky fantasies built during nights apart, silver links
binding them together, jewels hidden and found. Her
panting replies—her yes, yes, yes riding each gasp—
stoked the fire in him higher until his whole body felt
like molten metal in a flame.

And just when he thought he couldn't hold out any
longer before the heat consumed them both, Johanna
flew apart in his arms. Her cries of completion rolled
free, as uninhibited and natural as the woman in his
arms. The sweet clamp of her body pulsing around him
sent him over the edge with her.

As wave after wave crashed over him, he held her
closer, absorbing her aftershocks as he slowly came

back down to earth again. His arms gave way, and he rolled to his side, taking her with him.

With the wind kicking up a humid breeze and rain pattering outside, he willed his galloping heartbeat to return to normal. Except his hammering pulse wasn't cooperating. With each slug against his ribs, he knew.

He couldn't give Johanna up again, but there wasn't a chance in hell she would stay with him if she knew the worst of what he'd held back, the reason he absolutely could not fulfill her dreams and become the father of her children.

Johanna woke up to an empty bed.

She stretched under the Egyptian cotton sheets, the scent of lovemaking mingling with the ocean air blowing in through the window. Barks also echoed from outside along with the rumbling bass of Stone's voice shouting a ramble of "fetch" and "good girl."

The sun climbing high into the sky told her she'd slept in, not surprising since they'd made up for lost time throughout the night. In bed, in the shower, moving into the kitchen for food, then making love against the counter.

Her body carried the delicious ache of total satiation. Although she knew the moment she saw Stone, she would want him all over again, and she couldn't help but want to look her best. She shoved her hands through her tangled hair, which must be a complete mess since she'd gone to sleep with it still damp.

A quick glance at the clock had her rolling to her feet and racing to the bathroom. A fast washup later, she wrapped her hair and body in fluffy towels and opened the closet.

The packed full closet?

She stared at all the clothes that hadn't been there the night before. Tags showed they were all new and in her size. Stone had been busy. He'd ordered her a whole new wardrobe for the rest of their trip. He'd heard what she said about feeling uneasy and in his own way he was trying to ease that worry for her.

The barking dogs gave her only a moment's warning before Stone walked into the bedroom. So much for dressing up. She secured the towel around her and tugged the other off her head, shaking her hair free.

She skimmed her fingers along the rack of clothes. "You didn't have to do this, but thank you."

"Glad you're happy." He captured her hand and pulled her close. "And just so we're clear, it doesn't matter to me what you're wearing. In my eyes you're magnificent."

"Thank you." She arched up for a kiss. "You're one good cowboy, Stone."

"I'm trying, lady, I'm trying." He kissed her good-morning thoroughly before easing back. "I did hear what you said about going to formal functions before, and it's killing me to think you ever felt uncomfortable."

"I know a person's worth doesn't have anything to do with their bank balance."

"Damn straight." He dropped to sit on the foot of the bed, pulling her into his lap. "I imagine that's part of my grandmother's plan here, too, giving me a reality check when it comes to family values."

Her heart fluttered in her chest. He couldn't possibly be changing his stance on a family. Could he?

Afraid to wreck the moment by pushing, she changed the subject. "There's quite a range of clothes you've bought for me." She pointed to a rack with everything from jeans and slacks to sundresses and a couple of longer gowns. "Where else are we going?"

"My grandmother has a wide range of people lined up, even a couple of backups if someone doesn't work out."

She snagged an ice-blue lacy dress. "This looks fit for royalty."

"You're perceptive," he said with a grimace.

She rolled her eyes, certain she must have misunderstood. "Really? Royalty, in addition to a former secretary of state."

"Really."

She froze, realizing he was serious. "All right," she exhaled, sagging back against his chest. "If Sterling is going to the political powerhouse couple, that leaves Pearl and Ruby. Which one's getting the tiara?"

"Ruby. Enrique Medina lost both of his Rhodesian ridgebacks this year to old age. He and my grandmother are friends. He's even the one who recommended contacting General Renshaw about Sterling."

Royalty. Honest-to-God royalty. Nothing would surprise her about this family again. "What about Pearl? Is she going to the Pope?"

Stone snorted on a laugh. "I'm sure he's one of Gran's backups." He kissed her nose. "Seriously, though, I don't know as much about the last family other than that they live on a ranch in Montana."

"Are the formal gowns for the jewelers' convention that you mentioned?" Her stomach gripped at the thought. Even with the fancy clothes, she was still a farm girl who felt most at ease in her jeans, with braided hair and a horse.

"I canceled that. The variety of dresses are so we can go out to dinner somewhere nice. Just the two of us, to thank you for coming along this week to ease my grandmother's mind. Regardless of where we go from here, I will always be grateful for all you've done for Gran."

She couldn't help but be surprised again over how he was revealing more to her on this trip than she'd ever understood about him before. Had he suffered as much from their time apart? Or had confronting mortality with his grandmother's illness brought down some walls? Either way, she couldn't help but be drawn in by this man.

He tipped her chin for another kiss, one that couldn't go any further with the day slipping away, but God, she was tempted. Because she couldn't help but think these changes were too good to be true.

An hour later, Stone opened the hatch on their rental SUV to load up the dogs for their drive over to the Landis-Renshaw compound. Ruby loped into the back and he lifted scruffy little Pearl in, as well, a mesh barrier keeping them from taking over the front seat. He'd stowed their luggage in a cartop carrier. They looked like a regular family on vacation.

He rubbed the kink in his neck from lack of sleep, but he wouldn't change a moment of their night together.

The waves glistened under the power of the noonday sun and he wished they could just blow off his grandmother's plan and stay at the cottage for the rest of the week. He and Johanna had connected, just like in the past, and he was working hard to reassure her. Maybe he was deluding himself into hoping she could overlook the bigger issues if he corrected some other problems in their relationship.

To what end?

Did he really expect they would ride off into the sunset together? He had to be honest with himself and admit he wanted her back in his life on a permanent basis. But being equally honest, he wasn't sure that was possible no matter how many closets full of comfy clothes and easygoing outings he came up with.

The beach cottage door opened, and Johanna stepped out with Sterling cradled in her arms. She'd chosen a simple flowery dress, loose and classic. But she looked good in everything she wore. His assistant had ordered everything and assured him the task would be easy. Johanna had pulled her hair back in a jeweled clasp—a Diamonds in the Rough piece. And of course she wore his grandmother's horseshoe charm.

He struggled to resist the urge to scoop her up, carry her back inside and peel the dress off her. Instead, he held out his arms. "I'll take Sterling."

She shook her head, her ponytail sweeping along her spine the way his hands ached to do. "I'll hold him. I'm feeling sentimental about saying goodbye to him. I keep thinking about the day your grandmother got him as a puppy."

He closed the back hatch and walked around to open her door. "I always think of you as being there for the horses. I forget sometimes that caring for the dogs falls under your job description, as well." He leaned in the open door. "It will be tough for you to say goodbye to them, too."

"I don't have pets of my own...so yes." She stroked the Chihuahua-dachshund mix. "I have become attached. But your grandmother is wise to make sure they're placed. Too many animals end up at shelters when their owners pass away or go into nursing homes."

"We would have taken them all for her. She has to know that." Not a chance in hell would he have dumped Gran's pets at the shelter. He closed the door, perhaps a bit more forcefully than he'd intended, but the reminder of a world without Mariah cast clouds over his day.

He walked around the hood and took his place behind the wheel. He swept off his Stetson and dropped it on the console between them. Starting the car, he pulled his focus back in tight before he landed them nose first in a sand dune. Navigating the beach traffic was tough enough.

Johanna's hand fell to rest on his arm as he passed a slow-moving RV. "Clearly, Mariah has a plan in mind for them, and for your future, too. Never doubt for a second that she loves you."

He glanced at her. "She loves you, too, you know."

"Thank you—" she smiled "—but it's not the same. I'm not family."

"I'm not so sure." His hands gripped the wheel tighter, settling into their lane along the ocean side road. "She was mad as hell with me when we broke up."

"Why was she angry with you?" Johanna sat up straighter. "I was the one who ended our engagement. I made that abundantly clear to everyone."

Had she made the breakup public to spare him blowback from his family? He'd been so angry at her then, he hadn't given thought to the fact that a public breakup actually cast him in a more sympathetic light. He'd been too caught up in his anger—and hurt. "Gran said I had to have done something wrong to make you give back the engagement ring. And she was right."

The breakup had been his fault, and nothing significant had changed. He still didn't want children, and watching her cradle the dog, he couldn't miss her deep-seated urge to nurture.

He felt like a first-class ass.

Johanna adjusted the silver collar around Sterling's neck. "I'm sorry if I caused a wedge between the two of you."

"You have nothing to apologize for," he insisted, steering onto a bridge that would take them to their barrier island destination. "I'm an adult. My relationships are my own problem."

"She's trying to matchmake, sending us on this trip together." Johanna traced the top of his hat resting between them.

No kidding. "I'm sure that was a part of her plan, no matter what she said, but the rest is still true." Miles of marshy sea grass bowed as they drove deeper into the exclusive beach property of Hilton Head, the South's answer to Martha's Vineyard. "She doesn't trust me to see to the dogs, and she's right. I would have screwed it up."

"I seriously doubt that," Johanna said with a confidence he didn't feel when it came to this subject.

"I wouldn't have been as thorough as you've been." He'd been impressed and surprised during the meet and greet with the Donavans. "I wouldn't have even thought of half the things you've done to make sure Gem's in the right home and that the transition goes smoothly for her."

"Gem's going to miss your grandmother." She swept

a hand under her eyes and he realized she'd teared up. "There will be grieving on his part as well."

"Are you trying to make me just skip the rest of this trip and take the dogs home with us? Because I'm about five seconds away from doing that," he half joked. "In fact, much more of this and I'll even snatch Gem back."

She responded with a watery laugh. "Don't you dare. The Donavans are a fantastic family for Gem, as Mariah clearly already knew." She reached into her bag and pulled out dog treats. She passed two over the mesh to Pearl and Ruby, before offering another to Sterling. "They're not cutie pie little puppies anymore, and placing an adult dog can be difficult. And we definitely don't want someone taking in the dogs in hopes of gaining favor with your grandmother."

Protectiveness pumped through him. "I wouldn't let that happen."

"Of course not. You're a good man."

"Such a good man my grandmother has to test me and you dumped me flat on my ass," he said wryly.

She scooted closer, slipping her hand to the back of his neck. "I miss the happy times between us. Last night was…incredible."

What an odd time to realize she was "soothing" him the same way she soothed Sterling, using her dog whisperer ways on him. "So you do acknowledge it wasn't all bad between us."

"Of course it wasn't all bad," she said incredulously.

"Specifics." He might as well use this time to get whatever edge he could.

"Why?" Suspicion laced her voice. "What purpose will it serve?"

"Call it a healing exercise." And the hope of figuring out a way to have more with her tomorrow.

"Okay, uh…" Her hand fell back to the dog in her lap. "I appreciate the way you support my work. Like the time I'd already pulled extra hours on my shift, but the call came from a shelter in South Texas in need of extra veterinary help for neglected horses seized by animal control. You drove through the night so I could sleep before working." Her mouth tipped in a smile, her eyes taking on a faraway look. "Then you didn't sleep. You rolled up your sleeves and helped."

He had to haul his gaze away from the beauty of her smile before he rear-ended the car in front of them. "We accomplished a lot of good together that day."

"We did. And I know it was you who encouraged your grandmother to help sponsor this year's big charity event to help save the wild mustangs."

He shrugged, her praise making him itchy. "We needed a tax write-off."

"You're not fooling me." She swatted his arm.

He searched for the right words. "My family has worked hard and been very lucky. We're in a position to do good."

"Not everyone makes the same choices as your family. I don't even know that I'd fully thought about it in such concrete terms until now. Your grandmother instilled solid values in all of you."

"Very diplomatic of you not to mention what my mom or Amie and Alex's parents could have shared." Diplomatic and astute.

"I'm sorry that your mother couldn't be a true parent for you."

"Don't be." The warmth of the day chilled for him.

"She broke Gran's heart. And Uncle Garnet wasn't much better, but at least he tried to build a normal family life. He went to work every day even if he wasn't particularly ambitious." Or willing to stand up to his overly ambitious wife. "Gran always said she babied him and she wanted to be sure she didn't make the same mistake with us."

"Your aunt Bayleigh was ambitious enough for the both of them." She shuddered dramatically.

"True enough." There was no denying the obvious. "She pushed the twins for as far back as I can remember. Although I gotta confess, even their flawed family looked mighty damn enticing to me as a kid."

"You wanted to live with them."

She sounded surprised, which made him realize yet again how little of himself he'd shared with the woman who was supposed to have been the most important person in his life. If he wanted even a chance at being with her again, he had to give what he could this time.

"I did want to be their kid," he admitted. "Gran even asked them once if they would be interested in guardianship of me, but their plate was full."

She gasped. "That had to be so painful to hear."

To this day, he was glad no one had seen him listening in. He couldn't have taken the humiliation of someone stumbling on him crying. Looking back, he realized he must have only been in elementary school, but the tears had felt less than manly on a day when he already felt like a flawed kid no one wanted.

"It worked out for the best." He found himself still minimizing the pain of that experience. "Gran was a great parental figure. And my mother, well, she was a helluva lot of fun during her sober stints."

The words came out more bitterly than he'd intended. Thank God, they were pulling up to the security gate outside the Landis-Renshaw compound because he'd had about as much "sharing time" as he could take for one day. Much more of this and he would start pouring out stories about being a crack baby, who still cringed at the thought of all the developmental psychologists he'd visited before he'd even started first grade.

He was managing fine now, damn it, and the past could stay in the past.

The wrought-iron security gates loomed in front of them, cameras peeking out of the climbing ivy. He rolled down his window and passed over his identification to a guard posted in his little glass booth with monitors.

The guard nodded silently, passed the ID back, and the gates swung open. Now he just had to figure out how to say goodbye to another family pet and pretend it didn't matter that the only family he'd known would soon fall apart when his grandmother died. She'd been his strength and his sanity. She'd literally saved his life as a baby. She was a strong woman, like Johanna.

As he watched Johanna cuddle the dog in her lap, he realized he hadn't taken this dog placement trip seriously, which was wrong of him. He'd just followed Johanna's lead in shuffling his grandmother's pets to new families, not thinking overlong about the loss, just going through the motions. His grandmother, Johanna—the dogs—all deserved better than that from him.

For the first time he considered that perhaps his grandmother hadn't been matchmaking after all. Maybe she had been trying to help him understand why Johanna was better off without him.

Eight

Settled deep in the front seat of the SUV, Johanna wrapped her arms around the dachshund mix in her lap and wondered how she'd gotten drawn back into a whirlwind of emotions for Stone so quickly.

At least once they arrived, she had the next few hours with people around to give her time to regain her footing before they were in a hotel together or some other romantic setting on this trip designed to tamper with her very sanity. She had time to build boundaries to protect her heart until she could figure out where they were going as a couple. Was this just sex for the week or were they going to try for more again? If so, they still had the same disagreements looming as before.

She hugged the dog closer as she looked through the window to take everything in. Could this day be any more convoluted? She was seconds away from meeting a political powerhouse couple. The general was reputed to be on the short list for the next secretary of defense. Ginger was now an ambassador and former secretary of state. Her oldest son was a senator. Who wouldn't be nervous?

Stone, apparently.

He steered the car smoothly, but his mind was obviously somewhere else. "I never did know how Sterling ended up in my grandmother's pack."

His comment surprised her.

"One of her employees was older and developed Alzheimer's. The retirement home the woman's family chose didn't allow animals."

"That's really rough. How did I not know that story?" His forehead furrowed as he steered the SUV up the winding path through beach foliage to the main house. "I wish my grandmother would have trusted me more to see to the animals after she's gone so she could have the comfort of them now when she needs them most."

Johanna stayed silent. She agreed 100 percent but saying as much wouldn't change anything. The situation truly was a tough one. "It's sad Sterling should lose his owner twice."

"Life is rarely about what's fair," he said darkly before sliding the car into Park alongside the house.

He grabbed his hat and was out of the car before she could think of an answer. What was going on inside his head? This man never ceased to confuse her.

While she secured Sterling's leash, she studied the grounds to get her bearings before she stepped out of the car. The beach compound was grander than the rustic Hidden Gem Ranch and more expansive than the scaled-back Donavan spread. She'd seen photos from a *Good Housekeeping* feature when she'd searched the internet for more details on the Landis and Renshaw families, who had joined when the widowed Ginger Landis married the widower General Hank Renshaw. But no magazine article could have prepared her for the breathtaking view as Johanna stared through the windshield. The homes were situated on prime oceanfront property. The main house was a sprawling white three-story overlooking the Atlantic, where a couple walked along the low-crashing waves. A lengthy set of stairs stretched upward to the second-story wraparound porch that housed the double door entrance.

Latticework shielded most of the first floor, which appeared to be a large entertainment area, a perfect use of space for a home built on stilts to protect against tidal floods from hurricanes. The attached garage had more doors than an apartment complex.

A carriage house and the Atlantic shore were in front of them. And two cottages were tucked to the sides around an organically shaped pool. The chlorinated waters of the hot tub at the base churned a glistening swirl in the sunlight, adults and kids splashing.

It was a paradise designed for a big family to gather in privacy. The matriarch and patriarch of the family—Ginger and the general—appeared on the balcony porch looking like any other grandparents vacationing with their family. Relatives of all ages poured from the guest quarters. Three other dogs sprinted ahead. Not quite the careful, structured meet and greet that worked best, but clearly this home was about organized chaos.

She stepped out of the car, setting Sterling on the sandy ground while she held tight to the leash. The family tableaus played out in full volume now. She could hear a little girl squealing with laughter while her dad taught her to swim in the pool. A mom held a snoozing infant on her lap while she splash, splash, splashed a toe in the water. Voices mingled from a mother's lullaby to a couple planning a date night since grandparents could babysit.

Johanna saw her own past in the times her parents

had taken her swimming in a pond and saw the future she wanted for herself, but couldn't see how Stone would fit into it. She was killing herself, seeing all these happy families while was stuck in a dead-end relationship with a man who would never open up.

All luxury aside, this kind of togetherness was what she'd hoped to build for herself one day. Those dreams hadn't changed. Which meant she'd landed herself right back into the middle of a heartache all over again.

Stone sat at a poolside table with Ginger and Hank Renshaw, pouring over their adoption paperwork. If anyone had told him a week ago that he would be grilling them to be sure Sterling would be a happy fit for their family, Stone would have said that person was nuts.

Yet here he was, quizzing them and watching the way they handled his grandmother's dog— Correction. *Their* dog now. Sterling was curled up in Ginger's lap, looking like a little prince, completely unfazed by the mayhem of children cannonballing into the deep end while a volleyball game took place on the beach.

Stone nodded somberly, pulling his hat off and setting it aside. "It's important that Sterling get along with children."

"Amen," the general agreed, having stayed silent for the most part, a laid-back gramps in khaki shorts and a polo shirt. "We have double digits in grandkids. Christmases are particularly chaotic."

This wasn't chaos? Stone felt the weight of Johanna's eyes on him, the confusion in her gaze. He gave her a reassuring smile, and she warily smiled back, which too quickly had his mind winging back to thoughts of last night, of how damn much he enjoyed making her smile...and sigh.

He cleared his throat, and his thoughts, turning his focus back to the older couple who'd clearly found a second chance at romance.

Ginger touched her husband's arm, the former secretary of state completely poised in spite of the breeze pulling at her graying hair and loose beach dress. "Hank, we should have them test out the Rottweiler—Ruby—while they're here, as well, since he will be part of the family, sort of, by going to Jonah's father-in-law."

Ginger's youngest son had married a princess, no less. Stone looked out at the beach where Ruby splashed in the waves with another dog and a trio of preteens. "So far so good, I would say."

Ginger nodded, patting the cairn terrier in Johanna's lap. "I just wish we could take that precious Pearl, too. She's like a little Toto from *The Wizard of Oz*. The grandkids would love her and it would be wonderful to keep them together. But we know our limits."

Johanna set her glass of sweet tea back on the table. "We're going to be sure Pearl is well taken care of. Just knowing that Sterling is happy is a load off all our minds, especially for Mrs. McNair." She glanced sympathetically at Stone before looking back at Ginger. "Thank you."

The family matriarch twisted a diamond earring in a nervous fidget, genuine concern in her eyes. "I'm terribly sorry about Mariah.... There are no words at a time like this."

"Thank you, ma'am." Stone nodded tightly, emotion squeezing his chest in a tight fist. "You're offering exactly the kind of help my grandmother needs. Right, Johanna?"

He glanced at her, finding her gaze locked on a mother, father and toddler splashing through the surf together. The look of longing in her eyes slashed straight through him.

Johanna stood up quickly. "We brought a little gift, as a thank-you from Diamonds in the Rough. I'll just get it out of the car."

As he watched her race away he realized how their night together had messed with both of them. Last night had been different from their other times together, and his emotions were in revolt. He was starting to accept it wasn't totally because of his grandmother. His confusion had more to do with Johanna than he'd realized.

Strange how they'd swapped roles here, but he appreciated her interjecting. Talk of his grandmother and seeing this picture-perfect family echoed what he'd already begun to accept. Johanna was right to want this for herself. She shouldn't compromise for him.

On the plane headed for Montana for Pearl's meeting, Johanna struggled to figure out the shift in Stone this afternoon. She thought they'd reached a truce whereby they would indulge in no-strings sex for the week and deal with the fallout later. Yet, something had already changed for him.

And she had to confess, she didn't feel carefree about things, either. Watching the huge Landis-Renshaw family hurt. She couldn't lie about that.

The plane powered through the bumpy night sky and even though she knew where they were going literally, figuratively, she was now totally adrift.

She studied Stone sitting on the sofa with a sketch
pad, his forearm flexing as he drew. Pearl slept on a
cushion beside him, her head resting on his thigh. He
was so damn enticing, he took her breath away.

"What happens now?" Johanna asked.

He glanced up. "Well, in about two more hours, we
should land in—"

"That's not what I meant." Her hand fell to Ruby's
head as the Rottweiler slept at her feet. Johanna would
kennel them for landing or if the turbulence worsened,
but for now she wanted to make the most out of the remaining time with the dogs before they went to their
new homes. "Why are you avoiding talking to me? I
really don't want to think that now that you've gotten
lucky we're through."

His eyebrows shot upward. "You have a mighty jaded
view of mankind."

"You haven't said anything to change my mind tonight," she pushed.

Eyes narrowed, he set aside his sketch pad and rolled
his broad shoulders to stretch out a kink. "Who gave
you such a bad impression of men, and why didn't I pick
up on this when we were together before?"

"Maybe because I always gave you the answers you
wanted to hear." She was realizing she had to accept
some responsibility for their breakup and quit blaming
him for everything.

"And I accepted them rather than pressing," he conceded, bracing his feet through another brief patch of
turbulence.

"There's no great mystery to be solved." She
shrugged. The muted cabin lights, with only a reading lamp over Stone, cast intriguing shadows along his

rugged face. "My parents were great. My father was a good man. But for some reason, the men I chose to date always let me down. One wanted me to give up vet tech school to follow him right away, no waiting—"

"That was Dylan—"

"Yeah," she said, surprised that Stone remembered. He'd been intensely into making his mark at the company, so much so she'd decided she needed to get over her crush. She'd been living in an efficiency apartment, training to be a vet tech. It had seemed time to move forward with her life. "He couldn't even wait six more months for me to finish."

"Then he didn't deserve you."

"Damn right." She knew that now, and even then she'd felt a hint of relief since she didn't ever want to leave Fort Worth. "And the next guy I dated when I moved back to the ranch after school—"

"Langdon."

"You have a good memory." A part of her had wanted him to notice she'd grown up, had wanted him to see her as a woman rather than the pigtailed kid trailing around in the stables. Hindsight, that had been incredibly unfair to Langdon.

"When it comes to you? Yes, I have a very good memory."

"Langdon was the jealous type." And there had been reason for him to be jealous, but that still didn't excuse him going borderline stalker about it. "No need to say more."

"I disagree," he said darkly.

"Don't get caveman on me. You don't need to hunt him down. He didn't hurt me." She stared out into the murky sky for a moment before continuing, "But a look in his eyes made me uncomfortable. I could go on about the other guys in my life, but I just kept picking losers."

"Ouch," he snapped back with a laugh, scrubbing a hand along his five o'clock shadow. "That stings since I'm on that list of exes."

"One of my exes accused me of entering relationships destined to fail because I was secretly pining for you." The words fell out before she could recall them, but then, what did she have to lose at this point?

"Was that true?"

"You know I always had a crush on you." The crush had been so much easier than this.

"Crushing and loving are very different."

Her stomach lurched and it had nothing to do with the bump, bump of the plane over another air pocket. "I did love you when we got engaged."

"Past tense...." He rubbed his neck, and her fingers clenched at the memory of the warmth of his skin. "I'm still getting used to that. What about now?"

"I honestly don't know, and the way you're sitting over there all detached makes it even tougher to figure out what I'm feeling."

He stood, and her mouth went dry the way it always did when he walked her way. But instead of scooping her up, he simply moved into a large leather chair across from her. "When we were together at the beach, none of that was pretend. You can trust what we felt."

"It was real, but we're still learning things weren't as perfect as we thought they were the day we got engaged. It will take us both some time to trust anyone again."

His jaw flexed with tension. "The thought of you getting over me enough to be with someone else is not a heartening thought."

"Why do you naturally assume that the someone I should be with would have to be another person?" She wanted to grab him by the shoulders and shake him. What the hell was going on? He'd made it clear he didn't want to break up when she'd walked, and now that she was reaching out, he'd put up a wall between them. "Even after what we shared last night?"

"Is this really a discussion we should be having now?"

"If not now, when?"

Turbulence jostled the plane again, harder this time and Ruby scrambled for steady footing.

Stone rose quickly, no doubt welcoming the chance to avoid the tough conversation. "We should crate the dogs now."

Sighing, Johanna rose, too, walking to the sofa to pick up Pearl. The pup sat on top of the sketch pad, head tipped with total attitude, one ear up, one down. Johanna gathered the scruffy rascal and uncovered Stone's sketch pad.

A gasp hitched in her throat as she looked down at a page filled with all the fantasy jewelry pieces he'd described wanting to create just for her, and in the middle of it all, a drawing of her sitting in a field of bluebonnets with Pearl beside her. The attention to detail was mindblowing, even down to the weave of her French braid.

The whole time she'd thought he was pushing her away, he'd been focused completely on her.

Stone secured the latch on Ruby's crate. The Rottweiler stared back with droopy sad eyes as she curled up on her fluffy green dog bed. He plucked a dog biscuit from the bin beside the crates and passed a treat through. This week with Johanna was getting more and more complicated and he didn't know how to return to the connection they'd enjoyed while staying at the beach.

She knelt beside him, sliding Pearl into the smaller crate with a pink doggie bed and a couple of chew toys. Just as she locked the pup in, the plane jostled again. And again. Johanna tumbled against him, knocking him back. He twisted fast to cushion her fall with his body.

Johanna stretched out on top of him. "Oh, my, that was something."

He tugged her loose ponytail. "I'm not right for you and you shouldn't settle."

"I know that, and yet here we are."

God, he knew he wasn't good enough for her and still he could already hear that voice in the back of his mind insisting he try to repair the damage that had been done in the past and clear away obstacles to their future.

She wriggled against him enticingly. "Do we have enough time to slip away into the back cabin before we land?"

He clamped a hand on her bottom, acknowledging that he was still unable to resist this woman. He couldn't envision a time he could ever keep her at arm's length. So yeah, he was a selfish bastard. "Keep moving like that and we won't need much time at all."

Laughing, she leaned down to kiss him. The turbulence dipped the plane, and they rolled, slamming against the dog crates.

The captain's voice rumbled over the intercom, announcing the need to return to their seats and buckle in until they cleared the turbulence.

Stone's low curse whispered between them before

he levered off her. He extended a hand to help her up while bracing his other palm along her back protectively to steady her as they returned to the sofa and dug out the seat belts. He took the sketch pad, flipped it closed fast and tossed it aside.

She clicked the lap belt and tugged the strap. "I felt much better for Ruby after hearing the Renshaws' feedback. Makes me hopeful that will work well, too. I wish we knew more about Pearl's family in Montana."

"Honestly, I'm surprised my grandmother isn't keeping Ruby, since that's the one dog she chose rather than adopting from someone else. I never thought to ask Gran about Ruby's history. She just said she got Ruby at a shelter, nothing more."

"Your grandmother seemed lonely after she retired from the board at Diamonds in the Rough. So I took her to the animal shelter. She chose a new friend. Ruby was a stray, no known history, but they took to each other right away."

"You're a good woman, Johanna. I've always known that, though." His hand fell on her knee.

"Don't try the übercharmer act on me." She leaned closer and tapped him on the chin.

"It's not an act," he denied even as he slid his hand under the hem of her dress, ideas flourishing for ways to please her in spite of the seat belt. "If I were just trying to charm you, I would compliment your beautiful face or your hot body...." He skimmed up the inside of her thigh, welcoming the distraction from more serious talk and concerns. If only he could lose himself in her infinitely.

"Which is all true, of course," he continued. "That's what reeled me into asking you out. But the good woman part?" He squeezed her thigh without moving any higher. "That's what kept me around. That's why I proposed. And ultimately, that's why you left me."

"What are you trying to accomplish?" There was anguish in her beautiful eyes, but a whisper of hope that spurred him on and crystalized his thoughts.

"It's a warning, I guess," he said somberly, sliding his hand from under her dress to take her fingers in his. "You are a good woman, and you deserve better than what I have to offer. But that isn't going to stop me from offering and asking again."

Her throat moved in a slow swallow. "Stone—"

"Shh." He pressed a finger to her lips. "I don't want you to answer yet. You should think. And just so you know, all I can think about is peeling your clothes away piece by piece, then making love to you in a field of bluebonnets."

"Are you really suggesting we just have sex and... drift?"

"If that means I get more time with you, then yes," he answered without hesitation. "There is no one else I'll be spending my life with. You were it, Johanna. My one shot at the whole happily-ever-after gig."

He cupped her face and drew her to him, easy to do as she leaned into him. Her fingers fluttered along his cheek, falling to rest on his shoulders. Her light touch stirred him every bit as much as her most bold caress.

Damn straight, there was no one for him other than Johanna. He deepened the kiss, her soft lips parting for him, inviting him in to taste, take and give. The warmth of her seeped into him, fanning the flames that never died. She was in his blood, now and always.

He tugged the band from her hair and combed his

fingers through the strands. The feel of her hair gliding along his hands was pure bliss, like the wind sliding over him when he rode on the open land. He played it out along her back and over her shoulders before stroking down her arms.

His hand returned to her knee and tunneled under her silky dress, along her even silkier thigh. His knuckles skimmed her satin panties, already hot from her arousal, and he ached to know what color she wore—

The plane's phone rang from beside the sofa, jarring him from the kiss and the moment. Who would call in the middle of the night? Only family and only with an emergency.

With more than a little regret, he ended the kiss and pulled away from Johanna, alarms already sounding in his mind. He angled past her to snag the phone and read the screen. He glanced at Johanna, apprehension filling his gut as his suspicion was confirmed.

"It's Amie." He frowned, thumbing the on button and activating the speakerphone. "Amie, what's up? You're on speaker. Johanna's here with me."

"Gran's in the hospital." His cousin's voice trembled, and Stone exchanged a quick glance with Johanna. "She had a seizure, Stone. It… It was…horrible. We had to call an ambulance."

Dread hit him like a boulder. "I'm on my way. I'll have the pilot turn around, and we'll be there in a few hours. Hold on, okay, kiddo?"

He vaguely registered Johanna's hand smoothing along his back.

Amie hiccuped on the other end of the line. "I'm sorry to be such a mess. It was just really frightening." The sound of her shaky breath reverberated on the crackly connection. "Alex and I can hold down the fort until you get here. The doctor says she's past the immediate danger, but…"

"I'm on my way," he repeated, pulling his focus in tight. He was the head of his family. He should be home overseeing the business and the family affairs for his grandmother, not playing games.

He owed his grandmother and Johanna better. From this point on, he was 100 percent in when it came to taking care of his family, and Johanna was going to be a member of his family.

Whatever it took.

Nine

Johanna's stomach dropped as the hospital elevator rose, taking them to Mariah.

Fear for Mariah and grief for Stone had tumbled and tangled inside her ever since the panicked call from Amie came through. And no matter how much she worried, there was nothing she could do to console Stone or make this better.

They should be bonded in the moment, leaning on each other while they were both scared and hurting, but instead she could see him drawing inward. Rather than letting anyone close, Stone took on the leader of the pack mentality that had kept him at the office late so many nights. Since he'd hung up the phone, he'd been in motion. He'd moved up front with the pilot to discuss rerouting the plane. A limo had met them at the airport driving them to the ranch to drop off the dogs and grab a quick shower.

Now, medical personnel on the fourth floor milled around the nurses' station watching over their patients through cameras and observation windows. His grandmother had plenty of watchful eyes but Stone had already started researching other hospitals and doctors without even consulting the rest of the family. God, she hoped there wouldn't be a major argument with Stone and his cousins.

The head nurse waved him through before returning to her charts. Stone had called ahead to confirm the minute morning visiting hours began. She didn't even want to consider the fact that they could have arrived too late.

Mariah looked pale and small under the stark white sheet, sleeping. Only the steady rise and fall of her chest and the monitors beeping and clicking offered any reassurance that she was still alive.

Stone swept off his hat, set it on the rolling tray and moved closer to his grandmother. His boots thudded softly against the tile floors.

Mariah's lashes fluttered upward, her eyes surprisingly clear and alert, thank heavens. "You're here." She reached out a thin hand, her skin almost translucent. "I told your cousins not to worry you. Which one called?"

"I'm not ratting anyone out," he teased softly.

Mariah laughed softly. "You three always did stick together." She looked past him and smiled at Johanna, lifting her other hand with the IV line taped down. "Dear girl, come closer. You can both do away with those gloom and doom looks on your faces."

Johanna stroked Mariah's wrist. "Of course we're worried. You would feel the same if our positions were reversed."

"True enough," Mariah conceded. "But I'm okay. It was only a case of dehydration. Nothing to do with the tumor. I let myself get run-down and just needed a little boost. It's my own fault, and I'm so sorry they scared you into coming home unnecessarily."

"Gran, you don't need to lie to me." Stone's forehead furrowed, his face bristly since he'd rushed his shower and skipped the shave. "I already know you had a seizure."

"Damn it, I told Amie and Alex not to worry you, and don't bother denying one of them told you," she groused with enough spunk that Johanna relaxed a hint. "I'm not going to die this week, so you two don't need to park by my bed and babysit me. You have work to do."

Stone dropped into the chair by her bed. "They knew how angry I would be once I found out no one bothered to call me. And believe me, I would have found out."

"You're just like me." She smiled fondly. "Tenacious."

"I'm just glad you're all right, Gran." He glanced across his grandmother at Johanna, the strain of the past few hours showing in the lines fanning from his sapphire-blue eyes. "We both are."

Mariah squeezed Johanna's hand. "Tell me about your trip so far. The pictures are wonderful but I want to hear what you think, Johanna."

Mariah was shifting topics deftly, ensuring Stone wouldn't have to battle through weightier emotions right now. Or was it Mariah who wasn't ready to face those feelings today? Johanna had never fully appreciated how alike the two of them really were. But for now, she gladly distracted both of them with talk of a safe subject.

"Well, Gem loves the wide-open space of the Donavans' home, and their home in Monte Carlo has a fenced area, as well. Sterling is enjoying his life as a pampered lapdog. You chose well for both of them."

Her eyelids fluttered closed for a moment before she

looked up at Stone and Johanna again with a mist of tears in her eyes. "Thank you, and I truly mean that."

"Gran." Stone leaned in. "Are you sure you want us to continue with the placements? You could keep Pearl and Ruby. Trust that we will take care of finding them new homes, if the time comes—" He swallowed hard, his Adam's apple making a slow trip down the strong column of his throat. "If the time comes you can't care for them anymore."

Johanna had to blink her eyes hard. God, maybe it was her who wasn't ready to face the big emotions in the room today. Mariah had become so dear to her. A role model. A friend.

"I'm absolutely certain that I want you to continue the plan." She smiled sadly. "I already can't give them the attention they need. Call me a micromanager if you will, but I need to know where they are and who they're with."

"Gran—" Stone's phone cut him short and he cursed softly. He pulled out the cell and checked the incoming call, before silencing the chimes and tucking the phone back in his pocket.

His grandmother touched his wrist. "Who is it? Your cousins?"

He shook his head. "It's from Montana. Probably something about Pearl. I'll take it later."

"No," Mariah said with surprising strength. "That's important business to me."

His cheeks puffed out with an exhale. "Okay, Gran. If that's what you want, but I'll be right back."

Phone to his ear, head ducked, he strode out, door swooshing closed behind him.

Mariah patted Johanna's hand. "Pull up a seat and talk to me, Johanna. How is it really going, dear?"

"What do you mean?" she asked evasively, looking away under the guise of tugging a chair over.

"No need to be coy," Mariah tsked. "Are you and Stone a couple again?"

Johanna dropped into a seat. "Wow, you really cut to the chase."

"I don't have time to dillydally around the subject." Mariah pushed the controls to raise the head of the mattress. "Even at half speed in this hospital bed, I can tell the chemistry is alive and well. I see the exchanged glances. You have to know I was hoping your trip together would fix things between you. Did my matchmaking work?"

The optimism in the woman's face was unmistakable. Johanna didn't want to give false hope, and she wasn't sure where things stood with Stone right now. "I wish I could tell you what you want to hear, but I honestly don't know."

"The fact that you didn't deny it outright gives me hope."

Johanna sagged back, rolling her eyes. "But no pressure, right?"

"You're more confident now than you were a year ago." She nodded approvingly. "That's a good thing. Your parents would be very proud of you."

She couldn't deny that Mariah's words of encouragement meant a great deal to her. "Thank you. I appreciate that, but please just focus on taking care of yourself. You're important to a lot of people."

"You've always been dear."

Johanna scrunched her nose. "You make me sound wimpy."

"I just told you I see your confidence and I meant that." Mariah studied her with perceptive eyes. "But there is a gentleness to you that my grandson needs in his life. It softens his harsher edges."

Johanna found herself growing defensive on his behalf. "Why is it that everyone assumes because his mother named him Stone he's hard-hearted?"

Mariah smiled. "And that's why you're perfect for him."

Stone ended his phone call the second he saw Amie and Alex entering the visitors' waiting room. The muted sounds from a mounted television broadcasting a talk show mingled with the soft conversations from a handful of other people in the waiting area. Fake plants and magazine racks were tucked into one corner. A coffeepot gurgled in the other.

He and his cousins had spent little time alone together since their grandmother's announcement. His gut twisted at the realization they would be meeting up in waiting rooms like this many more times in the coming months.

In light of that, any bickering between them felt like a waste of precious time. And the frustration with the Montana family that had changed their mind about Pearl? He would deal with that later.

He had Johanna's reassurance that there was nothing between her and Alex, and Stone couldn't blame his cousin. Johanna was an amazing woman.

Alex stuffed his hands in his jean pockets and rocked back on his boot heels. "You've seen Gran already?"

Stone nodded, tucking an arm around Amie, her shoulders too thin beneath her silk blouse. "She seems alert, just tired. Thank you for calling me."

Amie hugged him back quickly before stepping away. "Alex said not to bother you."

Alex shrugged. "I've got things under control here, so you can finish up your business with the dogs."

Stone held back the urge to chew out Alex for being an ass. Even his quiet cousin would have blown a gasket if left out of the loop on news about Mariah's health.

Torqued at Alex's attitude, Stone couldn't resist jabbing, "Wait until you're the one turning your life upside down to make her happy. And you know damn well you both will."

He glowered at his cousin until he was sure Alex understood he wouldn't have appreciated being left in the dark about Gran. Then, hoping to distract Amie, he asked, "Any idea from Gran about what test she has in mind for the two of you?"

Amie shuffled from high heel to high heel, gnawing her thumbnail. "She hasn't mentioned it, but you know there's no rushing Gran. She has a plan and a reason for everything she does." She looked at her hand as if only just realizing she was chewing her nails down to nothing. She tucked her fist behind her back. "Have you told your mother yet?"

"Why would I?" Stone retorted quickly. "If Gran wants to see her, she'll tell her."

Alex lifted a lazy eyebrow. "Have you ever considered we should overrule Gran? Not just on this, but on other issues, as well. You have to confess that this test thing to decide the future of a huge estate is more than a little half-baked."

Stone stared at Alex in surprise. His cousin was a man of few words, so a speech that long carried extra weight.

Amie crossed her arms tightly, a wrist full of delicate silver bangles jangling. "You can't be saying what I think. You can't intend to have Gran declared unfit to manage her affairs."

"I think we should consider it," Alex said somberly. "She even said she planned this test for you because she was afraid the tumor might affect her judgment. What if it's too late?"

Stone hated even considering it. But had he disregarded warning signs about his grandmother out of a selfish need to have Johanna back in his life? "This isn't a question we can answer on our own. We need to speak with her doctors. Agreed? Alex?"

His cousin held up both hands. "Fair enough. And about contacting your mom?"

Damn. He scrubbed a hand along his jaw. "If you want to call my mother, do it, but I have nothing to say to her. And when she does something to hurt Gran—and trust me, my mother will—it will be on your conscience."

He pivoted away to end the conversation only to find Johanna standing behind him, her worried eyes making it clear she'd overheard at least part of their exchange. He slid an arm around her shoulders. "Johanna, let's go. We need to take care of Ruby and Pearl."

The weight of Alex's jealous gaze seared his back. For his entire life, his grandmother, the ranch and time with his cousins had been his stability, his grounding force. In the span of the week, all of that was being threatened. Without his grandmother as the glue, would their family hold together?

Johanna had accused him of not understanding how she felt when she lost her whole family. For the first time, he fully grasped what she meant. The impending sense of loss left a hole in his chest. And the prospect of having his mother roll into town creating havoc did little to reassure him.

He tucked Johanna closer to his side and wondered if he could dig deep enough to keep her this time.

Johanna curled against Stone's side, resting her head on his shoulder and soaking in the feel of his fingers stroking up and down her arm. The ceiling fan in her bedroom gusted cooling air over her bared flesh. So easily, they'd fallen into old habits, tossing aside their clothes the second they crossed the threshold of her cabin.

They hadn't even discussed it or questioned it. They'd sought the blissful escape of losing themselves in each other. The ease of that unsettled her. Eventually they would have to resolve the differences that had made her walk before. The past seven months had been hell, but they couldn't just pretend the future didn't matter, even if lounging in her lavender-scented sheets with him felt deliciously decadent.

Stone kissed the top of her head, the stubble on his chin catching in her hair. "My cousins brought up something at the hospital that I can't ignore, as much as I might wish otherwise."

She glanced up at him. "What's wrong?"

"I'm going to have to tell my mother about Mariah's cancer."

"Oh, wow, I hadn't even considered that..." The last she'd heard of his mother, Jade had been living with a boyfriend in Paris. "Is she still in France?"

As best as Johanna could remember, Jade had moved in with a wealthy wine merchant about four years ago and hadn't come home since. Johanna had gotten the feeling Jade was hiding as far away from her family as she could.

Stone shook his head. "She's in Atlanta now. She went through another rehab two months ago and decided to stay near her shrink rather than go back to her fast-living wine merchant sugar daddy. Having such a large trust fund can be a blessing and a curse. Too much cash on hand to feed the habit, but plenty of money to get the best care during the next detox."

She had few memories of his mom, most of them conflicted, depending on if she was in the middle of a frenetic drug binge or somberly drained from another stint in rehab. "How do you feel about that?"

He eyed her wryly. "How do you think I feel?"

"Not happy?"

"Mariah doesn't need the drama draining what strength she has."

Johanna slid her arm around him, hugging him, her leg nestled between his. "I agree, but eventually she'll have to be told."

He nodded, his chin brushing the top of her head again. A long sigh shuddered through him. "I was a crack baby."

His stark declaration caught her by surprise, stunning her still and silent. She scrambled for the right thing to say but could only hold him tighter to let him know she was here to listen. In fact, she wished he had trusted her enough to open up before now. "Stone, I don't know what to say."

"There's nothing to say. People assume it's a poverty issue, but that's not always the case. My mother was addicted to cocaine when I was born. I didn't know that until I was an adult and saw my medical records. I just thought I needed all those developmental therapists and tutors as a kid because I wasn't as smart as my cousins." He kept skimming his hand along her back as if taking comfort from the feel of her. "My first days on this earth were spent detoxing."

She pressed a kiss to his collarbone, still too choked up to speak. Her eyes burned with tears she knew he wouldn't want to see. Thank God, Mariah had been there for him.

His hand kept up the steady rhythm. "I don't like to take medicines. I figure with a junkie mom, genetics aren't on my side as a father," he said darkly, the deeper implication clear, explaining the mystery of why he seemed so determined to deny himself a family of his own. "And what if that early addiction is still there lurking, waiting to be triggered again?"

She blinked back the tears and tipped her head to look up at him. "What does your doctor say?"

His handsome features were strained, his jaw flexing. "Not to snort coke."

She skimmed her fingers over the furrows in his forehead. "How can you make jokes about this?"

"It's better this way." He captured her hand and pressed a kiss into her palm. "I want you to understand why I'm not comfortable being a father or passing along my genes to future generations."

"Why didn't you try to make me understand before?

You have to know I would have listened without judging." Although she had to wonder. Would she have been able to accept that he didn't want children? Or would she have pushed for him to resolve his feelings in order to have things the way she wanted them?

"I thought you would run if you knew. Then you ran anyway, which only confirmed my suspicion." He threaded his fingers through her loose hair, cupping the back of her head. "Now, there's nothing to lose."

Her parents' love had been such a grounding foundation for her all her life, giving her a confidence she carried with her even now that they were gone. She'd always thought about how lucky he was to have Mariah—Johanna hadn't considered the scars he must carry because of his mother's addiction. "I am so sorry for what you went through as a baby and for all you went through afterward with your mom."

He searched her eyes. "And you aren't upset that I didn't tell you before?"

Was she? She searched her heart and decided *upset* wasn't the right word. *Disappointed* fit better. That he'd held this back only reinforced her feelings that they hadn't been ready to commit before. For whatever reason, he hadn't been able to trust her, and she hadn't looked any deeper than the surface.

She understood now that he'd never be able to give her the family she craved. His resistance was rooted in something much deeper than she'd ever guessed. But even knowing that she wouldn't be able to move them to a healthier, happier place together, she couldn't help wanting to savor this time with him. She was deeply moved that he'd trusted her enough to share this. She just wished he loved her enough to address the problem. For now though, with her emotions ripped raw, she would take whatever tenderness she could find in his arms until she found the strength to move forward with her life again.

"Not angry." She kissed him once, lightly, before continuing. "Just glad you told me now."

"You're being too nice about this." He tunneled his hands through her hair again and again in a rhythm that both soothed and aroused.

"I'm seeing things from a new perspective, questioning if I really gave you the opening to share the darker corners of your life." She took in the handsome, hard lines of his face, thinking about all the times she'd fantasized about him as a teenager. She'd idealized him and idolized him for so many years; she hadn't given him much room to be human. "I created a fantasy crush image of you and expected you to live up to that. It wasn't fair to you."

"You truly are too forgiving."

"I have my limits," she admitted. "I'm human, too."

"I should let you go, but all I can think is that someone else would take advantage—" his voice went gravelly, his arms flexing a second before he tucked her underneath him "—and there's nothing in this world I want more than to keep you safe."

"You know what I want more than anything? I want to make love to you until you can't think of any more gut-wrenching discussions for us to have." She angled up to kiss him once, twice, distracting him so she could roll him to his back. "I want us to try to be normal for a while."

"You can absolutely feel free to console me with sex."

As much as he tried to joke, she could see the raw emotion in his eyes and knew he'd pushed so far outside his comfort zone, he would need time before he could go further. So she offered him the only comfort he would allow now—an escape, a reprieve that could be found in each other's arms.

She sealed her mouth to his again. His arms wrapped around her in a flash, his hands curving around her bottom and bringing her closer. She straddled him. The pressure of his erection against the core of her was a delicious friction. Already, a euphoric haze seeped through her veins, evicting her concerns—at least for this stolen moment together.

Ten

Johanna woke to the sound of voices. Or rather one voice and a couple of different barks.

She pushed her tangled hair off her face and sat up, sheet pooling around her waist in the empty bed. Blinking to clear her mind and vision, she saw Stone's boots still on the floor, his shirt tossed over a chair. Where was his rumbly voice coming from? Maybe he was in the kitchen?

Then she heard him…from the porch. Her window was open since the night had dipped into the seventies.

"Sit…. That's right, good girl," he said, a dog bark answering.

Pearl.

"Girl, this is the last treat. You've already had four. You're gonna get sick. Yeah, Ruby, I have another for you, too. Fair's fair."

She smiled affectionately. He was sweeter than he gave himself credit for. Although with his revelations the past few days, she could understand why he was so hesitant to let down his walls and be vulnerable. His mother had betrayed him on so many different levels from the start.

The details about his birth and early years still

rocked her. It also affirmed they hadn't been ready to get married before with such secrets between them, but it heartened her that they were making progress now. He was opening up to her, and she wondered what that could mean for them as the rest of this week played out. While she wasn't ready to think beyond the next few days, she also knew they'd moved past having a one-night stand for old times' sake.

Tossing aside the sheets, she left the bed and grabbed a silky robe from a hook on the bathroom door. The sun was only just rising, but usually she would already have her coffee in a travel mug as she headed to the barn. Being idle felt…strange.

She wrapped the knee-length robe around her and padded barefoot through the living area out to the covered porch. Stone sat in a rocker wearing jeans and nothing else. His hair stood up a little in the back with an endearing bed-head look that softened her already weakening emotions. She'd missed mornings like this with him. Ruby was lounging at his feet, and Pearl slept curled up on the porch swing.

Stone glanced back at her and grinned. "Good morning, gorgeous."

"Good morning to you, too. Any news on your grandmother?" Although she assumed there must not have been any bad updates, given his happy mood.

"Amie sent a text a half hour ago. Gran's resting comfortably and will be released this morning. Alex and Amie are arguing—as expected—over which one of them will bring her home."

"I'm relieved to hear Mariah's well enough to come home. Hopefully Alex and Amie will put their competitiveness on hold for the day." She leaned a hip against the door frame, watching the low hum of activity at the lodge in the distance. She had the added privacy of a circle of sprawling oak and pine trees since she lived here. A couple hundred yards away, beyond the trees, she could hear a couple of early risers talking over breakfast. Voices and hubbub from the stables echoed from the other side of the ranch house, but everyone was out of sight.

For the most part, she had Stone to herself. "What are you drawing?"

He tipped his head for her to join him. "Come see."

She walked out onto the porch and stopped behind his chair. Looping her arms around his neck, she peered over his shoulder, surprised to find he wasn't sketching the landscape after all. He had almost finished a sketch of Pearl on the porch swing. Even only halfway done, the likeness was impressive and heart tugging. He'd captured a sadness in the dog's eyes that mirrored the sadness she'd seen in Stone's since his grandmother's announcement. He patted her hand quietly but kept the pencil in motion.

She stepped around him and settled onto the porch swing beside the terrier. She tapped the swing into motion, staying silent while Stone lost himself in the drawing. She wanted to soak up the moment and ignore the fear that this was merely the calm before the storm.

Finally, he sighed and closed the pad, looking across at her. "Sorry if I woke you."

"I wake up earlier than this for work." She reached to touch the edge of the sketch pad on the table beside him. "I forget sometimes what a good artist you are."

"The jewelry design gene in my family takes many forms," he said offhandedly.

She smoothed her hand along Pearl's back, flattening her bristly fur. "Have you ever thought about offering more input on the designs?"

"That's Amie's realm. We try not to encroach on each other's territory. The last thing we need is more competition in this family." He scratched his collar bone, drawing her eyes to his bare chest. "Besides, this is my hobby, my way of relaxing."

Her mouth watered at the flex of his tattoo along his arm and the muscled expanse of his chest. "Did you destroy the drawings of me the way you promised when we broke up?"

"You mean the nude drawings." He grinned wickedly. "What do you think?"

She wasn't sure what she thought. In the past couple of days she'd come to realize he was very good at keeping secrets and she had been very good at dodging tough subjects in the interest of keeping her fantasy alive. "Should I trust you?"

"Absolutely," he said without question. "I'm trying to make things right. And as for the drawings, I don't need any help remembering every amazing inch of you."

He angled out of the chair to kiss her with a firm, sure confidence that swirled her senses. In a fast sweep, he lifted her and settled her onto his lap. "We have about an hour before we need to head over to the house. Any ideas how we can spend that time wisely?"

She teased the swoop of bed head in his hair. "I think you may need a shower. Are you sure you don't want to hurry and help Alex drive your grandmother home?"

"I'll just leave Alex and Amie to duke that out between them."

She leaned back against his chest. She'd missed moments like this, enjoying the steady thud of his heart. "They're both so competitive. It should be interesting to watch them once their test comes. I always felt sorry for them as a kid."

"How so?" he asked. "They had everything—money, parents, a family."

Really? He was that clueless? "They had a mom who trotted them out like prize horses and a father so tied to golf and hiding from their mom they barely saw him."

"The pageant thing was a little over-the-top," he conceded.

She couldn't hold back a laugh. "You think?"

"Amie never protested—" He held up a hand. "Wait. I take that back. She complained once. She wanted to go to some high school dance and it fell on the weekend of a pageant competition."

"Did she get to the dance?"

"Nope. She won her crown." A one-sided smile kicked a dimple into his cheek. "We found the tiara in the middle of a silver tureen of grits the next morning."

"Miss Texas Grits," she quipped. "I like it. Amie is full of grit, after all." Johanna had spent so much of her life idealizing the McNairs, minimizing their struggles, feeling sorry for them on some issues, but overall envying them.

The sound of an approaching taxi pulled her attention out of their bubble of intimacy. Johanna kissed Stone quickly then eased off his lap.

She extended a hand to him. "We should go back inside before the rest of the guests saddle up for the day. I don't want to have to fight off the tourists. They'll be drooling over a half-dressed cowboy."

Her half-dressed cowboy. The possessive thought
blindsided her.

The cab drove past the Hidden Gem Lodge and drew
closer, as if coming to her home. Johanna hesitated half
in, half out of her door. Sure enough, the taxi stopped
right at her fenced front lawn. Ruby and Pearl leaped
to their feet and flew off the porch, barking.

The back door of the vehicle opened and a woman
stepped out, one high heel at a time. Stone's quick gasp
gave her an instant's warning before recognition hit.

The reed-thin woman bore a striking resemblance to
Mariah and Amie for a reason. After four years away,
Stone's mother—Jade McNair—had come home.

Stone carried his mother's designer luggage into the
guest suite in the family's portion of the Hidden Gem
Lodge. He'd been on autopilot since the second he'd
seen his mother step out of the taxi. He vaguely recalled
Johanna filling the awkward silence with small talk
while he grabbed his shirt and boots. His mother had
said something about seeing him on Johanna's porch
so Jade had instructed the taxi driver to go to the cabin
rather than straight to the lodge.

His only thought had been to divert any crisis that
might upset Mariah.

He put the hang-up bag in the closet and dropped the
two suitcases by the leather sofa, onto the thick wool of
the Aztec patterned rug. She'd certainly brought enough
to stay for more than a weekend trip.

Pivoting, he found his mother standing in the middle
of the floor, shifting from foot to foot under the elk horn
chandelier. From nerves? Or in need of a fix? She was
as thin as a bird, her skin sallow and eyes haunted but

clear—her standard postdetox look. He'd seen it enough times to recognize it, and he'd seen it fall apart enough times not to bother hoping the new start would stick.

He cut straight to the chase. "Mariah needs peace, not drama. Cause her any heartache and I will throw you out myself."

Jade nodded nervously, her hand shaking as she pushed back a hank of dark hair with new threads of silver. "I'm not here to cause trouble. I heard the news about my mother's cancer from a friend."

"Are you here to make sure you're in the will?"

She sagged onto the upholstered bench at the foot of the bed. "I understand you don't have any reason to trust me, but I want to see my mother. I would also like to help if I can—and if she will let me."

She sounded genuine. But then she always did at this stage of the cycle.

"Jade, keep in mind what I said. Mariah's comfort and health come first." He turned for the door, wanting the hell out of here and back to Johanna's cabin with the dogs.

"Stone, wait," his mother called.

He stopped with his hand on the door handle. His shoulders sagged with a weary sigh. "Remember the part about no drama? The same goes in talking to me."

She stayed silent until he finally faced her again.

Jade still sat on the bench, hugging one of those fancy throw pillows women insisted on. "I'm sorry for not being a real mother to you. I regret that."

"Everyone has regrets." He understood she had to make amends as a part of the recovery process. She'd walked the steps again and again until he had the whole routine memorized. Too many times he thought she'd bottomed out enough that she'd finally begin a real recovery.

He wasn't falling into that trap again.

She looked at him uncertainly. "What? No telling me off? Handing over pamphlets for the latest, greatest rehab center? I just finished with one of the best, you know."

"So I hear. Congratulations." Time would tell, but he wasn't holding his breath.

"You've changed," she said sadly. "You're colder than ever, something else I need to make up to you."

"I'm an adult. I accept responsibility for who I am." He put his hand back on the door handle. "Now if we're done here…?"

Her eyes welled up. "My mother is dying. Can you cut me a little slack?"

"Yes, she is," he snapped, pushing past the lump in his throat. "And she doesn't need you sapping what strength she has left."

"Maybe I can bring her some comfort," Jade said with a shaky hope that hinted at the brighter spirit she'd been during some of the better times of her life. She toyed with a turquoise cascade around her neck, a piece her dad had made for her eighteenth birthday. "I have a small window here to get things right, and I'm not going to waste it."

"You can sit by her side as long as you're lifting her spirits. If you don't do that, you're gone." That's all he cared about. And hadn't he made that freaking clear the first time? Impatience gnawed at the back of his neck. "Now what else do you need from me?"

"Keep being the good man that you are." Her eyes went doe-wide as she launched into a facade he liked to call "the good mother." She deluded herself that she had something to offer. When he was a kid, this phase had been killer because it offered the false impression that she gave a damn.

"Right." He ground his teeth together, knowing Johanna would tell him to get through this. Keep the peace. At least, he thought that's what she'd say. He'd never given his mother that much airtime to know for sure.

"And Stone? Figure out how to be the kind of husband Johanna deserves because even I can see the two of you are meant to be together. I'm going to try to help here, but I know there's probably nothing I can accomplish better than you or your cousins."

Already this was seeping into drama-land. "Mom, can we stop? I need to go—"

She launched up and grabbed his arm. "You're the only hope I have left of making my mother happy. Even though I can't take credit for the man you've become—Mariah brought you up—I can take some pride in knowing I was your mother. At some point I must have done something good as your mom."

The pleading look in her eyes chipped away at him, catching him at a time when he was already raw from all the walls he'd torn down in the past couple of days. Johanna, with her healing spirit and love of family, would want him to try. She had helped so many—human and animals—without expecting anything in return.

For Johanna, he scrounged in his mind for a positive memory with his mother and came up with, "You helped me with my macaroni art project for kindergarten."

Blinking fast, she thumbed away a tear. "What did you say?"

He leaned against the closed door. "The teacher wanted us to use pasta to create scenes for the four seasons. I was mad because I wanted to draw horses so I blew off the 'homework.' The teacher sent a note home."

"You always were a good artist and smart, too," she said with pride.

He resisted the urge to say the crack baby rehab had probably shaved ten points or more off his IQ. A year ago, he would have opted for the joke. Instead, he opted for another Johanna-like answer. "You read to me. A lot. I remember that, too."

She sat on her suitcase. "What else do you remember about the macaroni art project?"

"After we finished—or so I thought—you said it needed sparkle." The memory expanded in his mind, making him smile even now in the middle of such a dismal morning. "We went into Grandpa's home studio and raided the jewel bags. You used a citrine stone for the summer sun. Silver shavings for winter snow. Tiny amethysts and rubies for spring flowers. And for autumn, we had—"

"A pile of leaves made of topazes." She clapped her hands and smiled. "When I heard you and Johanna were engaged, I called my mother and asked her to unearth those projects from a trunk I'd stored in the attic."

"You kept the project?" Stunned, he was glad he had the door at his back for support.

"All four seasons," she confirmed. "I got them framed, to be a wedding gift to you and Johanna. When you and Johanna broke up, I just kept them for myself. They're hanging in my living room. You can come see for yourself if you don't believe me." The hint of desperation in her eyes punched away a little more of his defenses.

"I believe you. That's really nice." And it was. Keeping kindergarten art didn't make up for the past but it meant something to him to know she'd held on to the memory, too.

He didn't think he could ever see her as a mother figure. That seemed disloyal to Mariah who'd done everything for him. Photos showed his grandfather had tried to fill the void of a father figure. From all he'd heard from Mariah about his grandfather, he would have kept that up....

That thought brought to mind other unfinished business between him and his mom. He'd learned time wasn't guaranteed, so he might as well go for broke. "I know who my father is."

Her McNair blue eyes went wide. "Is that a trick question where you try to get me to admit something?"

"No trick. I did the detective work and figured it out. A DNA test confirmed Dale Banks is my biological father." He still didn't know how he felt about that. Maybe it would have been better not to know than to continue to wonder what would happen if he ever confronted the guy with the truth.

Her jaw dropped. "Dale agreed to the test?"

"He didn't know about the test. I tricked him. But if I'm right, I think he already knew and didn't want to be a father, or he refused a test in the past."

She nodded.

Stone followed the rest of the thought to its logical conclusion. "And he wasn't interested in being a parent."

"I'm afraid not, son." She stood and reached to pat

his arm, but stopped just shy of actually touching him. "I'm so sorry."

He winced at the word *son* but decided to let it slide. "Apology accepted."

Yes, anger and betrayal churned inside him, but he refused to stir up drama right before Mariah came home from the hospital.

"Does that mean I'm forgiven?" Jade asked hopefully. "I know that I can't make up for what I put you through, but I would like to know you've found some peace. You deserved better."

"I have Mariah," he said without missing a beat. "I got the best."

No more blaming the past for current issues. He had to shoulder his own mistakes from now on. Which meant he had a final confession to make to Johanna, and with his blinders off, he understood she might well never forgive him. But lying to her through evasion was no longer an option.

The sun sank on the horizon like a melting orange Dreamsicle.

Johanna drew in the sweet fragrance from the field of bluebonnets. After a full day of walking on eggshells around the entire McNair family, she was more than ready to jump all over Stone's suggestion that they slip away for a ride before supper. She should have known he would choose to ride to his favorite patch of Mc-Nair land.

She slid from her horse, leather creaking. "What a great idea to come here to watch the sunset."

He swung a leg over and dismounted. He opened the saddlebag, pulled out a yellow quilt and passed it over to her. With a pat to his quarter horse's flank, he let Copper graze alongside Johanna's palomino.

She shook the quilt out onto the ground and dropped down to sit with an exhausted sigh. It seemed like aeons ago that she'd woken up to find Stone on the porch sketching doggie portraits.

"What does your grandmother want to do about Pearl since the Montana couple reneged?" She'd been surprised when he announced the family had changed their minds, but then she'd always wondered if Pearl should stay with Mariah.

He pulled two water bottles from the saddlebag before sitting beside her. He stretched his legs out, boots crossed at the ankles. "Gran expects us to proceed as planned with the backup families once we take Ruby to her princess digs."

"Sounds like Mariah really has her heels dug in deep." Johanna sipped the water, trying not to get her hopes up too high over how right this felt with his warm muscled thigh against hers while they sat shoulder to shoulder. "I have to admit, I'm surprised. I always thought Pearl was her favorite."

"Pearl was actually my mother's dog." He tipped back his water bottle, his throat moving with a long swallow.

"How did I not know that?" She thumbed the condensation on the outside of her water bottle. "I can only remember Pearl coming to Mariah about four years ago and Mariah saying offhandedly that Pearl had been abandoned by her owner."

"That's pretty much dead-on correct," he said drily. "My mother bought her from a pet store, paid a fortune for her. Thought she was getting her own *Wizard of Oz*

Toto. Once Pearl wasn't a puppy anymore, my mom didn't want her. Too much mess, too much nipping, too much trouble to take with her to France."

"That's sad to hear." Would the little terrier remember Jade? Be confused? "Shelters are full of older puppies just like that. Thank goodness your grandmother took her."

"Just like she took me."

She slid an arm around him. Jade showing up after so long must have rattled him. "Your grandmother did a great job with you. You're an amazing man."

He didn't smile or even look at her. He picked at a clump of bluebonnets and smashed them between his fingers. "It's crazy, but she blamed herself for the selfish decisions made by her adult children. I think she saw me as her second chance to get it right after my drug addict mother and my trust fund uncle who never worked a day in his life."

"You work very hard." Too hard, in her opinion.

"She still doesn't trust me to take over the company." He sprinkled the bits of bluebonnet leaves over her lap.

"She can't doubt your skills as the CEO of Diamonds in the Rough. You've expanded the company in a tough economy." She wasn't a business major, but she knew magazines had written glowing features on him.

"Mariah doubts my humanity instincts. Something you yourself have noted, as well," he pointed out. "And that stings more because I'm not sure it's something I can fix."

"Oh, Stone," she said, her heart aching over the hurt they'd caused each other. She shifted, swinging her leg over to straddle his lap. She took his face in her hands. "I never should have said that. Whatever our differences, I know you care about people. I guess that's what frustrates me most. Your refusal to see how good you are."

Unable to take the pain in his sky-blue eyes, she leaned in to kiss him, hoping he would feel all the emotion in her flowing into him. No matter how hard she'd tried to deny it, this was the only man she'd ever loved. The only man she ever would love.

His arms wrapped around her, his hands sliding up her spine and under her long braid. With deft fingers, he worked her hair loose, combing through it until her every nerve tingled to life. In a smooth sweep, he rolled her onto her back, her legs hooking around his waist. A fresh whiff of bluebonnet perfume wafted up from the press of their bodies. Already, she could feel the swell of his erection between them. What she wouldn't give to be with him, out here in the open.

"Stone," she whispered between deep, luscious kisses, "we should go back to my cabin."

"This is my land," he growled possessively, nipping along her jaw and up to her earlobe. "No one's going to find us."

"Yours?" Her head fell back, gasping. "I thought it was all jointly owned."

"We each have a section that belongs exclusively to us. This became mine on my twenty-first birthday."

"Why did you never mention that before when we came here for picnics?" She swatted his bottom lightly. God, she loved the way he filled out denim. "It would have been nice not to worry about people stumbling upon us."

He angled away, propping himself on one elbow to look directly into her eyes. "You pegged it when you said I was holding back. I planned to surprise you on our wedding day with plans for a home."

A pang shot through her chest at the fairy tale he'd tried to give her. As much as she knew she'd made the right decision then, she'd missed out on a lot of happy moments, too. Her throat burned until she cleared it.

"I would have liked that."

"Except there wasn't a nursery in my plans."

The burn in her throat shifted, moving down into a cold knot that settled in her stomach. "You know how I feel about that, and I'm beginning to understand why you feel otherwise. I've watched you for years as you helped out the staff with games for vacationers and I guess I always thought you would change your mind."

"Liking children and being a father are two different things."

She sifted through his words, wondering what he was trying to tell her by bringing her here, because clearly he had something on his mind. "But you want a space away from here, a home in your bluebonnet field."

"I never had a regular home like other kids." He picked up one flower petal after another and placed them in her hair. "Not with my mother zipping in and out of my life. A couple of times she even took me with her when she left."

"Jade 'took' you? That had to be confusing."

"Hell, yeah, it was. Especially the time the cops stopped us at the Mexican border and charged my mother with kidnapping. My grandmother had legal custody at that point."

She searched his face, shadows making it tougher with the sun surrendering fast. "Why Mexico?"

"Easier access to drugs, most likely." He said it so

nonchalantly her heart broke. "She dodged prosecution for custodial interference by agreeing to go into rehab. Again. But if we learned anything over the years, we know that unless the junkie is committed to coming clean…rehab is just a temporary, Band-Aid fix."

She kissed him again because there just weren't any words for all he'd been through with his mother. Having her here now when he was still reeling from his grandmother's cancer news had to be overwhelming. Johanna poured all her love into the kiss—and yes, she loved him so damn much, always had, ever since she was a teenager with a colossal crush that had matured into so much more.

Groaning, he trailed kisses along her jaw, her cheek, her forehead before burying his face in her hair. "Johanna, more than anything, I want to be with you out here, just us on a blanket in my field full of bluebonnets."

"Of course, I want that, too." She slid her hand between them, palming the length of his steely erection. A moist ache settled between her legs.

"Before we're together again, we need to be sure it's forever. No more pretending we could ever have a fling."

Her heart sped in her chest like a hummingbird. "I agree."

"So we need to clear up one last issue."

The little bird in her chest sped faster. The only remaining issue had to do with children. Where did she stand and how far was she willing to compromise?

"If we make love now, we don't need a condom."

She blinked in shock, certain she couldn't have

heard him right. Terrified to hope. "You've changed your mind about having children?"

"Hell, that's not what I meant, Johanna."

His eyes squeezed shut tight for an instant before he opened them again, sapphire-blue eyes so full of regret she only had a second to prepare herself before he continued.

"There's no easy way to say this. I've had a vasectomy."

Eleven

Stone knew he'd just lost Johanna. He could see it in her eyes. Just as he'd feared, once he told her everything, it was over.

That didn't stop him from trying to hold on to her. He wasn't giving her up so easily, not this time. So he sat on the quilt beside her and waited to take his cue from her. Her whole body was rigid. She shook just a little, trembling from the aftermath of a direct hit to her tender, sweet heart.

A heart he didn't deserve, no matter how much he wanted to claim it.

She blinked quickly, her eyes as green as clover even in the dimming day. "You…you did what?"

"Just what I said, and God, Johanna, I am sorry to have to say it at all." He took her hand, her fingers quivering, and he hated that he'd brought her this pain. "I had a vasectomy right after I met my biological father, which also happened to be around the time my mother checked out of rehab early again. I knew her next fall was inevitable. And I was right."

He'd been so damn sure of himself and his choices.

Her breath was as shaky as his hand. "You were so young. You still are."

Her words echoed the mandatory counseling session he'd been forced to sit through before the surgery. It made a whole hell of a lot of difference hearing it from the woman he loved instead of a well-meaning health care professional who'd made the same speech a hundred other times. He could have never predicted loving someone so much it made him question everything he'd ever believed.

"It was way before you and I started dating. Because I swear to you—" and he meant it with every fiber of his being "—if I'd had an inkling of what having you in my life this way would mean, I wouldn't have done it."

"Have you ever considered having the procedure reversed?" she asked, each word carefully enunciated, her breathing fast and shallow. Clearly, she was holding on by a thread.

"Not until I met you."

"How do you feel now?"

"If you want a child, I will do that for you." Even saying the words scared the hell out of him, but the thought of losing her scared him more. For Johanna, for their kid, he would figure it out. He refused to fail as a parent. "But you need to understand that the more time that lapses the less chance a reversal has of working. Do you have any issues with adoption?"

She shook her head, but there was still something about her stunned expression that made him uneasy. This was too much, too fast for her. She'd barely had time to process the first bombshell he'd dropped.

He waited for her to speak but she kept looking around the field of bluebonnets, the horses grazing, the circle of trees—anywhere other than at him.

Nerves strung tight, he pressed ahead. "I have two drug addict parents. I was born a crack baby. Consider me a broken model. As far as I'm concerned, I would rather fund orphanages and adoption agencies to help babies like me that didn't have a rich grandma to step in. But if you have faith I can handle being a parent, then I'm going to trust you."

"Thank you," she said woodenly. "I understand how difficult that was for you to say."

"Then why do I still see smoke coming out of your ears?"

"First of all. It's not just smoke. It's pain, Stone. Real, deep hurt." Her hands clenched into fists, and she drew her arms in closer to herself, away from him. She kept shaking her head slowly from side to side. "But yes, there's anger, too. All those months we were together using birth control, you were lying to me, letting me believe that you might be open to having a family some-day even though you knew otherwise." She shoved to her feet, dusting the flower petals off her jeans in angry sweeps. "It wasn't just one lie by leaving out something in your past. It was a lie *every time we made love.* I'm having a difficult time wrapping my brain around that."

She thrust her hands into her hair, pressing against her head as she paced.

"Yes, it was a cop-out on my part not telling you." He stood, walking off the quilt and toward her, wary. "I'm an even bigger jackass than you imagined."

She stroked her fingers through her horse's mane, a nervous habit he recognized well. "Stone, I'm… I don't know what to say other than I feel betrayed." She looked up at him, her eyes so full of pain the clover-green was dewy with unshed tears. "How could you say you love me? How could you propose to me and keep something *this* important from me?"

"I intended to tell you, even though I knew it would drive you away. Maybe that's why I delayed because I knew it would make you leave me." Just as it was doing now. The hole in his chest widened until he fought back the urge to howl in denial. "Then it was too late. Apparently, it still is."

She turned to him hard and fast, fire spitting from her eyes. "Don't you get it? It's not that you had the procedure. That happened before we were a couple. It's because you lied to me, again and again. Telling me now... I don't know if that's enough. I just don't know."

"God, Johanna." His voice cracked as he reached for her.

She yanked away, her horse sidestepping sharply. "I can't..."

"Can't what?"

"I can't process this. I need air—away from you." She hitched a foot in the stirrup and swung up onto her palomino.

He didn't bother to stop her. There wasn't any use. His worst fear had happened, just not for the reason he'd expected. She hadn't left him because he couldn't father her children. She'd left him because he hadn't trusted in their love enough to tell her.

Johanna gripped the reins tightly in her hands even though she knew Goldie could find her way back in the dark. The evening had started out on such a hopeful note only to end in total heartbreak. She'd even chosen

Mariah's horse to ride as a tribute to the woman who meant so much to them all. Now she could only think of everything they'd all lost.

Goldie slowed from a canter to a trot as they neared the stables. And, oh, God, on the lanai, a wedding was taking place. The trees were strung with lights. Sunflowers and wildflowers filled the space, a live band played as the happy couple walked back down the aisle. The whole ranch would echo with music all night with the reception in a special barn built for just such catered occasions.

She'd dreamed of a wedding just like this.

Squeezing her eyes closed, she let Goldie find her way back to the stables. The regular scents of hay and leather offered none of the normal calm she found here in the barn, her realm. The noise level didn't help with the reception in full swing and some kind of party going on in the hot tub, too. She could have sworn she heard someone calling her name....

She looked back over her shoulder.

Amie was walking fast in a whispery sequined sun dress and cowboy boots only someone like her could pull off. Her brother trailed behind her, hands in his jeans pocket.

"Wait!" Amie waved, bracelets sliding to her elbow. "Johanna, I have to talk to you."

There was no missing the panic in her voice, which launched an echoing wave of panic in Johanna. "Is something wrong with Mariah?" She slid from her horse, her own boots a dusty, scarred contrast to Amie's shiny black leather.

Amie shook her head, her long hair in two loose

braids swishing. "No, she's fine. We just got a surprise
visitor. The king—Enrique Medina—is in the lodge. He
wants to save us the trouble of delivering Ruby so he's
coming here." She clapped her hands, bracelets jingling.
"Thank God we had the presidential suite available because every other room is booked. But he's here and
he wants to meet Ruby, and Gran couldn't find you or
Stone, and you didn't have your cell phones."

Alex put a hand on top of his sister's head. "Amie.
Chill. Johanna's got it now. Right, Jo?"

Johanna looked back and forth between them and it
didn't appear they were joking. "The king that wants
Ruby is here now?"

Amie nodded quickly. "We can't keep him waiting
any longer."

Johanna looked down at the stained jeans and sweaty
white tank top. But he wanted his dog now. "Give me
five minutes to throw on a dress and pull back my hair.
I'll be right there."

She could do this. For Mariah, for Ruby, and yes,
even for herself. She could pull this off. What a time
to realize Stone had helped her unearth a confidence
in herself she hadn't known existed.

By the time Stone finished riding alone for an hour,
then brushing down Copper and returning him to the
stable, he still had no clue what—if anything—he could
say to Johanna to ease the pain he'd seen in her eyes.
Pain he'd put there. He loved her and yet he'd still fallen
short.

Music echoed from the barn on the other side of
the stable yard, and from the sound of things, it was a

wedding celebration in full swing. As if he didn't already feel lower than dirt. Had fate scheduled a wedding for tonight with the specific purpose of torturing him? Seeing the happy bride and groom stabbed at him with all he should have given Johanna She wanted a family. She deserved to have the family she dreamed of. She had such a loving, nurturing heart. Would she leave here altogether?

She loved the ranch as much as he did.

He hadn't thought about that before. She'd been tied to the land in one way or another for most of her life. Just because he held the deed to a piece of property didn't negate all the heart she'd poured into Hidden Gem.

The only thing that kept his feet moving right now was the need to check on his grandmother.

He darted from the stable to the main lodge, boots sending dust puffing with each heavy step. And damn it, he'd left his suitcase at Johanna's. But he wasn't willing to push his luck with her tonight. He needed to get his head together first and come up with a plan to ease her heart even if that meant he couldn't have her back. He wanted her happiness above everything.

Except plans were in short supply as he climbed the steps to the massive log cabin–style lodge that had been his home his whole life. He should have taken a side entrance but his feet were on autopilot. Staff cleared away the wedding decorations on the lanai.

Pushing through the large double doors into the great room, he nodded to all the staff but didn't pause long enough to give anyone a chance to speak. He vaguely registered there was a frenetic buzz to the place that didn't seem connected to the wedding celebration since that was all taking place outside. Yet nothing appeared out of the norm. Wealthy socialites curled up on the leather sofas with cocktails. Older couples played poker in a far corner by the massive granite fireplace. He could hear laughter from the hot tub outside. Alex's business ran smooth as silk.

Only a few more steps and he would be clear of people, period, and into the private wing. He could shut himself in his suite with…nothing. He had nothing left and had no one to blame but himself.

A door opened ahead of him and his gut clenched at the thought of another confrontation with his mother. Instead, his grandmother stepped out on her own two feet, with a cane, but walking. She even wore clothes instead of a robe, a simple dress but complete with a Diamonds in the Rough signature piece around her neck. Amie hovered beside her, as if his willowy featherweight cousin could catch their grandmother.

Stone charged ahead. "Gran, what are you doing out of bed? You should be resting."

She waved him back. "I'm fine. The doctor released me as long as I use the cane."

Amie interrupted, "A walker. But she would only agree to the cane since it's one of our designs."

Stone felt like his head was about to explode. "Let me walk you back to your room. We'll talk over tea or something while you *rest*."

His grandmother patted his hand. "Stone, the king is here. In the presidential suite."

"Run that by me again?"

"Stone, we need to get moving," Amie said. "Enrique Medina decided he would come to us for his dog to save you the trouble. Johanna is doing the meet and greet now because we couldn't find you and you weren't answering your damn phone." She swatted him on the arm. "Now let's get moving to help her."

He glanced at Alex. "Do you have Gran?"

His cousin nodded.

"Thanks." Stone sprinted down the hall. Johanna had freaked out over meeting the Landis-Renshaw family. This was going to be way outside her comfort zone. While he knew she was amazing and would handle the meeting smoothly, he hated that she would feel nervous or uneasy, especially after the emotional hell they'd both been through today.

He passed by familiar framed landscapes mixed with photos, images of famous people who'd stayed at the lodge or worn Hidden Gem pieces. Finally—thank God—finally, he made it to the presidential suite. The door was cracked open enough for him to see Johanna sitting next to an older gentleman in a suit with an ascot. Johanna held Pearl, and Ruby slept at the king's feet. If Stone hadn't known the man was deposed royalty, he would have thought she was talking to any prospective pet owner.

Johanna had changed from her jeans into a simple white dress and matching white leather boots, her hair in a side ponytail, trailing a wavy blond cascade over her shoulder. She was pure Texas but with a designer elegance and poise, smiling and nodding at something the king was saying.

Stone realized he wasn't needed here. Johanna had it totally under control. Not a single nerve showed through. She wasn't even fidgeting with the diamond horseshoe that dangled on the silver chain around her neck. Something had happened to her this week. She didn't need him for confidence or help, and God, she was magnificent.

She glanced at the door as if sensing he was there. Her eyes lost their sparkle but she kept her composure. "Come on in, Stone, and hear the good news from our honored guest."

Stone forced a smile onto his face and stepped into the presidential suite. "Sir, we're honored that you would come visit us at Hidden Gem."

The deposed king had a reputation for being a bit of a hermit who lived in an island fortress off the coast of Florida. "I am so sorry to hear Mariah is having health concerns. It is a joy to have one of her dogs and my honor to make things easier for her by coming to her directly."

"Thank you," Stone answered, his head spinning from this day, blindsiding him nonstop. "It appears Ruby has found a great new companion."

Johanna stroked Pearl, still perched in her lap. "He also shared more good news. General and Mrs. Renshaw have decided they want Pearl after all. The three dogs will get to see each other at family reunions. Isn't that wonderful?"

A roaring started in Stone's head, growing louder by the second. Thoughts of his fight with Johanna, his grandmother's illness, his mother's arrival—his whole world was falling apart and there was nothing he could do about it. His eyes landed on Pearl and he knew. His grandmother needed to have this pup with her. Mariah, who'd given so much of herself to others, needed her favorite dog and needed someone to stand up, to make the decision to put her needs first. He would adopt Pearl so his grandmother could keep her near.

Even if it cost him the position as CEO of Diamonds In the Rough, he loved the little mutt and he wasn't giving her up.

"I'm sorry, sir." He strode into the room, boots thudding against the thick rug patterned with a yellow rose of Texas theme. He swiped Pearl from Johanna's lap before she could stop him. He cradled Pearl in one arm. "She's staying with me after all."

Standing, Johanna gasped. "But your grandmother's requirements…"

"I'll talk to my grandmother. She needs Pearl now more than anyone. I'll take care of Pearl during Mariah's treatments—and afterward." That last part stuck in his throat but he didn't doubt his decision. After seeing Johanna through different eyes this week, he'd learned the meaning of real love. His arms wrapped tighter around the dog. He nodded to their guest. "Thank you again for helping us rehome Ruby. Let us know if there's anything you need to make your stay more comfortable."

And manners be damned, the whole company be damned, Stone left with his dog, a dog that carried the scent of bluebonnets from Johanna.

As she listened to Mariah make small talk with the deposed King, Johanna's heart was in her throat.

At least Mariah and the twins had joined them so she didn't have to carry the conversation on her own, but it was the most torturous hour of her life. Not because she was intimidated by royalty—the man was truly approachable and, truth be told, she felt more confident now. But wondering about Stone was tearing her apart.

She couldn't believe Stone had left with Pearl, that he'd made such a beautiful and selfless sacrifice for his grandmother. He'd ignored his grandmother's test because he knew Mariah needed the comfort. Anyone who knew Mariah would understand she didn't make frivolous threats. Her test might have seemed strange, but she'd known what she was doing.

Johanna toyed with the diamond horseshoe pendant and realized Mariah never did *anything* by accident. She'd meant this test for Johanna, as well. The McNair matriarch had treated Johanna as a daughter every bit as much as she'd treated Stone as a son. This journey had brought Johanna the self-confidence to push Stone for the answers she needed, as well as bringing about an openness between them they should have had long ago.

She kept replaying the look on his face as he'd left with Pearl, remembering him telling her the story of how Pearl had come to his grandmother. As a vet tech, Johanna had observed countless people with their animals. She recognized true affection and a connection when she saw it. He didn't often show his emotions, but she'd seen the sketches he'd made. Stone was the right one to care for Pearl so Mariah could keep her during her treatment, and he was the perfect one to take Pearl afterward. No question, Stone loved the scruffy little pooch.

She'd already realized there was much more to Stone than the cowboy Casanova, stony facade he showed the world. Yet she'd let him down, as well, today. He'd told her his secrets, owned up and offered to make amends as best he could, and she'd panicked. She'd walked out on a man who'd been abandoned by his mother and his father. A man who was willing to give up his life's work and billions of dollars to put his grandmother's happiness first. He loved his grandmother, and yes, he even loved the scruffy little pooch enough to risk everything.

That was the man for her and she didn't intend to wait another minute to get him back.

She stood, resting a hand on Mariah's shoulder. "Ma'am, would you like some refreshments sent in or do you need to rest?"

Mariah smiled at the king with a twinkle in her eyes. "We're having a lovely visit. Refreshments would be nice."

"Perfect. I'll let the kitchen staff know." Johanna grasped the excuse to leave with both hands.

"And Johanna?" Mariah's voice stopped her at the door. "Be sure to take something to that rebellious grandson of mine."

"Yes, ma'am." Johanna smiled back at the woman who wasn't just *like* family. She *was* family.

Racing through the lodge to the kitchen, she didn't have to wonder where to look for Stone. She angled through the lanai party group in full swing, vacationers and guests from the wedding filled the place to capacity.

She stepped clear of them into the starlit night, music from the live band at the wedding reception still filling the air. Stone loved this land and she understood the feeling. The land all but hummed under her boots as she saddled up the first horse she came to—a sleek gray quarter horse named Opal. A simple click launched the beautiful beast into motion, sure-footed even in the night with only the moon and stars lighting the way in a dappled path.

The wind tore through Johanna's wavy hair, rivulets of air rippling her dress along her skin. She'd never felt more alive and more afraid than right now. This was her chance for everything, if she could only find the right way to let Stone know how deeply she loved him.

Approaching Stone's favorite piece of land, the part that belonged to him, she ducked low under a branch. The moon shone down on Stone lying on the yellow quilt, staring up at the sky with Pearl curled up asleep beside him.

Her heart filled with tender feelings for the man who'd been let down by so many, yet still had a full heart to offer her.

Johanna dismounted. "Stone?"

"Do you know why this particular part of the land is my favorite acre?" he asked without moving, the night breeze ruffling Pearl's wiry fur.

She settled her horse alongside Stone's and walked to the blanket. "Why is that?"

"The bluebonnets. They remind me of you. The peacefulness and the sweet scent carrying along the breeze of home." His eyes slid to her. "That's you."

She sank down beside him, sitting cross-legged. "Stone, you take my breath away when you say things like that."

How many times had she imagined a future with him back when she'd been a fanciful girl? He was everything she'd hoped for and so much more. More real. More complicated and compelling. She wouldn't trade any part of him for the simple fantasies she'd once built around him.

"Good. You deserve the words and everything else. Whatever you want. Children. Home and hearth. Building a family. Don't settle." Even now, he fought to protect her.

He just didn't realize that she knew what was best for her now.

"I'm not settling." She wanted to reach for him but they had things to discuss first. Their reunion hadn't been a smooth, joyous coming together. It had been stilted steps toward each other because they couldn't stay away. But that was their path and she would keep on walking it. Toward her future with him. "I was hurt by what you told me today, but I shouldn't have run away. You opened up to me, and I let you down."

"You spoke the truth, though. I owe you more apologies than I can speak in a lifetime."

She hugged her knees to her chest and mulled that over for a minute, sifting through for the right words. "I guess we both aren't perfect. I tried to make you fit some high school fantasy and almost missed out on something so much better—the man you've become."

Sitting up, he captured a strand of her hair, his hand not quite steady. "Does this mean you forgive me?"

She nodded, tipping her face into his touch. "You told me you're willing to compromise with having one child—biological or adopted—however the cards land on that. I accept your beautiful offer."

He cupped her head and drew her toward him for a kiss, the closemouthed sort filled with a relief and intensity that seared straight through. "Johanna, I love you so damn much, I will do my best to be the man you deserve because, God help me, I can't live without you."

"I don't want to live without you, either," she admitted. "I've tried it. I don't like it."

"I don't want you making sacrifices for me."

"It's a bigger sacrifice to be without you." She knew that with a thousand percent certainty. No matter what the future held, she wanted Stone in her life, her heart and her home forever. He was her family.

His eyes held hers, his fingers smoothing her cheek and then tracing her lips.

"You don't know how much..." He took a deep breath and released it in a shuddering sigh. "I'll do everything I can to make this right. To give you the life you deserve."

"I know. We'll fill our home with dogs, and dote on our nieces and nephews, and yes, maybe a child of our own. But we're going to do it together."

He moved closer to her, Pearl huffing in irritation over being disturbed, then settling back to sleep. "I want to make sure you know what you're signing on for."

"What do you mean?"

"I realized tonight when I took Pearl here that somewhere along the way to being the CEO for Diamonds in the Rough, I lost sight of who I really am, lost sight of where I belong."

"And where is that?"

"I belong here, to the land, to the McNair land." He scratched his dog's ear. "I'm not a CEO who happens to be a cowboy. I'm a cowboy who happens to be an executive."

"Okay? And that means?" She wasn't certain, but

the fact that they were talking so openly gave her a new
hope for their future.

"It feels crystal clear to me." He cupped Pearl's
head. "My grandmother was right to give me this test.
It helped me to understand. I'm not meant to be the CEO
of Diamonds in the Rough."

"Whoa." She pressed a hand to his chest. "I'm completely confused."

"It's time for me to be my own man. This land, this
corner, belongs to me and it's time for me to follow my
destiny." He tapped her lips to silence her. "Before you
think you've hitched your wagon to a broken star, I have
a hefty investment portfolio of my own. And I don't see
stepping away from the company altogether. I've contributed designs to the company that have landed big."

"But your plans to take the company international?"

He shook his head. "That was ego talking, the need
to prove I'm better than my cousins even if I don't have
parents that give a damn about me."

She reached for him. "Stone—"

"Johanna, it's okay. It's not about competing. Not
anymore. It's about finding the right path. Mine is here.
I want to build a home for us. Ours. A place to start our
future. Not some wing at the Hidden Gem Lodge. But
a place of our own to build our family."

"You have this all thought through." And it made
beautiful sense.

"Even if we have a dozen children of our own, I
would still like us to consider..."

"What?" she prompted.

"There are a lot of children out there who need
homes, babies like I was, except they don't have a rich

grandmother to pick up the pieces for a newborn going through withdrawal. It's a lot to take on. What do you think?"

What did she think? She thought this was the easiest question ever. "I'm all-in, wherever the path takes us, as long as we're together, cowboy."

* * * * *

"I'm sorry to disappoint, but you're stuck with me today."

Gavin had screwed up last night, he could tell. Not in seducing her—that would never be a bad idea—but in forcing the idea of the apartment on her. Anyone else would jump at the offer, but to her, it was him imposing on her. Demanding they be closer so he could see his son more easily. Not once mentioning that he'd like *her* closer as well because that opened the door to dangerous territory.

Sabine was skittish. She scared off easily last time. He wasn't about to tell her that he wanted to see her more, because he was still fighting himself over the idea of it. He was usually pretty good at keeping his distance from people, but he'd already let Sabine in once. Keeping her out the second time was harder than he expected.

"That's scarcely a hardship," he said. "I find your company to be incredibly...s*timulating.*"

* * *

His Lover's Little Secret
is part of the No.1 bestselling series from
Mills & Boon® Desire™—Billionaires & Babies:
Powerful men...wrapped around their
babies' little fingers

HIS LOVER'S
LITTLE SECRET

BY
ANDREA LAURENCE

Published in Great Britain 2014
by Mills & Boon, an imprint of Harlequin (UK) Limited,
Eton House, 18-24 Paradise Road, Richmond, Surrey, TW9 1SR

© 2014 Andrea Laurence

ISBN: 978 0 263 91462 7

51-0414

Harlequin (UK) Limited's policy is to use papers that are natural, renewable and recyclable products and made from wood grown in sustainable forests. The logging and manufacturing processes conform to the legal environmental regulations of the country of origin.

Printed and bound in Spain
by Blackprint CPI, Barcelona

Andrea Laurence is an award-winning contemporary romance author who has been a lover of books and writing stories since she learned to read. She always dreamed of seeing her work in print and is thrilled to be able to share her books with the world. A dedicated West Coast girl transplanted into the Deep South, she's working on her own "happily ever after" with her boyfriend and five fur-babies. You can contact Andrea at her website: www.andrealaurence.com.

This book is dedicated to single mothers everywhere,
including my own hard-working mother, Meg.
You fight the good fight every day, often at the expense
of your own well-being. Thank you for everything
you do. (Treat yourself to some chocolate or
shoes every now and then!)

One

"You'd better get on out of here, or you'll be late to stand on your head."

Sabine Hayes looked up from the cash drawer to see her boss, fashion designer Adrienne Lockhart Taylor, standing at the counter. She had worked for Adrienne the past thirteen months as manager of her boutique. "I'm almost done."

"Give me the nightly deposit and go. I'll stay until Jill shows up for her shift and then I'll stop by the bank on my way home. You have to pick up Jared by six, don't you?"

"Yes." The day care center would price gouge her for every minute she was late. Then she had to get Jared home and fed before the babysitter got there. Sabine loved teaching yoga, but it made those evenings even more hectic than usual. Single motherhood wasn't for wimps. "You don't mind making the deposit?"

Adrienne leaned across the counter. "Go," she said.

Sabine glanced quickly at her watch. "Okay." She put the deposit into the bank pouch and handed it over. Thank goodness Adrienne had come by this afternoon to put together the new window display. The trendy boutique was known for its exciting and edgy displays that perfectly showcased Adrienne's flair for modern pinup girl fashions. Sabine couldn't have found a better place to work.

Most places wouldn't look twice at an applicant with a nose piercing and a stripe of blue in her hair. It didn't matter that it was a small, tasteful diamond stud or that her hair was dyed at a nice salon in Brooklyn. Even after she'd bitten the bullet and had the bright color removed and left the piercing at home, she'd been turned down by every store on Fifth Avenue. The businesses that paid enough for her to support her son in New York were flooded with applicants more experienced than she was.

She thanked her lucky stars for the day she spied Adrienne walking down the street and complimented her dress. She never expected her to say she'd designed it herself. Adrienne invited her to come by her new boutique one afternoon, and Sabine was enamored with the whole place. It was fun and funky, chic and stylish. High-class fashion with an edge. When Adrienne mentioned she was looking for someone to run the store so she could focus on her designs, Sabine couldn't apply fast enough. Not only was it a great job with above-average pay and benefits, Adrienne was a great boss. She didn't care what color hair Sabine had—now she had purple highlights—and she was understanding when child illness or drama kept her away from the store.

Sabine grabbed her purse and gave a quick wave to

Adrienne as she disappeared into the stockroom and out the back door. It was only a couple blocks to her son's day care, but she still had to hurry along the sidewalk, brushing past others who were leisurely making their way around town.

Finally rounding the last corner, Sabine swung open the gate to the small courtyard and leaped up the few steps to the door. She rang the buzzer at exactly three minutes to six. Not long after that, she had her toddler in her arms and was on her way to the subway.

"Hey, buddy," she said as they went down the street. "Did you have a good day?"

Jared grinned and nodded enthusiastically. He was starting to lose his chubby baby cheeks. He'd grown so much the past few months. Every day, he looked more and more like his father. The first time she'd held Jared in her arms, she looked into his dark brown eyes and saw Gavin's face staring back at her. He would grow up to be as devastatingly handsome as his father, but hopefully with Sabine's big heart. She should be able to contribute *something* to the genetic makeup of her child, and if she had her pick, that was what it would be.

"What do you want for dinner tonight?"

"A-sketti."

"Spaghetti, again? You had that last night. You're going to turn into a noodle before too long."

Jared giggled and clung to her neck. Sabine breathed in the scent of his baby shampoo and pressed a kiss against his forehead. He had changed her whole life and she wouldn't trade him for anything.

"Sabine?"

The subway entrance was nearly in sight when someone called her name from the restaurant she'd just passed. She stopped and turned to find a man in a navy suit drinking wine at one of the tables on the sidewalk. He looked familiar, but she couldn't come up with his name. Where did she know him from?

"It is you," he said, standing up and stepping toward her. He took one look at her puzzled expression and smiled. "You don't remember me, do you? I'm Clay Oliver, a friend of Gavin's. I met you at a gallery opening a couple years back."

An icy surge rushed through Sabine's veins. She smiled and nodded, trying not to show any outward signs of distress. "Oh, yes," she said. She shifted Jared in her arms so he was facing away from his father's best friend. "I think I spilled champagne on you, right?"

"Yes!" he said, pleased she remembered. "How have you been?" Clay's gaze ran curiously over the child in her arms. "Busy, I see."

"Yes, very busy." Sabine's heart began pounding loudly in her chest. She glanced over her shoulder at the subway stop, desperate for an escape. "Listen, I'm sorry I can't stay to chat longer, but I've got to meet the babysitter. It was good to see you again, Clay. Take care."

Sabine gave him a quick wave and spun on her heel. She felt as if she was fleeing the scene of a crime as she dashed down the stairs. She nervously watched the people joining her on the platform. Clay wouldn't follow her. At least she didn't think so. But she wouldn't feel better until she was deep into Brooklyn and far out of Gavin's sphere of influence.

Had Clay seen Jared closely enough? Had he noticed the resemblance? Jared was wearing his favorite monkey T-shirt with a hood and ears, so perhaps Clay hadn't

been able to make out his features or how old he was.
She hoped.

She leaped onto the train the moment it arrived and
managed to find a seat. Clutching Jared tightly as he
sat in her lap, she tried to breathe deeply, but she just
couldn't do it.

Nearly three years. Jared was fewer than two months
from his second birthday, and she had managed to keep
their son a secret from Gavin. In all this time she'd never
run into him or anyone he knew. They didn't exactly
move in the same social circles. That was part of why
she'd broken it off with Gavin. They were a world apart.
Unsuitable in every way. After she split with him, he'd
never called or texted her again. He obviously wasn't
missing her too badly.

But Sabine had never allowed herself to relax. She
knew that sooner or later, Gavin would find out that he
had a son. If Clay didn't tell him tonight, it would be the
next time she bumped into someone Gavin knew. Sitting in the park, walking down the street...somebody
would see Jared and know instantly that he was Gavin's
son. The bigger he got, the more of a carbon copy of his
father he became.

Then it was only a matter of time before Gavin
showed up, angry and demanding. That was how he
worked. He always got his way. At least until now. The
only thing Sabine knew for certain was that he wouldn't
win this time. Jared was her son. *Hers.* Gavin was a
workaholic and wouldn't have a clue what to do with a
child. She wasn't about to turn him over to the stuffy
nannies and boarding schools that had raised Gavin instead of his parents.

As the train approached their stop, Sabine got up and

they hurried to catch the bus that would take them the last few blocks to her apartment near Marine Park in Brooklyn, where she'd lived the past four years. It wasn't the fanciest place in the world, but it was relatively safe, clean and close to the grocery store and the park. The one-bedroom apartment was growing smaller as Jared grew older, but they were managing.

Originally, a large portion of the bedroom was used as her art studio. When her son came along, she packed up her canvases and put her artistic skills toward painting a cheerful mural over his crib. Jared had plenty of room to play, and there was a park down the street where he could run around and dig in the sandbox. Her next-door neighbor, Tina, would watch Jared when she had her evening yoga classes.

She had put together a pretty good life for her and Jared. Considering that when she moved to New York she was broke and homeless, she'd come quite a long way. Back then, she could live on meager waitressing tips and work on her paintings when she had the extra money for supplies. Now, she had to squeeze out every penny she could manage, but they had gotten by.

"A-sketti!" Jared cheered triumphantly as they came through the door.

"Okay. I'll make a-sketti." Sabine sat him down before switching the television on to his favorite show. It would mesmerize him with songs and funny dances while she cooked.

By the time Jared was done eating and Sabine was changed into her workout clothes, she had only minutes to spare before Tina arrived. If she was lucky, Tina would give Jared a bath and scrub the tomato sauce off his cheeks. Usually, she had him in his pajamas and in bed by the time Sabine got home. Sabine hated that he would be asleep when she returned, but going through his nightly routine after class would have Jared up way past his bedtime. He'd wake up at dawn no matter what, but he'd be cranky.

There was a sharp knock at the door. Tina was a little early. That was fine by her. If she could catch the earlier bus, it would give her enough time to get some good stretches in before class.

"Hey, Tina—" she said, whipping open the door and momentarily freezing when her petite, middle-aged neighbor was not standing in the hallway.

No. No, no, no. She wasn't ready to deal with this. Not yet. Not tonight.

It was Gavin.

Sabine clutched desperately at the door frame, needing its support to keep her upright as the world started tilting sharply on its axis. Her chest tightened; her stomach churned and threatened to return her dinner. At the same time, other long-ignored parts of her body immediately sparked back to life. Gavin had always been a master of her body, and the years hadn't dulled the memory of his touch.

Fear. Desire. Panic. Need. It all swirled inside her like a building maelstrom that would leave nothing but destruction in its path. She took a deep breath to clamp it all down. She couldn't let Gavin know she was freaking out. She certainly couldn't let him know she still responded to him, either. That would give him the upper hand. She plastered a wide smile across her face and choked down her emotions.

"Hello, Sabine," he said with the deep, familiar voice she remembered.

It was hard to believe the handsome and rich blast from her past was standing in front of her after all this time. His flawlessly tailored gray suit and shiny, sky-blue tie made him look every inch the powerful CEO of the BXS shipping empire. His dark eyes were trained on her, his gaze traveling down the line of his nose. He looked a little older than she remembered, with concern lining his eyes and furrowing his brow. Or maybe it was the tense, angry expression that aged him.

"Gavin!" she said with feigned surprise. "I certainly didn't expect to see you here. I thought you were my neighbor Tina. How have you—"

"Where is my son?" he demanded, interrupting her nervous twitter. His square jaw was rock hard, his sensual lips pressed into a hard line of disapproval. There had been a flash of that same expression when she'd left him all those years ago, but he'd quickly grown indifferent to it. Now he cared. But not about her. Only about their child.

Apparently news traveled fast. It had been fewer than two hours since she'd run into Clay.

"Your son?" she repeated, hoping to stall long enough to think of a plan. She'd had years to prepare for this moment and yet, when it arrived, she was thrown completely off guard. Moving quickly, Sabine rushed into the hallway and pulled the apartment door nearly closed behind her. She left just the slightest crack open so she could peek through and make sure Jared was okay. She pressed her back against the door frame and found it calmed her nerves just a little to have that barrier between Gavin and Jared. He'd have to go through her to get inside.

"Yes, Sabine," Gavin said, taking a step closer to her. "Where is the baby you've hidden from me for the last three years?"

* * *

Damn, she was still as beautiful as he remembered. A little older, a little curvier, but still the fresh, funky artist that had turned his head in that art gallery. And tonight, she was wearing some skimpy workout clothes that clung to every newly rounded curve and reminded him of what he'd been missing since she'd walked out on him.

People tended not to stay in Gavin's life very long. There had been a parade of nannies, tutors, friends and lovers his whole life as his parents hired and fired and then moved him from one private school to the next. The dark-haired beauty with the nose piercing had been no exception. She had walked out of his life without a second thought.

She'd said they weren't compatible in the long term because they had different priorities and different lives. Admittedly, they fell on opposite ends of the spectrum in most every category, but that was one of the things he'd been drawn to in Sabine. One of the reasons he thought she, of all people, might stay. She wasn't just another rich girl looking to marry well and shop often. What they had really seemed to matter. To mean something.

He'd been wrong.

He'd let her go—he'd learned early that there was no sense in chasing after someone who didn't want to be there—but she'd stayed on his mind. She'd starred in his dreams, both erotic and otherwise. She'd crept into his thoughts during the quiet moments when he had time to regret the past. More than once, Gavin had wondered what Sabine was up to and what she had done with her life.

Never in his wildest dreams did he expect the answer to be "raising his child."

Sabine straightened her spine, her sharp chin tipping up in defiance. She projected an air of confidence in any situation and had the steel backbone to stand behind it. She certainly had spunk; he'd loved that about her once. Now, he could tell it would be an annoyance.

She looked him straight in the eye and said, "He's inside. And right now, that's where he's staying."

The bold honesty of her words was like a fist to his gut. The air rushed from his lungs. It was true. He had a son. *A son!* He hadn't entirely believed Clay's story until that precise moment. He'd known his best friend since they were roommates in college, one of the few constants in his life, but he couldn't always trust Clay's version of reality. Tonight, he'd insisted that Gavin locate Sabine as soon as possible to find out about her young son.

And he'd been right. For once.

Sabine didn't deny it. He'd expected her to tell him it wasn't his child or insist she was babysitting for a friend, but she had always been honest to a fault. Instead, she'd flat-out admitted she'd hidden his child from him and made no apologies about it. She even had the audacity to start making demands about how this was going to go down. She'd been in control of this situation for far too long. He was about to be included and in a big way.

"He's really my son?" He needed to hear the words from her, although he would demand a DNA test to confirm it no matter what she said.

Sabine swallowed and nodded. "He looks just like you."

The blood started pumping furiously in Gavin's ears. He might be able to understand why she kept it a secret if she was uncertain he was the father, but there was no doubt in her mind. She simply hadn't wanted him involved. She didn't want the inconvenience of having to share him with someone else. If not for Clay seeing her, he still wouldn't know he had a child.

His jaw tightened and his teeth clenched together. "Were you ever going to tell me I had a son, Sabine?"

Her pale green gaze burrowed into him as she crossed her arms over her chest. "No."

She didn't even bother to lie about it and make herself look less like the deceitful, selfish person she was. She just stood there, looking unapologetic, while unconsciously pressing her breasts up out of the top of her sports bra. His brain flashed between thoughts like a broken television as his eyes ran over the soft curves of her body and his ears tried to process her response. Anger, desire, betrayal and a fierce need to possess her rushed through his veins, exploding out of him in words.

"What do you mean, no?" Gavin roared.

"Keep it down!" Sabine demanded between gritted teeth, glancing nervously over her shoulder into the apartment. "I don't want him to hear us, and I certainly don't want all my neighbors to hear us, either."

"Well I'm sorry to embarrass you in front of your neighbors. I just found out I have a two-year-old son that I've never met. I think that gives me the right to be angry."

Sabine took a deep breath, amazing him with her ability to appear so calm. "You have every right to be angry. But yelling won't change anything. And I won't have you raising your voice around my son."

"*Our* son," Gavin corrected.

"No," she said with a sharp point of her finger. "He's my son. According to his birth certificate, he's an immaculate conception. Right now, you have no legal claim to him and no right to tell me how to do *anything* where he's concerned. You got that?"

That situation would be remedied and soon. "For now. But don't think your selfish monopoly on our son will last for much longer."

A crimson flush rushed to her cheeks, bringing color to her flawless, porcelain skin. She had gotten far too comfortable calling the shots. He could tell she didn't like him making demands. Too bad for her. He had a vote now and it was long overdue.

She swallowed and brushed her purple-highlighted ponytail over her shoulder but didn't back down. "It's after seven-thirty on a Wednesday night, so you can safely bet that's how it's going to stay for the immediate future."

Gavin laughed at her bold naïveté. "Do you honestly think my lawyers don't answer the phone at 2:00 a.m. when I call? For what I pay them, they do what I want, when I want." He slipped his hand into his suit coat and pulled his phone out of his inner breast pocket. "Shall we call Edmund and see if he's available?"

Her eyes widened slightly at his challenge. "Go ahead, Gavin. Any lawyer worth his salt is going to insist on a DNA test. It takes no less than three days to get the results of a paternity test back from a lab. If you push me, I'll see to it that you don't set eyes on him until the results come back. If we test first thing in the morning, that would mean Monday by my estimation."

Gavin's hands curled into tight fists at his sides. She'd had years to prepare for this moment and she'd done her homework. He knew she was right. The labs probably wouldn't process the results over the weekend, so it would be Monday at the earliest before he could get his lawyer involved and start making parental demands. But once he could lay claim to his son, she had better watch out.

"I want to see my son," he said. This time his tone was less heated and demanding.

"Then calm down and take your thumb off your lawyer's speed dial."

Gavin slipped his cell phone back into his pocket. "Happy?"

Sabine didn't seem happy, but she nodded anyway. "Now, before I let you in, we need to discuss some ground rules."

He took a deep breath to choke back his rude retort. Few people had the audacity to tell him what to do, but if anyone would, it was Sabine. He would stick to her requirements for now, but before long, Gavin would be making the rules. "Yes?"

"Number one, you are not to yell when you are in my apartment or anywhere Jared might be. I don't want you upsetting him."

Jared. His son's name was Jared. This outrageous scenario was getting more and more real. "What's his middle name?" Gavin couldn't stop himself from asking. He suddenly wanted to know everything he could about his son. There was no way to gain back the time he'd lost, but he would do everything in his power to catch up on what he missed.

"Thomas. Jared Thomas Hayes."

Thomas was *his* middle name. Was that a coincidence? He couldn't remember if Sabine knew it or not. "Why Thomas?"

"For my art teacher in high school, Mr. Thomas. He's the only one that ever encouraged my painting. Since that was also your middle name, it seemed fitting. Number two," she continued. "Do not tell him you're his father. Not until it is legally confirmed and we are both comfortable with the timing. I don't want him confused and worried about what's going on."

"Who does he think his father is?"

Sabine shook her head dismissively. "He's not even two. He hasn't started asking questions about things like that yet."

"Fine," he agreed, relieved that if nothing else, his son hadn't noticed the absence of a father in his life. He knew how painful that could be. "Enough rules. I want to see Jared." His son's name felt alien on his tongue. He wanted a face to put with the name and know his son at last.

"Okay." Sabine shifted her weight against the door, slowly slinking into the apartment.

Gavin moved forward, stepping over the threshold. He'd been to her apartment before, a long time ago. He remembered a fairly sparse but eclectic space with mismatched thrift store furniture. Her paintings had dotted the walls, her portfolio and bag of supplies usually sitting near the door.

When he barely missed stepping on a chubby blue crayon instead of a paintbrush, he knew things were truly different. Looking around, he noticed a lot had changed. The furniture was newer but still a mishmash of pieces. Interspersed with it were brightly colored plastic toys like a tiny basketball hoop and a tricycle with superheroes on it. A television in the corner loudly played a children's show.

And when Sabine stepped aside, he saw the small, dark-haired boy sitting on the floor in front of it. The child didn't turn to look at him. He was immersed in bobbing his head and singing along to the song playing on the show, a toy truck clutched in his hand.

Gavin swallowed hard and took another step into the apartment so Sabine could close the door behind him. He watched her walk over to the child and crouch down.

"Jared, we have a visitor. Let's say hello."

The little boy set down his truck and crawled to his feet. When he turned to look at Gavin, he felt his heart skip a beat in his chest. The tiny boy looked exactly like he had as a child. It was as though a picture had been snatched from his baby album and brought to life. From his pink cheeks smeared with tomato sauce, to the wide, dark eyes that looked at him with curiosity, he was very much Gavin's son.

The little boy smiled, revealing tiny baby teeth. "Hi."

Gavin struggled to respond at first. His chest was tight with emotions he never expected in this moment. This morning, he woke up worried about his latest business acquisition and now he was meeting his child for the first time. "Hi, Jared," he choked out.

"Jared, this is Mommy's friend Gavin."

Gavin took a hesitant step forward and knelt down to bring himself to the child's level. "How are you doing, big guy?"

Jared responded with a flow of gibberish he couldn't understand. Gavin hadn't been around many small children, and he wasn't equipped to translate. He could pick out a few words—*school, train* and something close to *spaghetti.* The rest was lost on him, but Jared didn't seem to mind. Pausing in his tale, he picked up his favorite truck and held it out to Gavin. "My truck!" he declared.

He took the small toy from his son. "It's very nice. Thank you."

A soft knock sounded at the front door. Sabine frowned and stood up. "That's the babysitter. I've got to go."

Gavin swallowed his irritation. He'd had a whole two minutes with his son and she was trying to push him out the door. They hadn't even gotten around to discussing her actions and what they were going to do about this situation. He watched her walk to the door and let in a middle-aged woman in a sweater with cats on it.

"Hey, Tina. Come on in. He's had his dinner and he's just watching television."

"I'll get him in the bath and in bed by eight-thirty."

"Thanks, Tina. I should be home around the usual time."

Gavin handed the truck back to Jared and reluctantly stood. He wasn't going to hang around while the neighbor lady was here. He turned in time to see Sabine slip into a hoodie and tug a sling with a rolled-up exercise mat over her shoulder.

"Gavin, I've got to go. I'm teaching a class tonight."

He nodded and gave a quick look back at Jared. He'd returned to watching his show, doing a little monkey dance along with the other children and totally unaware of what was really going on around him. Gavin wanted to reach out to him again, to say goodbye or hug him, but he refrained. There would be time for all that later. For the first time in his life, he had someone who would be legally bound to him for the next sixteen years and wouldn't breeze in and out of his life like so many others. They would have more time together.

Right now, he needed to deal with the mother of his child.

Two

"I don't need you to drive me to class."

Gavin stood holding open the passenger door of his Aston Martin with a frown lining his face. Sabine knew she didn't want to get in the car with him. Getting in would mean a private tongue-lashing she wasn't ready for yet. She'd happily take the bus to avoid this.

"Just get in the car, Sabine. The longer we argue, the later you'll be."

Sabine watched the bus blow by the stop up the street and swore under her breath. She'd never make it to class in time unless she gave in and let him drive her there. Sighing in defeat, she climbed inside. Gavin closed the door and got in on his side. "Go up the block and turn right at the light," she instructed. If she could focus on directions, perhaps they'd have less time to talk about what she'd done.

She already had a miserably guilty conscience. It wasn't like she could look at Jared without thinking of Gavin. Lying to him was never something she intended to do, but the moment she found out she was pregnant, she was overcome with a fierce territorial and protective urge. She and Gavin were from different planets. He never really cared for her the way she did for him. The same would hold true for their son. Jared would be *acquired* just like any other asset of the Brooks Empire. He deserved better than that. Better than what Gavin had been given.

She did what she thought she had to do to protect her child, and she wouldn't apologize for it. "At the second light, turn left."

Gavin remained silent as they drove, unnerving her more with every minute that ticked by. She was keenly aware of the way his hands tightly gripped the leather steering wheel. The tension was evident in every muscle of his body, straining the threads of his designer suit. His smooth, square jaw was flexed as though it took everything he had to keep his emotions in check and his eyes on the road.

It was a practiced skill of Gavin's. When they were together, he always kept his feelings tamped down. The night she told him they were over, there had barely been a flicker of emotion in his eyes. Not anger. Not sadness. Not even a "don't let the door hit you on the way out." Just a solemnly resigned nod and she was dismissed from his life. He obviously never really cared for Sabine. But this might be the situation that caused him to finally blow.

When his car pulled to a stop outside the community center where she taught, he shifted into Neutral, pulled the parking brake and killed the engine. He glanced down at his Rolex. "You're early."

She was. She didn't have to be inside for another fifteen minutes. He'd driven a great deal faster than the bus and hadn't stopped every block to pick up people. It was pointless to get out of the car and stand in front of the building to wait for the previous class to end. That meant time in the car alone with Gavin. Just perfect.

After an extended silence, he spoke. "So, was I horrible to you? Did I treat you badly?" His low voice was quiet, his eyes focused not on her but on something through the windshield ahead of them.

Sabine silently groaned. Somehow she preferred the yelling to this. "Of course not."

He turned to look at her then, pinning her with his dark eyes. "Did I say or do anything while we were together to make you think I would be a bad father?"

A bad father? No. Perhaps a distracted one. A distant one. An absent one. Or worse, a reluctant one. But not a *bad* father. "No. Gavin, I—"

"Then why, Sabine? Why would you keep something so important from me? Why would you keep me from being in Jared's life? He's young now, but eventually he'd notice he didn't have a daddy like other kids. What if he thought I didn't want him? Christ, Sabine. He may not have been planned, but he's still my son."

When he said it like that, every excuse in her mind sounded ridiculous. How could she explain that she didn't want Jared to grow up spoiled, rich but unloved? That she wanted him with her, not at some expensive boarding school? That she didn't want him to become a successful, miserable shell of a man like his father? All those excuses resulted from her primary fear that she couldn't shake. "I was afraid I would lose him."

Gavin's jaw still flexed with pent-up emotions. "You thought I would take him from you?"

"Wouldn't you?" Her gaze fixed on him, a challenge in her eyes. "Wouldn't you have swooped in the minute he was born and claimed him as your own? I'm sure your fancy friends and family would be horrified that a person like me was raising the future Brooks Express Shipping heir. It wouldn't be hard to deem me an unfit mother and have some judge from your father's social club grant you full custody."

"I wouldn't have done that."

"I'm sure you only would've done what you thought was best for your son, but how was I to know what that would entail? What would happen if you decided he would be better off with you and I was just a complication? I wouldn't have enough money or connections to fight you. I couldn't risk it." Sabine felt the tears prickling her eyes, but she refused to cry in front of Gavin.

"I couldn't bear the thought of you handing him off to nannies and tutors. Buying his affection with expensive gifts because you were too busy building the family company to spend time with him. Shipping him off to some boarding school as soon as he was old enough, under the guise of getting him the best education when you really just want him out of your hair. Jared wasn't planned. He wasn't the golden child of your socially acceptable marriage. You might want him on principle, but I couldn't be certain you would love him."

Gavin sat silent for a moment, listening to her tirade. The anger seemed to have run its course. Now he just looked emotionally spent, his dark eyes tired. He looked just like Jared after a long day without a nap.

Sabine wanted to brush the dark strands of hair from his weary eyes and press her palm against the rough stubble of his cheek. She knew exactly how it would feel. Exactly how his skin would smell…an intoxicating mixture of soap, leather and male. But she wouldn't. Her attraction to Gavin was a hurdle she had to overcome to leave him the first time. The years hadn't dulled her reaction to him. Now, it would be an even larger complication she didn't need.

"I don't understand why you would think that," he said at last, his words quieter now.

"Because that's what happened to you, Gavin." She lowered her voice to a soft, conversational tone. "And it's the only way you know how to raise a child. Nannies and boarding schools are normal to you. You told me yourself how your parents were always too busy for you and your siblings. How your house cycled through nannies like some people went through tissue paper. Do you remember telling me about how miserable and lonely you were when they sent you away to school? Why would I want that for Jared? Even if it came with all the money and luxury in the world? I wasn't about to hand him over to you so he could live the same hollow life you had. I didn't want him to be groomed to be the next CEO of Brooks Express Shipping."

"What's wrong with that?" Gavin challenged with a light of anger returning to the chocolate depths of his eyes. "There are worse things than growing up wealthy and becoming the head of a Fortune 500 company founded by your great-great-grandfather. Like growing up poor. Living in a small apartment with second-hand clothes."

"His clothes aren't secondhand!" she declared, her blood rushing furiously through her veins. "They're not from Bloomingdale's, but they aren't rags, either. I know that to you we look like we live in squalor, but we don't. It's a small apartment, but it's in a quiet neighborhood near the park where he can play. He has food and toys and most importantly, all the love, stability and attention I can possibly give him. He's a happy, healthy child."

Sabine didn't want to get defensive, but she couldn't help it. She recognized the tone from back when they were dating. The people in his social circles were always quick to note her shabby-chic fashion sense and lack of experience with an overabundance of flatware. They declared it charming, but Sabine could see the mockery in their eyes. They never thought she was good enough for one of the Brooks men. She wasn't about to let Gavin tell her that the way she raised her child wasn't good enough, either.

"I have no doubt that you're doing a great job with Jared. But why would you make it so hard on yourself? You could have a nice place in Manhattan. You could send him to one of the best private preschools in the city. I could get you a nice car and someone to help you cook and clean and take care of all the little things. I would've made sure you both had everything you needed—and *without* taking him from you. There was no reason to sacrifice those comforts."

"I didn't sacrifice anything," Sabine insisted. She knew those creature comforts came with strings. She'd rather do without. "I never had those things to begin with."

"No sacrifices?" Gavin shifted in the car to face her

directly. "What about your painting? I've kept an eye out over the years and haven't noticed any showings of your work. I didn't see any supplies or canvases lying around the apartment, either. I assume your studio space gave way to Jared's things, so where did all that go?"

Sabine swallowed hard. He had her there. She'd moved to New York to follow her dream of becoming a painter. She had lived and breathed her art every moment of the day she could. Her work had even met with some moderate success. She'd had a gallery showing and sold a few pieces, but it wasn't enough to live on. And it certainly wasn't enough to raise a child on. So her priorities shifted. Children took time. And energy. And money. At the end of the day, the painting had fallen to the bottom of her list. Some days she missed the creative release of her work, but she didn't regret setting it aside.

"It's in the closet," she admitted with a frown.

"And when was the last time you painted?"

"Saturday," she replied a touch too quickly.

Gavin narrowed his gaze at her.

"Okay, it was finger paints," Sabine confessed. She turned away from Gavin's heavy stare and focused on the yoga mat in her lap. He saw more than she wanted him to. He always had. "But," she continued, "Jared and I had a great time doing it, even if it wasn't gallery-quality work. He's the most important thing in the world to me, now. More important than painting."

"You shouldn't have to give up one thing you love for another."

"Life is about compromises, Gavin. Certainly you know what it's like to set aside what you love to do for what you're obligated to do."

He stiffened in the seat beside her. It seemed they

were both guilty of putting their dreams on the back burner, although for very different reasons. Sabine had a child to raise. Gavin had family expectations to uphold and a shipping empire to run. The tight collar of his obligations had chafed back when they were dating. It had certainly rubbed him bloody and raw by now.

When he didn't respond, Sabine looked up. He was looking out the window, his thoughts as distant as his eyes.

It was surreal to be in the same car with Gavin after all this time. She could feel his gravitational pull on her when they were this close. Walking away from him the first time had been hard. They dated for about a month and a half, but every moment they spent together had been fiercely passionate. Not just sexual, either. They enjoyed everything to the fullest, from spicy ethnic foods to political debates, museum strolls to making love under the stars. They could talk for hours.

Their connection was almost enough to make her forget they wanted different things from life. And as much as he seemed enticed by the exoticness of their differences, she knew it wouldn't last long. The novelty would wear off and they would either break up, or he would expect her to change for him. That was one thing she simply wouldn't do. She wouldn't conform for her parents and the small-minded Nebraska town she grew up in, and she wouldn't do it for him. She came to New York so she could be herself, not to lose her identity and become one of the Brooks Wives. They were like Stepfords with penthouse apartments.

She had briefly met some of Gavin's family, and it had scared the hell out of her. They hadn't been dating very long when they ran into his parents at a restaurant. It was

an awkward encounter that came too early in the relationship, but the impact on Sabine had been huge. His
mother was a flawless, polished accessory of his father's
arm. Sabine was fairly certain that even if she wanted
to be, she would be neither flawless nor polished. She
didn't want to fade into the background of her own life.

It didn't matter how much she loved Gavin. And she
did. But she loved herself more. And she loved Jared
more.

But breathing the same air as Gavin again made her
resolve weaken. She had neglected her physical needs
for too long and made herself vulnerable. "So what do
we do now?" Sabine asked at last.

As if he'd read her thoughts, Gavin reached over to
her and took her hand in his. The warmth of him en-
veloped her, a tingle of awareness prickling at the nape
of her neck. It traveled like a gentle waterfall down her
back, lighting every nerve. Her whole body seemed to
be awakening from a long sleep like a princess in a fairy
tale. And all it had taken was his touch. She couldn't
imagine what would happen if the dashing prince actually kissed her.

Kissed her? Was she insane? He was no dashing
prince, and she had run from this relationship for a good
reason. He may have tracked her down and she might
be obligated to allow him to have a place in Jared's life,
but that didn't mean they had to pick up where they left
off. Quite the contrary. She needed to keep her distance
from Gavin if she knew what was good for her. He'd let
her go once, proving just how much she didn't matter to
him. Anything he said or did now to the contrary was
because of Jared. Not her.

His thumb gently stroked the back of her hand. Her

body remembered that touch and everything it could lead to. Everything she'd denied herself since she became a mother...

He looked up at her, an expression of grave seriousness on his face. "We get married."

Gavin had never proposed to a woman before. Well, it wasn't really even a proposal since he hadn't technically asked. And even though it wasn't candlelight and diamonds, he certainly never imagined a response like this.

Sabine laughed at him. Loudly. Heartily. For an unnecessarily long period of time. She obviously had no idea how hard it had been for him to do this. How many doubts he had to set aside to ask *anyone* to be a permanent part of his life, much less someone with a track record of walking away from him.

He'd thought they were having a moment. Her glossy lips had parted softly and her pale eyes darkened when he'd touched her. It should've been the right time, the perfect moment. But he'd miscalculated. Her response to his proposal had proved as much.

"I'm serious!" he shouted over her peals of laughter, but it only made her giggle harder. Gavin sat back in his seat and waited for her to stop. It took a few minutes longer than his pride would've liked. Eventually, she quieted and wiped her damp eyes with her fingertips.

"Marry me, Sabine," he said.

"No."

He almost wished Sabine had gone back to laughing. The firm, sober rejection was worse. It reminded him of her pained, resolved expression as she broke off their relationship and walked out of his life.

"Why not?" He couldn't keep the insulted tone from

his voice. He was a great catch. She should be thrilled to get this proposal, even as spur of the moment and half-assed as it was.

Sabine smiled and patted his hand reassuringly. "Because you don't want to marry me, Gavin. You want to do the right thing and provide a stable home for your son. And that's noble. Really. I appreciate the sentiment. But I'm not going to marry someone that doesn't love me."

"We have a child together."

"That's not good enough for me."

Gavin scoffed. "Making our son legitimate isn't a good enough reason for you?"

"We're not talking about the succession to the throne of England, Gavin. It's not exactly the horrid stigma it used to be. Having you in his life is more than enough for me. That's all I want from you—quality time."

"Quality time?" Gavin frowned. Somehow legally binding themselves in marriage seemed an easier feat.

"Yes. If you're committed enough to your son to marry his mother when you don't love her, you should be committed enough to put in the time. I'm not going to introduce a 'dad' into his life just so you can work late and ignore him. He's better off without a dad than having one that doesn't make an effort. You can't miss T-ball games and birthday parties. You have to be there when you say you will. If you can't be there for him one hundred percent, don't bother."

Her words hit him hard. He didn't have bad parents, but he did have busy ones. Gavin knew how it felt to be the lowest item on someone's priority list. How many times had he sat alone on the marble staircase of his childhood home and waited for parents who never showed up? How many times had he scanned the crowd at school pageants and ball games looking for family that wasn't there?

He'd always sworn he wouldn't do that to his own children, but even after having seen his son, the idea of him wasn't quite a firm reality in Gavin's mind. He had only this primitive need to claim the child and its mother. To finally have someone in his life that couldn't walk away.

That's why he'd rushed out to Brooklyn without any sort of plan. But she was right. He didn't know what to do with a child. His reflex would be to hand him off to someone who did and focus on what he was good at—running his family business. He couldn't afford the distraction, especially so close to closing his latest business deal.

And that was exactly what she was afraid of.

She had good reason, too. He'd spent most of their relationship vacillating between ignoring her for work and ignoring work for her. He never found the balance. A child would compound the problem. Part of the reason Gavin hadn't seriously focused on settling down was because he knew his work priorities would interfere with family life. He kept waiting for the day when things at BXS would slow down enough for him to step back. But it never happened. His father hadn't stepped back until the day he handed the reins over to Gavin, and he'd missed his children growing up to do it.

Gavin didn't have a choice any longer. He had a child. He would have to find a way—a better way than his father chose—to keep the company on top and keep his promises to his son and Sabine. He wasn't sure how the hell he would do it, but he would make it happen.

"If I put in the quality time, will you let me help you?"

"Help me with what?"

"With life, Sabine. If you won't marry me, let me get you a nice apartment in the city. Wherever you want to live. Let me help pay for Jared's education. We can enroll him in the best preschool. I can get someone to help around the house. Someone that can cook and clean, even pick up Jared from school if you want to keep working."

"And why would you want to do that? What you're suggesting is incredibly expensive."

"Maybe, but it's worth it to me. It's an investment in my child. Making your life easier will make you a happier, more relaxed mother to our son. He can spend more time playing and learning than sitting on the subway. And admittedly, having you in Manhattan will make it easier for me to see Jared more often."

He could see the conflict in Sabine's pale green eyes. She was struggling. She was proud and wouldn't admit it, but raising Jared on her own had to be difficult. Kids weren't cheap. They took time and money and effort. She'd already sacrificed her art. But convincing her to accept his offering would take time.

He knew Sabine better than she wanted to admit. She didn't want to be seen as one of those women who moved up in social status by calculated breeding. Jared had been an accident, of that he was certain. Judging by the expression on Sabine's face when she opened the door to her apartment, she would've rather had any man's son but his.

"Let's take this one step at a time, please," Sabine said, echoing his thoughts. There was a pained expression on her face that made him think there was more than just pride holding her back.

"What do you mean?"

"You've gone from having no kids to having a toddler and very nearly a fiancée in two hours' time. That's a big change for you, and for both Jared and me. Let's not uproot our lives so quickly." She sighed and gripped his hand. "Let's get the DNA results in, so there are no questions or doubts. Then we can introduce the idea of you to Jared and tell our families. From there, maybe we move into the city to be closer to you. But let's make these decisions over weeks and months, not minutes."

She glanced down at the screen on her cell phone. "I've got to get inside and set up."

"Okay." Gavin got out of the car and came around to open her door and help her out.

"I have tomorrow off. If you can make an appointment for DNA testing, call or text me and we'll meet you there. My number is the same. Do you still have it?"

He did. He'd very nearly dialed it about a hundred times in the weeks after she'd left. He'd been too proud to go through with the call. A hundred people had drifted in and out of his life, but Sabine leaving had caught him by surprise and it stung. He'd wanted to fight, wanted to call her and convince her she was wrong about them. But she wanted to go and he let her.

Now he could kick himself for not manning up and telling her he wanted her and didn't care what others thought about it. That he would make the time for her. Maybe then he would've been there to hear his son's heartbeat in the doctor's office, his first cries and his first words. Maybe then the mother of his child wouldn't look at him with wary eyes and laugh off his proposal of marriage like a joke.

He made a point of pulling out his phone and confirming it so she wouldn't think he knew for certain. "I do."

Sabine nodded and slowly started walking backward across the grass. Even after all this time apart, it felt awkward to part like strangers without a hug or a kiss goodbye. They were bonded for a lifetime now, and yet he had never felt as distant from her as he did when she backed away.

"I'll see you tomorrow, then," she said.

"Tomorrow," he repeated.

He watched as she regarded him for a moment at a distance. There was a sadness in her expression that he didn't like. The Sabine he remembered was a vibrant artist with a lust for life and experience. She had jerked him out of his blah corporate existence, demanded he live his life, not just go through the motions. Sabine was nothing like what he was supposed to have but absolutely everything he needed. He'd regretted every day since she'd walked out of his life.

Now, he regretted it more than ever, and not just because of his son. The sad, weary woman walking away from him was just a shadow of the person he once knew. And he hated that.

The outdoor lights kicked on, lighting the shimmer of tears in her eyes. "I'm sorry, Gavin," she said before spinning on her heels and disappearing through the doors of the community center.

She was sorry. And so was he.

Three

Gavin arrived at the office the next morning before seven. The halls were dark and quiet as he traveled to the executive floor of the BXS offices. The large corner office had once belonged to his father and his grandfather before him. Gavin's original office was down the hallway. He'd gotten the space when he was sixteen and started learning the business and then passed it along to his younger brother, Alan, when Gavin took over as CEO.

Opening the door, he walked across the antique rug and set his laptop bag and breakfast on the large wooden desk. The heavy mahogany furniture was originally from his great-grandfather's office and was moved here when BXS upgraded their location from the small building near the shipping yards.

His great-grandfather had started the company in

1930, Depression be damned. What began as a local delivery service expanded to trains and trucks and eventually to planes that could deliver packages all over the world. The eldest Brooks son had run the company since the day it opened. Everything about Brooks Express Shipping had an air of tradition and history that made it one of the most trusted businesses in America.

Frankly, it was a bit stifling.

Despite how he'd argued to the contrary with Sabine last night, they both knew this wasn't what he wanted to do with his life. The Brooks name came with responsibilities. Gavin had been groomed from birth to one day run BXS. He'd had the best education, interned with the company, received his MBA from Harvard... Each milestone putting him one step closer to filling his father's shoes. Even if they were too tight.

Sabine had been right about some things. He had no doubt his family would assume Jared would one day be the corporate successor to his father. The difference would be that Gavin would make certain *his* son had a choice.

He settled in at his desk, firing up his computer. He immediately sent an email to his assistant, Marie, about setting up a lab appointment for their DNA testing. With it, he included a note that this was a confidential matter. No one, literally no one, was to know what was going on. He trusted Marie, but she was friendly and chatty with everyone, including his father, who she used to work for. Gavin had barely come to terms with this himself. He certainly wasn't ready for the world, and especially his family, to know what was going on.

Marie wouldn't be in until eight, but she had a corporate smartphone and a long train ride in to work. He was certain she'd have everything handled before she arrived.

That done, he turned to the steaming-hot cup of coffee and the bagel he picked up on his way in. The coffee shop on the ground floor of the building was open well before most people stumbled into BXS for the day. Gavin spread cream cheese on his toasted bagel as he watched his in-box fill with new messages. Most were unimportant, although one caught his eye.

It was from Roger Simpson, the owner of Exclusivity Jetliners.

The small, luxury jet company specialized in private transportation. Whether you were taking a few friends for a weekend in Paris, transporting your beloved poodle to your summer home or simply refused to fly coach, Exclusivity Jetliners was ready and waiting to help. At least for now.

Roger Simpson wanted to retire. The business had been his life, and he was ready to finally relax and enjoy the fruits of his labor. Unlike BXS, he didn't have a well-groomed heir to take his place at the head of the company. He had a son, Paul, but from the discussions Roger and Gavin had shared, Roger would rather sell the company than let his irresponsible son drive it into the ground.

Gavin quickly made it known that he was interested. He'd been eight years old when his father let him ride in the cockpit of one of their Airbus A310 freighters. He'd immediately been enamored with planes and flying. For his sixteenth birthday, his parents had acquiesced and got him flying lessons.

He'd even entertained the idea of joining the Air Force and becoming a fighter pilot. There, sadly, was where that dream had died a horrible death. His father had tolerated Gavin's "hobby," but he wouldn't allow his son to derail his career path for a silly dream.

Gavin swallowed the old taste of bitterness on the back of his tongue and tried to chase it with his coffee. His father had won that battle, but he wasn't in charge anymore. He clicked on the email from Roger and scanned over the message.

BXS was about to offer a new service that would push them ahead of their shipping competitors—concierge shipping. It would appeal to the elite BXS clientele. Ones who wanted their things handled carefully and expeditiously and were willing to pay for the privilege.

The fleet of small planes from Exclusivity Jetliners would be transformed into direct freight jets that would allow the rich art lover to see to it that their new Picasso bought at auction over the phone would arrive safely at their home the same day. It would allow the fashion designer to quickly transport a dozen priceless gowns to an Academy Award nominee while she filmed on set two thousand miles from Hollywood.

It was a risk, but if it worked, it would give Gavin something he'd been wanting his whole life—the chance to fly.

Sabine had encouraged him years ago to find a way to marry his obligations and his passions. It had seemed impossible at the time, but long after she was out of his life, her words had haunted him.

Just as her words had haunted him last night. He'd lain in bed for hours, his brain swirling with everything that had happened after he'd answered Clay's phone call. Sabine had always had the innate ability to cut through his crap. She called it like she saw it, as opposed to all the polite society types who danced around delicate subjects and gossiped behind your back.

She didn't see Gavin as a powerful CEO. The money and the privilege didn't register on her radar at all, and really it never had. After years of women chasing after him, Sabine was the first woman he was compelled to pursue. He'd spied her across an art gallery and instantly felt the urge to possess her. She had no idea who he was or how much he was worth at first, and when she did, she didn't care. He insisted on taking her out to nice dinners, but Sabine was more interested in making love and talking for hours in bed.

But she couldn't ignore their differences. They'd lasted as long as they had by staying inside the protective bubble of the bedroom, but he could tell it was getting harder for Sabine to overlook the huge, platinum gorilla in the room. She didn't see his power and riches as an asset. It was just one thing on a list of many that made her believe they didn't have a future together. She would rather keep her son a secret and struggle to make ends meet than to have Jared live the life Gavin had.

What had she said? ...*You know what it's like to set aside what you love to do for what you're obligated to do.*

He did. Gavin had done it his whole life because of some misguided sense of duty. He could've walked away at any time. Joined the Air Force. Sacrificed his inheritance and what little relationship he had with his parents. But then what would happen to the company? His brother couldn't run it. Alan hadn't so much as sat down in his token office in months. Gavin wasn't even sure if he was in the country. His baby sister, Diana, had a freshly inked degree from Vassar and absolutely no experience. His father wouldn't come out of retirement. That meant Gavin ran BXS or a stranger did.

And no matter what, he couldn't let that happen. It was a family legacy. One of his earliest memories was of coming into this very office and visiting his grandfather Papa Brooks would sit Gavin on his knee and tell him stories about how his great-grandfather had started the company. Tears of pride would gather in the old man's dark eyes. Gavin and his father might have their differences, but he wouldn't let his grandfather down. He'd been dead for four years now, but it didn't matter. BXS and its legacy was everything to Papa Brooks. Gavin wouldn't risk it to chase a pipe dream.

A chime sounded at his hip. Gavin reached down to his phone to find a text from Marie. She'd arranged for an appointment at 4:15 with his concierge physician on Park Avenue. Excellent.

He could've just copied the information into another window and included the location to send it to Sabine, but he found himself pressing the button to call her instead. It was a dangerous impulse that he wished he could ignore, but he wanted to hear her voice. He'd gone so long without it that he'd gladly take any excuse to hear it again. It wasn't until after the phone began to ring that he realized it was 7:30 in the morning. Sabine had always been a night owl and slept late.

"Hello?" she answered. Her voice was cheerful and not at all groggy.

"Sabine? It's Gavin. I'm sorry to call so early. Did I wake you?"

"Wake me?" Sabine laughed. "Oh, no. Jared is up with the chickens, no later than 6:00 a.m. every morning. I tease him that he's going to grow up to be a farmer like his granddaddy."

Gavin frowned for a moment before he realized she was talking about her own father. Sabine spoke very rarely of her parents. Last he'd heard they were both alive and well in Nebraska, but Sabine wasn't in contact with them. It made Gavin wonder if he wasn't the only one who didn't know about Jared.

"My assistant got us an appointment." Gavin read her the information so she could write it down, including the address of the doctor's office.

"Okay," she said. "We'll meet you there at a little before 4:15."

"I'll pick you up," he offered.

"No, we'll take the subway. Jared likes the train. There's a stop about a block from there, so it's not a problem at all."

Sabine was fiercely independent. Always had been. It had made him crazy when they were dating. She wouldn't let him do anything for her. He wanted to argue with her now, but he wouldn't. His afternoon schedule was pretty hectic, and he'd have to shuffle a few things around to drive out to Brooklyn and get them in time unless he sent a car. And yet, he wasn't ready to end the conversation, either.

"After the appointment," he said, "may I take you and Jared to an early dinner?"

"Um…" Sabine delayed her response. She was probably trying to come up with a reason why she couldn't, but was failing.

"A little quality time," he added with a smile, happily using her own words to get his way.

"Sure," she said, caving. "That would be nice."

"I'll see you this afternoon."

"Goodbye," Sabine said, disconnecting the call.

Gavin smiled as he glanced down at his phone. He was looking forward to his afternoon with Jared. And even though the rational side of his brain knew that he shouldn't, he was looking forward to seeing Sabine again, as well.

Sabine was surprised that it didn't take long at the doctor's office. The paperwork took more time than anything else. Gavin and Jared got their cheeks swabbed, and they were told the office would call with the lab results on Monday.

By four forty-five, they were standing on the sidewalk watching the traffic stack up on Park Avenue. Sabine secured Jared in the collapsible umbrella stroller she sometimes took into the city. It was too busy to let him walk, even though he was getting more independent and wanted to.

"What would you like to eat?" Gavin asked.

Sabine was pretty sure that the majority of places he was used to eating at were not equipped to feed a picky toddler. She glanced around, getting her bearings for where she was in the city. "I think there's a good burger place about two blocks from here."

Gavin's gaze narrowed at her. "A burger?"

She swallowed her laugh. "Let's wait until Jared is at least five before we take him to Le Cirque. They don't exactly have a kid's menu."

"I know."

Sabine shook her head and started walking toward the restaurant. Gavin moved quickly to fall into step beside her.

"You're used to taking people out to nice places and spending a lot of money for dinner. I suppose that's what people expect of you, but that's not how Jared and I roll. We'll probably all eat for less than what you normally pay for a bottle of wine. And that's fine by us. Right, Jared?"

The little boy smiled and gave a thumbs-up. He'd learned the gesture in day care a few weeks ago and since then, a lot of things had called for it. "Chee-burger!"

"See?" Sabine said, looking over to Gavin. "He's easy to impress."

The restaurant was already a little busy, but they were able to order and get their food before their toddler started to revolt. Sabine tried to keep her focus on Jared, making sure he was eating small bites and not getting ketchup everywhere. It was easier than looking at Gavin and trying to guess what he was thinking.

Things were still very up in the air between them. He was being nice to her. More polite than she expected, under the circumstances. But once the test results came back, Sabine was certain that things would start to change. Gavin had sworn he wasn't about to snatch her baby from her arms, but she was more concerned about it happening slowly. A new apartment in the city. A new school for Jared. New clothes. New toys. Even if he gave up the idea of marrying for their child's sake, things would change for her, too. He'd insist she stop working. He'd give her spending money. Suggest they just move in with him.

And when the time came that she decided to move out, she was certain he'd see to it that Jared stayed behind in the stable home they'd created for him there. She'd be unemployed and homeless with no money of her own to fight him for custody.

These were the thoughts that had kept her quiet throughout her pregnancy. The same fears that made her hide Jared from his father. And yet, she found herself smiling as she watched Jared and Gavin color on the kid's menu together. There was a hamburger with legs dancing on one side. Jared was scribbling green across the bun. Gavin was more cautious, making the meat brown and the cheese orange as he stayed between the lines.

That was Gavin for you. No matter what he did, he always stayed between the lines. He never got dirty. Or screwed up anything.

Opposites attracted, but they were polar to the point of near incompatibility. A lot of Sabine's clothes had paint splattered on them from her art. She embraced that life was messy. You had to eat a little dirt before you died. Gavin was polished. Tailored. You couldn't find a speck of dirt beneath his fingernails.

How had she ever thought that dating Gavin was a good idea?

Her eyes drifted over his sharp features and thick, dark hair. His broad shoulders and strong jaw. In truth, that was why she'd let herself indulge. Gavin was a handsome, commanding specimen of a man. Every inch of him, from his large hands attempting to clutch a tiny crayon, to his muscular but trim frame, radiated health and power. He was interesting and thoughtful. Honorable and loyal to a fault.

If she'd *had* to get pregnant, her instincts had sought out a superior male to help her propagate the species.

Somehow, even that most scientific of thoughts spoke straight to her core. Her appraisal of Gavin had shot up her pulse. She felt a flush rise to her cheeks and chest.

The heat spread throughout her body, focusing low in her belly. She closed her eyes, hoping to take a private moment to wish away her desire and regain control.

"Do you need to do anything else in the city before I take you back to your place?"

No such luck. Sabine's eyes flew open to see Gavin looking at her with a curious gaze. "You don't have to take us back," she snapped. She wasn't certain she could take being so close to him in the car. At least not at the moment. "We'll take the subway."

"No, I insist." Gavin paid the check and handed his crayon over to Jared.

"Gavin, you have a two-passenger roadster with no car seat. You can't drive us home."

He smiled and fished into his pocket, pulling out the ticket for the garage attendant. "Not today. Today I have a four-door Mercedes sedan..."

Sabine opened her mouth to reiterate the lack of car seat when Gavin continued, "...with a newly installed combination car seat that Jared can use until he's eighty-five pounds."

Her mouth snapped shut. He was determined to undermine any arguments she might make. Sure, it was harmless when it came to rides home from dinner, but what about when the decisions were important? Would Gavin find a way to make sure he got his way then, too? He'd always seemed to win when they were dating, so she wouldn't be surprised.

Tonight, Sabine didn't feel like arguing. She waited with Jared while Gavin had the attendant retrieve his car. Admittedly, it was nice to just sit in the soft leather seats and let Gavin worry about the stressful exodus of traffic into Brooklyn. No running down stairs to the train platforms…no crowded, B.O.-smelling subway cars…

And when he pulled up right in front of her building and parked, trimming several blocks from her walk, she said, "Thank you."

"For what?"

"Driving us home."

Gavin frowned slightly at her. "Of course I would drive you home. There's no need to thank me for that."

Sabine glanced over her shoulder and found Jared out cold in his new car seat. "I think he likes it," she said. She glanced at her watch. It was a little after seven. It was earlier than Jared usually went to bed, and he'd probably beat the sun to rise, but that was okay. If she could get him upstairs, change his Pull-Up and take off his shoes without waking him up, she'd consider it a victory.

They got out of the car. Sabine walked around to the other side, but Gavin had already scooped up the sleepy toddler in his arms. Without waking, Jared put his head on Gavin's shoulder and clung to his neck. Gavin gently ran his palm over the child's head, brushing back the baby-soft strands of his dark hair and resting his hand on Jared's back to keep him steady.

Sabine watched with a touch of tears distorting her vision. It was sweet watching the two of them, like carbon copies of one another. It was only their second day together and already she could see Jared warming up to Gavin.

Gavin carried Jared through the building and into her apartment after she unlocked the door. Sabine led the way down the hall to the bedroom. Flipping on the lights, they were greeted with calming mint-green walls, cream wainscoting and a mural of Winnie the Pooh characters she'd painted above the crib. Her double bed was an afterthought on the opposite wall.

She slipped off Jared's shoes. His soft cotton pants and T-shirt would be fine to sleep in. She gestured for Gavin to lay him on the crib mattress and made quick work of changing him.

Jared immediately curled into a ball, reaching out for his stuffed dinosaur and pulling it to his chest. Sabine covered him with his blanket. They slipped out quietly, the night-light kicking on as the overhead light went out.

Sabine pulled the door closed gently and made her way back into the living room. She expected Gavin to make noises about leaving, but instead he loitered, his eyes focused on a painting on the wall over the dining room table.

"I remember this one," Gavin said, his fists in his pants pockets.

Sabine looked up at the canvas and smiled. "You should. I was painting that one while we were dating."

The background of the painting was intricately layered with a muted palette of white, cream, ivory, off-white and ecru. The design was extremely structured and orderly. The variations of the pattern were really quite remarkable if you could differentiate the subtle color differences.

It was Gavin on canvas. And across it, splatters of purple, black and green paint. Disorder. Chaos. Color. That was Sabine. It was a striking juxtaposition. One that when it was complete, was the perfect illustration of why as a couple they made good art, but not good sense.

"You weren't finished with it when I saw it last. Some of this is new, like the blue crosses. What did you end up calling it?"

The pale blue crosses were actually plus signs. The final addition to the work after seeing her own unexpected plus sign on a pregnancy test. "Conception," she said.

Gavin looked back at the painting and turned his head to look at it from a new angle. "It's very nice. I like the colors. It's a much-needed pop against the beige."

Sabine smiled. He didn't see the symbolism of their relationship in it at all and that was okay. Art was only half about what she created. The other half was how others perceived and experienced her work.

He turned back to her, his face serious. "You are a really talented artist, Sabine."

The compliment made her squirm a little. She was always uncomfortable with praise. Frankly, she wasn't used to it after growing up with parents who didn't understand why their daughter danced to a different drummer. "It's okay," she said with a dismissive wave of her hand. "Not my best work."

Gavin frowned and closed the gap between them. He clasped her hand in his and pulled it to the red silk of his tie. "No," he insisted. "It's not just okay. You're not just okay."

Sabine tried to pull away, but he wasn't having it. He bent his knees until he was at her eye level and she couldn't avoid his gaze.

"You are a gifted painter," he insisted. "You were then and you certainly are now. I was always amazed at how you could create such wonderful and imaginative things from just a blank canvas. You have a great deal of skill, Sabine, whether you think so or not. I hope our son has the same eye for the beautiful things in life."

The words were hard enough to hear when they were

about her, but knowing he wished the same for their son was too much for her to take. Her parents hadn't wanted her to be a painter. It was frivolous. They'd wanted her to stay home and work on the farm, grow up and marry a farmer, and then raise a brood of tiny farmers. She was absolutely nothing like they wanted. And the day she left for New York, they said as much.

Before she could change her mind, Sabine threw herself against the wall of Gavin's chest and hugged him tight. He seemed surprised at first, but then he wrapped his strong arms around her and pulled her close. "Thank you," she whispered into his lapel.

It felt good to be in his arms, surrounded in his warmth and spicy cologne. Good to be appreciated for her work even when she hadn't lifted a brush in two years. Good to have someone believe in her, even if it was the same man who let her walk away from him. She would be happy with his professional admiration if nothing else.

And yet, with her head pressed to his chest, she could hear his heart racing. His muscles were tense as he held her. He was either extremely uncomfortable hugging her or there was more than just admiration there.

Sabine lifted her head and looked up at him. Her breath caught in her throat as her eyes met his. They glittered with what could only be desire. His jaw was tight, but unlike last night, he wasn't angry. He swallowed hard, the muscles in his throat working hard down the column of his neck. She recognized the signs in Gavin. She knew them well but thought she'd never see him look at her like that again.

The intensity of his gaze flipped a switch in her own body. As it had in the restaurant, heat pooled in her cheeks and then rushed through her veins to warm every inch of her. She couldn't help it. There had been few things as exquisite in her life as being made love to by Gavin. It had come as a huge surprise considering how tightly buttoned-up he was, but there was no denying he knew just how to touch her. It was probably the worst thing she could do considering what was going on between them, but she wanted Gavin to touch her again.

He must have read it in her eyes because a moment later he dipped his head and brought his lips to hers. They were soft at first, molding to her mouth and drinking her in. Sabine gently pressed her hands against his chest, pushing up onto her toes to get closer to him.

His hands glided across her back, the heat of him penetrating through the fabric of her blouse and searing her skin. She wanted to feel those hands all over her body. It had been so long since someone had touched her that way. She didn't want it to stop. Not ever.

Sabine was about to lean in. She wanted to wrap her arms around his neck and press her body tight against his. As if he sensed the move, Gavin started to retreat. She could feel him pulling away, the cool air rushing between them and bringing with it reality. She pulled away, too, wrapping her arms across her chest to ward off the chill and its evidence on her aching body.

Gavin looked down at her and cleared his throat. "I'd better go."

Sabine nodded and moved slowly with him toward the door.

"Good night, Sabine," he said in a hoarse whisper. He took a step back, straightening his suit coat, and then gripped the brass knob in his hand.

"Good night," she whispered, bringing her fingers up to gently touch her lips. They were still tingling with his kiss as he vanished through her doorway. "Good night."

Four

"We have a date this afternoon. I mean a playdate. I mean, aw hell, I have no idea what's going on," Sabine lamented. She was folding a stack of shirts and paused with one clutched to her chest. "You know, a few days ago I was living my life like a criminal on the run, but I felt like I had a better grip on things."

Adrienne smiled at her and turned to change the outfit on the mannequin by the wall. "It's a big change," she said. "But so far, it's not a bad change, right?"

"That's true. I guess that's what worries me. I keep waiting for the other shoe to drop."

The boutique was open, but the foot traffic usually didn't pick up until closer to lunchtime on a Saturday. At the moment, Sabine and Adrienne were alone in the store and able to speak freely about the dramatic turn of events in her life. Normally, Sabine ran the shop alone until another employee, Jill, came in later in the day. Today, Adrienne came in as well to relieve Sabine so she could meet Gavin.

"I don't think he's going to steal Jared away from you, Sabine. It sounds like he's been pretty reasonable so far."

"I know," she said, folding the last shirt and adding it to the neat display. "But he doesn't have the DNA results back yet and won't until Monday. If he was going to make a move, it wouldn't be until he had the advantage. The Gavin I knew three years ago was…calculating and ruthless. He had absolutely no qualms about sitting back and waiting for the perfect moment to strike."

"This isn't a business deal and he's not a cobra. You two have a child together. It's different." Adrienne pulled out a pin and fitted the top of the dress to the form.

Sabine stopped and admired the outfit Adrienne had designed. The sexy sheath dress was fitted with a square neckline, but it had fun details like pockets and a bright print to make it pop. It was perfect for the summer with some strappy heels or colorful ballet flats. She'd been tempted to use her employee discount to buy it for herself, but there wasn't much point. That was the kind of dress a woman wanted to wear on a date or a night out with the girls. She hadn't had either in a very long time. And despite Gavin proposing one night and kissing her the next, she didn't think her Facebook relationship status would be changing anytime soon.

"Work and life are the same to Gavin. I mean, he didn't propose to me. Not really. It was more like an offer to buy out my company. A business merger. Just what a girl wants to hear, right?"

Adrienne turned and looked at Sabine with her hands planted on her hips. "And the kiss?"

The kiss. The one thing that didn't make sense. She knew he was her Achilles' heel so it didn't surprise her that she fell into his arms, but his motives were sketchy. "Strategy. He knows my weakness where he's concerned. He's just buttering up the competition to get his way."

"You really think that's all it was?" Her boss looked unconvinced.

Sabine flopped down onto an upholstered bench outside the changing rooms. "I don't know. It didn't feel like strategy. It felt..." Her mind drifted back to the way her body had responded to his touch. The way her lips tingled long after he'd left. She sighed and shook her head. "It doesn't matter what it felt like. The fact of the matter is that Gavin doesn't love me. He never has. His only interest in me back then was as a source of rebellion against his uptight family. Now, I'm nothing more than a vehicle to his son. And when he gets tired of the games, he'll remove the obstacle—*me*."

"You don't think he's interested in a relationship with you?" Adrienne sat down beside her.

"Why would he be? He wasn't interested the last time. At least not enough to so much as blink when it ended. I mean, I thought there was more between us than just sex, but he was always so closed off. I had no idea how he really felt, but when he let me walk out the door like I was nothing more than an amusement to occupy his time...I knew I was replaceable. Gavin never would've sought me out if it wasn't for Jared."

"You broke up with him," Adrienne reminded her. "Maybe his pride kept him from chasing after you. Listen, I'm married to one of those guys. They're all about running their little empires. They're the king of their own kingdoms. In the business world, showing weakness is like throwing chum in the ocean—the sharks start circling. They keep it all inside for so long that after a while, they lose touch with their own sense of vulnerability."

Her boss knew what she was talking about. Adrienne's husband was Will Taylor, owner of one of the oldest and most successful newspapers in New York. He came from a long line of CEOs, just as Gavin had. Even then, she'd seen Adrienne and Will together multiple times, and he was putty in her hands. And happily so. Will at work and Will at home were completely different people.

But somehow Sabine had a hard time picturing Gavin with a marshmallow center beneath his hard candy shell. They'd shared some intimate moments together while they'd dated, but there was always an element of control on his part. They were together only a short time, but it was an intense relationship. She gave so much and yet he held back from her. She had no way of knowing the parts he kept hidden, but more than likely, it was his apathy. "You're saying he let me walk away and cried himself to sleep that night?"

Adrienne chuckled. "Well, maybe that's taking it a little far. But he might have had regrets and didn't know what to do about it. Jared gives him a good reason to see you again without having to address any of those icky, uncomfortable feelings."

A pair of ladies came into the shop, so they put their conversation on hold for now. While the women looked around, Sabine moved over to the checkout counter and crouched down to inventory the stock of pink boutique bags with Adrienne's signature across the side. The passive activity helped her think.

Feelings were definitely not Gavin's forte. Or at least sharing them. She was certain he had them, he just bottled them up on the inside. But feelings for her? She doubted that.

Gavin might be attracted to her. The kiss they shared might've been him testing the waters of resuming a physical relationship. They'd always had an undeniable chemistry. She knew the minute she saw him the first time that she was in trouble. It was at a gallery showing for a local contemporary artist. Sabine had gotten lost in the lines and colors of one of the pieces and the rest of the world disappeared.

At least until she heard the low rumble of a man's voice in her ear. "It looks like an expensive mistake to me."

She'd turned in surprise and nearly choked on a sip of champagne when she saw him. He wasn't at all the kind of man she was used to. He wore an expensive suit and a watch that cost more money than she'd made in the past year. Men like Gavin typically turned their nose up at Sabine. But he'd looked at her with dark eyes that twinkled with amusement and desire.

Her pulse had shot up, her knees melted to butter beneath her, and she'd found herself without a witty response. Just that quickly, she was lost.

The weeks that followed were some of the greatest of her life. But not once in that time had he ever looked at her with anything more than lust. So as much as she'd like to think Adrienne was right, she knew better. He'd either been using their attraction to his advantage or using their situation to get laid.

One of the ladies tried on a blouse and then bought it, along with a scarf. Sabine rang her up and they left the store. The chime of the door signaled that her conversation with Adrienne could resume.

"So where are you guys going on your playdate today?" Adrienne called from the stockroom.

"We're going to the Central Park Zoo."

"That should be fun," Adrienne said, returning to the front with her arms full of one of her newest dress designs. "Was that his idea?"

"No," Sabine chuckled. She reached out to take several of the outfits from her. "He didn't have a clue of what to do with a two-year-old. I suggested the zoo because I wanted us to do something that didn't involve a lot of money."

Adrienne wrinkled her delicate nose. "What do you mean?"

They carried the dresses over to the empty rack and organized them by size. "I don't want Gavin buying Jared anything yet. At least not big, expensive things. He used to tell me that his father only ever took him shopping. I can't keep him from buying things forever, but that's not how I want to start off."

"Money isn't a bad thing, Sabine. I never had it until I married Will, and trust me, it takes some adjusting to get used to having a lot of it. But it can be used for good, too, not just for evil."

"It's also not a substitute for love or attention. I want Gavin to really try. Right now, Jared is still young, but before too long, he's going to be in the 'gimme' stage. I don't want Gavin buying affection with expensive gifts."

"Try to keep an open mind," Adrienne suggested. "Just because he buys Jared something doesn't mean he isn't trying. If getting him a balloon makes Jared smile, don't read too much into it. Just enjoy your afternoon." Adrienne stopped and crinkled her nose, making a funny face at Sabine.

"What's the matter?"

"I don't know. My stomach is a little upset all of a sudden. I think my smoothie is turning on me. Either that, or I'm nauseated by all your drama."

Sabine laughed. "I'm sorry my crazy life is making you ill. I've got some antacids in my purse if you need them."

"I'll be fine," Adrienne insisted. She looked down at her watch. "You'd better get going if you're going to meet him on time. Worry about having fun instead."

Sabine nodded. "Okay," she said. "We will have a good time, I promise."

She hoped she was right.

As Gavin stepped out of his apartment building onto Central Park South and crossed the street, he realized just how long it had been since he'd actually set foot in Central Park. He looked out at it every day but never paid any attention to the looming green hulk that sprawled out in front of him.

His first clue was that he was a little overdressed for a summer afternoon at the zoo. He'd left the tie at home, but he probably could've forgone the suit coat, too. A pair of jeans or khakis and a polo shirt would've suited just fine. He considered running his jacket back upstairs, but he didn't want to be late.

When he was younger, he'd enjoyed jogging along the paths or hanging out and playing Frisbee with friends in the Sheep Meadow. The more involved he got in the management of BXS, the less important trees and sun-shine seemed in his agenda. He and Sabine had taken a horse-drawn carriage through the park one evening when they were dating, but the closest he had gotten to it since then was a gala at the Met last year.

By the time he reached the front entrance to the zoo, he could feel the sweat forming along his spine. He slipped out of the jacket and threw it over his arm after rolling up his sleeves. It helped, but not much. He was supposed to meet Sabine and Gavin just outside the brick archways that marked the entrance, but he didn't see them anywhere.

He unclipped his phone from his belt to look at the time. He was a few minutes early. He opted to flip through some emails. He'd hit a little bit of a snag with the Exclusivity Jetliners merger. The owner's son, Paul, had found out about his father's plans and was throw-ing a fit. Apparently he wasn't pleased about watching his inheritance getting sold off. Gavin was paying a pretty penny for the company, but Roger's son seemed to fancy playing CEO. Roger was starting to second-guess the sale.

He fired off a couple quick emails, but his attention was piqued by the sound of a child's laughter in the dis-tance. It was one of those contagious giggles that made you smile just to hear it. He looked up in the direction of the sound and saw Sabine and Jared playing in the shade of a large tree.

Slipping his cell phone back in the holster, he made his way over to where they were. Sabine was crouched down beside Jared, dressed in capris and a tank top. Her dark hair was pulled back into a ponytail and a bright red backpack was slung over her shoulders.

Jared was playing with another one of his trucks. In the mud. Apparently, the kid had managed to find the only mud bog in the park. He was crouched barefoot in the brown muck, ramming his trucks through the sludge. He made loud truck noises with his mouth and then giggled hysterically when the mud splashed up onto his shirt. He was head-to-toe filthy and happy as a little piglet.

Gavin's instinct was to grab Jared and get him out of the dirt immediately. There had to be a restroom somewhere nearby where they could rinse him off. But then he saw the smile on Sabine's face. She wasn't even remotely concerned about what Jared was doing.

His mother would've had a fit if she had found him playing in the mud. His nanny would've had to hose him off outside and then thoroughly scrub him in the tub. When he was dry, he would've been given a lengthy lecture about how getting dirty was inappropriate and his nanny would've been fired for not keeping a better eye on him.

Jared dropped one of the trucks in the puddle and the water splashed up, splattering both him and Sabine. Gavin expected her to get upset since she'd gotten dirty now, but she just laughed and wiped the smear of muddy water off her arm. It was amazing. It made Gavin want to get dirty, too.

"Oh, hey," Sabine said, looking up to see him standing nearby. She glanced at her watch. "I'm sorry to keep you waiting. We got here a little early and Jared can't pass up some good mud." She stood up and whipped the backpack off her shoulders.

"Not a problem," he said as he watched her pull out

an assortment of things including wet wipes, a large, plastic zip bag and a clean shirt.

"All right, buddy," she said. "Time to go to the zoo with Gavin. Are you ready?"

"Yeah!" Jared said, immediately perking up at the suggestion of a new adventure.

"Give me your trucks first." She put all the muddy toys in the bag and then used his dirty shirt to wipe up a good bit of the muck off his hands and feet before shoving it in there, as well. The baby wipes made quick work of the rest, then the clean shirt and the little socks and sneakers she'd taken off went back on. "Good job!" she praised, giving him a tiny high five and zipping up the backpack.

Gavin was amazed by the process. Not only did she let Jared get dirty, she was fully prepared for the eventuality. He'd always just thought of Sabine as the artistic type. She was laid-back and went with the flow as he expected, but she also had a meticulous bit of planning underneath it all that he appreciated. She had the motherhood thing down. It was very impressive.

"We're ready," she said, bending down to pick Jared up.

Gavin had to smile when he noticed the speck of mud on Sabine's cheek. "Not quite yet," he said. Without thinking, he reached out to her, running the pad of his thumb across her cheekbone and wiping it away. The moment he touched her, he sensed a change in the energy between them. Her pale green eyes widened, the irises darkening in the center to the deep hunter green he remembered from their lovemaking. A soft gasp of surprise escaped her glossy pink lips.

His body reacted, as well. The touch brought on the

familiar tingle that settled between his shoulder blades and sent a shot of pure need down his spine. He wanted Sabine. There was no use in denying it. There was something about her that spoke to his most base instincts. Their time apart hadn't changed or dulled the attraction. In fact, it seemed to have amplified it.

That night at her apartment, he had to kiss her. There was no way he could walk out of there without tasting her again. Once he did, he could feel the floodgates giving way. He had to leave. And right then. If he had lingered a moment longer, he wouldn't have been able to stop himself.

Their relationship was complicated. There were a lot of proverbial balls still in the air. He wasn't dumb enough to get emotionally involved with Sabine again, but leaping back into a physical relationship with her, at least this soon, was a bad idea, too. For now, he needed to try and keep his distance on both fronts.

Why, then, was he standing in the middle of Central Park cradling Sabine's face with a throbbing erection? Because he was a masochist.

"A...uh...stray bit of Jared's handiwork," he said. He let his hand drop back to his side before he did something stupid in public. Instead, he turned to look at Jared. "Are you ready to see the monkeys?"

"Yeah!" he cheered, clapping his chubby hands together.

They bought their tickets and headed inside. Starting at the sea lion pool, they made their way around to visit the penguins and the snow leopards. He enjoyed watching his son's eyes light up when he saw the animals.

"Do you guys come here a lot?" he asked, leaning on

the railing outside the snow monkey exhibit. "He really seems to like it."

"We actually haven't been here before. I was waiting until he was a little older. This seemed like the perfect opportunity."

Gavin was surprised. Somehow he'd thought he had missed all his son's firsts, but there were more to be had than he expected. "I've never been here, either."

Sabine looked at him with disbelief lining her brow. "You've lived in New York your whole life and you've never been to the zoo?"

"Saying I lived here my whole life isn't entirely accurate. My family lived here, but I was gone off to school a lot of the time."

"So not even as a child? Your nannies never brought you here?"

"Nope. Sometimes we came to the park to play or walk, but never to the zoo. I'm not sure why. My boarding school took a field trip to Washington, D.C., once. We went to the Smithsonian and the National Zoo on that trip. I think I was fourteen or so. But I've never had the chance to come here."

"Have you ever been to a petting zoo?"

At that, Gavin had to laugh. "A petting zoo? Absolutely not. My mother would have a fit at the thought of me touching dirty animals. I never even had pets as a kid."

Sabine wrinkled her nose at him. "Well, then, today is your day. We'll head over to the children's zoo after this and you and Jared can both pet your first goat."

A goat? He wasn't so sure that he was interested in that. Sabine seemed to sense his hesitation. "Maybe we can start you off slow. You can hold a rabbit. They have places to wash your hands. I also have hand sanitizer in my bag. You'll be okay, I promise."

Gavin chuckled at Sabine. She was mothering him just the same as she did to coax Jared into trying something new. He wasn't used to that.

They were on their way to the children's zoo when he felt his cell phone buzzing at his hip. He looked down at the screen. It was Roger. He had to take this call.

"Excuse me one minute," he said.

Sabine frowned but nodded. "I'll take Jared to the restroom while we're waiting."

Gavin answered the phone and spent the next ten minutes soothing Roger's concerns. He didn't want this opportunity to slip through his fingers. Acquiring those private jets was as close to fulfilling his childhood dream as he might ever get. He had a plane of his own, but it was small and didn't have anywhere near the range of Roger's jets. He longed for the day when he could pilot one of those planes to some far-off destination. He was a falcon on a tether now. He wanted to fly free, and he wasn't going to let Paul Simpson's desire to play at CEO ruin it.

It was going well so far. He was able to address all of Roger's concerns. Things might be back on track if he could keep the owner focused on what was best for his family and his company. But it was taking some time. The conversation was still going when Sabine returned. She didn't seem pleased.

He covered the receiver with his hand. "I'm almost done. I can walk and talk," he said.

She turned and started walking away with Jared. He followed close behind them, but he was admittedly distracted. By the time he finally hung up, Gavin had already missed out on feeding the ducks. Jared was quacking and clumsily chasing one at the moment.

Sabine was watching him play with a twinkle in her eye. She loved their son so much. He could tell that Jared was everything to her. He appreciated that about her. His parents had never been abusive or cruel, but they had been distant. Busy. They weren't hands-on at all. Jared hadn't had all the privileges that Gavin grew up with, but he did have a loving, doting mother.

Who was frowning intently at Gavin.

"I'm sorry," he said. "It was important."

She shook her head and turned back to look at Jared. One of the zoo employees was holding a rabbit so he could pet it. "That's the most important thing, right there, Gavin."

Jared turned around and grinned at his mother with such joy it made Gavin's chest hurt. "A bunny," he exclaimed, hopping around on his little legs like a rabbit.

She was right. He needed to be in this 100 percent. Jared deserved it. And so did Sabine.

Five

There was a knock on the door early Sunday morning. Sabine was making pancakes while Jared played with blocks on the floor. Sunday was their easy day. There was no work or preschool. They were both still in their pajamas and not expecting company.

She was surprised to find Gavin on her doorstep. She was even more surprised to find he was wearing jeans and a T-shirt. It was a Gucci T-shirt, but at least it wasn't a suit. And it looked good on him. The black shirt fit his muscular frame like a second skin, reminding her of the body he hid beneath blazers and ties. And the jeans... they were snug in all the right places, making her mouth go dry in an instant.

He caught her so off guard, she didn't notice at first that he had a large canvas and a bag of painting supplies in his hands.

"Gavin," she said. "I wasn't expecting you this morning." After yesterday, she didn't figure she would see him until the test results came back. She could tell that he was trying yesterday, but his thoughts were being pulled in ten different directions. Even after he got off the phone, he was checking it constantly and replying to emails. He had a business to run.

And yet, here he was.

"I know. I wanted it to be a surprise."

Sabine wasn't big on surprises. With Gavin, it was more that he wanted to do something his way and to keep her from arguing, he wouldn't tell her until the last second. Surprise! But still, she was curious. "Come on in," she said.

Gavin stepped in, leaning the canvas against the bookcase. "Hey, big guy," he said to Jared. He got up from his blocks and came over to hug Gavin's leg. Gavin scooped the toddler up and held him over his head, and then they "soared" around the living room making airplane noises. Jared the Plane crash-landed onto the couch in a fit of giggles and tickling fingers poking at his tummy.

It had only been a few days, but she could tell that Jared was getting attached to Gavin. It was a good thing. She knew that. But still, she worried. He'd put in a decent effort so far, but could he keep it up for the next sixteen years? She wasn't sure. But she did know that he'd better not screw this up.

"I was making pancakes," she said, turning and heading back into the kitchen. "Have you had breakfast?"

"That depends," he said, pausing in the tickle fight. "What kind of pancakes are they?"

"Silver-dollar pancakes with blueberries."

"Nope." Gavin smiled. "I haven't had breakfast." He let Jared return to his blocks. "I'll be right back, big guy."

He followed her into the kitchen, leaning against the entryway. The kitchen was too small for both of them to be in there and get anything done. She tried to ignore his physical presence and how much of the room he took up without even entering, but she failed. The sight of him in those tight jeans was more than she could take. Her body instantly reacted to his nearness, her mouth going dry and her nipples pebbling against the thin fabric of her T-shirt.

She spun to face the stove before he could notice and decided to focus on pancakes, not the sexy man lurking nearby. Eyeing the batter, she decided she needed a larger batch to feed a man of his size. "So what brings you here this morning?"

Gavin watched her fold in another handful of dried blueberries. "I wanted to make up for yesterday."

Sabine tried not to react. She was happy that he was making the effort, but failing Jared and then making a grand gesture to appease his conscience was a dangerous cycle. She'd rather he just be present the first time. "How's that?"

"I saw in the paper that the Big Apple Circus is here. I got tickets for this afternoon."

Just as she'd thought. She had no problems with going to the circus, but he didn't ask her. He didn't call to see if that was something they might want to do. What if Jared was petrified of clowns? Or if they had other plans today? Gavin just bought the tickets and assumed that everything would go the way he'd planned.

But—he was trying, she reminded herself. "Jared

would probably enjoy that. What time do we need to leave for the show?"

"Well," Gavin said, "that's only part of the surprise. *We* aren't leaving. You're staying."

Sabine looked up from the griddle. "What do you mean?"

"I just got tickets for Jared and me. I thought you might enjoy an afternoon to yourself. I even brought you some painting supplies."

That explained the stuff he brought in with him. She'd been so thrown off by his unannounced arrival that she hadn't questioned it yet. She supposed that she should be excited and grateful, but instead, her stomach ached with worry. Gavin was taking her son someplace without her. She didn't really like the sound of that. He didn't know anything about children. What if Jared got sick? Or scared? Did Gavin even know that Jared wasn't fully potty trained yet? Just the idea of him changing dirty Pull-Ups started a rumble of nervous laughter in her chest that she fought down.

"I don't think that's a good idea," she managed to say.

Gavin's dark brow drew together in consternation. "Why not? You said you wanted me to be there. To be involved."

"It's been less than a week, Gavin. You've spent a couple hours with him, sure, but are you ready to take care of him on your own for a day?" Sabine turned back to the stove and flipped over the pancakes. She grabbed one of Jared's superhero plates and slid a couple tiny pancakes onto it beside the slices of banana she'd already cut up.

"You don't think I can handle it?"

She sighed heavily. Ignoring him, she poured some

blueberry syrup into the small bowl built into the dish and grabbed a sippy cup with milk from the refrigerator. She brushed past him to go into the living room. Jared had a tiny plastic table and chair where he could eat. She set down his breakfast and called him over. Once he was settled, she turned back to look at Gavin. He was still standing in the doorway to the kitchen looking handsome and irritated all at once.

"I don't know," she admitted. "I don't know if you can handle it or not. That's the problem. We don't really know one another that well."

Gavin crossed his arms over his chest and leaned against the door frame. His biceps bulged against the constraints of the shirt, drawing her eyes down to his strong forearms and rock-hard chest. It was easier to focus on that than the strangely cocky expression on his face.

"We know each other *very* well," he said with a wicked grin curling his lips.

Sabine approached him, stopping just short of touching him. "Your ability to give me an orgasm has no bearing on whether or not you can care for a toddler."

At the mention of the word *orgasm* his gaze narrowed at her. He swallowed hard but didn't reach for her. "I disagree. Both require an attention to detail. Anticipating what another person wants or needs. I don't think it matters if what they need is a drink, a toy or a mind-blowing physical release."

Mind-blowing. Sabine couldn't stop her tongue from gliding out over her lips. They'd gotten painfully dry. His gaze dropped to her mouth, then back to her eyes. There was a touch of amusement in his gaze. He knew he was getting to her.

"What if what they need is their poopy diaper changed? Or you gave them too much cotton candy and they spew blue muck all over the backseat of your Mercedes? Not quite as sexy."

The light of attraction in his eyes faded. It was hard to keep up the arousal with that kind of imagery. That's why she hadn't bothered dating in all this time. Maybe she should reconsider. She might not feel as vulnerable to Gavin's charms if she had an outlet that didn't involve him.

His expression hardened for a moment. He seemed irritated with her. "Stop trying to scare me away. I know taking care of a child isn't easy. It can be messy. But it's just a few hours to start. I can handle it. Will you let me do this for you? Please?"

"Do this for *me?* Shouldn't you be doing this for your son?"

"I am. Of course, I am. I want a relationship with Jared more than anything. But to do that, you have got to trust me. I will return him to you tonight, well fed, well cared for and, for the most part, clean. But you have to do your part. You have to let me try. Let me mess up. Enjoy your free afternoon. Paint something beautiful because you can. Go get a pedicure."

Sabine had to admit that sounded wonderful. She hadn't had an afternoon to herself since she went into labor. She didn't have any family here to watch Jared. She tried to only use Tina's services when she had to for classes. She hadn't had a day just to relax. And to paint...

She pushed past him into the kitchen to finish making pancakes. Gavin stayed in the doorway, allowing her the space to think, while also keeping an eye on Jared. She appreciated having someone to do that. She hadn't had another set of eyes to help before. Since Jared became mobile, she hadn't been able to shower, cook or do anything without constantly peeking out to check on him. Life was a little easier when he sat in his swing or bouncy chair while she did what needed to be done.

A whole afternoon?

She wanted to say yes, but she couldn't shake the worry. It was probably going to be fine. There was only so much trouble that could befall them in an afternoon at the circus. If Jared came home covered in blue vomit, the world wouldn't end. And it was a family-oriented event. She had no doubt that if another mother saw Gavin and Jared in a meltdown moment, she would step in to help.

Sabine finished the pancakes and turned off the burner. She slid a stack onto her plate and the other onto a plate for Gavin. Turning around, she offered one to him. When he reached for it, she pulled it back slightly.

"Okay," she said. "You can go. But I want you to text and check in with me. And if anything remotely worrisome happens—"

Gavin took the plate from her. "I will call you immediately. Okay?"

Sharing Jared with someone else was going to be hard, she could tell already. But it could be good, too. Two parents were double the hands, double the eyes, double the love. Right? "Okay, all right. You win. Just don't feed him too much sugar. You'll regret it."

Gavin couldn't remember being this tired, ever. Not when he was on the college rowing team. Not when he stayed up late studying for an exam. Not even after spending all night making love to a beautiful woman. How on earth did parents do this every day? How did

Sabine manage to care for Jared alone, work full-time, teach yoga...it was no wonder she'd stopped painting. He was bone-tired. Mentally exhausted.

And it was one of the best days of his life.

Seeing Jared's smile made everything worth it. That was what kept parents going. That moment his son's face lit up when he saw an elephant for the first time. Or the sound of his laughter when the clowns were up to their wacky antics.

The day hadn't been without its mishaps. Jared had dropped his ice cream and went into a full, five-alarm meltdown. Gavin knew Sabine didn't want him buying a bunch of things, but he gladly threw down the cash for the overpriced light-up sword to quiet him down. There was also a potty emergency that was timed just as they neared the front of the mile-long food line. Sabine had begun potty training recently and had told him that if Jared asked, they were to go, right then. So they did. And ended up at the end of the line, waiting another twenty minutes for hot dogs and popcorn.

But the world hadn't ended. There had been no tragedies, and he texted as much to Sabine every hour or so. The day had been filled with lights and sound and excitement. So much so that by the time they made it back to the apartment, Jared was out cold. Gavin knew exactly how he felt.

He carried the exhausted toddler inside, quietly tapping at the apartment door so as to not wake him up. When Sabine didn't answer, he tried the knob and found it unlocked. He expected to find Sabine frantically painting. This was her chance, after all, to indulge her suppressed creativity. Instead, she was curled up on the couch, asleep.

Gavin smiled. He had told her to spend the afternoon doing whatever she wanted. He should've guessed that a nap would be pretty high on the list. He tiptoed quietly through the living room and into the bedroom. Following the routine from Thursday night, he laid Jared in the crib and stripped him down into just his T-shirt and shorts. He covered him with the blanket and turned out the lights.

Sabine was still asleep when he came out. He knew he couldn't leave without waking her up, but he couldn't bear to disturb her. He eased down at the end of the couch and decided to just wait until she woke up.

He enjoyed watching Sabine sleep. She had always been one to work hard and play hard, so when she slept, it was a deep sleep and it came on quickly. There were many nights where he had lain in bed and just studied her face. Gavin had memorized every line and curve. He'd counted her eyelashes. There was just something about her that had fascinated him from the first moment he saw her.

The weeks they'd spent together were intense. He couldn't get enough of her. Sabine was a breath of fresh air to a man hanging from the gallows. She'd brought him back to life with her rebellious streak and quest for excitement. He'd loved everything about her, from her dazzling smile to her ever-changing rainbow-streaked hair. He'd loved how there was always a speck of paint somewhere on her body, even if he had to do a detailed search to find it. She was so different from every other woman he'd ever known.

For the first time, he'd allowed himself to start opening up to someone. He'd begun making plans for Sabine to be a permanent fixture in his life. He hadn't antici-

pated her bolting, and when she did, he shut down. Gavin
hadn't allowed himself to realize just how much he'd
missed her until this moment.

She didn't trust him. Not with her son and not with
her heart. Gavin hadn't appreciated it when he had it—
at least not outwardly. He never told her how he felt or
shared his plans for their future. That was his own fault,
and they missed their chance at love. But even with
that lost, he wanted her back in his bed. He ached to
run his fingers through her hair. Tonight, it was pulled
up on top of her head, the silky black and bright purple
strands jumbled together. He wanted to touch it and see
it sprawled across the pillowcase.

His eyes traveled down her body to the thin shirt and
shorts she was wearing. He didn't think it was possible,
but she was more beautiful now than she had been back
then. She wouldn't believe him if he told her that, but it
was true. Motherhood had filled out some of the curves
she'd lacked as a struggling artist. He remembered her
getting so engrossed in her work that sometimes she
would simply forget to eat. Gavin would come to the
apartment with takeout and force her to take a break.

Now she had nicely rounded hips that called to him
to reach out and glide his palms over them. He wanted
to curl up behind her and press her soft body into his.
He wanted to feel her lean, yoga-toned muscles flexing
against him. The sight of her in that skimpy workout
outfit had haunted him since that first night.

Her newly developed muscles didn't make up for the
mental strain, however. Even in her sleep, a fine line ran
between her eyebrows. She made a certain face when
she was frustrated or confused, and that line was the
result. There were faint circles under her eyes. She was

worn out. He was determined to make things easier for her. No matter how their relationship ended or his feelings where she was concerned, she deserved the help he could provide.

She just had to let him.

"Gavin," Sabine whispered.

He looked up, expecting to see her eyes open, but she was talking in her sleep. Calling his name in her sleep. He held his breath, waiting to see if she spoke again.

"Please," she groaned, squirming slightly on the sofa. "Yes. I need you."

Gavin nearly choked on his own saliva. She wasn't just dreaming about him. She was having an erotic dream about him. The mere thought made his jeans uncomfortably tight.

"Touch me."

Gavin couldn't resist. He reached out and placed his hand on the firm curve of her calf. He loved the feel of her soft skin against him. It made his palm tingle and his blood hum in his veins. Just a simple touch. No other woman had had this effect on him. Whatever it was that drew them together was still here, and as strong as ever.

"Gavin?"

He looked up to see Sabine squinting at him in confusion. She was awake now. And probably wondering why the hell he was fondling her leg. He expected her to shy away from his touch, but she didn't. Instead, she sat up. She looked deep into his eyes for a moment, the fire of her passionate dream still lighting her gaze.

She reached up, cradling his face in her hands and tugging his mouth down to hers. He wasn't about to deny her. The moment their lips met, he felt the familiar surge of need wash over him. Before when they'd kissed, he had resisted the pull, but he couldn't do it any longer. He wanted her and she wanted him. They could deal with the consequences of it later.

Her mouth was hungry, demanding more of him, and he gave it. His tongue thrust inside her, matching her intensity and eliciting a groan deep in her throat. Her fingers drifted into his hair, desperately tugging him closer.

Gavin wrapped his arms around her waist and drew her up onto her knees. He explored every new curve of her body just as he'd fantasized, dipping low to cup the roundness of her backside. The firm press of her flesh against his fingertips was better than he ever could have imagined. He didn't think it was possible, but he grew even harder as he touched her.

Sabine's hands roamed as well, sliding down his chest, studying the ridges of his abs and then reaching around his back. She grasped the hem of his shirt and tugged until their lips parted and it came up and over his head. She did the same with her own shirt, throwing it to the floor and revealing full breasts with no bra to obscure them.

Before he could reach out to touch them, Sabine leaned back, cupping his neck with one hand and pulling him with her until she was lying on the couch and he was covering her body with his. Every soft inch of her molded to him. Her breasts crushed against his bare chest, the hard peaks of her nipples pressing insistently into his skin.

Gavin kissed her again and then let his lips roam along her jaw and down her throat. He teased at her sensitive skin, nipping gently with his teeth and soothing it with his tongue. He brought one palm to her breast, teasing the aching tip with slow circles and then massaging it with firm fingers. Sabine gasped aloud, her hips rising to meet his.

"I want you so badly," Gavin whispered against her collarbone.

Sabine didn't reply, but her hand eased between their bodies to unzip his jeans. She brought one finger up to her lips to gesture for him to be quiet, then her hand slipped under the waistband of his briefs. He fought for silence as her fingers wrapped around the length of him and stroked gently. He buried a moan against her breast, trying not to lose his grip of control. She knew just how to push him, just how to touch him to make him unravel.

He brushed her hand away and eased between her legs. He thrust his hips forward, creating a delicious friction as he rubbed against her through the thin cotton of her shorts.

"Ohh…" she whispered, her eyes closing.

She was so beautiful. He couldn't wait to watch her come undone. To bury himself deep inside her again after all this time.

"Please," he groaned, "tell me that you have something we can use." Gavin got up this morning thinking he was taking his son to the circus. He wasn't a teenager walking around with a condom in his pocket all the time. He hadn't come prepared for this.

Her eyes fluttered open, their green depths dark with desire. "I had an IUD put in after Jared was born," she said.

"Is that enough?" he asked.

At that, Sabine laughed. "It's supposed to be 99.8 percent effective, but with your super sperm, who knows? The condom didn't work so well for us the last time."

"Super sperm," Gavin snorted before dipping down

and kissing her again. "Do you want me to stop?" he asked. He would if she wanted him to, as much as that would kill him. But she needed to decide now.

"Don't you dare," she said, piercing him with her gaze.

With a growl, he buried his face in her neck. His hand grasped at the waist of her shorts, tugging them and her panties down over her hips. She arched up to help him and then kicked them off to the floor.

Sabine pushed at his jeans without success until Gavin finally eased back to take them off. She watched him with careful study as he kicked off his shoes and slipped out of the last of his clothes.

He looked down at her, nude and wanting, and his chest swelled with pride. She was sexy and free and waiting for him. As he watched, she reached up and untied her hair. The long strands fell down over her shoulders, the ends teasing at the tips of her breasts.

He couldn't wait any longer. Gavin returned to the couch, easing between her thighs. He sought her out first with his hand. Stroking gently, his fingertips slid easily over her sensitive flesh, causing her to whimper with need.

"Gavin," she pleaded, her voice little more than a breath.

His hand continued to move over her until she was panting and squirming beneath him. Then he slipped one finger inside. Sabine threw her head back, a cry strangling to silence in her throat. She was ready for him.

Gavin propped onto one elbow and gripped her hip with his other hand. Surging forward, he pressed into the slick heat of her welcoming body. He lost himself in the pleasure for a moment, absorbing every delicious sensation before flexing his hips and driving into her again.

Sabine clung to him, burying her face in his shoulder to muffle her gasps and cries. She met his every advance, whispering words of encouragement into his ear. The intensity built, moment by moment, until he knew she was close.

Her eyes squeezed shut, her mouth falling open in silent gasps. He put every ounce of energy he had left into pushing her over the edge. He was rewarded with the soft shudder of her body against him, the muscles deep inside clenching around him. The string of tension in his belly drew tighter and tighter until it snapped. He thrust hard, exploding into her with a low growl of satisfaction.

They both collapsed against the couch cushions in a panting, gasping heap. No sooner had they recovered than Gavin heard Jared crying in the other room.

Sabine pressed against his chest until he backed off. She quickly tugged on her clothes and disappeared into the bedroom.

Things were officially more complicated.

Six

Jared went back down fairly quickly. Sabine changed his Pull-Ups, put him in his pajamas and he fell asleep in minutes. Even then, she stayed in her bedroom longer than necessary. Going back into the living room meant facing what she'd just done. She wasn't quite ready for that yet.

Damn that stupid, erotic dream. When she fell asleep on the couch, she never expected to sleep that long. Or that she would have a sexual fantasy about Gavin while he was sitting there watching her. When she opened her eyes and he was touching her with the spark of passion in his eyes, she had to have him. She needed him.

And now it was done. She'd refused his proposal of marriage because he didn't love her, yet she'd just slept with him. She was throwing mixed signals left, right and center.

But she had to go back out there eventually. Steeling

her resolve, she exited the bedroom and pulled the door shut behind her. She made a quick stop in the restroom first, cleaning up and smoothing her hair back into a ponytail. When she returned to the living room, Gavin was fully dressed and sitting on the couch.

"Everything okay?" he asked.

"Yeah," she said. "He's back to sleep now. He probably won't wake up again until the morning." She nervously ran her hands over her shorts, not sure what to do with herself. "Did you guys have fun today?"

"We did. He's a very well-behaved kid. Gave me almost no trouble. Almost," he said with a smile.

Sabine was glad. She'd worried so much about them that she couldn't paint. At least at first. She'd tried, but it had been so long since she'd painted that she didn't know where to start. Instead, she'd taken a long, leisurely shower and indulged in extended grooming rituals she usually had to rush, like plucking her eyebrows and painting her toenails. One of her favorite chick flicks was on TV, so she sat down to watch it, and the next thing she knew, she was nodding off. She'd only expected to sleep for a half hour or so.

"I'm glad it went well." She eyed the spot on the couch where she'd just been and decided she wasn't quite ready to sit there yet. "Would you like some wine? I'm going to pour myself a glass."

"Sure," he said with a soft smile.

Sabine could tell this was awkward for him, too. And yet, he could've turned her down and left. But he didn't. She disappeared into the kitchen and returned a few minutes later with two glasses of merlot. "It came out of a box, but I like it," she said.

Gavin smiled in earnest, taking a large sip, then another. "It's pretty good," he admitted with surprise.

She sat down beside him and took her own sip. The wine seemed to flow directly into her veins, relaxing her immediately.

He pointed over at the blank canvas. "I'm surprised you didn't paint at all today."

Sabine looked at the white expanse that had been her nemesis for a good part of the afternoon. She couldn't count how many times she'd put her pencil to the canvas to sketch the bones of a scene and then stopped. "I think I've forgotten how to paint."

"That's not possible," Gavin argued. "You just need the right inspiration. I put you on the spot today. I bet if you relax and let the creative juices flow without the pressure of time, the ideas will come again."

"I hope so."

"You're too gifted to set your dream aside. Even for Jared. We can work together to get you back to what you love. I mean, after we get the results and I have visitation rights, you'll have more free time to yourself."

That was the wrong thing to say. She had been nervous enough about tomorrow and the lab results that were coming in. Knowing he was already planning to "exercise his rights" and take Jared for long stretches of time just made her chest tight with anxiety. It was a sharp reminder that even after they'd had sex, he was really here for Jared, not her. He hadn't mentioned anything about *all* of them spending time together. Or just the two of them. Any fantasies she had about there being any sort of family unit cobbled out of this mess were just that.

"And what about you?" she said, her tone a bit sharper than she'd planned. "You seem as wrapped up in the business as ever. We couldn't get you off your phone yesterday. I'm thinking you don't have much time to get in the cockpit anymore."

"It's been a while," he admitted. "But I'm working on it. All those calls I was taking at the zoo," he said, "were about a big deal I'm trying to pull together. Things were unraveling and I couldn't let it happen."

Sabine listened as he described his plans for BXS and Exclusivity Jetliners. It really did seem like a brilliant plan. There were plenty of wealthy and important people who would pay a premium for that kind of service. That didn't mean she appreciated it interloping on their day out together, but she could see it was important to him and not just day-to-day management crap.

"I'm hoping to fly one, too."

Her brows went up in surprise. "Did you get demoted from CEO to pilot?"

"I wish," he groaned. "But I've always wanted a Gulfstream model jet. The ones we're acquiring could go over four thousand miles on one tank of gas. That could get me to Paris. I've always dreamed of flying across the Atlantic. But even if I can't manage that, I can take one out from time to time. Even if it's just to do a delivery. I don't care. I just want to get out from behind the desk and get up there. It's the only place I can ever find any peace."

She understood that. Yoga did a lot to help center her mind and spirit, but nothing came close to losing herself in her art.

"I want more time out of the office, and Jared finally gives me a real reason to do it. There's no point in work-life balance when you've got no life. But spending time with Jared needs to be a priority for me. I've already missed so much."

Sabine was impressed by his heartfelt words. Gavin had quickly become enamored with Jared, and she was glad. Part of her had always worried that he might reject his son. The other part worried that he'd claim him with such force that he'd rip her child from her arms. This seemed a healthy medium. Maybe this wouldn't be so bad. He was trying.

"I found a great apartment in Greenwich Village overlooking Washington Square Park," he said. "It has three bedrooms and it's close to the subway."

Sabine took a large sip of her wine. Here we go, she thought. "I thought you liked your apartment," she said, playing dumb. "Getting tired of living at the Ritz-Carlton?"

Gavin frowned. "What? No. Not for me. For you. I'd prefer you to be closer to me, but I know you'd rather live downtown. You work in SoHo, right? You could easily walk to work from this apartment."

Walking to work. She wouldn't even allow herself to fantasize about a life without a long train commute each day. Or three bedrooms where she didn't have to share with Jared. "I'm pretty sure it's out of my budget."

Gavin set his wine down on the coffee table. "I told you I wanted to help. Let me buy you an apartment."

"And I told you I wanted to take this slowly. I probably couldn't even afford the maintenance fee, much less the taxes or the mortgage itself. Homeowner's insurance. The utilities on a place that large would be through the roof."

He turned in his seat to face her, his serious businessman expression studying her. "How much is your rent here?"

"Gavin, I—"

He interrupted her with a number that was fewer than fifty dollars off the mark.

"Yes, pretty much," she admitted, reluctantly.

"Tack on a couple hundred for utilities and such. So what if I bought an apartment and rented it to you for the same amount you're paying now? That would be fair, right? You wouldn't have to worry about all the fees associated with owning the place."

She did have to admit that she preferred this idea. If she had to pay rent, she would continue working. She liked her job and wanted to keep doing it. But a three-bedroom apartment in the Village for the price of what she paid for a tiny place beyond the reach of the subway lines? That was insanity.

"That's a ridiculous suggestion. My rent is less than a tenth of what the mortgage on that kind of apartment would be."

Gavin shrugged. "I'm not concerned. You could live there rent-free for all I care. I just thought you would feel more comfortable if you contributed."

"There's a difference between helping us out and buying us a multimillion-dollar apartment."

"I want you close," he said. His dark eyes penetrated hers with an intensity that made her squirm slightly with a flush rising to her pale cheeks. Did he really mean *her*?

Sabine opened her mouth to argue, but he held up his hand to silence her protest. "I mean," he corrected, "living in Manhattan will make it easier to handle the custody arrangements and trade-offs. When he starts at his new school, he would be closer. It would be safer. More convenient for everyone."

Just as she thought. He wanted Jared close, not her. At least not for any reason more than the occasional booty call. "Especially for you," she snapped, irritably.

"And you!" he added. "If I got things my way, the two of you would just move in with me. That's certainly the cheapest option, since you seem so concerned about how much I spend, but I thought you would like having your own space better."

She must seem like the most ungrateful person on the planet, but she knew what this was. A slippery slope. He would push, push, push until he had things just the way he wanted them. If he wanted them—or Jared, she should say—living with him, eventually he would. This apartment in the Village would just be a pit stop to make it look as if he was being reasonable.

"I know it's a pain for you to drive all the way out here every time you want to see Jared. And I know that you and I just..." Her voice trailed off.

"Had sex?" he offered.

"Yes," she said with a heavy sigh. "But that doesn't change anything between us or about the things we've already discussed. We're not moving at all. Not in with you and not into that apartment. It sounds nice, but it's too soon. When we're ready, perhaps we could look together. I'd like some say in the decision, even if you're writing the checks. I'm pretty sure the place I pick will be significantly cheaper."

"I'm not concerned with the cost of keeping my child happy and safe."

A painful twinge nagged at Sabine right beneath her sternum. She should be happy the father of her child was willing to lay out millions for the health and welfare of their child. But a part of her was jealous. He was always so quick to point out that this was about their son. Each time he mentioned it, it was like he was poking the gaping wound of her heart with a sharp stick. She would benefit from the arrangement, but none of this was about her. The sex didn't change anything, just like it didn't change anything three years ago. He was attracted to her, but she was not his priority and never was.

"Thank you," she choked out. "I appreciate that you're so willing to create a stable, safe home for our son. Let's give it a week to sink in, all right? We've got a lot of hurdles to jump before we add real estate to the mix."

Gavin eyed her for a moment before silently nodding. Sabine knew this was anything but a victory. She was only pushing off the inevitable. He would get his way eventually.

He always did.

When Gavin arrived at Dr. Peterson's office at 10:00 a.m. Monday morning, Sabine was already there. She was lost in a fashion magazine and didn't notice him come in. "Morning," he said.

Sabine looked up and gave him a watery smile. "Hey." She looked a little out of sorts. Maybe she was nervous. Things would change after this and she probably knew it.

"Where's Jared?" he asked.

The smile faded. She slung the magazine she'd been reading onto the seat beside her. "At school, where he belongs. I'm sorry to disappoint, but you're stuck with me today."

He'd screwed up last night, he could tell. Not in seducing her—that would never be a bad idea—but in forc-

ing the idea of the apartment on her. Anyone else would
jump at the offer, but to her, it was him imposing on her.
Demanding they be closer so he could see his son more
easily. Not once mentioning that he'd like *her* closer as
well because that opened the door to dangerous territory.

Sabine was skittish. She scared off easily last time. He
wasn't about to tell her that he wanted to see her more
because he was still fighting himself over the idea of it.
He was usually pretty good at keeping his distance from
people, but he'd already let Sabine in once. Keeping her
out the second time was harder than he expected. Especially when he didn't want to. He wanted her in his
bed. Across from him at a nice restaurant. Certainly he
could have that and not completely lose himself to her.

"That's scarcely a hardship," he said, seating himself
in the empty chair beside her. "I find your company to
be incredibly...*stimulating*."

Sabine crossed her arms over her chest and smothered
a snort of disbelief. "Well, you'll be stimulating yourself
from now on. Last night was —"

"Awesome?" he interjected. Their physical connection could never be anything less.

"A mistake."

"Sometimes a mistake can be a happy accident. Like
Jared, a happy accident."

Her moss-green eyes narrowed at him. "And sometimes it's just a mistake. Like sleeping with your ex when
you're in the middle of a custody negotiation."

Gavin nodded and leaned into her, crossing his own
arms. She really thought last night was a mistake? He
hadn't picked up on it at the time. She was probably
just worried it would give him the upper hand somehow. Knowing just how to touch a woman was always

an advantage, but he didn't intend to use that knowledge against her. At least outside the bedroom.

"So I suppose you've got no business going to dinner with me tonight, either."

Her gaze ran over his face, trying to read into his motives. "Listen, Gavin," she started with a shake of her head. "I know I told you that I wanted you to put in quality time with Jared, but that doesn't mean you have to come see him *every* day. I know you've got a company to run and a life in progress before all this came out. I only meant that you had to keep your promises and make an effort."

She thought this was about Jared. Apparently he had not made it abundantly clear how badly he wanted her last night. Their tryst on the couch was nice, but it was just an appetizer to take the edge off three years apart. He wouldn't allow himself to fall for Sabine, but he wasn't going to deny himself the pleasure of making love to her. "Who said anything about Jared? I was thinking about you and me. Someplace dark and quiet with no kid's menu."

"That sounds lovely," she said, "but Jared isn't a puppy. We can't just crate him while we go out."

"I can arrange for someone to watch him."

A flicker of conflict danced across her face. She wanted to go. He could tell. She was just very protective and worried about leaving their son with a stranger. Hell, she hadn't even wanted to leave Jared with *him*.

"Someone? You don't even know who?"

"Of course I do. I was actually considering my secretary, Marie. She's got a new grandson of her own that she fawns over, but he lives in Vermont, so she doesn't see him nearly as much as she wants to. I asked her this morning if she was willing to watch Jared tonight. She'll even come out to your apartment so you don't have to pack up any of his things and he can sleep in his own bed when the time comes."

Sabine pursed her lips in thought and flipped her ponytail over her shoulder. "So you were so confident that I would go to dinner with you that you arranged a babysitter before you even bothered to ask if I wanted to go."

Her dream last night had tipped her hand. "Your subconscious doesn't lie."

Her cheeks flushed red against her pale complexion. She turned away from him and focused her attention on the television mounted on the opposite wall of the waiting room. "What if I have plans?"

"Do you have plans?" he asked.

"No," she admitted without facing him. "But that's not the point. You assume too much. You assume that just because we have a child together and we went too far last night that I want—"

"Brooks!" The nurse opened the side door and called out their name to come back.

Sabine's concerned expression faded, the lines disappearing between her brows. She seemed relieved to avoid this conversation. He wasn't going to let her off that easily.

"To be continued," Gavin said, looking her square in the eye. She met his gaze and nodded softly.

He climbed to his feet and offered his hand to help Sabine up. They made their way back to Dr. Peterson's personal office and sat in the two guest chairs across from his desk. It didn't take long before his physician strolled in with a file in his hands.

Dr. Peterson eased into his seat and flipped open the

paperwork. His gaze ran over it for a moment before he nodded. In that brief flash of time, Gavin had his first flicker of doubt. Jared looked just like him. There was no real reason to believe he wasn't his son, but Sabine had seemed nervous in the lobby. He didn't know anything for certain until the doctor told him the results. He hadn't even wanted a son a week ago, and now he would be devastated to know Jared wasn't his.

"Well," the doctor began, "I've got good news for you, Mr. Brooks. It appears as though you're a father. Congratulations," he said, reaching across the desk to shake his hand.

"Thank you," Gavin replied with relief washing over him.

Dr. Peterson pulled out two manila envelopes and handed one to each of them. "Here's a copy of the DNA report for each of you to give your lawyers."

This apparently was not the doctor's first paternity test rodeo. "Thank you," he said, slipping the envelope into his lapel pocket.

"Let me know if you have any questions. Good luck to you both." Dr. Peterson stood, ushering them out the door.

They were back in the lobby of the building before they spoke again. Gavin turned to her as she was putting the envelope into her purse. "Now about that dinner. You never answered me."

Sabine looked up at him. She didn't have the relieved expression he was expecting. She seemed even more concerned than she had going in. "Not tonight, Gavin. I'm not much in the mood for that."

"What's the matter?" he asked. Some women would be leaping with joy to have scientific evidence that their child was the heir to a multibillion-dollar empire. Sabine was a notable exception. "This was your idea," he reminded her.

She sighed. "I know. And I knew what the results would be, but I wasn't prepared for the finality of it. It's done. Now the wheels start turning and the child that has been one hundred percent mine for the past two years will start slipping from my arms. It's selfish of me, I know, and I apologize, but that doesn't make me leap for joy."

Gavin turned to face her, placing his hands reassuringly on her shoulders. It gave her no real choice but to look at him. "Sabine, what can I possibly say to convince you that this isn't a bad thing?"

Her pale green eyes grew glassy with tears she was too stubborn to shed in front of him. "There's nothing you can say, Gavin. Actions speak louder than words."

Fair enough. "How about this," he offered. "I'll get Edmund to start the paperwork and put together a custody proposal for you to look over. When you're happy with it, we'll share a nice dinner, just the two of us, to celebrate that the sky didn't fall and things will be fine."

Her gaze dropped to his collar and she nodded so slightly, he could barely tell she'd agreed. "Okay," she whispered.

"Clear your schedule for Friday night," he said with confidence. "I have a feeling we're going to be sharing a lovely candlelit dinner together before the weekend arrives."

Sabine curled up on the couch and watched Gavin and Jared play on the living room floor. They were stacking Duplo blocks. Gavin was trying to build a plane, but

Jared was determined to make a truck and kept stealing pieces off the clunky blue-and-red jet. It was amazing to see them together, the father and his tiny toddler clone.

It made her smile, even when she wasn't sure she should be smiling.

Gavin had done his best to reassure her that things would be fine. His lawyer had presented a very reasonable custody agreement. Her relief at reading the briefing was palpable. They were both giving a little and taking a little, which surprised her. Gavin got Jared on alternate weekends, rotating holidays and two weeks in the summer, but he would continue to reside primarily with Sabine. Her concession was to agree to move to Manhattan to make the arrangement easier on everyone.

They'd built in flexibility in the agreement to accommodate special requests, like birthdays. Unless Gavin pushed her, she intended to let him see Jared as often as he liked. How could she turn away a scene like the one playing out on her floor?

Tonight, they were telling Jared that Gavin was his father. It was a big moment for them. The DNA test had made it certain, but telling Jared made it real.

"Hey, big guy?" Gavin said.

Jared dropped a block and looked up. "Yep?"

"Do you know what a daddy is?"

Sabine leaned forward in her seat, resting her elbows on her knees. She agreed to let Gavin be the one to tell him, but she wasn't certain how much Jared would understand. He was still so young.

"Yeah," he said cheerfully, before launching into another of his long-winded and unintelligible speeches. Jared was a quiet child, slow to speak, although it seemed more that he didn't have a lot he wanted to say.

Only in the past few months had he started rattling on in his own toddler-speak. From what pieces she could pick out, he was talking about his friend at school whose daddy picked him up every day. Then he pointed at Sabine. "Mommy."

"Right." Gavin smiled. "And I am *your* daddy."

Jared cocked his head to the side and wrinkled his nose. He turned to Sabine for confirmation. "Daddy?"

She let out the breath she'd been holding to nod. "Yeah, buddy. He's your daddy."

A peculiar grin crossed Jared's face. It was the same expression he made when she "stole" his nose and he wasn't quite sure he believed her. "Daddy?" He pointed at Gavin.

Gavin nodded, having only a moment to brace himself before his son launched into his arms.

"Daddy!" he proclaimed.

Sabine watched Gavin hold his son as fiercely as if someone were going to snatch him away. She understood how he felt. And then she saw the glassy tears in the eyes of her powerful CEO, and her chest tightened with the rush of confusing emotions. It hadn't taken long, but Gavin was completely in love with his son.

She couldn't help but feel a pang of jealousy.

Seven

"**D**amn you for always being right."

Gavin stood on Sabine's doorstep holding a bouquet of purple dahlias. She had opened the door and greeted him that way, stealing his "hello" from his lips. Fortunately she was smiling, so he did the same.

He held out the bundle of flowers with the nearly black centers that faded to bright purple tips. "These are for you. They reminded me of your hair."

Sabine brought the flowers up to her nose and delicately inhaled their scent. "They're beautiful, thank you."

"So are you," he added. And he meant it. She looked lovely tonight. She was wearing a fitted white dress with brightly colored flowers that looked like one of her watercolor paintings. It was sleeveless and clung to every curve of her body.

She smiled, wrinkling her nose with a touch of embarrassment. The movement caught the light on the tiny pink rhinestone in her nose. It was the same bright color as her lipstick and the chunky bracelet on her wrist. "Let me put these in some water and we can go."

Gavin nodded and stepped across the threshold into the apartment. It was Friday night and as predicted, they were having dinner. Everything had gone smoothly. The paperwork had been filed in family court to add Gavin's name to the birth certificate. Along with the addition, Jared's last name would be updated to Brooks. He'd suggested making Jared's middle name Hayes, but she said the name Thomas was more important to her. He'd thought Sabine would pitch a fit on the subject of Jared's name, but it hadn't concerned her.

The custody proposal Edmund put together was approved by both of them on the first draft. He hoped that he would see Jared more than required, but this established a minimum they were both comfortable with.

He noticed Marie's coat hanging by the door when he came in, so he knew she was already there to watch Jared. Gavin looked around the apartment, but he didn't see Marie or Jared anywhere. "Where is everyone?"

Then he heard giggles and splashing from the bathroom. He smiled, knowing Marie was probably soaked. After they'd told Jared that Gavin was his daddy, he'd insisted *Daddy* give him his bath that night. Gavin had gotten more water on him than the toddler in the tub, he was pretty certain.

Aside from that, the night had gone pretty smoothly. Apparently toddlers didn't angst about things the way grown-ups did. Gavin was his daddy—*great*. Let's go play.

"Marie is giving Jared a bath, although I think they're

probably having more fun with the bathtub paints than actually washing."

Gavin wanted to peek in and say hello before they left, but he resisted. He'd gotten Sabine to agree to this dinner and the babysitter he provided. Right now, Jared was happy. If they went in to say goodbye, the giggles might disintegrate into tears. "Are you ready?"

She nodded, the luxurious black waves of her hair gracefully swaying along her jawline. "I already told Marie goodbye a few minutes ago so we could slip out. She seems to have everything under control."

Since it was just the two of them tonight, he'd opted for the Aston Martin. He held the door for her, noting the elegant curve of her ankles in tall pink pumps as she slipped inside. Gavin had no clue how women walked in shoes like that, but he was extremely thankful they did.

They had seven-thirty reservations at one of the most sought-out, high-end restaurants in Manhattan. He'd made the reservation on Monday, feeling confident they would come to an agreement in time, but even then, it had taken some persuading to get a table. Most people booked a table several months in advance, but they knew better than to tell a Brooks no. He tended to get in wherever he wanted to, and he made it worth the maître d's efforts.

They checked in and were immediately taken to an intimate booth for two. The restaurant was the brainchild of a young, up-and-coming chef who snagged a James Beard award at the unheard-of age of twenty-two. The decor was decidedly modern with lots of glass, concrete and colored lights that glowed behind geometric wall panels.

Their table was like a cocoon wrapping around them

and shielding them from the world. A green glass container on the table had a flickering candle inside, giving a moody light to their space. It was just enough to read their menus, but not enough to draw attention to who was inside the booth. It made the restaurant popular with the young celebrity set who wanted to go out but maintain their privacy.

"Have you ever been here?" Gavin asked.

Sabine took in all the sights with wide eyes. "No, but I've heard of it. My boss said her husband took her here for her birthday."

"Did she like it?"

"She said the food was good. The decor was a little modern for her taste, which is funny considering her clothing design has a contemporary edge to it that would fit right in."

"I've been here once," Gavin said. "It's fine cuisine, but it's not stuffy. I thought you'd like that."

Sabine smiled and looked down. "Yes, there aren't fifteen pieces of silverware, so that's a relief."

Gavin smiled and looked over the menu. He'd learned his lesson the first time they dated. His attempts to impress her with nice restaurants had only intimidated her and pointed out the wide gap of their social standings. She wasn't like other women he'd dated. A lot of women in Manhattan expected to be wined and dined in the finest restaurants in town. Sabine was just as happy with Thai takeout eaten on the terrace of his apartment, if not more so.

This place was his attempt at a compromise and so far, it seemed to be a good choice. There wasn't a fixed tasting menu like so many other restaurants. Foie gras and caviar wasn't her style, and she wouldn't let him pay two hundred dollars a head for a meal she wouldn't eat.

Here, diners got to mix and match their choice of Asian fusion dishes for the six courses.

The waiter brought their drinks, presenting him with a premium sake and Sabine with a light green pear martini that was nearly the color of her eyes. They ordered and the server disappeared to bring their first course selection.

"I'm glad we got everything worked out with Edmund. I've been looking forward to this night all week." He met her eyes across the table and let a knowing smile curl his lips. Gavin expected tonight to go well and for Sabine to end up back in his bed. He'd fantasized about her naked body lying across his sheets as he lay in bed each night.

Holding up his drink for a toast, he waited for Sabine to do the same. "To surviving the terrible twos," he said with a grin, "and everything else the future may hold."

Sabine tipped her glass against his and took a healthy sip. "Thank you for handling all of this so gingerly. You don't know how much I've worried."

"What are we drinking to?" A nasal voice cut into their conversation.

They both turned to find a blonde woman standing beside their table. *Ugh.* It was Viola Collins. The Manhattan society busybody was one of the last people he wanted to see tonight. She had a big mouth, an overabundance of opinions and a blatant desire for Gavin that he'd dodged for years.

"Viola," he said, ignoring her question and wishing he could ignore her, as well. "How are you?"

She smiled and showed off her perfect set of straightened, whitened teeth that looked a touch odd against her too-tan skin. "I'm just great." Her laser focus shifted toward Sabine, taking in and categorizing every detail with visible distaste. "And who do we have here?"

Gavin watched his date with concern. He wasn't certain how Sabine would react to someone like Viola. Some people might shrink away under Viola's obvious appraisal, but she didn't. Sabine sat up straighter in her seat and met Viola's gaze with her own confident one.

"Viola Collins, this is my date, Sabine Hayes."

The women briefly shook hands, but he could tell there was no friendliness behind it. Women were funny that way, sizing one another up under the cool guise of politeness.

"Would I have met you before?" Viola asked.

"I sincerely doubt it," Sabine replied.

Gavin couldn't remember if they had or not. "You may have. Sabine and I dated a few years back."

"Hmm…" Viola said. Her nose turned up slightly, although Gavin thought that might be more the result of her latest round of plastic surgery. "I think I would've remembered *this*. That's interesting that you two are dating again. I would've thought the novelty would've worn off the first time."

"Oh, no," Sabine said, a sharp edge to her voice. "I'm very bendy."

Viola's eyes widened, her tight mouth twisting at Sabine's bold words. "Are you?" She turned to Gavin. "Well, I'll have to tell Rosemary Goodwin that you're off the market. *For now,*" she added. "I think she's still waiting for you to call her again after your last hot date. I'll just tell her to be patient."

"You'll have to excuse me." Sabine reached for her purse and slipped out of the booth, deliberately sweeping the green martini off the table. The concoction splattered across Viola's cream silk dress. "How clumsy of me!"

she said. Ignoring the sputtering woman, Sabine bent down to pick up the glass and set it back on the table. "That's better." At that, she turned and bolted from the restaurant.

Viola gawked at Sabine as she disappeared, sputtering in outrage. The silk dress was ruined. No question of it.

Gavin didn't care. Viola could use a fist to the face, but no one wanted to pick up her plastic surgery tab to repair the damage. He got up, throwing cash onto the table for the bill and pressing more into Viola's hand for a new dress. "That wasn't your color anyway."

He jogged through the restaurant, pushing through the crowd waiting to be seated, and bursting out onto the street. He spied Sabine about a block away, charging furiously down the pavement despite the handicap of her heels.

"Sabine!" he yelled. "Wait."

She didn't even turn around. He had to run to catch up with her, pulling alongside and matching her stride.

"I should've known," she said, without acknowledging him. "You know there was a reason I ended this the last time. One of the reasons was that everyone in your world is a snob."

"Not everyone," he insisted. He wrapped his fingers around her delicate wrist to keep her from running off again and pulled her to a stop. "Just ignore Viola. She doesn't matter to anyone but herself."

She shook her head, the waves of her hair falling into her face as she looked down at the sidewalk. "It's the same as last time, Gavin. People in your world are never going to see me as anything other than an interloper. Like you're slumming for your own amusement. I don't fit in and I never will."

"I know," he said. "That's one of the many things that make you great."

Her light green eyes met his for a moment, a glimmer of something—hope, maybe—quickly fading away. "Stop fooling yourself, Gavin. You belong with someone like Viola or this Rosemary woman that's waiting on you to call again. We're all wrong for each other. You're only here with me now because of Jared."

"Let me assure you that if I wanted a woman like Viola I could have one. I could have *her,* if I wanted to. She's made that very clear over the years, but I'm not interested. I don't want her." He took a step closer, pulling Sabine against him. "I want you. Just as you are."

"You say that now, but you wouldn't answer her question," she said, resisting his pull on her.

"Answer what question?"

"She asked what we were drinking to. You don't want anyone to know about Jared, do you? Are you ashamed of him? Or of both of us?"

"Absolutely not!" he said as emphatically as he could. "I will gladly shout the news about my son from the rooftops. But I haven't told my family yet. If Viola found out, it would be all over town. I don't want them to hear it from her."

Gavin slipped his arms around her waist, enjoying the feel of her against him, even under these circumstances. "I'd like to tell them tomorrow afternoon. Would you be able to bring Jared to meet them? Maybe around dinnertime? That would give them some time to adjust to the idea before you show up."

"Why don't you just come get him?" she said. Her bravado from her interaction with Viola had crumbled. Now she just looked worn down.

"Because I want them to spend time with you, too,"

Gavin added. "I know you've met them before, but that was years ago. This is different."

"And say what, Gavin? 'Hey, everyone, you remember Sabine? Since you saw her last, she's had my son and lied to all of us for over two years. We've got that worked out now. Don't mind the nose ring.'"

"Pretty much," he said with a smile. "How did you guess?"

Sabine's gaze shot up to his. Red flushed her cheeks and she punched him in the shoulder. She hit him as furiously as she could and he barely felt it. He laughed at her assault, which only made it worse. She was like an angry kitten, hissing and clawing, but not dangerous enough to even break the skin. "I'm serious, Gavin!"

"I'm serious, too." He meant every word of it. Gavin had gone into this thinking that he could indulge in Sabine's body and keep his heart thoroughly out of the equation. She had no idea how badly she'd hurt him when she left, and he didn't want her to know. But he'd opened the door to her once. No matter how hard he fought, it was too easy to open up to her again. It wasn't love, but it was something more than his usual indifference.

Perhaps this time would be different. Even if they weren't together, they would always be connected through Jared. They would be constants in an ever-changing life and he welcomed it, even if he didn't know what they would do with it.

He slipped his finger under her chin and tipped her face up to him. "Serious about this."

Gavin's lips met hers before she could start arguing with him again. The moment he kissed her, she was lost. She melted into him, channeling her emotions into the kiss. Sabine let all of her anger, her frustration, her fear flow through her mouth and her fingertips. She buried her fingers through his dark hair, tugging his neck closer.

He responded in kind, his mouth punishing her with his kiss. His hands molded to her body, his fingers pressed hard into her flesh. The rough touch was a pleasure with a razor's edge. She craved his intensity. The physical connection made everything else fade away. At least for tonight. Tomorrow was...tomorrow.

"Take me to your place," she said.

Gavin reluctantly pulled away. "I'll have the valet bring the car."

Within a few minutes, they were strolling into the Ritz-Carlton Tower. They took the elevator up to Gavin's apartment. It had been a long time since she'd been here. She'd walked alone down this very hallway after she broke up with him. Pregnant and unaware of that fact. It felt strange to traverse the same carpeting after all these years.

Inside the apartment, little had changed. The same elegant, expensive and uncomfortable furniture that was better suited for a decorating magazine than to actually being used. The same stunning view of Central Park sprawled out of the arched floor-to-ceiling windows. There was a newer, larger, flatter television mounted to one wall, but that was about it.

"You've done a lot with the place since I saw it last," she said drily.

"There's new additions," he insisted. He pointed to a corner in the dining room where there was a stack of children's toys, new in the packages, and the car seat from the Mercedes. "I'm also doing some renovations to one of the bedrooms."

Gavin led her down the hallway to the rooms that had once functioned as a guest room and his office. Inside the old guest room, a tarp was draped over the hardwood floors. Several cans of paint were sitting in the middle of the floor, unopened. Construction was under way for some wainscoting and a window seat that would cover and vent the radiators. Jared was too young to enjoy it now, but she could just imagine him curling up there, looking out over Central Park and reading a book.

"You said his favorite color was red, so I was going to paint the walls red." He gestured over to the side. "I'm having them build a loft with a ladder into this niche here, so he'll have his own tree house–like space to play when he's older. They're delivering a toddler bed in a few days with a Spider-Man bedding set and curtains."

"It's wonderful," Sabine said. And it was. A million times better than anything she could afford to get him. "He will love it, especially when he gets a little older. What little boy wouldn't?"

Sabine took a last look and moved back out into the hallway and past the closed door to his home office. She didn't begrudge her son anything his father gave him, but it was hard for her to face that Gavin could provide Jared with things she couldn't. "What's this?" she asked, pointing toward a touch panel on the table near the phone.

Gavin caught up with her in the living room. "It's the new Ritz-Carlton concierge system. We didn't have dinner. Would you like me to order something?"

"Maybe later. It's still early." Sabine kicked off her heels and continued through the apartment to the master suite. She reached behind her and began unzipping her dress as she disappeared around the corner.

She'd barely made it three feet inside before she felt Gavin's heat against her back. He brushed her hands away, tugging her zipper down the curve of her spine. His fingertips brushed at the soft skin there, just briefly, before he moved to her shoulders and pushed her dress off.

Sabine stepped out of her clothing, continuing across the room in nothing but the white satin bra and panties she'd worn with it. There were no lights on in that room, so she was free to walk to the window and look outside without being seen.

She heard Gavin close the door behind them, ensuring they were blanketed in darkness. The moonlight from outside was enough to illuminate the pieces of furniture she remembered from before.

She felt Gavin's breath on her neck before he touched her. His bare chest pushed into her back, his skin hot and firm. He swept her hair over her left shoulder, leaning down to press searing kisses along the line of her neck. One bra strap was pushed aside, then the other, before he unhooked the clasp and let the satin fall to the floor.

Sabine relaxed against him, letting her head roll back to rest on his shoulder and expose her throat. She closed her eyes to block out the distraction of the view and focus on the feeling of his lips, teeth and tongue moving over her sensitive flesh. His palms covered her exposed breasts, molding them with his hands and gently pinching the tips until she whimpered aloud with pleasure.

"Sabine," he whispered, biting at her earlobe. "You don't know how long I've waited to have you back in my bed." He slid his hands down to her hips, holding her steady as he pressed his arousal into her backside with a growl.

The vibration of the sound rumbled through her whole body like a shock wave. Her nipples tightened and her core pulsed with need. Knowing she could turn him on like this was such a high. She never felt as sexy as she did when she was with Gavin. Somehow, knowing she could bring such a powerful man to his knees with desire and pleasure was the greatest turn-on.

Sabine turned in his arms, looking up at the dark shadows across his face before she smiled and slipped out of his grasp. Her eyes had adjusted to the light. It made it easy for her to find her way to the massive bed in the center of his room. She crawled up onto it, throwing a glance over her shoulder to make sure he was watching the swell of her backside peeking out from the satin panties. Of course he was.

"This bed?" she asked sweetly, although she felt anything but sweet.

Gavin had his hands balled into fists at his side. "What are you trying to do to me?"

He was fighting for control, but she didn't want him to win. She wanted him to break, to lose himself in her. It would only require her to push a little bit harder. She climbed up to her knees and hooked her thumbs beneath her panties. Looking him in the eye, she bit her lips and glided the slick fabric over her hips.

His breath was ragged in his chest, but he held his place. Gavin's burning gaze danced between the bite of her teeth into her plump pink lips to her full, pert breasts, to the ever-lowering panties. When the cropped dark curls of her sex peeked out from the top, he swallowed hard. His hands went to his belt. His eyes never left her body as he removed the last of his clothes.

Now they were both naked with no more barriers between them. She was ready for him to unleash his passion on her.

With a wicked smile, Sabine flicked her dark hair over her shoulder and curled her finger to beckon Gavin to come to her. He didn't hesitate, surging forward onto the bed until she fell backward onto the soft comforter.

Every inch of her was suddenly covered by the massive expanse of his body. The weight of him pressed her into the mattress, molding her against him. He entered her quickly as well, causing Sabine to cry out before she could stop herself.

"Yes," Gavin hissed in encouragement. "Be loud. You can scream the walls down tonight." He thrust hard into her again. "I want hotel security knocking on the door."

Sabine laughed and drew her knees up to cradle him. When he surged forward again, he drove deeper. She groaned loud, the sound echoing off the walls of the room. He wanted her loud and she would be happy to oblige.

Eight

Sabine rang the doorbell with her elbow, fighting to keep ahold of her son. Jared squirmed furiously in her arms, and she didn't blame him. For their trip to see Gavin's parents she'd dressed him in his best outfit—a pair of khakis, a short-sleeved plaid shirt and a little bow tie. Adrienne had bought the outfit for him and he looked adorable in it. When he stopped squirming. His two-year-old heart much preferred hoodies and T-shirts with cartoon characters on them.

Putting him on the ground, she crouched down to his level and straightened his clothes. "Hey, buddy," she said. "I know you don't like this, but I need you to be a good boy today. You're going to see Daddy and meet some nice people who are very excited to see you."

"Don't wanna." He pouted, with one lip sticking out so far, she was tempted to kiss it away. "Want truck."

"I've got your truck in my bag, and you can have it later. If you're a good boy today, we'll get ice cream on the way home, okay?"

The dark, mischievous eyes of her son looked up at her, considering the offer. Before he could answer, the door opened and Sabine looked up into the same eyes. Gavin was in the doorway.

"Hi, Jared," Gavin said, his whole face lighting up at the sight of his son. He knelt down and put out his arms, and Jared immediately stopped pouting and ran to him. Gavin scooped him up and swung him in the air while Jared giggled hysterically.

Sabine stood and smiled, nervously readjusting her purse on her shoulder and smoothing a hand over her hair. She'd pulled the black-and-purple strands back into a bun at the nape of her neck. The violet highlights were still visible, but not so "in their face." Adrienne had insisted she wear one of her newly designed tops today, a silky, scoop-neck red top that gathered at the waist. She'd paired it with some black pants and a patent leather belt. It looked good on her, but it was hardly the armor she'd wanted going into this.

She sucked a deep breath into her lungs, trying to even out her frantic heartbeat, but it did little good. She was about to see Gavin's parents again, and this time, as the mother of their grandchild. They had been polite but distant the last time. Obviously, they hadn't felt the need to get invested in Gavin's latest dating novelty.

She didn't anticipate this going well. They might hate her for keeping Jared a secret. They might turn their noses up at her like Viola had. Only today, she couldn't dump a drink on the bitch and run out.

"How'd it go?" she asked.

Gavin settled Jared in his arms and turned to her. "Well, I think. They were surprised. Okay, *more* than surprised. But we talked a lot, and they've had some time to process it. Now I think they're excited at the prospect of their first grandchild."

It was too early for Sabine to feel optimistic. She was about to reply when she heard a woman's voice from inside the apartment. "Are they here? Ohmigosh, look at him!"

Sabine was expecting his mother, but instead, the face of a younger woman appeared over Gavin's shoulder. She had long, dark brown hair like his, but her eyes were a steely gray color. It had to be his sister, Diana.

Gavin turned toward her, showcasing his son. "This is Jared. Jared, this is your auntie Diana."

Jared played shy, turning his face into Gavin's shirt when Diana tried to coax him to say hello. More voices sounded inside with footsteps pounding across the floor. How many people were in there? A crowd of four or five people gathered, all fussing at Jared and Gavin at once.

"He looks just like you did at that age!"

"What a handsome boy!"

Sabine was happy to stay safely in the hallway and play spectator for the moment. It was easier. She always knew they would accept Jared. He was their blessed heir. The vessel that brought him into existence was another matter.

She could feel the moment the first set of eyes fell on her. It was Diana. She slipped around Gavin into the hallway, rushing Sabine with a hug she wasn't anticipating.

"It's so nice to finally meet you," Diana said.

Sabine patted weakly at the young woman's back and pulled away as soon as she could. "Finally?"

Diana smiled and threw a conspiratorial look over her shoulder. "Gavin had mentioned you to me when you were first dating. He just went on and on about you. I'd never heard him do that about another woman before. And then it ended and I was so disappointed. When he called and asked me to come over today to meet his son, I was so happy to hear that you were the mother." She grinned wide and nudged Sabine with her elbow. "I think it's fate."

Sabine tried not to laugh at the young woman's enthusiasm. She couldn't be more than twenty-two or twenty-three. She still believed in all that. And since Diana was the beautiful only daughter of a billion-dollar empire, Sabine was pretty certain no man had the nerve to break her heart. At least, not yet.

Diana snatched up Sabine's hand in hers and tugged her over the threshold of the entryway. The polished parquet floors were too slick for her to resist the movement and before she knew it, the door was closed and she was standing in the apartment of Byron and Celia Brooks.

Okay, apartment was a misnomer. This was a mansion slapped on the top of an apartment building. In front of her was a grand marble staircase with a gold-and-crystal chandelier twinkling overhead from the twenty-foot ceilings. On each side of the doorway were large urns filled with bouquets of fresh flowers that were nicer than the arrangements at some people's weddings.

That was all she could see with the press of people, but it was enough to let her know she wasn't in Nebraska anymore.

"Everyone, you remember Sabine Hayes. She's Jared's mother."

Sabine's chest tightened instantly, her breath going

still in her lungs of stone. Every eye in the room flew from Jared to her. His father's. His mother's. His brother Alan's. She tried to smile wide and pretend she wasn't having a panic attack, but she wasn't certain how convincing she was.

His mother stepped forward first. She looked just as she had the last time. Sabine and Gavin had run into them at a restaurant as they were going in and his parents were leaving. It had been an accidental meeting really, given their relationship hadn't called for the meeting of the parents yet. Sabine had been struck by how refined and effortlessly elegant his mother was. Today was no exception.

Celia's light brown hair was pulled back in a bun like Sabine's. She was wearing a gray silk dress with a strand of dark gray pearls around her neck and teardrops with diamonds from her ears. The dress perfectly matched her eyes, so much like Diana's. Her gaze swept quickly over Sabine from head to toe but stopped at her eyes with a smile of her own. "It's lovely to see you again, Sabine."

"Likewise," she said, politely shaking the woman's hand. Every description Gavin ever gave her of his mother had built an image of a cold, disinterested woman in Sabine's mind. Their meeting before hadn't been very revealing, but today, she instantly knew that was not the case. There was a light in her eyes that was very warm and friendly. Celia Brooks had just been raised well and taught early the rules of etiquette and civility that a woman of her class needed. Yes, she could've been a more hands-on mother and let her children get dirty every now and then, but that wasn't how she was brought up.

"Please, come in and meet everyone. You remember my husband, Byron, and this is my other son, Alan."

Sabine shook each of their hands and was amazed at how much alike the Brooks men looked. Thick brown hair, eyes like melted dark chocolate, strong builds. Just one glance and Sabine could tell exactly how Jared would look when he was twenty-five and when he was fifty-five.

"Nora has refreshments set up for us in the parlor," Celia said, ushering everyone out of the hallway.

The farther they went into the apartment, the more nervous Sabine became. Not because of his family, but because of their stuff. Every item her eyes lit upon looked fragile and priceless. "Do not put him down," Sabine whispered to Gavin.

At that, Gavin chuckled. "Do you have any idea how many things my siblings and I have broken over the years? I assure you, if it's important, it's not sitting out."

"Oh, yes," Celia insisted. "Don't worry about a thing. It has been quite a while since we had a youngster here, but we'd better get used to it, right?" She got a wistful look in her eye and glanced over at Jared. "A grandchild. What an unexpected and wonderful surprise."

Sabine wasn't quite sure what to say. She expected the other shoe to drop at any moment. But time went on, and it didn't. They chatted and nibbled on treats their housekeeper, Nora, made. His family asked questions about her with genuine interest. Jared was turned loose and managed not to break anything. To her shock, Byron, the former CEO of BXS, got on the floor and played with him and his dump truck.

She had made herself sick worrying about today. Thinking they would hate her. That they'd never accept her or her son. But as time went by, she found herself to be incredibly at ease with his family. They were polished and polite, but not cold and certainly not blatantly rude like Viola. It was nothing like she'd expected.

It seemed Sabine was as guilty of prejudice as she worried they would be. Just as she feared they would look at her and make snap judgments, so had she. She had this idea of what rich people were like. Gavin's stories of his distant, workaholic family had only reinforced the image in her mind.

But she was wrong. And it made her angry. People like Viola had made her believe that she could never have Gavin. That she would never fit in. She was angry at herself, really. She was the one who was too afraid to find out if their wicked whispers were true. She pushed away the only man she'd ever loved, deprived him of his son for two years, because she was certain they could never last.

She was wrong. At least in part. They might never truly be together as a couple again, but they could be a family and make it work.

Sabine had wasted so much time being afraid. She wasn't about to make the same mistake twice.

"You don't have to keep trying to take me out to dinner, Gavin."

"If at first you don't succeed, try, try again." Gavin smiled and helped her out of the car and onto the curb outside a restaurant.

"You didn't fail the last time." Sabine slowly approached him, pressed herself against the length of his body and wrapped her arms around his neck. "I seem to recall that evening ending in quite a...spectacular fashion."

"Spectacular, eh?" Gavin growled near her ear. "I'm

glad you seemed to think so. But—" he planted a kiss on her neck and whispered to her "—we never actually ate."

"That was okay with me." She looked up at him with her wide green eyes and a wicked smile curling her lips. "We could have the same thing tonight, if you'd like."

He smiled and let his hands roam across the silky fabric of her dress. She was trying to lure him back to bed, but he wouldn't let her. Couldn't let her. At least not tonight. "Well, as tempting as that is, I'll have to pass. You see, I brought in reinforcements to make sure this meal was a success. We can't stand up our guests."

Sabine frowned at him, her nose wrinkling. "Guests?"

"Sabine!"

She pulled away from Gavin and turned to find Adrienne and Will behind her. "Adrienne? Will? What are you two doing here?"

Adrienne leaned in to give her a hug with an amused smirk on her face. "Gavin invited us to have dinner with you tonight. Did he not tell you?"

"Uh, no, he didn't." Sabine looked over her shoulder at Gavin, who appeared appropriately admonished, at least for the moment. "How did you even know how to get in touch with either of them?"

"Gavin and I have been acquaintances for several years," Will said. "We play the occasional game of racquetball together."

Sabine just shook her head. "So…what? Do all young, rich guys know each other? Is there some kind of club or something where you all hang out and be rich together?"

"Yes, we have a support group—Rich and Sexy Anonymous," Gavin offered with a smile. "Let's get inside or we'll be late for our reservation."

They were seated at a table for four near the window.

He'd known Will for several years but hadn't connected that the Adrienne that Sabine worked for was the same Adrienne that married Will the year before. When the pieces finally clicked, he thought having dinner together would be nice. Not even Viola would have the nerve to come up to a table like this and make a fuss. They were guaranteed a fun night out with people that he already knew would make Sabine comfortable.

He had also been curious to meet Adrienne in person. He'd read about her in the newspaper a few years ago after her plane crash and the scandal that followed. She had lost her memory for weeks, and everyone thought she was Will's fiancée, who actually died in the wreck. It was the stuff of dramatic movies, but she had made herself into quite the success story. Her clothing line had soared in the past year, and her boutique was one of the most popular destinations for the young and hip in Manhattan. He just never thought to look for his runaway girlfriend behind the counter of the store.

The waiter came to take their drink orders. "Is anyone interested in some wine?"

"None for me," Adrienne said.

"We can order something sweeter," Sabine offered. "I know you like a Riesling or a Moscato, right?"

"I do normally—" she smiled "—but I'm not drinking at all for the next eight months or so."

The sharp squealing noise that followed was nearly enough to pierce Gavin's eardrums. Sabine leaped up from her chair and ran around to embrace Adrienne. That kicked off a rapid-fire female discussion about things that Gavin would rather not be privy to. Instead, he ordered sparkling water for Adrienne and wine for everyone else.

"Congrats, Daddy," he said to Will.

Will chuckled. "Congrats to you, as well. It seems to be going around."

"It has. I can assure you that mine was more of a surprise, since my child was walking and talking by the time I found out about it."

"Yeah, but you lucked out. You missed the morning sickness, the wild hormonal swings, the Lamaze classes, the birthing room where she threatens to castrate you. After the child is born there's the midnight feedings, the colic…"

Gavin listened to Will talk for a moment and shook his head to interrupt. "I'd gladly take all that and more in exchange for the rest of what I missed. I also didn't get to be there when she heard his heartbeat or saw his image on the sonogram for the first time. I missed his birth, his first steps, his first words…. Enjoy every moment of this experience with Adrienne. Things that don't seem very important now will be the very stuff that will keep you up at night when you're older. One day, you'll look up from your BlackBerry and your kid will be in high school."

Gavin couldn't stop the words from flying out of his mouth. Every single one of them was true, although he'd barely allowed himself the time to think about what he'd missed. He tried to focus on what was ahead. Jared wasn't going to drift in and out of his life like so many others, so he had no excuse. If he missed moments going forward, it was his own fault. He didn't want any more regrets.

The waiter brought their wine, and Gavin took a large sip. "Sorry about that," he said.

"No, don't be," Will answered. "You're right. Time goes by so quickly, especially to guys like us. The priorities start to change when you fall in love and even more so when kids come into the picture. I'll try to keep it in perspective when she's sending me out in the night on strange cravings runs."

"Gavin is taking us to look at apartments on my day off," he heard Sabine say.

"There's an apartment down the street from us that's for sale," Adrienne said. "A really nice brownstone. It's on the second floor, so there's some stairs, but not many."

"I think I'd prefer her to be in a building with a doorman and some security. It would make me feel better."

"It's not like my current apartment has surveillance cameras and security," Sabine said.

"It doesn't matter. If you continue to refuse living with me, I want you in someplace secure. I don't want just anyone strolling up to your door. This can be a dangerous town sometimes, and I want you and Jared protected when I can't be there."

"Yes, that viciously dangerous Upper West Side," Sabine said with a smile. "I actually read that the Village has one of the higher crime rates, but you seemed okay with that."

"Hence the doorman."

"Okay, fine, no brownstones." The two women exchanged knowing looks and shrugged.

They placed their orders and continued chatting easily during the meal. Given they actually got as far as having food on the table, this was their most successful dinner yet. At this point, Gavin was thinking of opening a door to a line of conversation he was extremely interested in. He hadn't brought it up to Sabine—she would likely shoot him down—but with Will and Adrienne as backup, he might be successful.

"So, are you guys planning to take any romantic pre-baby vacations sometime soon?"

The couple looked at each other. "That's not a bad idea," Will said. "We honestly haven't given it much thought. It really will be a challenge to travel with little ones. Honey," he said, turning to Adrienne, "we should definitely do something. Let's go somewhere glamorous and decidedly un-kid-friendly to celebrate. We're going to be making pilgrimages to the Mouse from now on, so we need to enjoy an adult vacation while we can."

"You really should," Sabine echoed. "That escape to your place in the Hamptons this summer was the only vacation I've taken since Jared was born. You should take the time to pamper yourself now. The spring lines are almost finished for Fashion Week. You should definitely go somewhere after the show."

Gavin perked up at her words. That was exactly what he was hoping to hear. "You've only had one vacation in two years?"

"More than that, really," she admitted. "Since I had Jared, I haven't had the time. Before I had Jared, I didn't have the money. Adrienne twisted my arm into going this summer. Prior to that, the last real vacation I took was my senior trip to Disney World in high school."

"That hardly counts," Will pointed out.

"Yes," Adrienne agreed. "You need a vacation as badly as I do. Maybe more. Thank goodness I got you to come to the beach house. I had no idea you were so vacation-deprived."

"I save all my hours in case Jared gets sick. And I don't have anyone to watch him while I'm gone. Tina had him over the Fourth of July trip, but I think that was too much for her. I couldn't ask her to do it again."

"You wouldn't have to," Gavin said.

"Are you offering to watch him while I go on vacation?" she challenged with a smile.

"Not exactly."

Nine

"This one is nice."

Sabine was gripping the handles of Jared's stroller as she shot him a glance that told him he was incorrect. She wasn't impolite enough to say that in front of the Realtor, though.

They were in the seventh apartment of the day. They had crisscrossed Manhattan, looking at places uptown, downtown, east and west. This last apartment, in midtown, had three spacious bedrooms, a large kitchen, a balcony and a spa tub in the master bath. And of course, it did not impress her nearly as much as some of the others. Unfortunately, it was the closest of all the apartments to his own place.

She favored the West Village, and there was no convincing her otherwise.

"This is probably a no," he said. "And I think we're

done for the day. The kid is getting tired." That was an understatement. He'd been conked out in his stroller since they arrived at this building.

"I really do like the one in the Village. I just want to know what all my options are before we spend that much. It's more than we need, really."

The woman sighed and closed her leather portfolio. "I'll keep looking and contact you next week with a list of other options. I worry you might lose out on that place if you don't put an offer in soon."

The Realtor was eyeing him from the other room. She was far too eager to push him into an expensive sale, and he wouldn't be rushed. Sabine would have what she wanted, and for the price he was willing to pay, this lady needed to find it for them.

"There are two million apartments in Manhattan," Gavin said. "We'll find another one if we have to."

They were escorted out of the apartment and downstairs. After they parted ways with the Realtor, they started strolling down the block. The street sounds roused Jared from his nap just as they neared Bryant Park.

"Could we take Jared over to the carousel? He loves that."

"Absolutely."

They took Jared for a spin on the carousel and then settled onto a bench to enjoy the nice afternoon. Gavin went to buy them both a drink, and when he returned, Jared was playing with another child who'd brought bubbles to the park.

"I've got a surprise for you."

Gavin had to smile at the mix of concern and intrigue on Sabine's face. He was excited about the prospect of what he had planned, but he also enjoyed watching her twist herself into knots trying to figure out what he was doing. She hated not knowing what was going on, which made him all the more determined to surprise her.

"Really?" Sabine turned away, feigning disinterest and watching Jared play with the bubbles.

It had been a couple days since she'd met his family. Things seemed to be going well on all fronts. Edmund said the custody and other legal paperwork should be finalized any day now. Gavin and his legal team were signing off on the merger agreement with Exclusivity Jetliners next week. Roger Simpson's son had finally stopped his loud protests about the acquisition, and things were moving forward.

Everything was going to plan, and Gavin wanted to celebrate the best way he knew how—an exhilarating flight and a luxurious weekend on the beach. For the first time in his life, he wanted to share that experience with someone else. He wanted Sabine beside him as he soared through the clouds and buried his toes in the sand. He just had to talk her into going along with it, which would be harder than securing an Exclusivity Jetliners jet and reserving a private beachfront bungalow in Bermuda on short notice.

"When you go home tonight, I want you to pack for a long weekend away."

Her head snapped back to look at him, a frown pulling down the corners of her pink lips. "I have to work this weekend, Gavin. I've already taken off too much time from the store. I can't go anywhere."

"Yes, you can," he said with a wide smile. Did she really think he would make a suggestion like this without having every detail handled? He ran an international shipping empire; he could manage taking her away for the weekend. "The lovely Adrienne and I spoke about my plans at dinner while you were in the ladies' room. She seemed very enthusiastic about it. You have the next three days off. She told me to tell you to have a good time and not to worry about anything."

Red rushed to Sabine's pale cheeks as her brow furrowed and she started to sputter. "What? You—y-you just went to my boss and made arrangements without asking me? Seriously? Gavin, you can't just make decisions like this and leave me out of them."

"Relax," he said, running a soothing hand over her bare shoulder. She was wearing a sleeveless blouse in a bright kelly green that made her eyes darken to the color of the oak leaves overhead. It was almost the same shade as when she looked at him with desire blazing in her eyes. "I'm not trying to take over your life. I'm just trying to take you on a little surprise getaway. You wouldn't do it if I didn't twist your arm."

His fingertips tingled as they grazed over her skin, rousing a need inside him that was inappropriate for the park. He hadn't made love to Sabine since they went to his apartment. She might have her concerns, but he was determined to take her to a tropical location where he could make love to her for hours, uninterrupted.

He wasn't sure whether it was his words or his touch, but the lines between her brows eased up. With a heavy sigh, she turned her attention back to the playground. "What will we do about Jared? You haven't mentioned him coming with us."

It was all handled. "My parents have volunteered to keep him for the weekend. They're quite excited about the prospect, actually."

Sabine's lips twisted as she tried, and failed, to hold in her concerns. "Your parents? The ones who left you with nannies, refused to let you get dirty or be loud or do anything remotely childlike? I don't see that going very well, to be perfectly honest."

Gavin shrugged. What was the worst that could happen? His parents had all the resources in the world at their fingertips. They could manage any contingency, even if it meant breaking down and hiring in someone to help them for the weekend. "I think it will be fine. This is completely different. From what I hear, being a grandparent has a different set of rules. They were distracted by work and responsibilities when I was a kid. Now, they've got nothing but time, cash and two years of indulging to catch up on. Worst-case scenario, we come home to a spoiled-rotten brat."

A soft chuckle escaped Sabine's lips as she turned back to the playground again. He followed her line of sight to the patch of grass where Jared and another little boy were chasing bubbles and giggling hysterically.

She was a great mother. She worried about their son and his welfare every second of the day and had done so for two straight years all on her own. A mother's protective nature never really went away, but Sabine needed a break. A weekend trip wouldn't hurt anything. In fact, she might come home refreshed and be a better parent for it.

"If it helps," Gavin added, "Nora, the housekeeper, used to work as a nanny. She's great with kids. If my parents need reinforcements, she'll be there to help. Nothing will go wrong. You deserve some time to relax."

"I don't know, Gavin. When you took him to the circus, I was nearly panicked the whole time. That was the first time he'd gone somewhere without me aside from day care. And now you want to take me on a trip? How far are we going?"

"Only a short plane ride away."

"Plane?" she cried, turning on the bench to face him full-on. "I really don't want to be that far from him, Gavin."

"It's only about a two-hour flight. If we drove to the Hamptons it would take just as long to get back home with summer traffic." He reached out and took her hand, relishing the cool glide of her skin against his. She had such delicate, feminine hands, more so than he remembered. He was used to them being rough with calluses from her wooden brushes, with paint embedded under her nails and along her cuticles. He hadn't managed to get her back to painting yet, but this trip was a sure start.

"Please let me do this for you. Not only will you have a great time, but it's my chance to share my passion with you the way you once shared your painting with me."

Her green eyes met his, and he felt some of her resistance fading away. She knew how important this was to him. "You're flying us there?"

Gavin smiled and nodded. It hadn't been an original part of his plan, but when he asked Roger about chartering one of his jets, he'd laughed and told him they were practically his already. If he wanted to take one, he was welcome to it, and he could fly it himself.

"Roger is loaning me one of his jets for the trip. I've been dying to fly one, and I really want you to be up there with me when I do. That would make the experience that much more special."

He loved to fly. Soaring through the air was the greatest high he'd ever experienced. It wasn't the same when you weren't sitting at the controls. The only thing that could make it better would be sharing it with her. Somehow, the idea of having Sabine beside him in the cockpit made his chest tight. He wanted to share this with her. He wanted to spoil her. She just had to let him.

She finally let the slightest smile curl her lips. He'd won, he could tell. The tiny smirk made him want to lean in and kiss her until she was blushing again, but this time with passion instead of irritation. But he'd have time soon enough. He wanted her in a swimsuit, her skin glistening with suntan oil. He couldn't wait to feel the press of her bikini bottom against him as he held her in the ocean. They both needed this trip away for a million different reasons.

"I suppose you're not going to tell me where we're flying to."

"Nope." He grinned.

"Then how do I know what to pack?"

"Dress for sizzling-hot days lounging on the beach and cool nights overlooking the ocean. Throw a couple things in a bag and leave the rest up to me."

Sabine wasn't a big fan of flying, but she wasn't about to tell Gavin that. It was his big love, like painting was for her, so she took her Dramamine, packed her bag and hoped for the best.

"You look nervous," Gavin said after locking the door and sliding into the cockpit beside her.

"Me?" she asked with a nervous twitter of laughter. "Never." She was thankful she'd worn large sunglasses today. Maybe he wouldn't notice her eyes were closed the whole time.

The taxi down the runway wasn't so bad. Gavin

seemed very at ease with his headset on and vast display of controls in front of him. He had given her a headset of her own to wear so she could hear the air traffic controllers talking. She heard the tower give them clearance to take off.

"Here we go," Gavin said with an impish smile that reminded her of Jared when he thought he was getting away with something naughty.

Gavin eased the accelerator forward and the jet started down the runway. At that point, Sabine closed her eyes and took a deep breath. She felt the lift as the plane surged into the sky, but she didn't open her eyes.

"Isn't it beautiful?" Gavin asked after a few minutes.

"Oh, yeah," she said, seeing nothing but the dark inside of her eyelids.

"Sabine, open your eyes. Are you afraid to fly?"

She turned to him with a sheepish smile. "No, I'm afraid to crash. You know my boss survived a plane crash a few years ago, right? When you know someone it happened to, it makes it more real in your mind." It was then that she looked through the glass and noticed nothing but ocean around them. He hadn't mentioned flying over the ocean. She swallowed hard. She could do this. She didn't really have a choice.

"We're not going to crash."

"No one plans to."

"Just breathe and enjoy the freedom of zooming through the sky like a bird. Soaring above everyone and everything."

She pried her gaze away from the vast stretch of ocean that surrounded them and decided to focus on Gavin instead. His eyes were alight with excitement. Her serious businessman was grinning from ear to ear like a child with his first bicycle. He adjusted the controls like a pro, setting the cruising altitude and putting them on a course to...*somewhere.*

It was an amazing transformation. Sabine had seen Gavin happy. Angry. Sad. She'd watched his face contort in the pinnacle of passion and go blank with deep thought. But not once had she ever seen him truly joyful. It suited him. He should've joined the Air Force. He might not have a thirty-million-dollar apartment on Central Park South, but he would've been happier. Sometimes you have to make the hard choices to chase your dream. She'd left her entire family behind to follow hers and had rarely regretted the decision.

Two hours later, Gavin started talking into the headset again, and they were granted permission to land although she didn't see anything but miles of blue sea. The plane slowly dropped in altitude. The ocean lightened to a bright turquoise blue, and mossy-green islands appeared through the clouds. She closed her eyes when they landed, but Gavin did a great job at that.

They taxied around the small island airport, finally passing a sign to help her figure out where she was. Welcome to Bermuda.

Bermuda!

At the hangar, they were directed to a location to leave the jet. Gavin shut all the equipment down and they opened the door, extending steps to the ground. Sabine was excited about the trip but grateful to finally have her sandals touching the earth again.

Gavin directed a couple men to unload luggage from the cargo hold and move it to a black town car waiting outside. The driver then whisked them through the narrow, winding streets. After a while, they turned off the main road to a sand-and-gravel drive that disappeared through the thick cover of trees. The world seemed to slip farther away with every turn until at last they came upon a secluded two-story home right on the beach. The house was bright yellow with a white roof and white shutters around each window.

The driver carried their bags inside, leaving them on the tile floor of the master bedroom suite. Sabine followed behind him, taking in every detail of their home away from home. It was decorated in a casual beach style with bright colors and lots of light. There were large French doors off the living room that opened onto a deck. She walked outside, stepping onto it and realizing that it actually extended out over the water.

Sabine leaned against the railing and looked all around her. She didn't see another house or boat anywhere. There was nothing but palm trees, black volcanic rock, clear blue water and pink sand. It was unexpected, but peachy-pink sand stretched out on either side of them.

"The sand is pink," she said, when she heard Gavin step out onto the patio behind her.

"I thought you'd like that." He pressed against her back and wrapped his arms around her waist.

Sabine sighed and eased against him. She could feel the tension start to drift away just being here in his arms. He was right. As much as she'd protested, she needed this vacation.

"I didn't even know such a thing existed. It's beautiful." Her gaze fell on some multicolored glittering stones in the sand. "What is that?" She pointed to the beach. "Shells?"

"Sea glass. They have some beaches here that are just covered in it."

Sabine had the urge to walk along the beach and collect some glass to take home. Maybe she could work it into her art. She hadn't done any painting yet, but she had begun allowing herself to think about it again. The ideas were forming, waiting for her to execute when she was ready. Sea glass might very well feature prominently in the first piece.

"This place is amazing. I want to paint it."

Gavin nuzzled his nose along the shell of her ear. "Good. I want you to paint. I even brought supplies with me."

Sabine turned in his arms with a small frown. "I didn't notice any canvases."

He grinned and planted his hands on the railing to trap her there. "That's because they're body paints. I'm your canvas."

"Oohhh…" Sabine cooed, the possibilities flowing into her mind. This could certainly be fun. "When can we start my next masterpiece?"

Gavin captured her lips with his own, coaxing her blood to move faster and her skin to flush with the heat of desire. One hand moved to her waist and slid beneath her shirt to caress her bare skin. "Right now," he whispered against her lips.

He took her hand and led her back inside. In the bedroom, his luggage was open, and sitting on the dresser was a box of body paints. Gavin must've unpacked it after their driver left. She picked up the pink box and eyed it with curiosity. "You didn't mention it was edible."

"I thought it might bother you to destroy your own creation."

Sabine pulled a jar of strawberry-flavored red paint

from the box with a wicked grin. "Given I'd be destroying it with my tongue, I don't mind so much."

She advanced toward the bed, Gavin stepping backward until his calves met with the mattress. Sabine set down the paints long enough to help him slip out of his clothes and lie out on the king-size bed.

There wasn't anything quite as inspirational as seeing his powerful, naked body sprawled in front of her. His arms were crossed behind his head, his rock-hard chest and chiseled abs just waiting for her artistic improvements. This was an exciting new canvas, and unlike the one he brought to her apartment, there was no blank, white surface to mock her.

Easing onto the bed beside him, she arranged her jars and pulled out the brush that came with it. It wasn't exactly the highest-quality equipment, but this wasn't going to hang in the Louvre one day.

Thinking for a moment, she dipped the brush into the blueberry paint and started swirling it around his navel. He hissed for a moment at the cold paint and then smiled. Next, she added some strawberry paint. Then green watermelon and purple grape. She lost herself in the art, mixing the colors around his skin until he looked like her own twisted, edible version of an abstract Kandinsky painting.

After nearly an hour, she sat back on her heels and admired her canvas. She liked it. It really was a shame it wouldn't last through his next shower.

"I like watching you work."

Sabine turned to look at him, his face one of the only parts of his body that didn't look like a unicorn had thrown up a rainbow on him. "Thanks."

"You get this intensity in your eyes that's amazingly

sexy." He sat up to admire his body. "I can say with certainty that this is probably the greatest abstract art piece ever created with edible body paints. And," he added with a grin, "the only one that smells like a bowl of Froot Loops."

She reached out with her brush and dabbed a dot of purple paint on his lips, then leaned in to lick it away. Her tongue glided slowly along his bottom lip, her gaze never leaving his. "Tasty."

He buried his fingers in her hair and tugged her mouth back to his. His tongue dipped inside and glided along her own. "Indeed. The grape is very tasty."

Sabine smiled and pushed him back against the bed. "That was fun, but now it's time to clean up."

She started with his chest, licking a path across his pecs and flicking her tongue across his nipples. She made her way down the flavorful canvas, teasing at his rib cage and the sensitive plane of his stomach. When she glanced up, she noticed Gavin watching just as eagerly as when she was painting.

"I told you I liked watching you work," he said with a grin.

Sabine dipped lower to the firm heat of his erection and wiped away his smile with her tongue. Taking it deep into her mouth, she worked hard to remove every drop of paint, leaving Gavin groaning and clutching at the blankets with his fists.

"Sabine," he whispered, reaching for her wrist. He found her and tugged until her body was sprawled across his. "You're wearing too much clothing," he complained.

Sitting astride him, Sabine slipped out of her top and bra and then stood to push down her capris and panties. She tossed everything onto the floor and crouched back down. With little effort, she was able to take him into her body and thrust him deep inside.

His hands moved quickly to her hips, guiding her movements. Sabine closed her eyes and tried to absorb the sensations, but found that without the distraction of painting, her emotions were starting to creep in.

From the moment he first kissed her, Sabine had worried that she was fighting a losing battle. Not for custody of Jared, but for custody of her heart. No matter how many times she told herself that none of this was about them, that it was about his son, she couldn't help but think it was more.

Sure, everything he offered would make her a happier mother for their child. But he didn't need to bring her here, to make love to her like this. He didn't have to be so supportive of her art when no one else was. It made it seem like more. And she wanted it to be more. She was just afraid.

Sabine loved him. She always had. There were plenty of reasons why they wouldn't make a good couple, but in the end, only one reason mattered. She left because she loved him enough to change for him—the one thing she swore she'd never do. She'd been disowned by her family for her unwillingness to bend, and yet she would be whatever Gavin wanted her to be. And it scared the hell out of her. So she made her excuses and ran before she did something she might hate herself for.

There was no running from Gavin now. He would forever be a part of her life. And she didn't have the strength to keep fighting this. He might never love her the way she loved him. But she couldn't pretend that this meant nothing to her.

Gavin groaned loudly, pulling her from her thoughts. He moved his hand up to cup her breast, the intensity of their movements increasing with each moment that went by. She wouldn't be able to hold out much longer.

Opening her eyes, she looked down at Gavin. His eyes were closed, his teeth biting down on his lip. He was completely wrapped up in his desire for her. For *her*. Just the way she was. He'd told her that the night she fought with Viola, but she wasn't ready to listen. Perhaps he really meant it. Perhaps he wouldn't ask her to change and she wouldn't betray how weak she was by giving in to his demands.

Perhaps one day he might love her for being herself.

That thought made her heart soar with hope and her body followed. The pleasure surged through her, her cries echoing in the large, tile-floored room. Gavin quickly followed, digging his fingers into the flesh of her hips and growling with satisfaction.

When their heartbeats slowed and they snuggled comfortably into each other's arms, Sabine spoke. Not the words she wanted to say, but the ones she needed to say. "Thank you."

"For what?"

"For the paint. And all of this, really. But mostly the paint."

"I assure you, the pleasure was all mine."

Sabine laughed and nestled tighter against his still somewhat rainbow-colored chest. "That's not what I meant. You've always been such a big supporter of my work. I haven't..." Her voice trailed off as tears crept into her words. She cleared her throat. "I haven't always had that in my life.

"After I had Jared and stopped painting, I began to worry that I might lose my touch. When you brought that canvas the other day and the ideas didn't come, I was re-

ally worried my art career was done. Today showed me
that I still have the creativity inside me. I just need to
not put so much pressure on myself and have fun with it
again. It doesn't seem like much, but those body paints
were a big deal. For me."

"I'm glad," Gavin said, holding her tight. "I have to
say it's the best fifteen bucks I've ever spent at the adult
novelty store."

Ten

"We should really call and check in on Jared."

Gavin tugged her tight against him and shook his head. They had made love, showered off her artwork, eaten—as body paints are not a replacement for real food—made love again and taken a nap. He wasn't anywhere near ready to let go of her. Not even just so she could grab her phone from the other room.

"I told my parents to call if there was a problem. I want you one hundred percent focused on enjoying yourself and relaxing. They've got it under control. We've only been gone for eight hours."

He could feel her start to squirm, but he wasn't budging. "How about we call in the morning?"

"Okay. I'm sure everything's fine, but I'm just a nervous mama. I worry."

"I know. But remember, our parents raised us, at least

yours did. Mine hired very qualified people to do it. They know what they're doing."

"I'd rather you not use my parents as an example of good parenting."

Gavin had never heard Sabine speak at length about her family or where she grew up. He knew it was somewhere in the Midwest, but she always seemed hesitant to talk about it. Since she opened the door, he'd take the opportunity. "Do your parents know about Jared?"

He felt Sabine stiffen in his arms. "No," she finally said.

"Why not?"

She wiggled until he allowed her to roll onto her back and look at him. "They are very religious, very hard-working Midwestern farmers. They worship God, the Cornhuskers and John Deere, in that order. I grew up in a small town that was nothing but cornfields and the occasional church for miles. From the time I was a teenager, I started to divert from the path they all followed. My parents tried their hardest to guide me back, but it didn't work. They decided they didn't want anything to do with me and this crazy life I wanted to lead. I refuse to expose Jared to grandparents that would just look at him as my shameful illegitimate son that my wild city life earned me."

"What happened between you and your family?" Gavin asked.

Sabine sighed, her kiss-swollen lips pursing in thought. She didn't really want to talk about it, but she needed to and they both knew it.

"Like I said, I wasn't the child they wanted. I wasn't willing to change who I was or what I dreamed of for them. They wanted me to be a quiet, mousy girl that would get up at dawn to cook for my husband and the other farmhands, take care of a brood of children and be content to sit on the porch and snap green beans. My two sisters didn't see anything wrong with that, but it wasn't what I wanted for my life. They couldn't understand why I wanted a nose ring instead of a wedding ring. The first time I dyed my bangs pink, my mother nearly had a heart attack. My art, my dreams of New York and being a famous painter...that was all childish nonsense to them. They wanted me to 'grow up' and do something respectable."

Gavin knew what it was like not to have his family support his choices. But he hadn't been brave like Sabine. He'd caved to the pressure. He envied her strength, especially knowing the high price she'd paid for her dreams. She had no contact with her family at all?

"You don't even speak to your sisters, then?"

"Very rarely. They're both older than I am, but the younger of the two talks to me on Facebook now and then. When we do talk, it's like chatting superficially with an old friend from junior high you barely remember. We don't share much. I don't post anything about Jared online, so none of them know about him. It seems that when I refused the life they chose I was insulting them, too. In trying to make myself happy, I made everyone else mad."

"So how did you end up in New York?"

"After graduation, I was toying with the idea of leaving Nebraska. I was working as a checkout girl at the grocery store and hoarding every penny I made. My parents had started this ridiculous parade of eligible farmers through the house each week at Sunday dinner just like they had with my older sisters. I could feel my opportunity to leave slipping away. If I wasn't careful, eventually one of the men would catch my eye. Then I'd end up pregnant or married, and I'd never get to New York.

"One night, after I walked the latest guy out, I returned to the living room and announced to my parents that I was moving out. I'd finally saved up enough to get there and a little money to live on. I told them I had a bus ticket to Manhattan and I would be leaving in the morning. It scared the daylights out of me, but I had to do it."

Gavin noticed the faint shimmer of tears in her eyes. The room was dark, but there was enough moonlight to catch it. Her parents hurt her and he hated them for it. "What did they say when you told them?"

She didn't reply right away. When she finally spoke, the tears had reached her voice, her words wavering with emotions. "They said to go on and go, then. Why wait for the morning? My dad grabbed the bag I had packed and threw it in the back of his truck."

Sabine sniffed delicately and wiped her eyes. "They were done with me. If I wasn't going to be the daughter they wanted me to be, then I just wouldn't be their daughter. My mama didn't say a word. She just shook her head and went to do the dishes. That's all she ever did was clean that damned kitchen. So I climbed into the truck and left. I wasn't even finished packing, but I couldn't make myself go upstairs to get the last of my things. I ended up sleeping in the bus station that night because I couldn't change my ticket."

"Just like that?"

"Just like that." She sighed, pulling her emotions back into check. "They disowned me. I don't know if they secretly thought I would fail and come running home, or if they were just tired of dealing with my eccentricities.

I wasn't the town tramp. I wasn't pregnant or on drugs. I was smart, I graduated high school with good grades. I worked and did my share around the farm. But I didn't fit this mold they tried to force me into.

"That was the last time I saw or spoke to my parents. The saddest part is that despite the fact that I wanted to go, I wanted them to ask me to stay. But they didn't. They just let me walk out like I meant nothing to them."

Gavin felt a sick knot start to form in his stomach. He'd done the exact same thing to her. All this time, he'd only focused on the fact that Sabine had left like everyone else in his life. He'd never considered that she might stay if he'd asked. And he'd wanted to. Every nerve in his body was screaming for him to say something—do *something*—to keep Sabine from leaving him, but he'd sat quietly and let her walk away.

"You know, people make mistakes. I'm willing to bet that they love you and miss you. Maybe they thought they were giving you one of those hard life lessons thinking you would come back and be more grateful for what you had. And when you didn't…they didn't know what to do. Or how to find you."

"I'm not that hard to find. Like I said, I'm on Facebook. For a while, I even had a website for my art."

Gavin shook his head. "It's not always as easy as that, especially when you know you're in the wrong. I mean, I did the same thing, didn't I? I was stupid and stubborn and let you walk away. I had a million idiotic reasons for it at the time, but none of them held up the moment that door slammed. Whenever I think back on that day, I wonder what would've happened if I'd run after you. If I'd pulled you into my arms and told you that I needed you to stay."

"You wanted me to stay?"

There was such astonishment in her voice that made him feel even worse. She thought he didn't care. All this time. A part of her probably still did. He hadn't asked for more than her body. Perhaps that's all she thought he wanted. It was all he thought he wanted, until this moment.

"Of course I wanted you to stay. I was just so caught off guard. I had let myself believe that you were different, that you wouldn't leave because you cared about me. When you broke it off, my world started to crumble. I just didn't know how to ask you to stay. You know that I'm not good with that kind of thing. Feelings…" His voice drifted off as he shook his head. He sucked at the emotional stuff.

"It's easier than you think."

Gavin planted a kiss against the crown of her head. "It is?"

"Yes." She propped up onto one elbow and looked him in the eyes. "All you had to say is 'stay.' Just that one word is enough."

"If I had said it the day you left…" He hated to ask, but he had to know.

"I would have stayed."

Gavin swallowed hard and nodded. So many people had come and gone from his life. How many of them might still be around if he'd had the nerve to ask them to stay? Some things were out of his control, but at least he could've salvaged the past few years with Sabine.

It was hard to face the fact that one little word could've changed their entire lives. But sometimes that was all it took. He looked down at the beautiful woman in his arms, the mother of his child, and he vowed he would never let something that insignificant get in the way again.

* * *

Sabine stretched out on the lounge chair and sighed. Gavin was snoozing in the chair beside her as they both soaked in the warm sunshine and light breeze. She was really enjoying this little vacation. They had eaten too much, drank too much, slept late and made love more times than she could count. Gavin had even taken her to the Bermuda Botanical Gardens and the art museum there. She'd lost herself in room after room of paintings and sculptures, lighting the fires of her long-cold creative flames.

It was all too perfect.

She couldn't believe how wrong she'd been. About everything. From the day she took that first pregnancy test, she worried that Gavin would take over her life, steal her son and leave her powerless to stop him. So far, he'd wanted to help, wanted to have his time with his son, but had respected her boundaries. Things would change, but they would compromise on the decisions. There would be no boarding schools, no nannies taking the place of loving parents…

She'd thought Gavin didn't want her, only to find out he'd been devastated when she left. He hadn't told her that he loved her, but she could tell he had feelings for her. They might not be as strong as what she felt for him, but it was more than she ever expected to have.

She thought that she would never fit into Gavin's world or be the woman he wanted her to be. Now, she realized he didn't want her to fit in. He wanted her to be herself. There would always be people with something rude to say, but if his family welcomed her with open arms, she didn't really care what anyone else thought.

Things were going amazingly well.

A soft chirp distracted Sabine from her thoughts. It was Gavin's cell phone. It had been remarkably quiet since they'd arrived. He'd done well in focusing on their vacation, too. She watched him reach for it and frown at the screen before answering.

"Hi, Dad," he said. "Is everything okay?"

Immediately, Sabine's stomach sank. They had called yesterday to check in and everything was fine. He'd told her that his parents would only call if there was a problem. She tried to will herself to relax as she listened to half of the conversation.

"What?" Gavin's tone was sharp and alarmed. He shot up on the lounge chair, his worried gaze searching the ocean for answers he wouldn't find there. "Are you sure? Did you look in all the closets and under the beds? He likes to play hide-and-seek."

Sabine sat up in her chair, swinging her legs over the side to turn toward him. "What is it? Is Jared okay?"

Gavin wouldn't look at her. He was totally focused on the call. "How did they get in the apartment?"

They? Her heart was racing.

"Did you call the police?"

"Gavin!" Sabine cried, unable to stand not knowing what was going on any longer. If Jared fell and skinned his knee, the police wouldn't be involved. This was something far worse than she could imagine.

"No, that was the right thing to do. We'll be home in three hours." Gavin turned off his phone and finally looked at her. He had the shimmer of glassy tears in his eyes as he spoke. "Jared is gone."

A strangled cry escaped her throat. "Gone? He's missing? How?"

Gavin shook his head softly. "Not missing. Kidnapped. A ransom note was left."

Sabine's brain started to swim in panic. She could barely follow his words. She couldn't possibly have heard him right. No one would take Jared. Why would anyone take Jared? "What?" she said, but she couldn't understand his answer. Nothing made sense.

Gavin stood up and offered his hand to her, but she didn't know why. "Sabine, please," he said at last. "We have to get back to New York."

She took his hand, standing slowly until she was looking into his eyes. His eyes. Just like her son's. That's when the fog in her brain cleared, and all that was left behind was red fury.

Her baby had been taken. Her sweet little boy, who had been nothing but safe under her care. Until now. Until he became the son of one of the wealthiest men in Manhattan. Then he was just a pawn in the games of the rich.

"Sabine?"

Her gaze locked on his, her lips tightening with anger. Gavin reached out to touch her face, but she swatted his hand away. "Don't you touch me," she warned through gritted teeth. "This is all your fault."

It was as though she'd slapped him across the face. He flinched and stepped back. "What?"

"I never should've listened to you. You said he would be safe with your parents."

"Of course. Why would I think someone would kidnap our son?"

"Because that's the world you live in, Gavin. You might be appalled by the way we lived with our tiny apartment and our old, worn furniture, but you know what? Jared was safe! He was a safe, happy little boy who didn't know what he was missing. And now he's a rich little boy, scared and alone because being *your son* made him a target."

"You think I'm the reason he was kidnapped?"

There was hurt in Gavin's eyes, but she ignored it. She was too deep in her rage to care. "You are *absolutely* the reason he was kidnapped. What did the ransom note say? Did they want millions of dollars? They wouldn't have gotten that from me, no matter what. I have nothing to offer, nothing anyone could possibly want, unlike you."

"I don't know what the ransom note said aside from the fact that they would call with instructions at 5:00 p.m. If we leave now, we can get back in plenty of time. Can you stop yelling long enough to pack and get on the plane?"

"You bet I can. I don't want to be on the island with you for another minute anyway." Sabine spun on her heel and ran from him, kicking pink sand as she headed for the stairs. She leaped up them two at a time until she reached the deck and raced for the master bedroom.

"What is that supposed to mean?" he said, charging in behind her.

"It means I wish I'd never run into Clay on the street. That the last two weeks had never happened. I should've gone home to Nebraska so you could never find me. If you weren't a part of Jared's life, I would have my son with me right now. This is exactly why I didn't tell you that you were a father."

The hurt expression on Gavin's face quickly morphed into anger. His dark eyes narrowed dangerously at her. "That is a load of crap and you know it. You didn't tell me about Jared because you're a control freak who couldn't stand someone else being involved in decisions for *your* son. You didn't tell me because you're selfish and you wanted him all to yourself, no matter what the cost to him."

"You bastard! I was protecting him from the life you hated."

"Yes, because it was so much better to suffer for your child and get sympathy than to give up your child dictatorship. Martyrdom doesn't look good on you, Sabine."

Her cheeks flushed red with anger. She didn't know what to say to him. There wasn't anything else to say. She turned her back on him and focused on packing and getting home to her son. She threw open her bag and chucked everything within reach into it. Whatever was too far away wasn't important enough to worry about. By the time she had her things together, so did he. He was standing at the front door, a car waiting for them in the driveway.

She couldn't speak. If she opened her mouth, she would say more horrible things. Some she meant, some she didn't. It was probably the same for him. Yelling made her feel better when she felt so helpless. Instead, she brushed past him to the car, giving her bags over to the driver and climbing inside.

The ride to the airport was just as silent. Her anger had begun to dissipate; this wasn't the time to start blaming and arguing. That time would come later, when Jared was home safely and she could think of something, anything, but her son's welfare.

The plane was well on its way back to New York before she so much as looked in Gavin's direction. There was only a foot between them, but it could've been miles. "Listen, fighting isn't going to get us anywhere, so let's call a truce until this whole mess is over."

Gavin's fingers flexed around the controls with anger

and anxiety, but the plane didn't so much as waver under his steady command. "Agreed."

"What else did your parents say when they called?"

"They had taken him to the park and then brought him home to take a nap before lunch. My mother said she fell asleep herself on the chaise in the living room. When she got up to check on him, he was gone and the ransom note was left on the bed."

"No one else was home?"

"My father was in his office. Nora had gone out to pick up groceries."

Sabine shook her head and focused her gaze on the miles of ocean between her and her baby. "How can someone just walk into a multimillion-dollar apartment building and walk out with our son? Did no one see him? Not even the doorman? Surely there are cameras everywhere."

"Whoever it was didn't go through the front door. They probably went in through the parking garage. There are cameras all over, but it requires a police request for them to pull the surveillance tapes."

"And?"

"And," Gavin said with a heavy sigh, "we haven't called the cops yet. The note threatened Jared's safety if we involved the police. I want to wait and take the kidnapper's call tonight. Then we might have a better idea of who we're working with here. At that point, we might get the NYPD to come in."

Sabine wasn't sure if she liked this plan or not. This was her first involvement with a kidnapping outside episodes of *Law & Order,* but calling the cops always seemed to be step number one in those situations. But perhaps Gavin had more insight into this than he was sharing. "You said 'a better idea of who we're working with.' Do you know who might be involved in this?"

Gavin shrugged, the dismissive gesture making her angrier than she already was. "It might not be anyone I know. With this kind of thing, it could just be some random creep out to make a quick buck in ransom money. You were right to say that claiming my son made him a target. It did. I hadn't really considered that until now.

"But I can't help but think this is someone I know. Jared isn't common knowledge yet. I can't be certain, but I've got a pretty short suspect list. Despite what you might think, I don't go around ruining my competitors and giving them reason to hate me."

"Who, out of those people, would despise you enough to kidnap your son?"

"Three, tops. And that's a stretch."

"And how many," Sabine asked with a tremble in her voice, "would be willing to *kill* your son for revenge?"

Gavin turned and looked at her, the blood draining from behind his newly tanned skin. "No one," he said, although not with enough confidence to make her feel better. "No one."

Eleven

Truthfully, Gavin only had one suspect on his list. As the time drew close for the call from the kidnappers, he was fairly certain who would be on the other end.

They had arrived safely at the airport and made their way to his parents' apartment as quickly as they could. His parents looked nearly ill when they walked in. His father's larger-than-life confidence had crumbled. His mother looked paper-thin and fragile. This had shaken them and it was no wonder. Their home, the one they'd shared for over thirty years, had been tainted by someone bold enough to stroll inside and walk out with the most precious treasure in their possession.

Sabine and his mother hugged fiercely and then went to sit together on the couch. His father paced in the corner, staring out the window at the city that had somehow betrayed him. Nora brought a tray with hot tea and nibbles that no one could stomach touching. Gavin just sat and waited for the call.

When the phone finally rang, Gavin's heart leaped into his throat. He answered on the second ring, gesturing for silence in the room. They had not called the police, but if the four nervous adults swarming him weren't quiet, the kidnapper might think the mansion was overrun with investigators and hostage negotiation teams.

"Hello?" he choked out.

"Gavin Brooks," the man said with an air of confidence that bordered on arrogance. Gavin didn't recognize the voice, but he hadn't spoken to his primary suspect. "So glad you could come home from your luxury vacation for our little chat."

"I want to talk to Jared," Gavin demanded as forcefully as he could.

Sabine leaped up and sat beside him on the couch. They hadn't really spoken much since their fight, and things might be irrevocably broken between them, but in this moment, they were united in finding their son and making sure Jared returned home safe and sound. He reached out and took her trembling hand in his. He was just as nervous, just as scared as she was, but he was better at not showing it. Holding her hand and keeping her calm was like an anchor on his own nerves. It kept the butterflies in his stomach from carrying him off into the sky.

"I bet you do. But you're not in charge here. I am. And you've got a couple hoops to jump through before that's even on the table."

"How do I know that you really have him?"

"If I don't...who does? You haven't misplaced your son, have you?"

"Is he okay?"

"For now. I haven't harmed a hair on his handsome little head. If you want to keep it that way, you'll do exactly as I ask and not involve the police. If you call the cops, we're done negotiating and you'll never see your little boy again."

Gavin nervously squeezed Sabine's hand. She smiled weakly at him, confusing his gesture as one of reassurance. He felt anything but sure. "I'm not calling the police. I want to keep this between you and me. But I have to know. What, exactly, do you want, Paul?"

The man on the other end of the line chuckled bitterly. "Aww, shoot. I was hoping it would take longer for you to figure out who was behind this. How did you guess it was me? I thought you'd be ruining the lives of half a dozen people right now, but you narrowed the field pretty quickly."

Paul Simpson. He had been right on the money with his original guess. Roger's irresponsible only son was the heir to Exclusivity Jetliners. At least until his father signed over the company to Gavin on Tuesday. The looming deadline must have pushed Paul too far. He had no choice but to act. That left little question of what his ransom demand would be.

"Only a handful of people knew I was going out of town. Even fewer knew that I had a son. That's not common knowledge yet."

Gavin had mentioned the trip to Roger when they spoke on the phone Thursday. He'd mentioned taking Sabine to Bermuda and that his parents would be watching Jared. That's when Roger had graciously offered the jet. If Paul was listening in on their conversation, all he had to do was wait for the right moment to slip in and steal away their son. He had handed his enemy the ammunition to attack him and didn't even realize it.

The only plus to this scenario was that Paul was spineless. Or so he seemed. Roger didn't have much faith in his son. When he snapped, Paul jumped to attention. That said, Gavin wouldn't have given him the credit to plan a scheme like this, so maybe he was wrong. He wouldn't push Paul to find out.

"Ahh. Well, mistakes are bound to be made in a scenario like this. Fortunately, we don't have to worry about any of that because this is going to go smoothly and without issue."

Somehow, Gavin doubted it. "What do you *want*, Paul? You still haven't told me what you're after with all this, although I have a pretty good guess."

"It's simple, really. First, you're going to call my father. You tell him that you have to back out of the merger deal. Give him whatever excuse you want to. Aside from blackmail, of course. But end it, and now."

The sinking feeling in his gut ached even more miserably than it had before. His dream of having his own jet fleet was slipping through his fingers. Everything he'd worked for, everything he'd built toward in the past few years would be traded away for his son. Gavin hadn't been a father for long, but he would do anything to keep Jared safe. If that meant losing Exclusivity Jetliners, that was the price he would pay. But that didn't mean it wouldn't hurt.

He should've seen this coming. Paul had silenced his complaints about the sale recently. Roger had thought that he had finally convinced his son to see reason, but

the truth was that Paul was quietly looking into alterna-
tives to get his way. Going around his father was the best
plan. But it wouldn't solve all of his problems.

"If I don't buy the company, your father will just sell
it to someone else."

"No!" Paul shouted into the line. "He won't. If this
falls through, he'll give me the chance to try running
the company on my own. Then I can prove to him that
I can do it and he won't sell."

Gavin wanted to tell Paul he was delusional, but he
couldn't. The moment Jared was safely in his arms, he'd
have the NYPD swarming this guy and hauling his ass
to Rikers Island for the foreseeable future. He wouldn't
be running a company anytime soon.

"After I call Roger and cancel the deal, we get our
son back?"

"Not exactly," Paul chuckled. "First, I have to confirm with my father that the merger is out for good. After
that, I need a little financial insurance. I expect to see
you at the bank bright and early in the morning—and
yes, I am watching you. You'll withdraw a million in
small bills and put it into a backpack. I'll call again in
the morning with the rendezvous point."

"And then we get Jared back."

"And then," Paul sighed in dismay, "yes, you get your
precious little boy back. But first, phone my father and
call off the deal. I'll be calling him in half an hour, and I
expect him to share the disappointing news when I speak
to him. You'll hear from me at 10:00 a.m. tomorrow."

The line went dead.

Gavin dropped the phone onto the table and flopped
back into the cushions of his couch. He was fighting

to keep it together, but inside, it felt as if his world was crumbling. His son was in danger. The one person he believed was in his life for good could be permanently snatched away on the whim of a ruthless man. His dreams of owning private jets were about to be crushed. The woman he cared for blamed him for all of it and might never forgive him if something went wrong. She was already one foot out of his life, he could tell.

But nothing he could say or do would guarantee that Jared would be handed over, unharmed. Or that Sabine would ever look at him with love in her eyes again.

She was watching him silently from the seat beside him. He was still clutching her hand, worried if he let go, he'd lose her forever. "Well," she said at last. "What did you find out?"

"Is Jared okay?" his mother asked.

"Yes, I think so. I know who has orchestrated this and why. I don't have any reason to believe that he won't return Jared to us safe and sound as long as I meet his demands."

She breathed a visible sigh of relief. "Who has him?"

"Paul Simpson. No one you know."

"What did he ask for?" His father finally entered the conversation.

"A million-dollar ransom, delivered tomorrow in exchange for Jared."

"Our accountant can make that happen," Byron confirmed.

"And today," Gavin continued, "the cancellation of my latest business deal."

Sabine gasped and squeezed his hand even tighter. "The one you were working with the private jet company?"

Gavin nodded, his gaze dropping down to his lap.

"Yes. I hope you enjoyed riding in that plane to Bermuda. That will probably be the last time."

"Oh, Gavin, I'm so sorry." Her pale eyes, lined with worry, were at once glassy with tears. For a moment he was jealous that she could cry for what he was losing and he couldn't. "I know how important that was to you. Maybe you can still—"

Gavin pulled his hand away and held it up to silence her. He wasn't in the mood to deal with the maybes and other consolations she could offer. It wouldn't matter. "Even if this all works out, I think my dealings with the Simpson family are over."

"We can acquire more planes, son."

He shook his head at his father. "Finding another company with a quality fleet I can afford is nearly impossible. The shareholders won't back a more expensive merger. The whole concierge plan is dead."

He turned away from his family and picked up his phone. He needed to call Roger, but that would wait a few more minutes. More important was calling his accountant. He didn't exactly leave thousands of dollars just lying around, much less a million. Some things would need to be shifted around so he had liquid assets for the ransom. His accountant would get everything together for him with little fuss.

The awkward call to his accountant took only a few minutes. The man seemed confused by the sudden and out-of-ordinary request, but he didn't question it. The money would be ready for pickup in the morning. That done, he couldn't put off the inevitable any longer.

Gavin slowly dialed the familiar number of Roger Simpson. With every fiber of his being, he didn't want to back out of this deal. It was everything he'd desired, and it was mere days from being his at last. He wasn't even sure how he would say the words out loud. His tongue might not cooperate. He'd rather shout at Roger about how his son was volatile, if not plain disturbed. But he wouldn't. Not while Jared's life was in another person's hands.

"Gavin?" Roger answered. "I didn't expect to hear from you today. You're back early from Bermuda. Did something happen? Was something wrong with the jet I loaned you?"

"The jet was fine. Don't worry about any of that. Something came up and we had to come back ahead of schedule." He just couldn't tell him that the something involved blackmail and kidnapping. "I—I'm sorry to have to make this call, Roger. I'm afraid I have to withdraw my offer to buy Exclusivity Jetliners."

"What?" Roger's voice cracked over the line. "You were thrilled about the offer when we last spoke just a few days ago. What's wrong? What happened to change your mind so suddenly? Did you find a better company to meet your needs? Our arrangement is completely negotiable."

"No, please, Roger. I'm sorry, but I can't really elaborate on the subject. I hate that I have to do this, but I must. I'm sorry for the trouble I'm causing you, but I have to go."

Gavin hung up the phone before Roger could grill him for more information. He did what he had to do for Jared's sake, but he didn't have to like it. Dropping his phone onto the coffee table, he got up, brushing off the questions and sympathetic looks of Sabine and his family, and walked out of the room. He needed some space to mourn his dreams, privately.

* * *

It was 10:00 a.m. and Gavin had returned from the bank with the million-dollar ransom a few minutes ago. The whole family was gathered around the phone waiting for Paul's call and the instructions for today's trade-off.

Sabine hadn't slept. They had all stayed at the Brooks mansion, but even an expensive mattress with luxury linens couldn't lure her to sleep. And from the looks of it, Gavin hadn't slept, either. Never in her life had she seen him look like he did right now. His eyes were lined with exhaustion and sadness. Gray smudges circled beneath them. He wasn't frowning, but he wasn't smiling, either. He had shut everything off. She recognized that in him. There was too much to deal with, too much that could go wrong, so he had chosen to numb himself to the possibilities.

She knew it was hard on him. Not only because of his concern for Jared but what it cost him to ensure his son's safety. That jet acquisition had meant everything to him. Seeing him in the cockpit of that plane had been an eye-opening experience. She had experienced what she thought was the pinnacle of passion when she made love to Gavin. But for him, there was a higher joy, a greater pleasure.

He'd been so close to merging his work and his dreams. And he'd been forced to throw it away.

Sabine placed a reassuring hand on his knee, and he covered it with his own. The warmth of his skin against hers chased away the fears that threatened from the corners of her mind. She wouldn't allow herself to indulge those thoughts. She'd be no good to her son if she was a hysterical mess.

As much as she'd yelled at Gavin, and blamed him for this whole mess, she was glad to have him here with her during this. No one should have to deal with this sort of thing alone. He had handled everything, and well. There were benefits to having a take-charge man in her life, even when it was sometimes frustrating.

Gavin would do whatever it took to see that their son came home safely. Jared was their number one priority.

The phone rang. The loud sound was amplified in the silent room, sending Sabine straight up out of her seat. Gavin calmly reached out and hit the button for the speakerphone. Sabine hated listening to only half the conversation and had asked him to let her listen this time, as well.

"Yes?"

"I'm surprised, Gavin." Paul's voice boomed through the speaker. "You've done everything I've asked so far without a whisper to the police. My father was quite disappointed that your deal fell through. It was hard not to laugh in his face. You've been so cooperative you must really care about this brat. Funny, considering you've only known about him for two weeks."

Sabine fought back her urge to scream profanities into the phone. They were too close to getting Jared home safely. She could say or do whatever she wanted after that.

"I've got the money," Gavin said, ignoring his taunts. "What now?"

"Meet me in an hour in Washington Square Park. I'll be waiting by the arch with junior. You hand over the backpack, I hand over the kid."

"I'll be there."

"If I so much as smell a cop, we're done. And so is the kid."

Paul hung up, leaving them all in a stunned silence. After a moment, Celia started crying. Byron put his arm around her.

"Don't worry, dear. He doesn't have the nerve to actually hurt Jared, no matter what he says."

Gavin stood up and nodded. "He's right. Roger told me once that Paul didn't have enough ambition to get out of bed before noon most days. This is just the quickest, easiest way to make some money and get his father to do what he wants." He slung the backpack with the money onto his shoulder. "I'd better go."

Sabine leaped up, as well. "I'm going with you."

Gavin's jaw tightened. He looked as though he wanted to argue with her, but he didn't. Gavin might be able to get his way when it came to unimportant things, but that was because most times, Sabine didn't care. She cared about this, and she wouldn't take no for an answer.

"Okay. Let's go."

Sabine grabbed her own red backpack. It had a change of clothes, Pull-Ups, dry cereal, Jared's favorite stuffed dinosaur and one of his trucks. She wanted to have everything she needed to clean him up and comfort him the minute she could finally get herself to let go.

Gavin had a car drive them downtown. It let them off about a block from the park and would circle until he called to be picked up. If all went well, this shouldn't take long.

Sabine's heart was pounding wildly in her chest as they walked through the park and headed toward the arch. She could barely hear the sounds of the traffic and people surrounding them. Gavin clutched her hand in his, steadying and guiding her to the rendezvous point.

They were about five minutes early. She didn't know what Paul Simpson looked like, but Jared was nowhere in sight.

The minutes ticked by. Anxiously waiting. Then she heard it.

"Mommy!"

Like an arrow through her brain, Sabine immediately recognized the voice of her child amid the chaos of downtown. Her head turned sharply to the left. There, an older man was walking toward them carrying Jared in his arms.

She broke into a sprint, closing the gap between them. It wasn't part of the plan, but Sabine didn't care. She could hear Gavin running behind her. She stopped herself short of the man, who looked nothing like she expected him to. He was in his late fifties easily, in a nice suit. He also immediately lifted Jared from his hip and handed him into her arms.

Something about this didn't seem right, but it didn't matter. All that mattered was the warm, snuggling body of her baby back in her arms. Jared clung to her neck, his breathing a little labored as she nearly squeezed the life out of him. When she could finally ease up, she inspected her son for signs of his abduction. He was clean. Rosy-cheeked. Smiling. He actually didn't appear to think anything was awry.

What the hell was really going on?

"Roger?"

Sabine pried her attention away to listen to Gavin's conversation. Roger? That was Paul's father. Was he involved in this, too?

"Gavin, I am so sorry. You have no idea how disturbed I was to find out what was really going on. My son…" His voice trailed off. "It's inexcusable. There are no words to express how horrified I am. This must have been a day of pure hell for you both."

"What happened, Roger? We were supposed to be meeting Paul here." Gavin's dark eyes flickered over Sabine and Jared, but he didn't dare try to hold his son. He'd have to pry him from Sabine's dead arms.

"After your call last night, I got concerned. When I went into the office this morning, I heard Paul talking to someone in the day care center of our offices. He doesn't have children, so there was no reason for him to be there. Later, I overheard him talking on the phone to you. After he hung up, I confronted him and he confessed everything to me. My wife and I have been concerned about him for a while, but you never believe your children could ever do something as horrible as this."

"Where is he now?"

"He's in one of my jets on his way to a very expensive long-term rehab facility in Vermont. It was that or I disinherited him. If you want to press charges, I completely understand. I can give you the facility address for the police to pick him up. I just wanted to start getting him help right away. It seems he had more problems than even I knew, including an expensive drug habit. He owed his dealer quite a bit and had worked out a deal where he would let them use our planes to import and export drugs. That was the only reason he wanted the company. Can you imagine?"

"I'm sorry to hear that, Roger."

The old man shook his head sadly and looked over at Jared. It must be hard to know your child did something terrible when all you can see is them when they were little.

"I want you to know your little boy was in the best possible care the entire time he was gone. Paul put him in the Exclusivity Jetliners day care center. We run a twenty-four-hour facility for our employees who might have to go on long flights or overnight trips. Jared spent the last day playing with the other children. I personally guarantee there's not a scratch on him."

Sabine felt a wave of relief wash over her. No wonder Jared seemed perfectly contented. He thought he had spent the day at school with new friends and had no clue he was a kidnapping victim. Thank goodness for that. She ran her palm over his head, messing up the soft, dark hairs and standing them on end.

Jared rubbed his hair back down with both hands. "Dinosaur?" he asked.

Sabine crouched down, settling him on his feet and pulling her bag off her shoulder. "He's right here." She pulled out the plush triceratops from their trip to the American Museum of Natural History.

Jared happily hugged the dinosaur and leaned against her leg. He wasn't traumatized by the whole ordeal, but Mommy was gone a little too long for his taste. She wasn't going to be out of his sight for a while, and she knew exactly how he felt.

"I want to make this up to you," Roger said. He was shuffling awkwardly in his loafers. "At least I want to try. I doubt anything can make it better."

"Don't beat yourself up over this, Roger. You can't control what your kids do when they're adults."

"No, Gavin. I'm taking responsibility for this whole mess. I kept waiting for him to grow up, and I let things go too far. Now I want to change what I can. If you're still interested, I want to make sure you get these planes you're after. There's no way in hell I want my son to ever have his hands in the company—rehab or no. Because of everything that happened, I'd like to sell it to you for twenty percent less than we previously negotiated. How's that sound?"

Sabine watched Gavin's eyes widen in surprise. Twenty percent of the money they were talking about was apparently a huge amount. She couldn't even imagine it.

"Roger, I—"

"And I'll throw in *Beth*."

"No." Gavin shook his head. "Absolutely not. That's your private jet. You named it after your wife!"

Roger smiled and patted Gavin on the shoulder. "My first wife," he clarified. "She's not a part of the Exclusivity Jetliners fleet, I know. But I want to give her to you. Not to BXS, but to *you*. Even if the merger is off the table. I know you've always wanted your own jet, and it doesn't get much better than my *Beth,* I assure you."

"What about you?" Gavin asked.

"I'll take some of the money I make off the sale and maybe I'll buy a smaller plane. I don't need such a big one anymore. Anyway, I don't want to give Paul too many options. Maybe I'll just get a nice yacht instead and take the missus to Monaco."

"Are you sure?"

"Absolutely. I'll have my lawyers redraft the agreement and we'll be back on for Tuesday." Roger smiled and looked down at Jared with a touch of sadness in his eyes. "Again, I'm sorry about all of this. Please, take your son home and enjoy your afternoon with him."

Then he leaned in closer to Gavin. "And for the love of God, stop by the bank and get that cash put back someplace safe. You can't just walk around with a million dollars in a backpack."

Twelve

"Well," Gavin said, breaking the long silence. "Tomorrow I'm going to call the Realtor and let her know that the apartment overlooking Washington Square Park is out."

"Out? Why?" Sabine asked from the seat beside him. The town car had picked them up after Roger left and was taking them back uptown to his apartment.

"I'm not paying five million dollars for a place that will do nothing but remind you of all of this every time you look out the window. This location is tainted."

Sabine sighed. "We looked at over half a dozen apartments last week, and that was the only one I really liked. I understand your concerns, but I hate to start over."

Thankfully, Gavin had no intention of putting her through all that again. There was only one apartment she needed to tour. It had taken him a long time to come to this conclusion, but now his mind was made up. "We're not. A place has come available that no one knows about yet. I think you're really going to love it."

Her brows arched in question, but she didn't press him. At least not now. She was too busy holding a squirming Jared in her lap. After the past twenty-four hours of hell, she probably didn't think apartment hunting was high on their agenda. She would question him later.

Besides, they hadn't spoken—really spoken—since their fight on the beach. They were angry with one another and then they set that aside while they focused on getting Jared back. Now, with all of that behind them, they had nothing to do but deal with each other and the fallout of their heated and regretful words.

Gavin wasn't ready to start that awkward conversation yet. He was much happier to watch Sabine and Jared interact as they drove home. Occasionally she leaned down and inhaled the scent of his baby shampoo and smiled, very nearly on the verge of tears. How could she ever have thought he could split the two of them up? It was an impossible task.

And as time went by, splitting Gavin from Sabine and Jared was an even more impossible task.

He'd signed off on the custody agreements because they were fair and reasonable, but he didn't like them. He wouldn't see Jared nearly enough. And aside from the occasional custody trade-off, nowhere in the pile of paperwork did it say how often he would get to see Sabine. There was no such thing as visitation with the mother.

At this point, she might not want anything else to do with him. They had both said terrible things to each other. He hadn't meant a word of it. He'd been hurt by her blame and flung the most convenient insults he could find. He could tell her that. But he knew Sabine. She wouldn't pay any attention to his apologies. They were just words, and she had told him more than once that actions spoke louder.

Now was the time for action.

The car finally pulled up outside of the Ritz-Carlton. He ushered them both inside through the crowd of tourists and over to the residential elevator. He swiped the card that had special access to his floor of the hotel. In his apartment with the door locked, Gavin finally felt secure again. His family was safe and intact and he was never going to let them out of his sight again.

Once they settled in, he called his parents to let them know Jared was okay. He should've called from the car, but he needed time to mentally unwind and process everything that happened.

Jared was playing with his dinosaur on the floor when he got off the phone. Sabine was staring out the window at Central Park, her arms crossed protectively over her chest.

"Sabine?" She turned to look at him, an expression of sadness on her face. "Are you okay?"

She nodded softly. "Yes. I wanted to tell you that I'm sorry about everything I said to you. I was upset and scared when I found out something had happened to Jared. Blaming you was the easiest thing to do. It was wrong of me. Your son was in danger, too."

"I said things I didn't mean, too."

"Yes, but you were right. I was being selfish. I was so afraid of not having Jared all to myself that I kept him from you. I shouldn't have done that. I'm glad that Clay saw me and told you about him. It was a step I couldn't make on my own. I'm really glad you're going to be a part of his life."

"What about your life?"

Sabine's eyes narrowed. "Of course Jared is already a huge part of my life. Any more, he is my life."

Gavin took a few steps closer to her. "I wasn't talking about Jared. I was talking about me. Will I get to be a part of your life, too?"

She sighed and let her gaze drop to the floor. "I don't know, Gavin. The last few weeks have been nice, but it has been a lot, and fast. We have a lifetime of sharing our son. I don't want anything to mess that up. I know how important he is to you."

"*You're* important to me," he emphasized. "Both of you. Not just Jared. All this time, all that we've shared together these weeks… It wasn't just about our son or wooing you into giving me what I wanted. You know that, right?"

Sabine looked up at him, her pale green eyes still sad and now, a touch wearier than before. "I want to believe that, Gavin. Truly, I do. But how can I know anything about our relationship when you won't tell me how you feel? You'd rather let me walk away than tell me you want me to stay. I can't spend all our time together guessing. I need you to talk to me."

"You know that's hard for me. I've never been good at voicing my feelings. I've spent my whole life watching people walk away and never come back. My parents were always busy, foisting me and my siblings off on one nanny after the next until I was old enough for boarding school. They were so worried about keeping up appearances that I changed schools every few years to move on to a more prestigious program. It didn't take long for me to learn to keep my distance from everyone."

"Not everyone is going to leave you, Gavin."

"You did. You said that you would've stayed if I had asked, but how do I know that for certain? What if I told them how I felt and they left anyway? I'm not good with words. Can't I just show you how I feel?"

"More kisses? More gifts and fancy dinners? That doesn't mean anything to me. I need more, Gavin. I need to hear the words coming from your lips."

He reached out for her hand. "I'm offering more. But first, please, I want to show you something." He tugged gently until she followed him down the hallway toward Jared's newly renovated bedroom.

"You already showed me Jared's room."

"I know. This time I want to show you the other room."

Gavin turned the knob and pushed open the door to what used to be his office. When he flipped on the light switch, he heard Sabine gasp beside him.

"Remember in the car when I said that I knew of an available property that you would love? This is it. I had the old office done up for you. An art studio just for you to work. You don't have to share it with a toddler or storage boxes or cleaning supplies. It's all yours for you to do whatever you like."

Sabine stepped ahead of him into the large, open room. He'd had the hardwood floors refinished. The walls were painted a soft, matte green very close to the color of her eyes. "The consultant I worked with told me that this shade of green was a good choice for an art studio because it wouldn't influence the color of your work and would provide enough light with the off-white ceilings."

There was one large window that let in plenty of natural light and several nonfluorescent fixtures that he was told were good for art. A leather love seat sat along one wall. Several cabinets lined the other, each filled with every painting supply he could order. Several easels were already set up with blank canvases perched on them, and a few framed paintings were hanging on the walls.

"That shade of green also looked wonderful with the paintings I had of yours."

"It's beautiful. Perfect." Sabine approached one of the three canvases hanging on the wall and let her finger run along the large wooden frame. "I didn't know you had bought any of my work. Why didn't you tell me?"

"Because I bought the pieces after you left me. It was my way of keeping you in my life, I guess."

She spun on her heel to face him, her brow knit together with excitement tampered by confusion. "When did you decide to do all this?"

"Three years ago."

"What?" she gasped.

"The room was nearly finished when you broke it off. I was planning on asking you to move in with me and giving you the room as a housewarming gift. I decided to go ahead and complete it, and then I didn't have the heart to do anything else with it. I've just kept the door shut."

"You wanted me to move in with you?" Sabine's hands dropped helplessly at her sides. "I wish to God you would've said something. I didn't think I mattered to you. I loved you, but I thought I was a fool."

"I was the fool for letting you walk away. I wanted you here with me then, and I was too afraid to admit to myself that I still wanted you here with me now. I would've bought you any apartment you chose, but I knew you were meant to be here with me."

"Why didn't you tell me about it when you showed me Jared's new room?"

Gavin took a deep breath. "I thought it was too soon to show it to you. We were slowly rebuilding our relationship. I didn't know where we would end up. I thought that I might scare you away if you saw it. Too much, too soon."

"Why would you think that?"

"You'd already laughed off my proposal and shot down any suggestion of moving in with me."

"To be fair, it wasn't much of a proposal."

"True. Which is why I worried you would think the studio was my way of trying to bribe you into moving in with me after you told me no already. It's not a bribe. It's a homecoming gift. I started working on this place years ago because I wanted it to be a home for us. Now, a home for *all* of us. Not a part-time, alternate weekends and holidays home. For every day. All three of us together."

He watched tears start welling in her eyes and didn't know if it was a good or bad sign. He decided to go with it. The moment felt right even though he wasn't as prepared as he would like to be.

"Sabine, I know I'm no good at talking about my feelings. I built this space for you because I…I love you. I loved you then and I love you now. This was the only way I could think of to show you how I felt."

"You love me?" Sabine asked with a sly smile curling her lips.

"I do. Very much."

"Then say it again," she challenged.

"I love you," he repeated, this time without hesitation. A grin of his own spread wide across his face. It was getting easier every time he said it. "Now it's your turn."

Sabine leaned into him, her green gaze focused intently on him. "I love you, Gavin," she said without a moment's indecision. Then she placed her hands on his face and leaned in to kiss him.

Gavin wrapped his arms around her, thankful to have this again after two days without her touch or her kisses to help him get through it. He'd worried that he'd ruined it again.

"I'm glad you do," he said. Gavin pulled her hands from his face and held them in his. "That will make this next part less embarrassing. I want to ask again if you'll marry me, but this time, even if the answer is no, please don't laugh. A man's ego can't take that twice."

"Okay," Sabine said, her face now perfectly solemn in preparation for his query.

Gavin dropped down to one knee, her hands still grasped in his own. "Sabine Hayes, I love you. And I love our son. I want us to be a family. There is nothing on this earth—not a jet, not money—that I want more than for you to be my wife. Will you marry me?"

Sabine could barely withstand the rush of emotions surging through her. She really was on an emotional roller coaster. She'd experienced the highest of highs and the lowest of lows all in a few hours' time. If Gavin wasn't looking up at her with dark, love-filled eyes, she might start nervously twittering with laughter again simply from the stress of it all.

But she couldn't laugh. Not this time. Gavin wanted to marry her and there was nothing funny about that.

"Yes. I will marry you."

Gavin stood back up and swept her into his arms. His mouth eagerly captured hers, sealing their agreement with a kiss that made her blood sizzle through her veins. She wanted to make love to him on the leather couch of her new studio. The sooner she could start creating memories in her new home, the better.

Of course, that would have to wait for nap time.

Instead, she looked up into the dark eyes of her fiancé. The man she loved. The father of her child. There, in his arms, everything felt right. This is what she'd missed, the thing that made all those other apartments seem cold and unappealing.

"Gavin, do you know why I didn't like any of the apartments we looked at?"

He gave her a lopsided smile in response to her unexpected question. "You wanted crown molding and granite countertops?"

"No. Guess again."

He shrugged. "I'm out of guesses. Why didn't you like them?"

"Because they were all missing something—*you*."

Gavin laughed. "Of course. There's only one apartment in Manhattan that comes equipped with Gavin Brooks. It's a very exclusive address. The only way to get into the place is through marriage."

"Well, wouldn't you know that THE Gavin Brooks just asked me to be his wife?"

He picked up her left hand and eyed the bare ring finger. "This won't do. The first thing everyone will do when you tell them we're engaged is look at your hand. We need to get you an engagement ring."

"Right now?"

"We're two blocks away from Tiffany's. Why not right now?"

Sabine sighed. It had been an exciting couple of

days. Too exciting if you asked her. She was happy to spread out some of the big moments to later in the week. "There's no rush. I know you're good for it. There's a million dollars in cash lying around on the living room floor in a JanSport."

"Okay, you win. What about tomorrow?"

"I have to work tomorrow morning."

Gavin eyed her with dismay. "No, you don't."

"Yes, I do. I'm not going to abandon my wonderful, pregnant boss when she needs me. You're the one that suggested a vacation. I at least have to stay at the store long enough for her to take one."

"What about if we go early, before the boutique opens?"

"Okay," Sabine relented. If he wanted so badly to put a dangerously expensive rock on her hand, she would let him. "But make sure you don—"

"Spider-Man!"

Sabine and Gavin turned to find Jared standing in the doorway of his new bedroom. He flung the door the rest of the way open and charged in the space that was custom-made for a little boy with dreams of being a superhero.

The workers had done an excellent job on the room. It was just as Gavin had described. Red walls, a loft with a rope swing for an adventurous young boy, and a comic-book motif sure to please. All it needed was his favorite toys from their place in Brooklyn and it would be perfect.

Jared crawled up on the new bed, bouncing ever so slightly on the new Spider-Man comforter. "Big bed!"

"Yep, it's a big boy bed."

"Mine?"

"It is," Gavin replied. "Do you like it?"

Jared flipped two thumbs up. "Love Spider-Man!"

Sabine was nearly overwhelmed by the joy and excitement on their small son's face. Gavin turned to look at her and frowned when he noted the tears pooling in her eyes.

"And I love you," she said.

"More than Spider-Man?" Gavin asked.

"Oh, yeah," she replied, leaning in to kiss him and prove her point.

Epilogue

Sabine was exhausted. There wasn't really another word to describe the state a woman was in immediately following childbirth. The messy business was over. The doctors and nurses had cleared out and the family went home. Now it was just Sabine and Gavin in a quiet hospital suite.

Well, make that just Sabine, Gavin *and* the brand-new Miss Elizabeth Anne Brooks in a quiet hospital suite.

Beth made her arrival at 4:53 p.m., weighing seven pounds, two ounces and shrieking with the finest set of lungs to ever debut at St. Luke's Hospital. They named her after Gavin's private plane—*Beth*—and Sabine's mother, with whom she'd recently reconciled.

Gavin's parents, siblings and the housekeeper had left a few hours ago with Jared in tow. Their son had been very excited to see his new sister, but the novelty wore off pretty quickly when she didn't do anything but sleep.

He insisted that Grandpa and Grandma take him for ice cream and when visiting hours ended, they relented.

It had been a long day filled with excitement, nerves, joy and pain. And now, she was enjoying a private moment she would remember for her whole life.

Gavin was beside her in the reclining chair. Beth was bundled up in a white blanket with pastel stripes. She was perfect, tiny and pink with Sabine's nose. The nurses had put a hat on to keep her head warm. It hid away the wild mohawk of dark hair she'd been born with. Gavin said her crazy hair was from Sabine, too. Beth had fallen asleep with her small hand clutching his pinky finger, content, warm and safe in her daddy's arms.

But the best part was watching Gavin.

The past nine months had been an adventure for her husband. Since he'd missed out on her first pregnancy, Gavin wanted to be a part of every moment from sonograms to Lamaze classes. Sometimes she wondered if he regretted getting so immersed in the details of the process.

He could handle running shipping empires and flying jets, but preparing for the arrival of a new baby— and a girl at that—nearly did him in. During labor, he was wide-eyed and panicked. Occasionally even a little green around the gills. It was pretty adorable.

Then she was born, shouting her displeasure to everyone in the maternity ward. Of course, Sabine looked at her baby first, cataloging fingers and toes and noting how beautiful and perfect she was. But the moment Beth was laid on her chest, Sabine's eyes went to Gavin. The expression on his face was priceless. It was quite literally love at first sight.

And now, while he held her, a marching band could parade through the room and Gavin probably wouldn't notice. He couldn't tear his gaze away from his daughter. It was as though the answers to all the questions in the universe were wrapped up in that blanket. It was the most precious thing Sabine had ever seen.

"You're my hero."

Sabine didn't realize Gavin was looking at her until he spoke. "Your hero?"

"Absolutely. You were amazing today." Gavin stood slowly so he didn't wake their daughter and carried Beth over to her.

Sabine accepted the bundle and smiled up at him. "Eh, piece of cake. I think I only threatened your life once."

"Twice, but who's counting?" Gavin eased down to sit on the edge of the bed and put his arm around her shoulders. "Seriously, though, I don't know how you did it. *Before.* With Jared. I mean, I knew that *I* had missed a lot, but one thing I never really considered was how it was for you. To do this all alone..."

It certainly was different this time. Before, one of her gallery friends came by the next day. That was it. This time, she had an entire cheering squad waiting in the next room, a crew in Nebraska staying up to date on Facebook and a husband holding her hand. What a difference a few years could make.

"That was the choice I made." She shrugged. "The wrong one, obviously. It was definitely better with you here."

Gavin leaned in to place a kiss on her lips and another on Beth's forehead. "I have to say I agree."

They both spent a moment looking down at their daughter. "She looks like you," Gavin said.

"That's fair since Jared looks like you. Besides, it would be unfortunate for a girl to have your chin."

"I can tell she's going to give me trouble. If she's half as beautiful and smart and talented as her mother, the boys will be lined up the block."

"She's four hours old. I don't think you need to start polishing the shotgun just yet. You've got years of ballet recitals and princess parties before we need to start worrying about that."

Gavin smiled and leaned his head against hers. "I'm looking forward to every pink, glittery second."

* * * * *

A sneaky peek at next month…

PASSIONATE AND DRAMATIC LOVE STORIES

My wish list for next month's titles…

In stores from 18th April 2014:

❏ The Sarantos Baby Bargain – Olivia Gates

& The Last Cowboy Standing – Barbara Dunlop

❏ From Single Mum to Secret Heiress
    – Kristi Gold

& Your Ranch...Or Mine? – Kathie DeNosky

❏ A Merger by Marriage – Cat Schield

& Caroselli's Accidental Heir – Michelle Celmer

2 stories in each book - only £5.49!

Available at WHSmith, Tesco, Asda, Eason, Amazon and Apple

Just can't wait?

Visit us Online

You can buy our books online a month before they hit the shops!

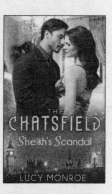

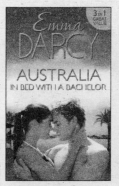

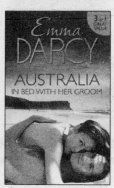

Join the Mills & Boon Book Club

Want to read more **Desire™** books?
We're offering you **2 more** absolutely **FREE!**

We'll also treat you to these fabulous extras:

- **Exclusive offers and much more!**

- **FREE home delivery**

- **FREE books and gifts with our special rewards scheme**

Get your free books now!

visit www.millsandboon.co.uk/bookclub
or call Customer Relations on 020 8288 2888

FREE BOOK OFFER TERMS & CONDITIONS
Accepting your free books places you under no obligation to buy anything and you may cancel at any time. If we do not hear from you we will send you 4 stories a month which you may purchase or return to us—the choice is yours. Offer valid in the UK only and is not available to current Mills & Boon subscribers to this series. We reserve the right to refuse an application and applicants must be aged 18 years or over. Only one application per household. Terms and prices are subject to change without notice. As a result of this application you may receive further offers from other carefully selected companies. If you do not wish to share in this opportunity please write to the Data Manager at PO BOX 676, Richmond, TW9 1WU.

Discover more romance at

www.millsandboon.co.uk

- 💜 WIN great prizes in our exclusive competitions

- 💜 BUY new titles before they hit the shops

- 💜 BROWSE new books and REVIEW your favourites

- 💜 SAVE on new books with the Mills & Boon® Bookclub™

- 💜 DISCOVER new authors

PLUS, to chat about your favourite reads, get the latest news and find special offers:

- 📘 Find us on facebook.com/millsandboon

- 🐦 Follow us on twitter.com/millsandboonuk

- 💜 Sign up to our newsletter at millsandboon.co.uk